The Other Side of Silence

Natasha Mostert

coronet

CORONET BOOKS
Hodder & Stoughton

Copyright © 2001 by Natasha Mostert

First published in Great Britain in 2001 by Hodder and Stoughton
First published in paperback in Great Britain in 2002
by Hodder and Stoughton
A division of Hodder Headline

The right of Natasha Mostert to be identified as the
Author of the Work has been asserted by her in accordance
with the Copyright, Designs and Patents Act 1988.

A Coronet paperback

2 4 6 8 10 9 7 5 3 1

A CIP catalogue record for this title is available from the British Library.

ISBN 0 340 76800 2

Printed and bound in Great Britain by
Mackays of Chatham plc, Chatham, Kent

Hodder and Stoughton
A division of Hodder Headline
338 Euston Road
London NW1 3BH

. . . it would be like hearing the grass grow and the squirrel's heart beat and we should die of that roar which lies on the other side of silence.

George Eliot, *Middlemarch*

CONTENTS

ACKNOWLEDGEMENTS

The problem of perfect tuning and the Pythagorean Comma is a complex one and any discussion of this topic usually becomes highly esoteric. I have simplified some of the issues involved in order to meet the demands of a work of fiction. I apologise in advance to knowledgeable readers who may find this approach unsatisfying.

The Other Side of Silence required extensive research on music and sound and I read more books and articles on the subject than I can remember. However, four sources were of particular assistance to me: Jamie James' delightful and witty book, *The Music of the Spheres*; Mickey Hart's thrilling account of *Drumming on the Edge of Magic*; Brenda Sullivan's moving exposition of the *Spirit of the Rocks* and David Tame's thought-provoking thesis on *The Power of Music*.

I wish to thank my agent, Harvey Klinger, for his steady guidance and unflagging efforts on my behalf. A special word of thanks to his associate, David Dunton, who believed in this book right from the start. Always enthusiastic and encouraging, but with a keen eye for flaws and inconsistencies, Carolyn Caughey is the kind of editor writers are grateful to have. Many thanks to her and her associate, the ever-cheerful Julie Crisp. Dr Jeanne Zaidel-Rudolph is a gifted musicologist, teacher and composer and I'm indebted to her for reading through the manuscript and sharing with me her formidable expertise.

I'm blessed in having family and friends who are supportive and generous with their time. Many thanks to my mother-in-law, Joan Mostert, and to Dianne Hofmeyr, Riette Malherbe and Gaynor Rupert. Thanks to my brother Stefan, whose wicked sense of humour was always there when I needed it. A very special thank you to my brother, Frans, and my sister-in-law, Catherine. Their input on the computer aspects was crucial and despite their gentle exasperation with my 'fuzzy thinking', they were always willing to help me get the book back on track whenever I wrote myself into a corner.

My husband, Frederick, is my biggest supporter. I can never thank him enough for his love, caring and patience. He beats my heart.

To Hantie Prins, my mother, I dedicate this book. I have never come across a finer musical mind and I am forever grateful that she made my childhood a place where music was a constant joy. She first introduced me to the concept of the Pythagorean Comma and throughout I relied heavily on her extraordinary understanding of music. She cheered me on; she assisted me in so many ways. Without her, this book simply would not have happened.

My life is much richer because of music. To borrow a phrase by Thomas Carlyle: Music is well said to be the speech of angels.

QUOTED REFERENCES

The author has been given permission to quote extracts from the poem *Ballade van die Bose* (Ballad of Evil) from *Gestaltes en Diere* by N.P. van Wyk Louw. Copyright by Tafelberg Publishers. Reprinted by permission. Translated from the Afrikaans by Natasha Mostert.

Aristotle. *Aristotle: Metaphysics. Books I–IX.* Translated by Hugh Tredennick. Harvard University Press, 1979.

Byron, George Gordon, Lord. *Don Juan.* Edited by T.G. Steffan, E. Steffan and W.W. Pratt. With revisions by T.G. Steffan. Penguin, 1977.

Campbell, Joseph. *The Hero's Journey: Joseph Campbell on his Life and Work.* Edited by Phil Cousineau. Element, 1999.

Confucius, as quoted in *An Encyclopedia of Quotations about Music.* Compiled and edited by Nat Shapiro. David and Charles, 1978.

Cowan, David and Anne Silk. *Ancient Energies of the Earth: A Groundbreaking Exploration of the Earth's Energy and how it Affects our Health.* Thorsons, 1999.

Dryden, John. *Selected Poems.* Edited by Donald Thomas. J.M. Dent, Everyman's Library, 1993.

Eco, Umberto. *Foucault's Pendulum.* Picador, 1990.

Eliot, George. *Middlemarch.* Penguin, 1965.

Emerson, Ralph Waldo. *Journals of Ralph Waldo Emerson. Vol 4, 1836–38.* Constable, 1910.

Glazerson, Matityahu. *Music and Kabbalah.* Jason Aronson, 1997.

Hart, Mickey with Jay Stevens and Fredric Lieberman. *Drumming on the Edge of Magic: A Journey into the Spirit of Percussion.* HarperSanFransisco, 1990.

Hart, Mickey and Lieberman, Fredric. *Spirit into Sound: The Magic of Music.* Grateful Dead Books, 1999.

Hayes, Michael. *The Infinite Harmony: Musical Structures in Science and Theology.* Weidenfeld, 1994.

Henderson, William J. Review of Edgar Varèse's, '*Hyperprism.*'. *New York Herald Tribune*, March 11, 1923.

Hollander, Lorin. 'Will you join the dance? Music, Vision and the Future' from *Music and Miracles*. Compiled by Don Campbell. Quest Books, 1992.

Hykes, David. Quoted from print material accompanying CD, *David Hykes and the Harmonic Choir: Hearing Solar Winds.* Ocora, 1994.

James, Jamie. *The Music of the Spheres: Music, Science and the Natural Order of the Universe.* Abacus, 1993.

Kerven, Rosalind. *The Mythical Quest: In Search of Adventure, Romance and Enlightenment.* The British Library, 1996.

Lewis, C.S. *Perelandra: A Novel (Space Trilogy).* Scribner, 1996.

Mutwa, Vusamazulu Credo. *Song of the Stars: The Lore of a Zulu Shaman.* Edited by Stephen Larsen. Station Hill Openings, Barrytown, 1996.

Mellers, Wilfrid. *Bach and the Dance of God.* Faber and Faber, 1980.

Melville, Herman. *Moby Dick.* Barnes and Noble, 1993.

Munch, Edvard. *The Frieze of Life.* Edited by Mara-Helen Wood. National Gallery Publications London, 1992.

New Scientist. 'Radio hum may herald quakes' by Bob Holmes. 23/30 December 1995.

The Oxford Companion to Music. Scholes, Percy A. Tenth Revised Edition, edited by John Owen Ward. Oxford University Press, 1970.

Pascal, Blaise. *Pensées.* Translated by Martin Turnell. Harvill, 1962.

Plato. *The Republic.* Translated by H.D.P. Lee. Penguin, 1955.

Sagan, Carl. *Broca's Brain: Reflections on the Romance of Science.* Ballantine, 1979.

The Song of Songs which is Solomon's. *The World English Bible (WEB).* Rainbow Missions, Inc. *http://www.worldenglishbible.org.*

Shakespeare, Nicholas. *Bruce Chatwin*. Vintage, 1999.

Sullivan, Brenda. *Spirit of the Rocks*. Human and Rousseau, 1995.

Tame, David. *The Secret Power of Music: The Transformation of Self and Society Through Musical Energy*. Destiny, 1984.

Tennyson, Alfred, Lord. *Idylls of the King*. J.M. Dent, 1934.

The Upanishads. Translated by Juan Mascaró. Penguin, 1965.

Van Wyk Louw, N.P. *Gestaltes en Diere*. Tafelberg, 1975. (Quotes from the poem *Ballad of Evil* translated from the Afrikaans, *Ballade van die Bose*, by Natasha Mostert.)

Waldrop, Mitchell M. *Complexity: The Emerging Science at the Edge of Order and Chaos*. Penguin, 1992.

Zappa, Frank. 'Rock and Other Four Letter Words' as quoted in *An Encyclopedia of Quotations about Music*. Compiled and edited by Nat Shapiro. David and Charles, 1978.

PROLOGUE

Fluisterwater
Northern Province
South Africa

The day started out so well.

She woke up feeling clearheaded and calm. The silence was a miraculous blessing. She lay with her eyes shut and she could almost visualise the quiet: a beautiful glinting thing – silvery, insubstantial – stretching into every nook and cranny of the room, creeping into every nook and cranny of her mind.

She placed her feet into the slippers next to the bed and draped the thin robe over her shoulders. As she stood up, she glimpsed her moving form in the mirror on the dressing table. These days she usually avoided looking at herself: the wild-eyed woman staring back at her made her feel afraid. But perhaps today would be different. She looked into the eyes in the mirror. Yes, the face was serene.

It was still early. The air was cool and the sky not yet intensely blue. She slid the bolt from the back door and sat down on one of the shallow steps. Breathing deeply, she inhaled the smell of grass and growing things wet with dew. From here she could see all the way across the vast expanse of yellow veld to the thin black line of the road pointing south, snaking up a far hill and then disappearing from sight. It showed no sign

I

of life: but then, it rarely did. It was five miles to the nearest neighbour; another ten to the nearest town.

Today, though, she was expecting a visitor. Tia was driving over from Johannesburg. She smiled at the thought. She had come to rely so much on these weekly visits from her daughter. When the pounding in her head became intolerable, the sounds around her toxic and magnified beyond all imagining, Tia's presence calmed her fears. She needed to feel Tia's small hand holding her own; to hear her say, 'Hang in there ... We'll fight this together.' Poor Tia. How distressing it must be to watch your mother do battle with invisible demons.

But today would be a happy day. They'd have lunch together, maybe go for a walk. Sit outside on the verandah at nightfall and watch the moon rise slowly in a sky crazy with stars. And all would be quiet.

The phone rang. The silence shattered. For a moment she tensed, but then got to her feet quickly, killing the urgent, sharp ring of the phone by snatching the receiver from the stand.

She spoke carefully into the mouthpiece: 'Hello, Klio speaking.'

'Mum?' Tia's voice sounded hoarse. 'It's this bug. It's going around campus; everyone has it. I feel really ill ... Actually,' she paused for a moment and the words came out in a rush, 'I don't think I'll be able to make it today.'

Klio slumped against the wall. But when she spoke she kept her voice light.

'That's OK, sweetheart. I'm having a really good day. And Maria will be over later to help me clean the house.'

'A good day?' The hesitation in Tia's voice was scarcely noticeable. But Klio knew her daughter. She could picture Tia's face at this moment. She would be concentrating intensely, trying to gauge every nuance of her mother's voice, her face completely still except for the tiny tick at the corner of one eyelid. It always acted up when Tia was troubled.

'Yes,' Klio said firmly. 'A good day. A very good day.'

'So, you're sure you'll be all right?'

'Absolutely. Not to worry.'

But Tia seemed unwilling to hang up. As they spoke for a few more minutes, Klio sensed her unease.

'I'm really OK, you know. And I promise I'll call you if I need to talk to you. You get some rest now. You sound terrible.'

'Yes.' Tia sniffed disconsolately. 'I feel terrible, too.'

'Make yourself a hot toddy. Then go to bed.'

'OK. I love you, Mum.'

Klio was still smiling as she hung up the receiver. She felt a sudden rush of love for her daughter. She never ceased to marvel at the strength of the bond between them. She would not have thought it possible, all those years ago when she was carrying Tia. It had not been a happy pregnancy. Nausea plagued her for seven months on end, and worse than the physical discomfort was the sense of resentment: one moment she was free, her life uncluttered. The next moment she was a pod.

But then Tia was born. She had looked into the face of her red-haired daughter, placed her hand underneath the tiny rickety neck. And kissing the soft blue-veined skin on her baby's forehead, she had lost her heart. Her daughter was a solemn-eyed child who grew up to become a quiet, reserved woman – but a woman capable of strength and unexpected warmth. Still, Klio worried about her. If only Tia had more confidence in herself, was able to break out of that shell of shyness, which sometimes made her seem aloof, stern almost.

She turned away from the telephone and walked into the kitchen, her slippers making a soft slurring noise as they brushed against the hem of her robe. Opening the kitchen cupboard, she took out a mug painted with bright yellow sunflowers. As she closed the door to the cupboard, she winced slightly as the hinges creaked. The sound was loud in that quiet room.

While she waited for the water to come to boil, she walked out into the garden. To her right was the long row of tall poplar trees, their tiny leaves coming alive with the slightest breath of air. She watched the tops of the trees as they swayed just a little and she squinted against the glare of the sun. With her eyes half-closed the trees seemed elongated, stretched into impossibly long smears of green.

She shook her head and rubbed her hand across her eyes. It was as she was starting to walk back to the house that she felt it. It came through the thin soles of her slippers: a pulse, like a heartbeat. She looked down. The earth underneath her feet was vibrating but the pulse was flawed and arrhythmic. And the silence in that quiet garden was no silence at all, but a hum like the ebb and flow of a giant spinning top.

'Nooo!' The cry tore from her breast, an ugly sound. She felt her lips stretch into a wide grimace. She placed her hands over her ears, but to no avail. There was a beating of wings inside her head and noisy invaders crashed through the deepest, most secret spaces of her mind. She felt nauseous, sick. She had to get back to the house, but where was it? She couldn't see the house because all around her were restless trees.

She started to run in the opposite direction, away from the trees and their hostile, whispering leaves. But the humming sound followed her and made the air seem alive to the touch. She ran, arms outstretched, into the yellow sea of waving grass. The white muslin gown, floating behind her, snagged on the tough stems and the tall grass cut her legs through the thin nightdress, drawing blood.

And as she ran, she knew she was hopelessly lost.

The Gongs

DAY ONE HUNDRED

The whole heaven [is] a musical scale and a number.

Pythagoras (according to Aristotle in *Metaphysics*)

The day was overcast. The slender stems of the Brixton and Hillbrow towers stretched into a sky the colour of mercury. As always, Tia felt her breath catch at the sight. There was something so ephemeral about the scene: a vast, sprawling city dumped in the middle of the open veld. She often had the feeling that one day she would steer her car around that corner only to find the city of Johannesburg reclaimed by tall tufted grass. And the skyscrapers, the shacks, the worked-out mine dumps with their black headgear, and the motorways, which twist and turn like the coils of a giant snake, would all be gone.

The road dipped beneath the wheels of the car and the square lawns and horseshoe-shaped building of the University of Johannesburg came into view. A few minutes later she pulled into the big parking lot at the back of B block.

She glanced at her watch. She was running late. But for just a moment longer she sat quietly, her fingers drumming uncertainly against the steering wheel. Then she opened her handbag and took out the slim bundle of letters.

In the right-hand corner of the letter on top was an address in the United States. The letter was dated two months earlier:

Dear Ms Theron,
    A mutual friend, Mr Ben Mbuyazi, suggested that I contact you. I shall be joining the staff of the University of Johannesburg in January as guest professor in Computer Science and Mathematics.
    My specific area of interest is resonance phenomena and as part of my research I hope to investigate the African granite boulders that were used by neolithic man as bells in religious rituals and ceremonies. Ben mentioned that you own a property in the Northern Province, which is home to four of these rocks. I would very much appreciate it if you would allow me the opportunity to study the rock gongs during my visit to South Africa . . .

The letter was signed Jon A. Falconer. The handwriting was dark and strong, the letters slanted forwards as if tripping over themselves with eagerness.

She flipped the page over and read through the copy of her own response, which was stapled to the back of the letter.

Dear Mr Falconer,
    Thank you for your letter. I regret that a visit by you to the rock gongs will not be possible.

Short and to the point. And such a terse response would have stopped most people in their tracks. But not this guy. No less than six additional letters had followed and she had lost count of the number of messages he had left on her answering machine. She had found such persistence not only annoying, but slightly disturbing. And to cap it off, last night her friend Ben had turned up on her doorstep: a man with a mission.

'Just meet with him, Tia.' Ben was at his most persuasive. 'He's a nice man. I met him during my visit to the States last year. He's not going to mess up the place with chocolate wrappers or carve his initials into the rocks, for God's sake.'

'Ben, that's not the point. You know why I don't have people over at that house any longer.'

'Yes, I know. But you've turned the place into a shrine. It's not healthy.'

'It's my business.'

'I'm not saying it isn't. And by the way, I haven't told Jon the reason you don't want people there. I respect your request to keep it private. But I promised Jon I'd put in a good word for him and I'm asking you as a personal favour. So please, for me. It can't hurt if you just have a cup of tea with him, now can it.'

Against her better judgment she had agreed, and here she was, on her way to meeting Mr Jon A. Falconer: American abroad. This was the first day of the new academic term and apparently he had arrived in the country only a week ago. They were to meet in the staff tea room. 'No pressure,' Ben had assured her. 'He just wants to talk to you. And I'll be there too.'

But she was angry with herself. She should not have allowed Ben to talk her into this. When was she ever going to learn how to say 'no' to him? She loved Ben and admired him, but he was simply too used to getting his own way.

For a moment she wondered what an American mathematician with an interest in rock gongs would look like. In her mind came the image of an eager face, thick glasses, a stooped figure kitted out in a Banana Republic outfit. She sighed. This was going to be a disaster.

Walking swiftly across the campus parking lot, she pushed past the swivel doors of B block. The air was humming with voices and she could sense that rowdy exuberance that the start of a new academic year always seems to bring. The air was thick with optimism. So many plans, so many ideas and at this time of the year, so few disappointments. As she brushed past a knot of female students dressed in minuscule tank tops, she got a whiff of youthful sweat and flowery eau de toilette. From within the depths of the student cafeteria came music turned to ear-splitting volume. An asexual voice was singing urgently about trust betrayed and love forever tainted. The music pursued her down the corridor and she found herself walking in step to the unrelenting confrontational thud of the drums. Turning right, she walked down a flight of shallow steps and into the long main corridor with its high triple-height dome.

It was quieter here and she shivered from the slight chill that pervaded the building at this level. The concrete made it feel cold. The ongoing joke on campus was that if you left the building, people on the outside would shout at you to close the door.

It was not a cosy place. With its soaring spaces, the light filtering in through slit-like windows, the overall impression was austere, cathedral-like. The place was a poem in concrete and steel: one enormous building in the shape of a horseshoe, separated from the five dormitories by two vast squares of lawn, so neat and green they looked painted. She herself disliked the wide, echoing corridors and high-ceilinged lecture halls. She longed for the traditional props of academic life: wood-panelled offices, leather-lined bookshelves, scarred wooden floors, blackboards, chalk . . .

But she supposed she had a reputation for being old-fashioned. Not only did she teach medieval poetry and culture but she was recently outed in the student paper as the only staff member in the whole of the university not to have an e-mail address. Actually, she did not even own a computer. It wasn't that she was computer illiterate – the university had forced all faculty members to take courses – but there was no doubt that computers intimidated her. Actually, she found them positively sinister. The fact that Jon Falconer was a computer geek did not count in his favour.

'He's not a computer geek,' Ben had protested last night. 'He's a fascinating man. A genuine celebrity, in fact.'

'Be still my heart. *I've* certainly never heard of him.'

'That's impossible. He designed *The Angels' Key*. You must have heard of him.'

'I have not.' Although this was not quite true. She had not heard the name Falconer before, but it was impossible not to know about *The Angels' Key*. A computer game, it was the hottest thing on the Internet right now. There was a lot of noise about the game, a lot of debate. The game was controversial with many parents claiming it to be a bad influence. The music generated by the game, they said, was unhealthily addictive and detrimental to young minds. Considering that young minds were routinely exposed to Marilyn Manson and Megadeath, this game must be really something. All of which still did not make her any more enthusiastic about meeting the man. And why on earth someone who wrote code for a living should be interested in prehistoric rocks was beyond her.

At the end of the long gently sloping corridor were leaded glass doors leading to the staff tea room. For just a moment she paused on the threshold. Then, leaving the shadowy hall behind her, she pushed open the door and saw Astrid Flemming, dressed in brightest red, waving at her from across the room.

Astrid was laughing: a throaty giggle, which meant that she was flirting and enjoying herself. The man with her stood with his back half-turned and Tia was unable to see him clearly. Dressed in jeans and a T-shirt, his hair growing thick and untidily around his ears, he stood out in the dark-suited crowd. Although she was too far away to hear every word he was saying, the accent was unmistakable. He had that peculiar American facility for making himself heard, without any conscious effort, above a number of less commanding voices. As she walked towards them, he turned around lazily.

He looked nothing like what she had expected. Despite his casual dress, he had a face that belonged to an earlier time. It made her think of a life lived in sumptuous drawing rooms where men dressed in velvet coats, lace foaming at the neck and wrist. She had seen that elongated face with the long thin nose, the thick brows above almond-shaped eyes, among the faces in an El Greco canvas. But those faces held an air of pious self-denial and melancholy. This man's smile was vital and swift and the smile of a man who certainly did not believe in denying himself anything.

'Well, finally,' Astrid gave Tia a peck on the cheek. 'We thought you weren't going to turn up after all.' She turned to the man at her side. 'Jon, here she is. Let me introduce you. Tia Theron. Jon Falconer.'

He smiled and held out his hand. It was warm, the skin surprisingly soft. Tia noticed with amusement that Astrid was sending out those signals women tend to send out when they stake their claim: touching his arm; brushing away an imaginary speck of dust from his shoulder. The message was clear as day. His smile showed that he was appreciative of the efforts made on his behalf. It was also clear, Tia thought wryly, that he was used to this kind of female attention.

'Thanks for coming.' His eyes were so dark she could hardly see the pupils. She folded her arms across her chest and then quickly unfolded them again. Crossed arms signalled aggression. She should at least try to look pleasant.

'Let me get you some coffee,' and before she could tell him that she never drank coffee, he was walking with long, easy strides towards the coffee machine.

'Where's Ben?' Tia asked Astrid. 'He said he'd be here.'

'And I am.' She felt a hand on her elbow. Ben, resplendent in a claret-coloured velvet jacket, was at her side.

She couldn't help smiling. She liked Ben a lot. He was shrewd and he could be very funny. He was also vain. When he slid his hand into the inside pocket to take out his spectacles, she saw that the inside of his jacket was lined with coral silk. He was in his early sixties but his skin – an even black, so dark it seemed tinged with blue – was still taut and looked almost polished. Ben was one of the most popular professors on campus. He taught anthropology and his lectures often had a Lyall Watsonish kind of isn't-it-incredible? flavour to them. The students loved it.

'So you made it.' He smiled at her.

'I said I would. But you owe me. And I haven't promised anything.'

'Fine. That's understood.'

Astrid's voice interrupted them. She was talking to Peter Sayles, a tall shy man – head of the chemistry department and her boss – who had just joined the group.

'Family ties,' Astrid was saying. 'They're the ties that bind and gag. Whoever said that had it about right.' Astrid had spent the Christmas holidays with her mother. A truly heroic deed, as far as Tia was concerned. She had met the elderly Mrs Flemming once before: a sharp-eyed woman with a tongue that took no prisoners.

'What did you do for Christmas?' Sayles nodded at Tia.

'Nothing exciting. Talked to my plants and tried to get some writing done.'

'How's that coming along?'

'Poorly, I'm afraid.' She frowned. 'My hero's turning out to be a wimp. I thought he was Spartacus but I've ended up with Hamlet. It's disheartening. And my other characters aren't talking to each other.'

'Writer's block. I sympathise.' Jon had returned and was handing her a cup of evil-looking black coffee.

'Thanks.' She took the cup from him gingerly.

He took a sip of his own coffee and looked down at her. The determined expression in his eyes made her sigh inwardly. Here it comes.

'Let me get straight to the point.' His voice sounded almost abrupt. 'You own this place out in the country.'

She nodded and noticed for the first time a small scar, like a welt, on the side of his face. It looked like a tiny fat slug clinging to the smoothness of his jaw.

'Astrid said it has a pretty name,' he continued. '"Babbling brook" or "burbling spring" – something like that.'

Tia's lips twitched. Astrid was a friend but she had a way of turning poetry into prose. 'It's called Fluisterwater. That means "Whispering Water".'

'Right.' He paused, cleared his throat. 'Anyway, as I told you in my letters, and as I'm sure Ben must have explained to you . . . I'm interested in rock gongs. Ben tells me there are four of them at Whispering Water. I'd like to take a look at them.' He made it sound like an order not a request.

'Well, as I told you in my letter and as I'm sure Ben must have explained to you,' she struggled to keep the sarcasm out of her voice, 'I rarely go to Fluisterwater these days and I don't have people over.'

'I've never seen a rock gong before.' He seemed to have a remarkable gift for listening only to what he wanted to. It was as though she hadn't spoken.

'I'm sorry. I can't take you there.'

'Why not?'

'I just can't.'

'Why not?'

'Look, I'm sorry. It's just not possible.'

'Why not?'

She couldn't decide what she found more provoking: his insistence or the studiedly patient tone of voice in which he spoke. As though he were talking to some querulous child. As if any objections she might have were bound to be frivolous. From the corner of her eye she could see Ben hovering anxiously, but enough was enough.

She placed her cup carefully on a wobbly side table where it rocked gently to and fro. Taking care to look Jon full in the face, she smiled sweetly.

'Why? Because it's a dangerous place.'

He frowned. 'Dangerous?'

'Yes. It's a place where people disappear.'

★　　★　　★

'It's a place where magic happens,' her mother would say. 'A special place where good and evil may unite into a harmonising force.' And then she'd smile and spread those square hands with the long white fingers in front of her.

'Fey' was a word often used to describe Tia's mother. 'Cooky', 'crazy' were words used by those who did not like Klio Theron. To Tia she was more a friend than a parent: a friend who was dazzling and fearless; impetuous, sometimes irresponsible.

Her father Tia could scarcely remember. Pieter Theron was a pilot with a passion for cars. Three years after she was born he took his Aston Martin for a breakfast run and lost control of the wheel. He was dead before the ambulance reached the hospital.

Tia grew up knowing him from the pictures that were scattered around the house. Pieter looking serious in a pilot's uniform at his passing-out parade; Pieter swinging his baby daughter above his head; Pieter and Klio together – her bare arms around his bare chest – a study in sensuality.

Klio had several lovers after Pieter's death, but she never remarried. 'Your father and I are connected still,' she told Tia. 'In another life, we'll find each other once more.'

Fluisterwater – 'Whispering Water' – was a gift from Pieter to his wife after she had given birth to Tia. It was their weekend home and would become the place where Tia spent most of her holidays. It was a wonderful place for a child: the brooding grandeur of the landscape adapting easily to a little girl's fantasies. Although there was broken terrain and many hills, the landscape was really a vast plain shaped by molten rock millions of years before and home to some of the oldest rocks on earth. During her school vacations Tia had played among these rocks, scuffing her knees on their roughness, finding secret hiding places for treasured objects, puzzling over the deep marks in the sandstone. The fossil footprints of ancient lizards, she had told herself.

And then there were the gongs. A good two hours' walk into the veld, miles away from roads and other houses, they were situated close to a deep ravine. When Klio first took her there, she had felt such awe. These rocks were objects from legend, but there they were: she could touch them, put her arms around them. Still, she had never been able to make them sing. And not even her mother, who was able to coax music from most things in life, had managed to release the sound within them. 'They must have lost their voice,' Klio explained sadly.

Tia loved Fluisterwater and, as for Klio, she was completely captivated by the place. Most people would find it a desolate spot – a house situated all by itself with the nearest neighbour more than five miles away. But to Klio it was magical. 'Don't you feel it?' she'd always say when she and Tia sat side by side on the verandah, the sky covered in stars and everything dead quiet except for the sound of the stream flowing at the edge of the dark garden. 'Don't you feel the energy? This is a place where evil and good will not be in opposition any more. Complete harmonisation. It's a place open to the music of the universe.' And Tia, delighting in these dreamlike thoughts, but not understanding and not really trying to, would merely nod and smile.

At any rate, she was used to her mother using music as a metaphor for her feelings. Before her marriage Klio had been a concert pianist and music continued to play a major role in her life. Some of Tia's earliest memories of Fluisterwater were of her mother bending over the keys of the beautiful old Steinway piano in the living room. Fluisterwater, in Tia's mind, became inextricably linked with complex harmonies and beautifully executed scales.

When she started college, Tia moved into her own apartment. At first she and Klio visited regularly and they drove out together to Fluisterwater at least every other weekend. But then came a period in which Tia was pushing to finish her dissertation and the visits to Fluisterwater, as well as to her mother's house in Johannesburg, became much more infrequent.

One morning she finished her last lecture and decided to pay her mother a quick visit. As she parked her car in front of Klio's house, Tia noticed as always at how quiet the neighbourhood was. No sound of the rush hour traffic seeped into the green seclusion of this, one of Johannesburg's oldest, most established suburbs. It wasn't a wealthy neighbourhood, but it had a feeling of permanence about it.

Tia had her own key to the house and she let herself in through the front door. For a moment she stood quietly in the living room. Through the window she could see her mother sitting on a wrought iron bench in the garden.

Klio had on a white linen dress and a large straw hat. Her hands were resting lightly in her lap. Something made Tia hesitate. The sun was so bright, it gave a sheen to the white of Klio's dress. The hat threw her face into shadow.

Klio was looking pensively ahead of her. Her face and body were completely relaxed. Tia looked at her mother's profile: at the clean, clear-cut sweep of the jaw, the long graceful neck.

Klio turned her head and her eyes met Tia's. And Tia felt her breath catch in shock.

Years afterwards Tia would still remember that moment when she had looked into her mother's face, and had seen for the first time the despair, the utter and incredible despair in those long-lidded eyes. And the fear. No, not fear. Panic. And then Klio had walked into the house, very slowly. 'I'm moving to Fluisterwater,' she informed Tia. 'And I'm not coming back.'

It took Tia a long time to coax her mother into telling her what lay behind this decision. But Klio's explanation left her feeling even more confused.

'I can't stay in Jo'burg any longer.' Klio's face was without colour. 'I can't think here. The noise. It's driving me crazy. That hum. You hear it? It just never stops.'

Tia tried to stay calm. 'What hum?'

'That hum. Listen,' and then, angrily when Tia did not respond, 'For God's sake. Open up your ears and listen for once. Really listen.'

Tia strained her ears, but all she heard were the put-put of the sprinkler in the garden; the drone of a far-off lawn-mower; the sing-song voice of a street vendor walking up and down these suburban streets selling her brooms. Safe sounds, familiar sounds.

But when she tried to reason with her mother, Klio become almost hysterical. 'Don't you dare tell me what it is I'm hearing. The sound – it's hurting my head. My eyes.' She drew a deep, shuddering breath. 'It's like I'm falling forward – forward into this dark chasm. And what I see in there . . .'

Tia insisted that Klio seek medical advice. Klio's GP was baffled. After two visits, he passed her on to a neurologist. The specialist referred Klio to a psychiatrist. The psychiatrist placed Klio on a regimen of drugs. After the first visit, he spoke to Tia alone and, alarmingly, murmured something about schizophrenia. But he also added carefully, 'Your mother's symptoms are, shall we say, a little atypical. But I'm afraid, Miss Theron, I'm very much afraid . . .'

The drugs turned Klio listless and sleepy. More worrying,

her creativity was affected. She never played the piano any more, did not try to compose any music. After four months she flushed the pills down the toilet and placed the Jo'burg house back on the market. 'Don't try to stop me,' she told Tia. 'I can't take those drugs any longer. I'm turning into someone else, a person I don't recognise. I need to be at Fluisterwater. It will be better there.' Tia saw the dark bruises underneath her mother's eyes and watched the hesitant, fluttering gestures. But for the first time in weeks, Klio's eyes were not glazed and lifeless. Tia found herself saying, 'OK. I'll help you.'

And once Klio had settled down at Fluisterwater it seemed as though things were indeed getting better. The old Klio returned: self-confident, strong. But there were times when Tia would walk in on her mother and find her sitting in front of the piano, her hands resting silently on the gleaming white and black keys as though her fingers lacked all strength. And there were those awful days when she'd find Klio curled up in a foetal position inside the closet; eyes closed tightly, hands clamped over her ears.

Tia made the journey from Johannesburg to Fluisterwater at least once a week. But one weekend she woke up with a burning throat and a high fever. She called her mother to tell her not to expect her.

'That's OK, sweetheart.' Her mother's voice had been cheerful. 'I'm having a really good day. And Maria will be over later to help me clean the house.'

A really good day. Her mother had actually repeated the phrase twice. But she should have known. She would never stop blaming herself for not getting into the car that day and driving over to Fluisterwater as planned. Because it was the last time she would ever speak to Klio and she never saw her again. That weekend Klio Theron vanished.

The police could find no evidence of foul play. No signs of a struggle. In the kitchen was a mug with a tea bag and a spoonful of sugar as if she had been about to make herself a cup of tea. Her shawl, the one with the pink roses embroidered on a background of pale yellow silk, was folded in a neat triangle on top of the pillow on her bed. In the last few weeks Tia had rarely seen her mother without it. When she saw it lying there, she had the strongest feeling that Klio might enter the room at any moment; wrap the shawl around her shoulders, pause in front of the dressing table and touch her hair with that playful feminine gesture a beautiful woman makes when she sees herself in the mirror.

Neigbours and friends were baffled and dismayed. Those who did not like Klio merely shrugged. After all, Klio Theron always did delight in doing the unexpected.

After her mother went missing Tia found herself suffering from insomnia. And she had nightmares. One dream in particular haunted her and this dream never changed. She would find herself at Fluisterwater, but a Fluisterwater that was desolate and empty and drained of colour. And she'd walk through the house, opening and closing doors and finding nothing.

The intervals between Tia's visits to Fluisterwater became longer and longer. 'When I'm there,' Tia told Ben, 'I dream too much.'

Tia changed very little at the house. She left the dresses, the blouses, the jewel-coloured velvet waistcoats as they were: draped around padded hangers and folded away in the scented drawers of the tall closets. The stacks of sheet music with Klio's pencilled notes in the margins lay undisturbed in the yellowwood chest next to the sofa. Maria, the char, continued to make the trip from the neighbouring farm once a week. But Maria did not so much as move a picture out of its place. Even the large arrangement of dried flowers was left untouched for fear of it crumbling to pieces. On her rare visits Tia would always find the dried proteas with a thickening sheen of dust on their stiff leaves.

The upkeep of the house was expensive, and the salary of an assistant professor only went so far. But she couldn't bring herself to sell Fluisterwater. And she became fiercely protective of the place. Almost to the point of paranoia. Visitors were not welcome. Why she felt so strongly that no one should disturb the place, she did not know. There was just something inside her that told her it would be wrong.

Six years earlier a young man had also vanished from the area. The police were not concerned. The young man had been a migrant worker from Swaziland and it was easy to believe he had simply packed up and returned home. But with Klio's disappearance people remembered. The farmhands on the neighbouring farms and the people from the local tribes started talking. The place of the Whispering Water, they said, has become a place where people disappear.

DAY NINETY-ONE

Wouldst thou know if a people be well governed, if its laws be good or bad, examine the music it practises.

Confucius

He noticed her immediately as she entered the drawing room. One moment he was still deep in conversation and the next moment there she was, hovering in the doorway, and suddenly nothing else in the room mattered.

Not that she was beautiful or eye-catchingly glamorous. And she was such a wisp of a thing. It was only that head of luminous red hair, which made her seem in any way remarkable. It was the first thing he had noticed about her the other day when they had met in the university's tea room. That and the wary, almost hostile look in her eyes. Her body language – the folded arms, the severe set of the shoulders – had sent out a clear message: Keep your distance.

'A place where people disappear.' He remembered the challenging tone of her voice, as though she was daring him to contradict her. And then, turning her back on him, she had walked off. Just like that. The rudeness of the gesture, as much as the oddness of her words, had taken him by surprise. For a moment he had considered walking after her, insisting that she continue their conversation. But then he decided to back off. It was the smart thing to do. Still, if she thought he was going to give up so easily, she was mistaken. He had made up his mind to study those gongs and once he made up his mind about something he always got what he wanted. Always.

In that he was lucky, he supposed. Whatever he set his heart on would somehow work out for him in the end. Academic achievement came easily to him. He had been a brilliant student and even during the tedious years of paying his dues as a junior professor, there was never any real doubt that he would get tenure. After flirting with quantum physics for a while, he had finally chosen the mathematics of resonance phenomena as his field of specialisation.

Sound fascinated him. 'Just think,' he would tell his students. 'Sound affects each one of us every single day of our lives. Music can drive up your blood pressure, lead to a drop in body temperature, a decrease in the skin's conductivity; interfere with your digestion, speed up your heartbeat . . . not to mention altering your mood. Loud sounds can put you at higher risk of having a heart attack. Certain frequencies can kill off bacteria. Some day – maybe not tomorrow – but some day in the future, scientists will be as concerned about sound pollution as they are about holes in the ozone layer.'

His academic work was controversial, to be sure, but respected. And now, with *The Angels' Key*, it looked as though he might just go down in history as the man who managed to crack one of the greatest mysteries in the science of sound. *The Angels' Key* was not just a computer game, of course. It was much, much more. And even though the game itself was only two years old, the research behind it had taken him and his friend Stephen Yale more than a decade to complete. After all these years the two of them were on the threshold of an extraordinary breakthrough.

So, he'd had a fulfilling life – professionally speaking, that is. His romantic life was less successful. He liked the company of women and he liked having them around. And he certainly did not like being alone. But none of the numerous relationships he'd been involved in had managed to go the distance. Before too long his single-minded obsession with his work would get in the way and whoever was sharing his bed at the time would get tired of having to make do with the fringes of his life.

In a way, Stephen was to blame. Stephen Yale: best buddy and exacting taskmaster. Stephen was the one who had first presented him with the challenge of *The Angels' Key* and ever since then his life had been consumed by it. For thirteen years he had worked on the problem of *The Key* night and day, thinking of little else.

Until last year. Until about four months ago when he was introduced to a visiting professor from South Africa. An anthropologist who had told him a story of sacred rocks that produced a sacred sound. A sound which had enormous healing properties. A sound so powerful, ancient cultures believed it could avert even the advent of drought and war.

There were gongs scattered throughout the whole of the African continent, Ben had told him, but they were not in use any more and their whereabouts were secret. Except that he, Ben, knew of four of these gongs: they were to be found on a piece of land in the far Northern Province of South Africa, a piece of land that belonged to a friend of his . . .

The story had enthralled him. He was a mathematician, but like many mathematicians he believed mathematics and mysticism to be complementary approaches to the same reality. And he had known suddenly and with absolute conviction that he had to see these rocks, study them. Hear for himself the magic sound. Without thinking it through or allowing anyone the chance to talk him out of it, he had taken a three-month sabbatical from his teaching job in New York. With Ben's help he had managed to secure a teaching position in Johannesburg.

Stephen, understandably, was furious. 'It's insane,' Stephen had said, his face paper-white, the British accent even more clipped than usual. 'How can you simply put your entire life on hold? And what about *The Key*? You're placing everything we've accomplished in jeopardy. That's thirteen years' work we're talking about. And for what? To chase after some prehistoric stones. A myth; a legend. It's illogical. Crazy. I don't understand it.'

Illogical. Crazy. Yes, it was certainly all of that. And he didn't really understand it himself. All he knew was that since Ben had told him about the gongs, he had become obsessed with the idea of them: with the idea that somewhere out there in Africa were rocks which had the magic ability to heal; rocks as old as time itself.

But there was one obstacle he had not counted on. He had not counted on being thwarted in his quest by a girl with fairy hair and eyes that were wide and distrustful. A girl who even now was pretending that she had not noticed him and was keeping firmly to the other side of the room.

Ben had arranged this dinner party at his house with the express purpose of bringing him and Tia together again. 'I'll invite some other people as well,' Ben suggested. 'I usually have a party this time of the year, so Tia won't feel she's being stalked.'

'Wouldn't it just be possible for you to drive me to Fluisterwater yourself? So that we can sneak a quick look at those rocks? What she doesn't know can't hurt her, right?'

Ben looked at him reprovingly. 'I wouldn't dream of abusing Tia's confidence in that manner. Besides, the rocks are situated in a very isolated spot. I wouldn't know how to get there on my own. No, you're just going to have to win her over. It's up to you, dear boy. At the party you should try and get her alone for a few minutes and this time I advise you to come on less strongly. A little small talk, first? And lay on the charm a bit.'

Well, he was willing to lay on the charm with trowels if only he could get within three feet of her. But he'd had some bad luck. One of Ben's guests, a horsy-looking woman with flabby arms, had cornered him and was not about to let him go. Ever since she had found out that he was the creator of *The Angels' Key*, she had pinned him down. And she wasn't an admirer. The way she talked about the game, you'd think it was evil incarnate.

'This computer game has really changed my Susan. She used to be such a happy girl.'

'Well, the teenaged years are difficult.' Her husband, a

diffident man with shy eyes had joined them and was placing a placating hand on his wife's arm.

'Don't be ridiculous, Simon.' The hand was shaken off with an impatient shrug of one bony shoulder. 'I've spoken to some of the other mothers as well and it's the same thing. The children are hooked on that game. It's all they do from the time they get home from school until they go to bed. Susan used to be an A student. Not any more. And that music . . . *Angel* music? It's devil music. And it's sickening.'

Sickening? Jon sighed. 'I'm sorry you disapprove,' he said, trying to keep his voice as even as possible. 'But we actually designed the game to be quite educational. The players get to compose their own music, you know. And I'm sure you'll agree that as far as violence goes, it's not a violent game. Compared to some of the other stuff out there, like *Carmageddon* or *Quake*—'

'Mr Falconer, I'm sorry. I know what I know.' She pursed her lips together and deep furrows appeared on her upper lip. 'I haven't played the game myself, of course . . .' Of course not, he thought, that would imply that she actually knew what she was talking about. 'But you must be aware that I'm not alone in my views. I read in *Time Magazine* the other day that almost a third of parents interviewed were concerned about *The Angels' Key*. And the fact that it's free on the Net is the biggest worry. The only way I'd be able to stop Susan from playing that game would be to take away her computer, which is impossible, of course. And I was shocked to find that you can now even buy that terrible music on CD. So when she's not in front of the computer, she's listening to it on her Discman. Or on the radio. There's no escaping it.'

He had to get away. Flight rather than fight seemed to be the appropriate response here. No use trying to argue with the woman. That was one thing he'd learnt from the stacks of hate mail he'd received over the past year.

'It's always good to get feedback,' he said vaguely, edging away. 'But if you'll excuse me I see a friend over there I really need to talk to . . .' Smiling at poor Simon who was still looking crushed, he started to make his way firmly towards the other side of the room.

Tia didn't seem to be having much fun either. She was part of a group which included Joe Modise, one of Ben's anthropology colleagues. Jon had already met Joe and, although he liked him, there was no getting away from the fact that the man was long-winded. Tia had a slightly vacant look in her eyes. As he watched, she suddenly nodded and smiled and was obviously excusing herself, because the very next moment she had slipped out the tall French doors leading to the patio.

Now was his chance. Picking up a fresh glass of champagne from one of the many side tables, he followed her outside.

It had felt stuffy inside the living room, but out here the air was fresh and scented with a sweet-smelling fragrance. The lights from the house lay in bright shards across the dark lawn and reached all the way to the back wall.

For a moment he watched Tia from behind. Even out here her hair seemed to catch the light. She was leaning against a pillar and there was suddenly something about the way she tilted her head and held her shoulders, which disturbed him. She seemed . . . lost.

She must have sensed someone behind her, because she turned around with a suddenness that surprised him. For a moment they stared at each other. Her face had sharpened when she saw who it was. In her eyes was that same watchful look he remembered from their first meeting.

He held out the glass of champagne at her.

She hesitated for only a moment. 'Thank you.' Her fingers were cool as they touched his. Then she turned away from him and stared out into the dark garden once again.

He glanced at her profile and realised with a mixture of irritation and amusement that he was actually nervous. It was a new feeling. Not many women managed to intimi- date him.

'Beautiful night, isn't it.' He gave her his best smile.

She didn't even bother answering. This was going to be tough.

'Are those roses?' He gestured at the outline of some bushes in the dark.

'Bourbon roses. They're Ben's passion.'

Silence again.

'So how's the book? Has your spineless hero come to a decision yet?'

At least this produced a faint smile. Hallelujah. He felt like wiping his forehead.

'Actually,' she said and the smile widened, 'he's got more backbone than I thought. If only I can get the heroine to think so too.'

He returned her smile. So far so good. Now to keep the conversation flowing smoothly and then . . .

But the next moment she surprised him again. She seemed to have the knack of keeping him off-balance. 'I'm not going to take you to Fluisterwater, you know,' she said calmly. 'But I feel I should apologise. I was a real pain the other day. I don't know what came over me. I was rude. I'm sorry.'

'That's OK. I understand.'

'What do you understand?'

'Well,' he said, feeling awkward once more. 'Astrid told me there had been some kind of . . . um . . . some kind of family tragedy.' Actually what Astrid had said was, 'Tia's lost it. Since her mother's disappearance she's behaving like Fluisterwater's some weird kind of Bermuda triangle or something. I love that girl to death and I'm sorry about her mother and all that, but *seriously*.' Sometimes listening to Astrid was like being caught in a shower of thought confetti. But seriously.

He turned and faced Tia directly. Maybe it was time for a different approach. Like begging.

'Look, I know your mother went missing while living there and I'm truly sorry. But I wish you'd reconsider. I don't want to intrude and I hate pestering you, but I desperately need to see those rocks. Please, won't you take me with you?'

'I see Maggie Page took you hostage.'

'What?' He was thrown by the abrupt switch in topic.

Tia jerked her head backwards. 'The lady who spoke to you so earnestly.'

'Oh, yes. Redoubtable woman. Let's just say I pity her poor husband.'

'Simon.' She nodded. 'He has sweaty palms.'

Her tone of voice made him smile. Obviously sweaty hands were not allowed. She continued, 'But you're right, I feel sorry for him too.'

'For all we know they're deeply in love.'

'You think?' She shrugged. 'You may be right. I've never understood marriages. Certainly not my own.'

She was married? Ben never mentioned it. Maybe that was the problem, then.

'Your husband . . .' he started cautiously.

'I'm divorced.'

'Oh.'

Another long silence.

'So who was he? Why did you marry him?'

If she was taken aback by the personal nature of the question she did not show it. 'He was a rugby player,' she said, as though that explained everything. And for all he knew, in this country maybe it did.

'He was like all rugby players: a god.'

He could feel his eyebrows rising. Before he could think of a response that could be considered even remotely appropriate, she continued. 'You're American, so you won't understand what I mean. But rugby – it's this really brutal game – these guys have no protection, you know: no helmets or shoulder pads or whatever, but it's all about speed, tremendous power and beauty. Out there on the field they're gazelles. Even though in the scrum they'll break each other's backs and take a bite out of the nearest ear.'

'It sounds completely disgusting.'

'Well, it is, of course. But it's also thrilling as hell. And the first time I saw him he had just finished a game and was dripping with blood and sun-baked sweat. Awesome.'

He couldn't decide if she was pulling his leg, and this was

not quite the conversation he had had in mind, but at least they were communicating. He should try to keep it going.

'So if he was that awesome, how come you left him?'

'Awesome isn't always enough.' And suddenly her voice was remote again without a hint of warmth and she turned her head so that he was only able to see the thick fall of bright hair and the tip of her nose.

In the room behind them, he heard laughter. The last guests must have arrived. Through a side window he could see one of the hired waiters putting the finishing touches to the long mahogany dining table decked in white, glinting with silver and porcelain. And suddenly he felt tired and a little depressed. It was beginning to dawn on him that he might not succeed in getting to see those gongs after all. What had he been thinking of anyway? Packing up and chasing after some rocks on a continent thousands of miles away? Without any guarantees that he was actually going to be able to study them once he got there? Stephen was right. The whole thing was insane.

In one corner of his mind he knew that what he was feeling was probably to be expected. He was suffering from a bad case of overload. The past three weeks had been intense. First the fifteen-hour flight from New York to Johannesburg, then a new country and new experiences following fast and furious. All in all he had been pleasantly surprised at the relative ease with which he had slipped into his new life here. Still, every now and then it would be as though he would put his foot down to find no solid surface beneath it. And he would suddenly realise that the land in which he found himself was, after all, deeply alien and the people around him strangers in every sense.

He looked away from her and towards the back of the garden. The long thin shadow of some kind of giant fern moved slowly against the garden wall. It looked for all the world like a withered hand.

'Let's go in,' he said abruptly.

She looked surprised, but nodded. As they walked up the steps, he looked back over his shoulder. The shadow against the wall was motionless now. But still he pulled his shoulders forward as though cold, and turned his face determinedly towards the warmth and the light inside.

★ ★ ★

He continued to feel out of sorts all throughout dinner. Not that dinner itself wasn't superb. The room, illuminated by two pierced brass incense-burners, gave the scene the illusion of an Arabian Nights fantasy, with Ben presiding over the bountiful dishes like a benevolent genie. But he couldn't shake the feeling of melancholy that clouded his thoughts.

Next to him Joe Modise was talking over the merits of the red wine with a rather stunning blonde going by the incongruous name of Toy. He half-listened to the lyrical, slightly pretentious phrases they were batting back and forth: 'soft-textured plumminess; dry, classy finish; tight, taut tannins.' Joe held his glass to the light and the heavy fragrant liquid lapped crimson against the fragile crystal.

Taking a sip from his own glass, his eyes moved slowly around the room. The decor was unusual to say the least. The flocked wallpaper was overpoweringly Victorian, as were the glass display cases from which the blind eyes of stuffed birds and reptiles followed one around the room. But the art on the bookshelves and against the walls, he had been told, came from all over the African continent: bronzes from Benin; highly polished wooden neck-rests from Uganda; Shoowa cut-pile embroidery from the Kuba kingdom in the Congo. And scattered throughout the large room were tall old-fashioned cases with a multitude of flat thin drawers. What did Ben keep in there, Jon wondered: long forgotten letters; exotic insects pierced by coloured pins; sheets of poetry?

He suddenly realised that the blonde was speaking to him. 'Pardon?'

'I said,' she replied patiently, 'I'm a level nine warrior.'

Well, what do you know. A genuine fan. After Maggie Page's ambush earlier, this was a relief. And a level nine? There must be a lot more to Toy than platinum hair and great cheekbones. He smiled at her, aware that Tia, on the opposite side of the table, was listening, even though she was looking the other way.

'I'm impressed. That means, you've travelled through the Shadows of Angels.'

'Definitely. And I've tasted the Poison Grass.'

He looked around the table. Most of the faces were blank. He suddenly realised that for those who had never played *The Angels' Key*, it must sound as though he and Toy were reminiscing about some kind of druggy trip.

But at least Tia had grasped what it was about. 'Tell me about the game. What's so special about it?'

'Unless you've played *The Key* yourself, I don't think you would understand.' There was just a hint of condescension in Toy's voice and he saw with amusement that Tia was bristling slightly. 'Try me,' she said, her tone sharp.

Toy shrugged. 'It's the music. That's what special about it.'

'The music is the hook,' Jon agreed. He turned his head and spoke to Tia directly. 'We deliberately designed the game that way. You see, in this game, if a player manages to pass from one level of skill to the next, he's rewarded with these digital sounds – I guess you can call it a kind of techno music, but it goes beyond that—'

'It's a crazy sound,' Toy interrupted. 'Very, very eerie. I've never heard anything like it in my life. After a while you find you're playing just so you can listen to it. You can buy the music on CD as well, and there are some live *Angel* techno acts, but nothing beats playing the game. It's as if the music in the game is continually evolving, changing. It's powerful.'

'All music is powerful.' Ben had entered the conversation. He spoke slowly, reflectively. 'It's something worth remembering. Actually, since meeting Jon, I've become inspired. I'm now thinking of teaching a course on vanishing soundscapes and the role of music in society. You know, a kind of historical perspective. Modern man tends to forget the impact that music has on the human mind, but the old ones knew very well its power.'

Ben drew deeply on his cigar. As he exhaled, the smoke seemed to curl from his mouth, his ears, his eyes. On the wall behind him hung a Dan mask carved from wood. The spherical eyes, daubed with white, the flattened cheekbones and the broad nose with its fastidious curl to the nostrils gave the mask an expression of stern serenity. For just a moment, as the smoke left Ben's lips in fragile tendrils, he showed an uncanny resemblance to the carved features on the wall behind him. He looked like a sage, Jon thought, about to impart a profound secret.

'In many ancient cultures nothing was more important than sound. Nothing.' Ben nodded for emphasis. 'And not just here in Africa. The ancient Chinese, for example, actively lived out their belief that sound forms the cornerstone of civilisation.'

Ben flicked off the ash from his cigar with one practised tap of the finger. It was suddenly quiet in the room.

'So serious were they about the power of music,' Ben continued, 'that certain chords, certain sounds were *verboten* – never to be heard. Confucius himself protested against the introduction of alien music into the kingdom. If the music of the kingdom was contaminated, so he believed, or if music fell into the hands of the wicked or the stupid, society would suffer dire consequences.'

'Like what?'

'Oh,' Ben said, 'like war. Aggression. Strife and conflict among the territories.' He placed his cigar on the edge of the heavy silver ashtray and the smoke spiralled upwards into the shadows on the ceiling.

In the pause that followed, the grandfather clock in the hallway struck the hour, the soft chimes unfurling slowly down the dark passage. It was getting late.

'The ancients believed that if sound is abused a great catastrophe might happen.' The soft vowels of Ben's native Zulu sounded through the English phrases and painted the words with a darkly beautiful timbre. 'The careless use of sound can lead to great misery, they said. Destruction. Death. And the slaughter of the innocents.'

DAY NINETY-ONE

9 P.M. EASTERN STANDARD TIME

Evansville
Pennsylvania
United States

'Mom says you have to take out the trash.'

Sebastian hardly glanced at his brother Ray who was leaning listlessly against the doorpost. The little pest has been bugging him the entire evening. First he needed help with his homework, then he wanted to play one on one. The kid was looking for attention. Usually Sebastian didn't mind too much. His kid brother was probably the only human being on this planet who admired him; who didn't think he was a loser. But tonight Sebastian felt strangely irritated and on edge.

He leaned forward and tapped a few keys on his computer. The screen in front of him blinked. Music was coming from the speakers: a low slow swell of sound. He placed his hand on the mouse, carefully moving it to one side. He clicked and the tiny red-hatted figure on the screen in front of him immediately touched his hand to a secret panel in the wall. It swung open. Cre-a-ak.

Sebastian smiled. The sound effects in this game were really amazing. And the music. Major cool. After two months of playing, he had only managed to get to level three of the game, but he knew from *firingsquad.com* and from the on-line chat room for *Angel* warriors that when you reach level five you can start composing your own stuff. He could hardly wait.

For as long as Sebastian could remember, music was the one thing in the world that made sense to him. Every penny of his pocket money was spent on buying music: his CD collection was wicked. Most of his friends were starting to think about SATs and leaving this town behind them, but he had no ambitions. If he could spend his entire life holed up in his room, earphones stuck to his head – his mind totally spaced out by Deftones or Massive Attack – he'd do it. That and playing computer games. Especially *The Angels' Key*. This game was something else.

He wished he could travel to New York City this weekend – there was an *Angel* Concert in the Park coming up – but his Mom would never allow it. But he just knew it was going to be awesome. Techno deejays at Glastonbury and the Love Parade started the trend about a year ago, combining *Angel* music with trance and techno. He had downloaded the music from the Internet and had seen the video. The crowd at Glastonbury had gone crazy. They had entered the zone.

He tapped the enter key on his computer. The red-hatted figure was now in a maze. He'd better watch out. According to Mike, there was a trapdoor somewhere in these subterranean caves just waiting to swallow up his hero. If that happened he would have to use one of the magical numbers that was keyed to a shaman song to get the hero out of trouble, but that would mean sacrificing a power chant and moving down a level. No way was that going to happen.

The music coming from the speaker was changing. There it was, Sebastian thought, his stomach clenching with excitement: a power chant. His mother hated the sound: it really freaked her out. But he loved it. It gave him a rush so strong it almost scared him. Now how to keep the chant going, that would be the trick . . .

Ray's whining voice interrupted his thoughts. 'Sebastian, Mom says—'

'Shut the fuck up!' Sebastian spun his chair around and made a grab for his brother who looked at him with shocked wide-open eyes, his mouth a stiff O.

For a moment they stared at each other. Sebastian could hear the blood thundering in his ears. His mouth tasted strange. The sudden rage inside him was so great, he had difficulty breathing.

Then Ray moved swiftly to one side, twisting free from Sebastian's grasp. Sebastian heard his feet clatter down the stairs, his voiced raised to a high-pitched, frightened bleat: 'Mo-o-m.'

Oh, man. Now his mother would go ballistic. He didn't need this.

Sebastian placed his hand against his forehead. He was surprised to feel it slick with sweat. And he felt like he wanted to puke. For a moment there with Ray he had almost lost it. He swivelled his chair slowly back and faced the computer.

What the hell was happening?

DAY NINETY

Screw thee high My heart: up to The Angels' key
What if thy strings all crack and flye?
On such a Ground, Musick 'twill be to dy.

Clemant Paman (as quoted by Wilfrid
Mellers in *Bach and the Dance of God*)

When Tia returned home from Ben's party, it was after mid-night. She was light-headed from too much wine, heavy with too much rich food, happy to fall into bed and draw the stiff, white sheets up to her chin. Before her eyelids even closed, she had stepped out into the silver coolness of dream.

Even though she knew she was dreaming, it all seemed very real. She was standing outside a house. She recognized the sweep of the thatched roof and the thick stone walls. But everything was different from what she remembered. The house looked run-down. The paint on the window frames was peeling, the panes smudged. Instead of the tall, yellow grass that usually grew around the house, there was sand – desert – for as far as the eye could see. But the sky; she had never seen a bluer sky.

She walked up the steps to the front door, which stood wide open. The house was empty. Just one echoing room after another.

As she pushed open the back door, she was surprised that

it did not creak. That door has always creaked, ever since she was a little girl.

Up to this moment, the dream had been familiar. She had walked through this house in many previous night visits. But now, as she stepped out, she suddenly found herself in the green lushness of Ben's garden. She was standing next to the fishpond, looking at a marble statue of an infant angel. It was a charming piece, the expression not overly cute or cloying. It appeared to her as though she could see the veins, blue and threadlike, underneath the marble skin of the tiny arm that held the lyre. She stretched out her hand but the figure receded before her touch. Then the eyes clicked open, the doll-like head falling to one side. The marble lips moved. The angel opened his mouth and screamed: a soundless scream, which made the trees bend and heave as if in a strong wind.

Tia jerked awake. Sunlight was streaming into the room. From three blocks away, the sound of the traffic in Empire Avenue seeped into the house.

Behind her eyes was an ache. She'd had far too much to drink at Ben's party the night before. And she had been dreaming. An empty derelict house. A sense of total loss. And that feeling of disquiet that always lingered afterwards.

She walked into the bathroom and winced at the face in the mirror. She looked terrible. Her thick red hair — usually her best feature — was a tangled mass with no lustre or gloss. There were dark rings around her eyes and her skin had that mottled look that usually signalled that she's had a late night out. What was that old joke? A vision the night before and a sight the day after. There was a time when she could have partied all night long without her looking the next morning like the ghost of Christmas Yet to Come. Not that she ever really did party all that much, not even when she was married to Mr Party Time himself. She had always felt awkward around his rugby-playing friends — all of them beautiful and strong with slightly brutal eyes — and after a while he hadn't bothered taking her along with him any more.

She remembered Jon Falconer's question the night before. 'If he was that awesome, how come you left him?'

How come indeed. She could have answered: because he made me feel inadequate, a loser; because we had nothing to say to each other – never really had, not even when we were still fresh to each other and eager to explore. She could have gone into the details of his endless drinking sessions with the boys and the rows that followed with mind-numbing predictability. Not that it had been a horrendous marriage: no drag-down kicking and clawing at each other's soft spots; just boring and slightly desperate at the same time. A marriage like so many other marriages. And when she had found him in bed with another woman, what had – shockingly – hurt the most, was that the woman was not that good-looking. She could even be called plain. A busty blonde with a gorgeous smile – Tia could have handled that. But as it was, she had never felt more of a failure.

Leaning forward, Tia placed her hands at the side of her face, drawing the eyes into an oriental slant. 'You're getting old,' she told the face in the mirror severely. As though there was anything she could do about it.

But by the time she arrived at campus for work she was feeling better. She had had yet another cup of coffee and a cold shower and while getting dressed, she had listened to Nina Simone singing *Feeling Good*, followed by Mozart's *Clarinet Concerto in A minor*. The combination of Simone and Mozart always made her feel terrific. Voluptuous sophistication and crystalline purity: it never failed.

As she stepped out of the elevator on the eighth floor, she hesitated for a moment. Then, instead of turning right towards her office, she continued across the skywalk that linked C block with B block. When she got to the other side she walked down the wide corridor and past the glassed-in labs where rows of students sat praying over their terminals.

Tia moved her shoulders slightly at the sight of those hunched-over figures in front of their computers. She still used a typewriter and often wrote first drafts with an old-fashioned nibbed pen. She knew her colleagues regarded her pen as an affectation, a kind of inverse snobbery. But she found genuine pleasure in the almost ritual aspect that comes with using the pen: feeling its elegant balance in her hand, dipping it into the silver inkwell, blotting up the excess ink with paper as soft as cotton.

In front of the door that carried the nameplate Prof. J. Falconer, she stopped and knocked. There was no answer. She turned the handle cautiously and stepped into the room.

It was a spacious office with a nice view of the athletic fields. In the distance, smudged with smog, were the glass towers of downtown Jo'burg.

She looked around her. Jon's jacket, tweed with worn leather patches on the elbows, hung shapelessly over the back of his chair. A somewhat insanitary-looking canvas bag rested on top of his desk. The words *Grateful Dead* were stencilled on the front flap and next to the words was a picture of a grimy rose from which sprouted a dazed-looking skull.

Against the one wall were two posters. One was a photograph of Frank Gehry's Experience Music Project in Seattle: Paul Allen's 'swoopy' fantasy. The other was a poster with the words ANGELS' KEY FESTIVAL printed at the top in fluorescent script. She moved closer and looked at it curiously. It was an aerial shot of thousands of swaying bodies and what looked like the biggest outdoor stage she had ever seen.

She turned her attention back to the desk. A framed photograph was facing towards the room and she picked it up. It was a black and white photograph of Jon and two other men. The picture was just the tiniest bit out of focus. The one man, heavy shouldered and wearing wire-rimmed glasses, had his arm around Jon's neck. They both had their eyes narrowed against the sun. The other man was on the very edge of the photograph. He had his face turned almost completely sideways so that one only got the impression of a strong jaw and decisive mouth and nose. She turned the picture around. On the back someone had written: 'Jon, Richie and Stephen. May the force be with us!'

'Can I help you?'

Tia turned around to find a student with a spectacular head of dreadlocked hair behind her. He had an enquiring look on his face.

'I'm the TA,' he said. 'If you're looking for Professor Falconer, he's having his fencing practice.'

'He fences?'

The student grinned and showed a row of perfect teeth. 'Yeah. Regular Zorro. If it's urgent – you can catch him at the gym. Otherwise I'll give him a message.'

'No. Thanks. I'll track him down.' The gym was at the other end of campus and she had to teach the next class, but she wanted to talk to Jon before she had time to change her mind.

Ten minutes later she walked into the gymnasium. As she stepped inside, she had to blink her eyes against the sunlight that was falling in broad bands of yellow onto the piste where two figures in white were fencing. Tia watched fascinated. The two masked figures were engaged in a formal, highly disciplined dance. Despite the thrust and parry of the swords there was a stillness, a remoteness, about the scene.

The two men separated and lowered their blades. Jon took off his mask and tucked it under his arm. Turning sideways, he looked over to where she was standing. In the honeyed light, with his heavily lidded, hooded eyes, and the long mouth with the full lower lip hinting at sensuality, he looked more than ever to her like a figure who might have been captured on canvas. Some Spanish nobleman, maybe, enmeshed in a world of secrecy and intrigue.

He peeled off the long white leather glove from his sword hand. 'You looking for me?'

'I didn't know you fenced.'

He shrugged. 'Just a little make-believe on my bread.'

'That's how you got the scar then.' She looked at the welt on his chin, which she had noticed when they were introduced to each other for the first time.

He touched it. 'This? Souvenir: courtesy of a friend of mine.'

'So that's what friends do to each other?'

He grinned. 'Only if they're best friends.'

He stooped and retrieved a gym bag from behind a chair. 'It happened way back when we were young and into this Heidelberg macho bullshit,' he continued, slinging the strap of the bag over his shoulder. 'You know, fencing without masks and that kind of thing. I wouldn't dream of doing it any more. Although Stephen might. But then he's crazy. So,' he said abruptly and looked at her appraisingly, 'to what do I owe the pleasure?'

She swallowed. She felt nervous. 'Actually,' she paused. 'Actually, I'm thinking of going to Fluisterwater for the long weekend.'

She glanced at him. He didn't say anything.

'So, I was thinking – if you're still interested, you're welcome to come along.'

'What made you change your mind?'

She looked into those pitch black eyes. 'I don't really know.' And that was true. Even as she was talking, she was aware that one part of her brain was protesting against her decision. The sane part.

They had been walking in the direction of the locker room and from behind the door in front of them came the sound of running water and high-pitched shouts of laughter.

'I'd be happy to come,' he said almost formally. Then his face broke into a delighted grin. 'This is great. Great,' he repeated.

'There's just one thing . . .'

'Yes?'

'The gongs – I hope you're not going to be disappointed.'

'Why would I be disappointed?'

'The sound they make is not that compelling. It's not really a big sound at all. At least that's the way I remember it. But then, I haven't visited the gongs in years.'

'I'm sure it's going to be wonderful,' he said confidently. 'Don't worry about it.'

'I'm just saying, after you've seen them there won't be

anything else for you to do. And we're going to be there for three days. You might get bored.'

'I never get bored.'

She wondered if that were true. There was something in his eyes, a restless energy, which made her suspect that it might not be.

'Well, I'll let you know nearer the time what the arrangements are,' she said and turned around to leave. 'I'm asking Ben to come along as well.'

'Tia.'

She glanced back over her shoulder.

'Thanks,' he said. 'I can't wait.'

DAY EIGHTY-SEVEN

Great Lakes region
Burundi
Central Africa

Jabulani Lumbwe was worried. Of course he couldn't even remember a time when he had not been scared. Ever since his entire family were wiped out in the great massacre, he had not been free of thoughts of death. Still, during the last few years, things had been relatively peaceful in this village in the north of Burundi and he had managed to relax; just a little. Until now. Something was wrong.

Jabulani didn't know why, but his heart was heavy with dread. He watched a giant moth settle close to the yellow light of the kerosene lamp. Its outsized shadow fell on the clay wall: a startling shape. The air inside the thatched roof hut was close and humid. The night has brought scarcely any relief from the heat.

The villagers were sleeping. It was quiet. Quiet, except for the tinny sound of his neighbour's radio that has been playing non-stop for days now. Always the same station. And the same kind of music. Jabulani did not care for that kind of music. It was unlike anything he had ever heard and it made him tired just listening to it. He had thought of asking his neighbour to switch it off, but he was wary of the man. He didn't trust him. And for the past few days the man's eyes had been bloodshot.

43

It could simply be a case of too much home-brewed beer, but Jabulani sensed that something else was going on: something he did not understand.

He sighed and walked towards the door of his hut. It was so hot, he would have liked to have left the door open, but his chest was tight with fear. Just before he closed the door and bolted it tightly, he paused. He placed his hand behind his ear so that he could hear better. Maybe he had imagined it, but no, there it was again.

A sound: like a hum.

DAY EIGHTY-SIX: AFTERNOON

I stood in the woods for long periods of time, my ear to the trunk of a tree . . . trying to push the edges of my sound envelope. I realized that everything must be making sound; the process of photosynthesis must be producing vibrations, if only we had sensitive enough ears. I began hearing the sacred in the music.

Mickey Hart, *Drumming at the Edge of Magic*

The long weekend did not officially start until Saturday, but the exodus of students and staff members was already in full swing by Friday morning. When Tia pulled the office door shut at two o'clock that afternoon, the corridors were almost empty. Here and there a voice echoed from downstairs.

For a moment she looked over the railing down into the main well to where she could see a few students moving around on the ground floor. The feeling of nausea pushed up warm and familiar in her throat. Heights did this to her. Which was why, perversely, she always looked. It was a compulsion: one she has had since childhood. She'd force herself to look down stairwells or peer out over balconies, but always with that scared, scared 'who-do-you-think-you're-kidding' feeling at the back of her mind. 'You don't need to prove anything,' Klio used to say. 'Fear of heights is nothing to be ashamed of.' But she couldn't help it, she did feel ashamed – intensely ashamed – of this fear so stupidly senseless and debilitating.

The elevator was empty and the ride down smooth and uninterrupted. She opened the glass door that gave access onto the parking lot. It was good to feel the sunshine on her face, to leave the chill of the high vaulted ceilings and empty echoing corridors behind her. She glanced at her watch. She would have to hurry. Jon was probably already waiting for her.

Since their conversation in the gym she had bumped into him only twice: once in the cafeteria and once when he was in Astrid's company.

Later that day Tia had made a point of talking to Astrid. 'Why don't you come along as well? You've never visited Fluisterwater before.'

Astrid looked at her thoughtfully. 'Any other time I would have jumped at the opportunity. You've always been so secretive about that place. But I don't think this is the right time. I don't think Jon would want that.'

'But I thought you two—'

'Yes. That would have been nice. But no, it didn't work out that way. Not for lack of trying, though: at least on my part.' Astrid hesitated. 'Actually, to be honest, I'm a little relieved as well.'

Tia looked at her sharply. 'Relieved?'

'Some people – some men; you shouldn't get too close to. They draw you in, completely. Their concerns become your concerns: your *only* concerns. I can see that happening with Jon. I just think it would be exhausting. I'd have to be constantly alert not to lose myself. That's a tiring way to live. Much better to just be friends.'

The conversation left Tia feeling uneasy. And, to tell the truth, now that she had gotten herself into it, she wished she could back out of the whole thing. If only Ben were going on this trip as well, but he had begged off at the last minute: an out-of-town relative had appeared on his doorstep unannounced. So here she was, all on her own, on her way to pick up Jon at his apartment. She still couldn't believe she was doing this.

Jon had told her that he had signed the lease on a one-bedroomed flat in a building that was situated close to Rockey

Street in Yeoville. It was an area that hovered uncertainly between sexy and sleazy. With its tattoo parlours, ethnic restaurants and hard rock clubs, Rockey Street could seem deliciously bohemian and liberatingly different from the staid green suburbs of northern Johannesburg. But the street life here was truly bizarre at times and the crime rate in the area was rising steeply. The building in which Jon lived was a rather tired-looking apartment block called Drake House, but as she stopped the car outside the entrance, she noticed that the street itself was pleasant: leafy with wide sidewalks.

As she had expected, he was already waiting for her. She leaned over to unlock the back door so that he could stow a battered-looking overnight bag and a black laptop computer onto the back seat. They pulled away from the kerb and he started opening the window on his side.

'Don't do that,' she said automatically.

He stopped, surprised. 'Why not?'

'Car hijackings. Someone should have warned you by now. Wait till we're out of the city.'

They were quiet as they waited at a pedestrian crossing. Across the street from them was a huge billboard advertising the current hot topic on talk-radio: the possible reintroduction of the death penalty. Next to a gigantic mockup of a hanging noose were the words 'COULD A SNAP DECISION PUT AN END TO CRIME?' The inane faces of the breakfast talk show hosts grinned down at them. 'TUNE IN TO THE CEREAL KILLERS. ONE MAN. ONE QUOTE.' Tia winced.

The sun beat down on the tarred surface of the road. Even inside the car she could smell that sweetish smell that she always associated with the city: a musky odour of dust, sweat and overheated bodies. A girl in a school uniform – slender, with a beautiful long neck – glided by with the haughtiness of a ramp model. Behind her followed a youth with a severely acne-scarred face. As he passed the car he slammed his fist on the bonnet and gave Tia a blind look. She recoiled involuntarily before the blank anger in his eyes.

She had often thought about moving away from Johannesburg.

47

In many ways it would be a relief to leave behind the filthy streets, the endemic violence. But it was addictive: this city pulsing with greed and need and high expectations. A city holding within its heart all of the continent's dark potential for self-destruction but also energy, ambition and a creativity that dazzles. The contradictions kept her hooked. Living in Jo'burg, she always thought, was like being with a man for whom you feel a strong passion. You're disenchanted with his messy habits, you're threatened by his anger. But you find excuses not to leave him because he never ceases to intrigue.

She glanced over at Jon. She wondered what he was thinking of the place. It must be very different from what he was used to.

'How are you settling in? Is Jo'burg what you expected?'

He turned his head towards her and smiled. 'I'm not sure what I expected. I left New York in a hurry. Didn't really have time to develop any ideas about what was waiting for me. Probably a good thing. The only thing I thought about were those rocks.'

'The gongs.'

'Yes.'

From the corner of her eye she saw him move in his seat so that his back was against the door and he was almost facing her. 'Tell me about the place. About Fluisterwater.' He pronounced the word carefully, as if each syllable held a special significance.

'Not much to tell, really. It used to be one of the largest farms in the district. But at the turn of the century, during the Anglo–Boer War, the farm became a casualty of the scorched-earth policy of the British.'

'And then?'

She shrugged. 'It's not a happy story. The owner at the time was a man called Zacharias Botha. He returned home after the war to find the fields black and the house a ruin. His wife and three of his seven children had died in a British camp so I suppose it's not surprising he decided his luck lay elsewhere. He sold off most of the original farm, but he wanted to hold on to the water-rights so he kept the house and a piece of the original land – it's still quite big and runs for several miles. As far as I know he eventually died in a mining accident. Many years later, one of his surviving children had the burnt-out house rebuilt. He lived there till his death and it was his son who finally sold Fluisterwater to my father. My father agreed to keep the land as an animal and plant conservation area.'

'And the gongs?'

'Oh, they've been there forever. The local people know about them, but that part of Fluisterwater is extremely isolated – miles away from anywhere – and the rocks have not been disturbed at all.'

'Is it pretty there?'

She thought for a moment. 'Pretty? It's beautiful . . . but austere. You'll see.'

'Are you an only child?'

She glanced over at him, surprised. 'Yes. Why do you ask?'

'I was just thinking: it must have been lonely growing up there.'

'I only spent weekends and vacations at Fluisterwater. But I've never minded the isolation.' She paused. 'And you? Do you have any brothers or sisters?'

'Richie. My younger brother. Actually, I spoke to him only this morning. He's thinking of coming out here himself. Poor guy is nursing a broken heart: he just split up with his girlfriend. As a matter of fact – she used to be my girlfriend.'

She glanced at him again. 'You just decided to pass her on to your brother?'

'Of course not. She's a lovely girl. Her name is Cassidy. Tall, athletic, blonde. She looks like she's stepped out of *Baywatch*.'

'So she looks like a genetic experiment.'

He laughed, genuine amusement in his voice. 'Well, let's say a genetic experiment that worked out really well.'

'So what was the deal with you two?'

'After we dated for a while, she fell for Richie instead.'

'This is very sad.'

49

'Well,' Jon said lazily, 'he's much more her type. She's into crystals and New Age and all that. I'm into mysticism myself, but I can't hold a candle to Richie. He's the quintessential space cadet.'

'Space cadet?'

'Yeah. He's not into any of the mainstream religions, but he's constantly looking for spiritual meaning in his life. He can recite pages from the Carlos Castaneda books. When *The Celestine Prophecy* was published, he practically slept with it under his pillow. He was all fired up about energy flow, the new evolution and human beings vibrating themselves into a different dimension.'

'I saw a photograph in your office the other day. You were on it and two other guys—'

'Oh sure,' he said immediately. 'That's Richie and my friend Stephen Yale. The one with the glasses is Richie. And I don't know how well you remember that picture, but the one looking away from the camera is Stephen.'

Tia recalled the clear-cut profile and the slim figure, which nevertheless gave an impression of whippy strength.

'You're pretty close, aren't you?'

'Three musketeers. Or were there four? That picture was taken on a special day.'

'Special how?' she asked, when he did not continue.

'It was the day we started work on *The Angels' Key*.'

'So you're all working on it together.'

'Well, it's really Stephen and me. But Richie's a good programmer. He's been doing some of the legwork. Still, it's not really his baby. I'm sorry to have to say that he has misgivings about the whole thing.'

'What do you mean by "misgivings"?'

'He doesn't like the hysteria. The cult following that's developed around the game. He's squeamish that way.'

'And you're not.'

'Of course not. It's great. There's no such thing as bad publicity.'

'So why aren't you making money out of this? The game

is free, right? Anyone plugged into the Net can play? I'm sure if you charge for it you could make a fortune.'

'Maybe later. Not now. Right now it's not the money that interests us.'

He suddenly yawned noisily and quite unashamedly. 'Sorry,' he said and yawned again. 'I've worked throughout the night. How long before we get there?'

'Another three – four hours at least.'

'In that case, would you mind if I took a nap? I could do with the sleep.'

And despite the awkward angle at which he had to fold his long legs and the uncomfortable position of his head, he fell asleep almost immediately. Tia, suffering as she did from insomnia, her sleep plagued by dreams, found it fascinating: this facility he had for simply closing his eyes and dropping out of the world around him. He slept with an almost intense concentration.

Once outside the city, she put her foot down and drove the car to its limits. She loved speed. It was, as far as she could tell, the only thing she had inherited from her father. That and his red hair and an exasperating tendency to freckle.

Jon did not wake up once as the car sped through the long miles of yellow farmland. He did not even wake up when she stopped at a gas station. Whenever she glanced over at him, she was surprised by the wary, almost secretive look on his face. The line of his mouth was taut, not softened by sleep. But his body was relaxed and his hands, resting on his knees, were turned palms up, as if in supplication.

★   ★   ★

By the time she turned the nose of the car into the long dirt-packed driveway leading up to Fluisterwater, the sun was setting and the stone walls of the house were turning pink.

She searched for the key among the pot plants above the ledge, awkwardly balancing a box of groceries on her knee.

'Is it wise to leave the key there?' Jon asked, looking around him.

'Probably not. But there's nothing so frustrating as making the trip from Jo'burg and finding that I haven't brought it with me.'

'Mind you,' he said as she fitted the key to the lock. 'There can't be many people around here.'

'The nearest neighbours are about five miles away. They run a guest house and private nature resort. If you climb to the top of that hill, you can see the house. They're nice people. I've known them since childhood. They keep an eye on this place for me.'

The house was cool inside. The thatched roof made the temperature inside the house comfortable, even on the hottest day.

'This is so pretty,' Jon said, as she switched on the light. He sounded as though he meant it. But then she supposed it was a nice room. Everything in it looked a little shabby, a little worn. If you sat on the sofa, you sank almost to the floor. The springs were shot and the down cushions refused to fluff any longer. But it was a calm room and there was a big wood-burning fireplace. Soft lamps and many books lined the walls. From one of the bay windows came the rich gleam of a piano.

It was a large house, but simply designed. Two separate wings flanked the living room, which formed the centre of the house. The guest bedroom was in the wing closest to the front entrance. Tia walked down the passage and turned the handle to one of the doors. She motioned to Jon to walk in.

Jon dropped his satchel and travel bag onto the wooden floor. Lifting the lid off the carved chest at the foot of the brass bed, Tia took out some folded sheets.

She glanced over to where Jon was standing at the window, his back half-turned. He was looking out into the garden where the shrubs and flowers were turning from green to grey in the gathering dusk.

She placed the pile of sheets at the foot-end of the bed.

'Make yourself at home,' she said. 'Bathroom's at the end of the passage.'

'Thanks.'

'Anything else I can get you?'

'No, thanks.' His voice was absent-minded. Then he glanced over his shoulder, 'It's very quiet here, isn't it.'

'I suppose so.'

He looked as though he were about to say something else, but then changed his mind.

'I'll heat us some soup later on,' she said as she walked to the door. He nodded. Before she had even left the room, he had turned his head towards the window once again.

Her room was in the opposite wing of the house. It was a spacious room but sparsely furnished. A double bed with a cream quilt, two night tables and a small dressing table with an oval mirror were the only pieces. A rag rug on the timber floor supplied some colour to the monochromatic colour scheme. She had made that rug herself as part of a project for her home economics class in high school. She was not good with her hands and had found the project a chore. Klio, however, had insisted that the rug was a masterpiece.

She opened the small overnight bag. She had brought only a few things with her. She unpacked carefully, taking her time. She refolded the blouses and the one sweater. She arranged the toiletries into little clumps and placed her brushes in a neat row on top of the dressing table. When she looked up, she found herself staring at her reflection in the oval mirror. Her face seemed pale to her.

She supposed she couldn't postpone it any longer. She walked out into the passage and stopped in front of the next door down. After a moment's hesitation, she turned the knob.

Her feet made no sound on the thick pile of the oriental carpet. Klio's bedroom. As usual she felt the presence of her mother strongly. It wasn't just the gold framed photograph on the night stand that reminded her of her mother – the entire room glowed with the jewel colours Klio preferred: amethyst, teal, ruby and coral. Every tapestry, every rug and ornament told of her mother's love for colour and texture.

She walked over to the tall closet and opened the heavy door. The dresses felt cool when she slid her hands between them. And faintly, more imagined than real, was the scent of cedar and sandalwood.

Sometimes she missed her mother more than she would have thought possible. She closed her eyes. She could see Klio in front of her holding out her arms, but she herself was small and wobbly on her feet and her mother seemed immensely tall. Then the arms came swooping down towards her, and she had her face in her mother's neck and the vanilla smell of her mother's skin filled her mind.

She opened her eyes. The sleeve of a silk robe was clenched in her hand. She opened her fingers and the sleeve fell silently back into place, the fragile fabric crumpled.

On the top shelf, next to a soft pile of stacked sweaters, was a shoe box. Tia lifted the lid. The box held a jumble of objects: a week-at-a-glance diary, the pages covered with pencilled-in notes; Klio's ID documents and her passport; a small bundle of report cards of Tia's first years in school.

Tia paged through them with idle curiosity. '. . . Tia is a well-behaved child who pays attention in class. She is a shy girl and seems to have difficulty making friends . . .'; '. . . no trouble, but a reserved little girl . . .'; '. . . increased tendency to daydream.'

Klio had been so dismissive of these comments. 'Nonsense, she's not shy. She's independent. With a strong imagination.' And Tia, unable to argue against the certainty in her mother's voice, had kept the frequent moments of awkwardness, of tongue-tied, stammering shyness to herself. The shyness that had bedevilled her school years and which even today, she knew, could make her seem solemn and watchful. She had kept this shyness hidden from her mother. And anyway, in Klio's company she had always felt like a different person. Klio had that effect on people. The effervescence of her personality was such that it overflowed like champagne, and if you were lucky enough, some of the sparkling drops fell on you.

Tia sensed someone behind her and turned around. Jon was leaning his shoulders against the doorway. How long he had been standing there, was impossible to know. Her first feeling at seeing him was one of resentment. A sanctuary had been breached.

His voice when he spoke was gentle. 'You miss her.'

She didn't answer. She replaced the shoe box and closed the closet door with a loud click.

'So this was her room.'

'Yes.'

Jon picked up the framed photograph of Klio from the wicker night stand. It was a studio photograph with clever lighting throwing the planes of her mother's face into relief, accentuating the high cheekbones, the wide forehead. Klio was looking over her shoulder. She was wearing a dress Tia remembered well. Black velvet with almost no back at all.

'What was she like?'

'She was beautiful. And strong.'

He turned his head towards her and gave her a measuring glance before looking back at the photograph in his hands.

'We aren't at all alike.' Tia wished her voice didn't sound so defensive. 'She didn't have the red hair. She was so fair, and tall. And fun-loving. Nothing scared her.'

She stopped. She wasn't telling the truth. She remembered Klio's panic at hearing terrifying sounds that lived only inside her own mind. Sounds that were driving her insane. 'Almost nothing scared her,' she amended.

She took the photograph from Jon and replaced it on the night stand. Then she walked to the door and waited for him to follow her out into the passage. Giving one last glance around the room, she switched off the light.

'Everything OK?'

She looked over her shoulder to where Jon was waiting, an enquiring look on his face.

'Everything's fine.' She pulled the door firmly shut.

DAY EIGHTY-SIX: LATE EVENING

Despite all Sunday-school teaching, life is necessarily a compromise; perfect truth is unattainable, and so is perfect tuning.

The Oxford Companion to Music, Tenth rev. ed.

It was so quiet Jon could almost hear every thought as it clicked over in his brain. And the darkness was incredible. Even with the curtains open, he was scarcely able to discern the outline of the armchair, the bulge of his overnight bag where it lay propped up against the wall underneath the window.

The room had just the hint of a musty smell to it: the same smell that clung to the sheets Tia had given him for the bed. The room had obviously not been used in a long time. But like the rest of the house the air felt strangely charged: as though the house was holding its breath expectantly – waiting for something, someone.

Despite his nap in the car he was tired, and had welcomed the opportunity to turn in just after dinner. But the strangeness of his surroundings and the smothering silence had kept him awake. This was unusual for him. He usually had no problem whatsoever going to sleep. But for the past hour or so he'd been lying on his back, arms folded underneath his head, eyes wide open.

A cigarette would be a sure-fire way of relaxing, but quitting was one of the goals he had set himself when he left New York.

Without Stephen around he might actually be able to do it. Stephen was a chain smoker and he had picked up the habit himself during those late night sessions when the two of them would sit back to back, poring over their work; cigarettes, coffee and Coca-Cola their engine fuel. He wondered what Stephen was doing at this moment. Probably slouched behind his desk in front of his computer, the tip of the cigarette burning red in the darkness, his hands moving over the keys like a master pianist. Stephen had a very specific way of tapping the computer keys: a kind of rhythm that was fluid, almost musical. He had always thought he'd be able to identify Stephen's keystroke blindfolded from among the keystrokes of a hundred other hackers.

It was strange to think that this was the first time in thirteen years that the two of them had been apart from each other for any length of time. They had met in college and, ever since, *The Angels' Key* had kept them inseparable.

The Angels' Key. An obsession. A magnificent obsession, he had always thought. But since leaving New York he felt just a little lethargic whenever his thoughts turned to this project he's been working on almost his entire adult life. The idea of it still excited him, but the sense of urgency had abated. Maybe it was burn-out. Thirteen years is a long time. Maybe it was because he was no longer within Stephen's orbit; was no longer exposed to the intensity of Stephen's single-mindedness.

The world thought of *The Angels' Key* as an entertaining computer game producing some cool music. But it was so much more. It was a tool, an incredibly wonderful tool, which would ultimately allow him and Stephen to find the solution to a deeply challenging mathematical problem. A problem that had kept them occupied for more than a decade now.

There was no doubt that Stephen was the one who had given the entire project life. Even though he, Jon, would probably be the one who got the credit. In a way it was unfair. If it hadn't been for Stephen, the problem that lay at the heart of *The Angels' Key* would still be only an elegant mathematical riddle: a problem that students of music and mathematics would examine and then put aside as one puts aside an impossibility – like trying to square the circle.

Except that the circle was just about to be squared.

He still couldn't believe it. He, Jonathan Adam Falconer, would be responsible for solving one of the greatest puzzles the science of sound had ever known. A puzzle that had confounded brilliant minds over the centuries. Pythagoras, Bach. Even though they tried, neither one of these geniuses had been able to give the world the gift that was now his to bestow: the gift of perfect musical tuning.

He was so used to the concept, it always surprised him how few people were aware of the fact that it is actually impossible to tune a modern musical instrument with one hundred per cent accuracy. Even an expert piano tuner in laboratory conditions would not be able to tune a piano to acoustic perfection. Each and every instrument was always tuned just the tiniest bit off-key in order to accommodate a mathematical blip – a flaw. This mathematical flaw had been christened the Pythagorean Comma by musicologists and was the reason why perfect musical tuning did not exist in this world. The reason why the world was filled with musical instruments that were all slightly off-key. Only a perfect musical scale from which the Pythagorean Comma had been eliminated would ensure perfect tuning. But no one has ever been able to create such a scale.

Over the ages a number of solutions had been proposed to resolve the imperfection in musical intervals. He and Stephen had studied them all and found them wanting. Pythagoras gave the world a scale based on perfect fifths that was acoustically flawless but which did not allow for musical innovation – so it had to be abandoned. Bach compromised. His system of equal temperament allows for modulation, but is acoustically flawed. The system of 'just intonation', with its perfect thirds does not take care of the Comma problem either. Every solution that had been dreamt up over the millennia had turned out to be a compromise. And compromise was not perfection. And perfection was the goal: it was what he and Stephen had set their hearts on.

Perfect tuning. A perfect musical scale. It was within their reach. For years he and Stephen had painstakingly pieced together the various pieces of the puzzle. And over the past eighteen months they had designed the computer game as the final key with which to unlock the entire mystery. Very soon the means would exist to create musical instruments tuned to absolute perfection. And he would be responsible. He and Stephen.

Poor Stephen. *The Angels' Key* was his whole life. There was something poignant about his dedication, because Stephen was handicapped. An accident in his youth had left him partially deaf and suffering from severe tinnitus. But here was someone with a hearing problem, willing to devote his entire life to solving one of the most intricate mysteries in the science of sound. It always made him sad to think of it. Not that Stephen would welcome his pity. Stephen was a proud man.

Jon sighed and turned his head to look at the illuminated alarm clock on the bedside table. He really should try to get some sleep. He moved restlessly, flinging the top sheet away from him. It was no use. Sleep was impossible. He was going to have to give in to temptation and light up. He swung his legs over the edge of the bed and searched for the light switch on the old-fashioned lamp that perched lop-sidedly on the night table.

The light was soft and barely illuminated the far corners of the room. He stood up and padded barefoot to where his jacket lay on the weathered pine desk. As he pushed his hand into the inside pocket, groping around for his cigarettes, he kept his eyes on the row of black-framed photographs on the wall. They were mostly landscapes: long, wide-angled shots of sunburnt veld. One picture showed a toddler in a red dress standing underneath a grey-barked thorn tree. He wondered if it could be Tia. It was not a close-up shot and the shadows of the spreading tree branches were too deep for him to see the colour of her hair. But he rather thought it might be her. It wasn't so much her features, but something in the way she held herself that seemed familiar. Even at that age, she already had the aura of being a deeply private little person. And she already seemed to exhibit that same mixture of defencelessness and resoluteness, which to his mind was her most outstanding characteristic. He had been particularly aware of it earlier tonight in her mother's bedroom. The slender neck, the shoulders slightly drooping, made her seem vulnerable; but the look in her eyes had said: no sympathy necessary thank you. He sensed a mental toughness there, a courage that impressed him. Gallant. That was the word he's been looking for. She was a gallant person.

He wondered what the mother had been like. Beautiful, Tia had said. And strong. He recalled the clear planes and fresh smile of the face in the picture, and agreed. The mother was a stunner. But Astrid had used the word 'strange' in her description of Klio Theron. 'She was a really strange woman. Very charismatic, of course, and she had an incredible musical mind, but her ideas were decidedly odd. I must say, I was not altogether surprised when she simply disappeared like that. It was sort of in character.'

Lighting his cigarette, Jon walked over to the window and looked out into the darkness. There were millions of stars in the sky. Their brightness was of an intensity he had never seen before, but their icy glitter did not seem to shed any light. The darkness was almost tangible. If you got lost in it, he thought, you might never find your way back again. He suddenly shivered even though the air was warm. To tell the truth, although he was looking forward to finally seeing the gongs tomorrow, he had to admit that he found the house, the whole place, unnerving. There was just something about it which made him feel deeply uneasy. He was amazed that Tia would spend weeks here at a time, unfazed by the isolation. Especially after her mother's disappearance. He certainly hoped he would never have to spend any length of time here on his own.

He shivered again and felt as though something was prodding at his mind, urging him to pay attention. A feeling like a warning, a premonition.

He shrugged. He was getting fanciful in his old age. Drawing deeply on his cigarette, he flicked the butt out the window and watched the tiny red coal trace an arc through the blackness before dying in the grass outside. He reached forward and pulled the window firmly shut.

DAY EIGHTY-FIVE: MORNING

In this Dark Age of vested interests, space probes and computerised everything, it is difficult to accept the nebulous concept of simple rocks throbbing with an uncanny, but usable power. Yet there they are, many still in good working order, like power points for electric plugs.

Brenda Sullivan, *Spirit of the Rocks*

Tia drew back the curtains and swung open the window as far as it would go. They were in for a scorcher. It was cool outside, but there was a hint in the air of heat to come and the dew on the grass was already drying.

Cautiously she opened the door of the room and tip-toed across the living room so as not to wake Jon. When she entered the kitchen, however, there were bread crumbs on the work top and the smell of coffee percolating.

'Good morning,' Jon said and emerged from behind the open fridge door. 'Sleep well?' He had already showered and dressed, she noticed. His hair was slightly damp.

She moved from one bare foot to the other, feeling awkward, and tried to smooth her hair. 'Hi. Yes, I did, thanks.' Actually, she was surprised at how deeply she had slept. The idea of someone else in the house would normally have kept her from a truly deep slumber. But last night she had been dead to the world.

'I've made some coffee for myself. But you drink tea, right? Tea bag in a cup all right with you?'

He was observant, she thought. She had never told him she didn't drink coffee. She accepted the mug with its limp tea bag and also a slice of toast, meticulously cut into two triangles.

'So what's the plan for today?' He looked at her expectantly.

'Well,' she gingerly took a sip of the hot liquid. 'I called Isaiah yesterday and asked if he'd mind if I took you to see the gongs.'

'Who's Isaiah?'

'He's the keeper of the gongs. The guy who watches out for them.'

'I don't understand. I thought the gongs belonged to you. That they were on your property. Why do you need his permission?'

'It's not permission really. It's more a gesture of respect. Isaiah is a sangoma – a witch doctor – I suppose you'd call him, and he's been the keeper of the gongs ever since I can remember. Sacred sites always have their guardians. Even sites that are not in use any more – like this one. Anyway, I didn't actually get to speak with him, but his assistant seemed to think there shouldn't be a problem. So we need to set out before the sun gets too high. It's going to be a hot day.'

Jon poured himself another cup of coffee. She watched with amazement as he added an incredible six spoonfuls of sugar to the brew. He had beautiful hands with long fingers, slightly tapered. There was a hint of spendthrift generosity in the flamboyant sweep of the thumb. She always noticed a man's hands. This did not make her any different from most women, she supposed. Considering the important part a man's hands played in love-making, it wasn't surprising that women found them a turn-on.

She suddenly realised what she was thinking and her face started to tingle, the heat spreading all the way to her hairline. She put her hand to her neck and closed the top button of her robe. Jon was looking at her oddly, she thought, and blushed again.

She slid off the high stool. 'If you'll excuse me, I need to take a shower. I won't be long.'

'Sure.' He waved a casual hand. 'Take your time.'

When she emerged from the bathroom half an hour later, she found the kitchen neat and tidy, the house silent. In the small rucksack she kept for hiking she packed two bottles of water, a tube of sunblock and a bar of chocolate. She took the soft broad-rimmed hat from the coat rack, the hat Klio had used for gardening, and let herself out the front door.

She looked around her, wondering where Jon was. Then she saw him wave at her. He had climbed to the top of the gently sloping hill to the back and side of the house. When she joined him, they were silent for a moment as they looked out over the surrounding landscape.

The sky, oyster grey when she woke up, had turned to blue. The jaunty red roof of the neighbouring homestead and the long line of adjacent guest cottages peeked out from behind a neat clump of trees a few miles to the right. On a map, Fluisterwater looked like a dagger, thrust in between the two neighbouring properties. But when her father had bought the land, turning it into a conservation area, he had removed all the fences and Fluisterwater now blended in seamlessly with the environment. Tia would have found it difficult to point out the borders. Farms in this part of the country were big and Fluisterwater itself, even after the largest part of the original farm had been sold off, was still a sizeable property indeed.

To the east, the horizon was marked by a dark line of vegetation, more sensed than seen. Thin as a pencil line, it signalled the end of the dry grassy plateau which stretched to all sides of them for as far as the eye could see. On the other side, she knew, lay the land of Modjadji, the Rain Queen, and the Great Letaba River. A soft land where the hills were green and shrouded in mist, and water was the colour of honey. Just before her mother became ill they had gone hiking in that area. It was the last trip the two of them had made together.

But green was not the colour of the immediate landscape. The knee-high grass through which they were walking was a tawny yellow and brown. The landscape alternated between gently sloping hills, towering outcrops of rock and long flat stretches of grass and rich red soil. Without warning, you could stumble onto a donga, a dusty trench worn into the earth through erosion, and there were ravines too, narrow but deep and choked with brush and undergrowth and trees that clung fantastically to the steep sides. As a child she had once slithered down one of these ravines and she still remembered the chill on her skin as she had descended cautiously, little by little, until the glare of the sun was blocked by the lacework of leaves above her head. She didn't see, but she could sense very well that there was other life in the undergrowth: tiny animals, reptiles, bigger animals even. Just thinking about it now made the hairs on her neck rise.

Jon was walking with an easy rhythm, he was obviously used to hiking. He kept a step behind and to her side, his shadow following hers. She stuck close to the river, but after a while the river went underground and she had to concentrate hard on finding her way. The gongs, she remembered, were positioned over a blind spring and close to a deep ravine. But she was getting anxious. She hadn't been this way in a long time.

After about an hour's walk, they stopped for a rest in the patchy shade of a mopane tree. Jon took a big greedy gulp of water before stretching out on his side and propping himself up on one elbow. Tia turned on her back and looked straight up into the sky.

White clouds and blue sky. Blue sky and white clouds. If you looked long enough they made you dizzy. This place was so different from Johannesburg. She loved the city, but in the city she was conscious of the passing of time some- times to the point of panic. In the city she often thought of the lives she could have led, the things she might have done. The teetering skyscrapers, the busy streets: everything seemed fragile and impermanent. But over here there was only a sense of sun and wind and baked earth that would be here tomorrow, and the next day and in the millennia to come.

'What are you thinking?' Jon was watching her with an expression that was hard to read.

She shook her head. He had such an intent way of looking at her. As though he knew what was going on inside her mind.

He suddenly reached over and picked up the rucksack next to her. For a moment his arm touched hers. Drawing back, he rummaged with one hand through the bag. She watched as he picked out the chocolate bar and peeled off the wrapper. The chocolate had melted in the heat and he licked the soft brown sweetness off the tip of his fingers.

He really had such graceful hands. Slender, but strong. And then on the back of the hands the tangle of hair growing thick and black. His hands would be sure in their touch: patient, knowing . . .

Stop it, she told herself savagely. This was not like her. She was behaving like some stupid teenager: everything from the butterflies in the stomach to the sweaty palms and flushed face. And she didn't even know the man. Silly wasn't the word for it. Pathetic was closer to the mark.

'Maybe we should get going again.' She stood up abruptly. He looked up, surprised, but got to his feet without argument.

The heat was now becoming seriously uncomfortable. Her scalp itched underneath her hat. Her feet felt bruised and, as she walked, her ankles ached. Jon had dark sweat stains under his arms and down the back of his shirt. But at last she saw the black outline of the massive outcrop of rock she had been searching for. She stopped and put her hand above her eyes.

She had begun to think that she might be seriously mistaken in her sense of direction. But there it was: the enormous outcrop of rock that clung to the precipice of a ravine. She had never climbed to the top of that rock pile, although the view from up there must be stupendous. But it was too high for her. Way too high. And the ravine down below, way too deep and dark.

'There they are,' she said.

Jon looked at her, his face wiped clean of any expression.

Tia pointed to the granite boulders about five hundred yards to the left of the rocky outcrop.

There were four boulders. Three of them were clustered together, deeply embedded into the ground. The fourth lay by itself a little distance away.

They were big, these stones, at least five feet in diameter. But because they stood in the shadow of that massive pile of stone behind them, they seemed smaller than they really were. They were also fairly unremarkable to look at, until one noticed the deep dents on their surfaces. There was no doubt these dents were man-made. They were evenly spaced and regular, not the work of wind or water.

Jon picked up a stone as big as his fist and knocked it on a dent in the rock. It produced a faint, hardly audible whisper of sound.

He walked over to the second boulder and tried again. Again the sound was that of rock on rock, muffled and dull.

The expression on his face had been expectant, but as he knocked against the third boulder, she saw the excited look replaced by one of puzzlement and then the corners of his eyes creasing with disappointment.

'Not much of a sound,' he said slowly.

'I did warn you.'

'So you did.'

She squatted down next to the boulder. Despite the heat of the day, the surface of the rock was strangely cold to the touch. She let her fingers travel gently across its scaly roughness. The coolness of the rock and its abrasive texture made her feel as though she were touching the skin of some immensely old reptile.

Jon opened his satchel and rummaged around in its capacious depths. Finally he extracted what looked like a long, gleaming, very thick nail with slightly rounded edges.

'Let's try again.'

He lowered himself to the ground and placed one arm around the rock in a kind of embrace. His ear was pressed tightly against its surface. In his other hand he held the nail with which he tapped gently at one of the hollows carved into the boulder. This time there was a soft ringing sound, but so tiny, she could hardly hear it.

He lowered the edge of the nail into the next hollow down and tapped again. Again there was a musical sound, and it seemed to her as though this time the pitch was slightly different. But she could be mistaken. The sound was too small to be sure.

There were nine dents altogether and they were scattered across the entire surface of the boulder. She watched as Jon tapped lightly at each of the hollows. And now she was certain of it. The sound – the pitch and the quality – was different each time.

He lifted his head and smiled at her. 'Come closer,' he said.

She moved cautiously towards him but he suddenly stretched out his arm and with one movement had pulled her so close that their heads were almost touching.

He drew the tip of his finger across the surface of the rock. 'See,' he said, 'this part of the rock is smooth. There are no dents, which means that this section of the rock has never been struck by man. But I'll bet you anything you like that it'll make a sound if you direct a blow at it.'

It was difficult to think clearly with him so close to her. She could feel his warm breath on her cheek. She didn't answer and merely watched as he tapped the nail against a smooth spot in the rock about twelve inches to the left of one of the hollows. And it was unmistakable. There was a musical echo there. Not as clear-cut as the sound that was released from the man-made hollows, but a delicate bell-like sound nevertheless.

'And here,' Jon tapped against another part of the boulder that was also smooth and pit-free. 'Hear that? This gong holds many more notes than have been used over the ages.'

'Why do you think these notes weren't used?'

'I don't know. Maybe each age was thought to have its own sound. That's what the ancient Chinese believed anyway. See, some of these hollows where the rock has been struck are deeper and more worn than the others.' He rubbed his fingers across several of the hollows in the rock's surface. Then he touched two other dents, which did indeed seem somewhat shallower. 'I think these deeper holes may be older than the shallow ones. I think with the advent of each age, new notes are struck. Every age has a new note added to the mix.'

He paused. 'Just think; somewhere in here . . . somewhere . . . may lie the sound of the third millennium.'

The sun was very bright. A row of black ants moved in a long glistening column across the base of the boulder. The wind moved languidly through the tall grass.

He got to his feet. Positioning the nail into the deepest of the hollows, he forcefully hit the back of it with the stone he had used earlier. But instead of a ringing sound, the rock only vibrated with that hollow remarkably non-resonant thud that had escaped it when Jon had struck at it the very first time. As soon as force was used, it seemed, the rock would not respond.

'I don't understand this.' Jon's words were stained by frustration. 'Ben told me that according to his research a gong like this would have been heard for a distance of at least seven miles around. No one is going to hear this, that's for sure.'

'The rocks will not sing like that.'

The voice was so unexpected, Tia felt her breath catch audibly in her throat.

She spun around. At first she could not determine where the voice had come from. But then the tall grass stirred slightly and her eyes picked out the beaded head-dress from amongst the fawn and brown vegetation.

Her pent-up breath exploded from her lips in a sigh of relief.

'Don't worry,' she said to Jon who was looking alarmed. 'It's Isaiah.'

He had been squatting on his heels, but now he stood up straight. Isaiah's ankles were thin, but he walked with a strong loping stride.

'*Unjani.*'

'*Unjani wena,*' she returned his greeting. 'How have you been?'

He turned up his ash-coloured palms and made an expressive gesture, which seemed to indicate that if life was not good, it was not bad either.

Isaiah was a man of few words. She had known him since childhood and in that time he had never spoken more than he absolutely had to. His mother had been a Zulu from the Natal province, but his father was a Venda. Although Isaiah's understanding of English was excellent, his spoken command of the language was imperfect. Between his broken English and her schoolgirl Zulu, it made communication between them sometimes a slow and intuitive affair.

Isaiah was one of the many local izangoma – medicine men and diviners. He owned a muti or medicine-shop in town and the farm hands and tribesmen in the area would not dream of going to a medical doctor with their ailments without consulting Isaiah or one of his colleagues first. He had also been Klio's main supplier of seeds for her herb garden. His knowledge of the medicinal properties of these plants was extensive and this was a subject in which Klio was quite proficient herself. She and Isaiah used to exchange notes.

The last time Tia had seen him must have been all of two years ago, but he hadn't changed. His face was still unlined and his movements supple. This despite the fact that he was elderly – actually, she looked at him more closely, he must be old.

As always he was wearing the multi-coloured beaded head-dress that signified his status as a qualified traditional healer. Around his neck hung a straight cross within a circle. This circle, Tia knew, was a circle of power and embraced the cardinal points of the four seasons and the elements of fire, earth, air and water. Around one arm was a brass bracelet of a coiled serpent.

'This is Jon,' she said to him. 'My friend. He works with me at the university in Johannesburg.'

'What does he want with the stones?' Isaiah spoke in Zulu.

She struggled to explain. 'He's interested in sound.'

'What does he think to hear?'

'You must ask him yourself.' She turned to Jon. 'He wants you to explain your interest in the gongs.'

Jon made an uncertain gesture with his hands. 'I am interested in sound. Sacred sound.'

'Sacred?'

Jon searched helplessly for an explanation. 'Healing,' he finally said. 'Sound that heals. Sound that creates. I came all the way from America to hear these rocks.'

Something very much like recognition came to Isaiah's eyes. He started to move slowly around Jon until he had made a full circle. He stopped and slapped his thighs with an urgent excited sound. When he looked at Jon he had an expression of expectation on his face. He nodded sharply a few times, as if impatient of Jon's silence; as if trying to persuade Jon to say something.

Jon looked at Tia with a slightly embarrassed, puzzled frown. She shrugged. She didn't herself know what was going on. She had never seen Isaiah behave in this way before. He was usually as cool as a judge. This was the first time she had seen him display this kind of almost agitated impatience.

When Jon still did not respond, Isaiah clicked his tongue impatiently. He bent over and gingerly put his hand into a crevice underneath one of the boulders as though careful of insects or snakes that might lurk in there. When he extracted his hand, he held two stones that were long and just slightly curved. He turned around and walked to the second boulder on springy ankles.

He beckoned to Jon and held out the hammers. Jon took the two stones hesitantly. Isaiah took Jon's hands and directed them as he struck the rock. The two pairs of hands started to pound the hollows together: first one, then another, in an unbroken rhythmic pattern.

As the rock started to sing, Jon's face became blank with wonder. The corners of his mouth puckered with concentration.

At first the sound was as muted as before, but then, without warning, the air filled with a deep, silvery drone. Every time they hit a hollow, a glinting tone was released. It hung in the air, as if waiting to merge with the next tone to escape from the rock's embrace. After a while Isaiah moved away, leaving Jon in sole possession of the hammers.

If one listened carefully, Tia thought, the tones were separate, like the leaves of a book. But when she gave herself up to the sound it became one throbbing, fundamental note that engaged the senses like a potent memory.

Jon stopped. His face was glistening with sweat and some of his fingers were bleeding from where the skin had scraped against the rock. She walked over to him and he looked up. He placed his hand on her wrist. She could smell the sweat on him and see the faint outline of dark circles under his eyes. The scar on his chin stood out white against the flushed skin. For one moment she had the extraordinary feeling that she could not only feel the pulse in his fingertips, but also hear the blood as it pushed strongly through his veins.

It was so overwhelming that she pulled away.

'Thank you,' Jon turned his head towards Isaiah. 'Thank you.' He placed the hammers into Isaiah's outstretched palms.

Isaiah took the two stones and looked at them for a few moments. With a sudden gesture he held them out at Jon again. 'For you,' he said in English.

Tia put her hand on Jon's arm. 'When you take it, cross your hands right over left. It shows respect to the ancestors who inspired the gift.'

Jon rubbed his fingers over the two oblong stones. Then he looked directly into Isaiah's eyes. 'Why me?'

Isaiah spoke quickly.

'What's that?' Jon looked questioningly at Tia.

'He says you have *nyama amandla*.'

'That's a good thing?'

She smiled. 'Yes. As far as I know it means you are divinely protected and have much wisdom.' She lifted an eyebrow. 'And great skill in oratory.'

72

'Oh.' Jon sounded at a loss. 'That's nice of him.'

Isaiah spoke again and this time Tia frowned in frustration. 'I don't know . . . I don't quite understand. Something about you being very late. But that he knows you and knows of your . . . task?' She shook her head. 'I'm sorry. I don't quite follow.'

Isaiah's face has assumed its habitual calm. His eyes now seemed uninterested. He nodded once.

Tia noticed that he threw no shadow. She looked up into the sky and saw that the sun was at its highest point. When she looked back at him, he had already turned around and was walking away on silent feet.

DAY EIGHTY-FIVE: EVENING

[The tuning system of] temperament is a musical allegory of the Fall and is, like Adam's mea culpa, *simultaneously a sign of evil and of potential grace.*

Wilfrid Mellers, *Bach and the Dance of God*

He was sitting outside in the swing chair, sipping a glass of wine. After the heat of the day the evening air was cool.

Jon took a sip of his wine; tried to relax. Tia was inside, taking a bath. While waiting for her, he had suddenly found the house claustrophobic and had headed outdoors. But neither the wine or the quiet could make him unclench. His muscles felt tense; his mind restless.

He knew what it was, of course. Now that he had seen the gongs, now what? He had been so sure that once he had heard the gongs, he would somehow be able to understand where the sense of urgency had come from that had caused him to pack up his stuff and head over the ocean. But instead, here he was, sitting in the middle of nowhere, being eaten alive by mosquitos and without a clue what he should do next.

He thought again of the sound of those gongs: a persistent drawn-out drone. Not a large sound, but a sound that pressed almost tangibly against the tender membrane of the ear. Throughout the day the sound had stuck in his mind. It seemed to him as though the memory of it still clung to the air and was even now fading into the rustle of leaves of the giant poplars growing in a straight row outside the kitchen door.

Just to have heard that sound was probably worth the trip. And it was certainly going to be interesting to study the gongs' resonance frequencies. He might even get an article or two out of it. But was that it? He had expected more, somehow.

There was, of course, Isaiah's oracle-like pronouncement. He grimaced. The whole episode still seemed unreal. And he couldn't help feeling just a little silly. When the old man had popped out of the grass like that he had felt like someone in a Tarzan movie. The head-dress, the cryptic utterances: it was all too much. Although this kind of stuff was apparently not unusual over here. 'In South Africa izangoma are common,' Tia had told him on their way back. 'Eighty per cent of black patients visit their traditional healer before going to the doctor. And a growing number of whites are making use of their services as well. In Soweto alone there are more than eight thousand traditional healers and in rural areas like this they're very much a part of everyday life. Isaiah is by no means the only healer around here. You should ask Ben. He'll be able to tell you a lot more about these guys. They fulfil a very important function: sort of medicine man and priest rolled into one.'

'Nyama amandla.' Divinely protected and much wisdom. And he was late for his task. Yeah, right. Like Keanu Reeves in The Matrix. He wouldn't have been surprised if the old man had muttered, 'You're the one' or something equally hokey.

But he was grateful for the gift. He pushed his hand into the inside pocket of his jacket and took out the gong hammers. They certainly did not look like much – just two stones slightly curved. If he had seen them lying on the street somewhere he would not have given them a second glance. He rubbed them between his fingers. They felt rough to the touch but strangely tactile. He intended dropping them off at the university's geology and palaeontology department. Maybe a geologist could provide the answer as to why the gongs would only respond to the touch of these particular stones.

The waterpipes of the house were groaning and there was

the sound of water flowing into an outside drain. The next moment a square of light leapt out onto the dark lawn. It was coming from one of the bedrooms. On the creamy wall above the bed he could see a shadow. It was Tia. She was drying herself.

For a few long moments he stared. Then she stretched out her arm and drew the white shutters tight across the window: shutting out the light; the velvet shadow. Feeling suddenly short of breath, he leaned back against the swing chair once again.

The air around him had come alive with secret nocturnal sounds. The whirr of a night bird's wings. The stealthy rustle of some small animal in the underbrush. The tiny high-pitched scream of a bat as a shadow detached itself from the roof, falling in a swift heart-stopping arc towards the ground before climbing effortlessly back into the sky. A frog croaked once, twice and then stopped abruptly. Even though light still glinted on the horizon, the slanting shadows of the tree trunks were only marginally darker than the surrounding blackness.

He took another sip of his wine and looked straight ahead through the opening of the sliding glass doors giving access to the drawing room. Tia had entered the room. She was standing in front of the book case, her back towards him, her hair a halo of light. She had taken down a book from one of the shelves and was staring at it intently.

He placed his glass on the grass beside him and walked noiselessly across the lawn and into the room.

'What are you reading?'

He had startled her. She almost dropped the book. This close he got the clean scent of her: soap and her hair had the fragrance of lemons. In the light of the lamp her skin seemed almost transparent. He leaned forward and took the slim volume from her nerveless fingers.

The pages were well-thumbed and the cover was creased and stained. On the very first page she had written her name in a careful neat hand and below it the date. She had been a young girl when she wrote that. The book was fifteen years old. He noticed that she had written her name with a rather self-conscious curl to the letter T.

It was a book of poetry, that much he could make out, but he couldn't read the words: the language was alien.

'Read it to me' he said, holding the book out at her.

'It's not in English.'

'Just read.'

The spine of the book was broken and it fell open in her hand. She cleared her throat.

> *'Ken jy my nou?*
> *Het jy die spieel gesien*
> *en ken jy jou?'*

She looked over at him.

'Don't stop.'

She continued reading, not glancing at him even once, her eyes veiled by long lashes tipped with gold. She spoke slowly and her voice had taken on an eerily languorous tone. He listened spellbound. The words he did not understand, but their sound conveyed to him a sense of creeping wickedness.

'What does it mean?'

'It's titled "The Ballad of Evil". The poet explores the idea that evil has existed from the very first moment of creation and that evil is merely the flip side of good.'

She put her finger on the page. It left a tiny smudge mark. 'It's difficult to translate word for word,' she said, 'but I'll try.

> *'Do you know me?*
> *Have you looked into the mirror*
> *and do you know yourself?*
>
> *When you try to flee*
> *from the city that burns*
> *then I flee with you*
> *like a woman hand in hand.*

The many think they know my face,
but I am too radiant,
I hide too close to the light,
if they try to warn you
give you advice,
my voice lingers
in the echo of their words.'

She paused, then shook her head. 'I'm not doing it justice. You know what they say: to translate is to betray.'

'How does it end?'

'It ends the way in which it begins,' she answered without looking at the page. 'Evil is inescapable. It is God's shadow. It is the red umbilical cord to which we are attached. If you wish to recognise evil, then look in the mirror.'

Behind her, high on the wall, a tiny lizard scurried into the shadow of one of the exposed beams. Outside the window the sun finally died in a streak of scarlet.

She slid the book back into place on the shelf. 'It's been a long day,' she said. 'I think I'll turn in.'

He put out his hand as though to stop her from leaving. But then he let it fall to his side. 'Sure. Sweet dreams.'

'You too,' she said and left him there in the darkening room.

⋆   ⋆   ⋆

Five hours later he was still wide awake. He could feel his body begging for sleep – the long hike of the morning had certainly tired him out – but there was just something about this house that made it impossible for him to relax.

He peered once again at the illuminated arms of the alarm clock. This was becoming a habit. Two in the morning. Ghost time. But only seven p.m. in New York. If Stephen was on-line, they could have a chat.

The door was clearly visible in the moonlight that fell in

large blocks of white across the wooden floor. But the passage outside the door was dark.

The door did not creak when he opened it wider. For a moment he listened, but all was quiet.

He did not switch on the light in the drawing room. The moonlight was strong enough for him to recognise his laptop where it sat hooked up to the phone.

He eased himself into the chair and switched on the computer. The sound of the modem scratched noisily through the quiet of the room. And as he had expected, Stephen was on-line.

Hi, Kojak.

He smiled. Whenever their brains would gum up with fatigue during those long hours they worked together, he and Stephen would watch reruns on cable TV. *Kojak. The Rockford Files. Charlie's Angels.* The blander the better. It had become a game to see who could best mimic the dialogue of Jill and Sabrina; the speech habits of Kojak and Jim.

He tapped the keys lightly: Hi, Crocker.

How are things?

Saw the rocks today.

There was a longish pause. He could picture Stephen's face. The eyes narrowed. Slight irritation thinning his lips. To say that Stephen did not share his enthusiasm for the gongs was putting it mildly.

And?

It was great. But maybe you're right. I was a little crazy coming out here.

Yes.

I think we should speed up work on the *Angel* project.

You're not jerking me around?

No. You were right. We're so close we should finish it off.

Yes! Yes! Yes!

So send me the number four file through tomorrow.

You're beautiful. So when are you coming back?

Would like to finish the term. It doesn't matter though. We can work while I'm here. We'll use encrypted mail.

OK. I'll set up PGP.

How's that other koochie koo doing?

Still miserable. Cassidy really creamed him. And he misses his big brother.

Tell him to be a man.

I'll buy him a lollipop.

Got to go. Don't forget the file.

Who loves you baby.

The screen went blank and he logged off. As he closed the laptop he saw something move from the corner of his eye. He swung around and his elbow brushed violently against the telephone directory on the table and sent it flying to the floor with an almighty crash.

'Good God,' he was breathing heavily. 'You scared the shit out of me.' For one terrifying moment he had thought he'd seen a ghost. Probably that white thing she was wearing. It was sort of floating.

'What are you doing?' Tia was standing in the door. Her voice was sharp. 'It's after two in the morning.' She unerringly put out her hand and switched on the light. He blinked in the sudden glare.

'Not in New York, it's not. I was having an on-line conversation with Stephen.' He suddenly laughed. 'For a second there I almost screamed. That would have been a serious blow to my macho image.'

Tia started moving towards the door. 'Wait,' he said. He reached out and put his hand on her shoulder. Through the thin cotton night dress he felt the warmth of her skin. 'I'm sorry if I woke you.'

She didn't say anything. She only looked at him with those wide lost eyes.

Carefully, deliberately, so as not to frighten her, he took her hand and placed it against his cheek.

She kept her eyes on his face, staring at him unblinkingly. He sensed the tension in her. If he wasn't careful, she would bolt any second now.

Still holding her wrist, he brought it up to his mouth. He

could see the pulse in her throat. Softly, very softly, he pressed his lips against her palm.

When he pulled her into his arms, ever so slowly, she did not resist.

DAY EIGHTY-FOUR

Evansville
Pennsylvania
USA

He had a headache. These days it seemed like he always had a headache. Sebastian squinted. The sunlight in the classroom was unusually strong. He wished the bell would go so he could get out of there. Usually he liked history class – Miss Davis was quite a fox – but today the sound of her voice was almost unbearable. Just a long, non-stop drone. He could hardly stand it.

Maybe he should tell his mom about the headaches; but then, what was the use? He knew what she would say. Stop playing those games. Go to bed early. And there was no way he was going to stop playing *The Angels' Key* now. He had reached level eight. Just one level to go and he'd be a real *Angel* warrior instead of just a low-level wannabe.

Man, he felt like shit. There was this funny hum in the air, which hurt his head, but it didn't seem to bother anyone else. He turned his head and saw Lowell Boyer mouth an obscenity at him. The prick had been on his case for weeks now, ever since that thing with the locker.

Anger suddenly flooded through him. Who the hell did this kid think he was? Before he knew it, he was standing up, pushing back his chair with such force that it slammed into Kathy Sullivan's desk behind him. He was going to *kill* the little fucker.

For a moment all the sound in the room disappeared. It was like he was under water. Miss Davis was walking towards him, a frown on her face, her hands held out at him. She seemed to move in slow-motion. But when she touched him, it was as though an electric shock went off inside his body. He couldn't help himself; he drew back and violently slapped her hand away from him.

His last thought before he passed out was that all the sounds that had disappeared were back: and they were all exploding at once inside his head.

DAY EIGHTY-THREE

I stood there trembling with anxiety and I felt a great, infinite scream pass through nature.

Edvard Munch, Thoughts on painting *The Scream*

She was sitting at a small mosaic-topped table. In front of her was a teapot, cup and saucer, and the remains of a glazed pastry clinging to a brightly coloured plate. Her head was bowed, she was reading from a book on her lap. The sun was so strong, it seemed to bleach out any colour from her skin, but somehow the red of her hair appeared more vibrant than ever.

He himself was lurking at a far corner table in the shadow of the café's awning. Jon felt foolish. The dark glasses, the big rubber plant behind which he had taken up his station – he felt like a second-rate spy in a second-rate novel. And he was intensely irritated with himself. This was not his style at all. Furtively following the object of his desire, watching her surreptitiously . . . it hardly oozed class. But what was he to do? She refused to take his calls. She avoided him on campus. He couldn't understand what the hell was going on. They had actually ended up spending the night together at Fluisterwater and he had certainly found it a delightful experience . . . until the next morning. He woke up to find Tia cold and distant and brittle. She had hardly spoken to him on their way back to Johannesburg. His ego was certainly taking a beating here.

He was not used to women treating him this way after the first night of intimacy. Tia must have found the entire episode utterly underwhelming.

But why the hell should he care? So the lady was not interested in pursuing a relationship. Fine, she only had to say so. He could handle it. Or . . . could he?

He watched her. She was reading with an unwavering concentration that brooked no distractions. She was surrounded by people and voices and only a few yards away a street performer was putting on a show which included fire and juggling, but she never even looked up.

But suddenly she slapped the book shut and pushed back her chair. She started to walk towards the bus stop, her bag swinging rhythmically from her hand.

He followed cautiously. When the big double-decker bus drew up, he slipped in at the back and took a seat a few rows behind her.

Even though she'd have to twist around completely before he'd be in her line of vision, he tried not to stare at her. He didn't want her to get that indefinable feeling one gets when you're being watched. Still, the red of her hair was a bright streak at the corner of his eye and when she started moving in her seat a few minutes later, he anticipated her next step and was able to get off the bus along with her. For a moment he was worried that she might spot him, but there were a large number of people leaving the bus, and she never even glanced at her fellow passengers.

He had no idea where he was. It looked like a residential suburban neighbourhood. She was walking briskly down a sidewalk shadowed by huge trees, her eyes fixed straight ahead of her. He followed at a distance, moving from one tree to the next, feeling more ridiculous with every passing moment.

Suddenly she stopped and glanced up and down the road. He had just enough time to dart behind a tree trunk. Then she pushed open a big, elaborately curlicued wrought iron gate and disappeared behind it.

He waited a few minutes, but she did not come out again.

He walked towards the gate and read the sign attached to it. Lepworth House. And below it opening and closing hours.

A museum. Just his luck. He certainly did not feel like staring at a bunch of dreary exhibits. He looked in the direction of the house, which could be glimpsed through the lush foliage of a thick hedge. The architecture was interesting. Victorian red brick, turrets and tall bay windows. A big house. Very big indeed.

He hesitated, but then pushed open the gate and walked up the neat gravel driveway towards the front door. The loose pebbles scrunched beneath the soles of his shoes.

The woman sitting behind the till in the shadowy entrance hall was nodding sleepily over a paperback. He paid the entrance fee and received a ticket and a leaflet in return. There were no other people around. Of Tia there was no sign.

He looked down at the leaflet in his hand. The house seemed to have belonged to one of Johannesburg's gold magnates more than a century before. The leaflet assured him that the wealth of the owner had been immense and that the house had once been famous for the parties that had taken place within its walls.

Jon looked around him. The place seemed forlorn and almost empty of furniture. The wide corridors stretching to either side of him were uncarpeted, the timber floorboards unpolished. Only the elaborate architecture and sweeping staircase told of wealth and a fabulous life style.

He walked hesitantly down the one hallway, stopping every now and then to peek into one of the many doorways opening off the passage. The rooms seemed sad. Yellowed wallpaper. Thick claret-coloured drapes hanging heavily in dusty folds. A velvet chaise-longue, the rich fabric faded and fraying. Next to it, a tarnished but beautifully scrolled harp, the strings so starkly still they appear never to have felt the touch of a hand. A classically proportioned ballroom with a stunning, many-tiered chandelier. And still no sign of Tia.

He was on the top floor now and he stopped for a moment in front of the beautiful tall window that dominated the landing.

Through the dusty panes he was able to look down at the exquisite formality of the landscaped garden outside. Stone benches, clipped hedges, squares of emerald grass hedged in by weathered footpaths. Standing there it was easy to imagine the sound of laughter, the clink of glasses, light spilling through the casement windows and richly attired guests floating like midnight ghosts through a darkened garden.

He moved away from the window and turned the corner. But almost immediately he jerked back. Tia was standing at the very end of the passage.

Very cautiously he peered around the corner once again. She was facing the wall, staring at a painting. From where he stood he could not see the image Tia was looking at, but her body language disturbed him. She was tense, her shoulders pulled up high, one hand clutched into a fist next to her side and the other resting on her breast.

She must have stood there for at least another five minutes, eyes fixed unwaveringly on the picture. He waited, baffled. He did not understand this eerie, all-consuming interest. Suddenly she stepped back. She opened her handbag and took from it a handkerchief with which she dabbed at her eyes. She was crying? He found the idea so unexpectedly unpleasant that he almost walked towards her, intent only on offering comfort. But the next moment she had turned away and was disappearing around the far corner.

He was very aware of the loud hollow sound of his footsteps on the plank floor as he walked towards the painting. It was not a big picture and, as he got closer, he saw that it was hanging from the wall by a dusty velvet ribbon. The gold leaf frame was thick and beautifully moulded, but it was the image it contained that made him stop in his tracks.

The face of a woman. A woman in distress. It showed in the open, naked mouth and the tendons tight as wires at the base of her throat. She was weeping, the tears glittering diamonds against her cheeks. Her hands, out-of-proportion large, were raised, but not towards her streaming eyes. The long pale fingers were pressed against the sides of her head, covering her ears.

The spidery signature in the corner of the painting meant nothing to him. The date told him the painting was more than a hundred years old. An old painting then, and indeed the woman's dress was Victorian prim, her hair arranged in tight ringlets. But the feel of the painting was strangely modern: the despair and dislocation captured in the agonised gaze suggestive of a very contemporary sense of alienation.

'So this is what you do in your spare time?'

Tia was standing behind and to the side, one hand resting on her hip, the elbow forming an aggressive triangle. The light was behind her and he could not see the expression in her eyes, but he did not need to. The tense line of her slight body shouted outrage.

For a moment he was speechless, then he said lamely: 'What do you mean?'

'What do I mean?' She spoke with a terrible emphasis on each word. 'You've been following me, haven't you? Stalking me.'

'I have not been stalking you. Don't be so damn melodramatic. Anyway, how do you know I haven't wanted to visit this place ever since I arrived in South Africa?'

'Oh, really.' She walked a step closer. 'So what's the attraction? No gongs around here, I assure you.'

He didn't answer, he merely looked at her. She had on not a speck of make-up and there were shadows under her eyes, but he suddenly had the most overwhelming desire to pull her close, to kiss her mouth until the tightness around her lips disappeared . . . either that or shake her really hard.

She raised her eyebrows. 'So?'

He sighed. 'OK. I followed you. But it's your fault. I've been trying to get in touch with you ever since we got back from Fluisterwater. Why won't you take my calls?'

'Why won't you take a hint?'

'Tia.' He stopped. This wasn't going to get them anywhere.

'So who was she?' He nodded his head at the painting behind him in a vain attempt to change the subject.

She looked at him challengingly. 'Are you truly interested?'

'I am. I am truly and deeply interested.'

She gave a short, abbreviated half-shrug. 'Her name was
Emmaline. She was the wife of the first owner of this house. By
all accounts she was a very talented and lovely woman. She was
much admired as a hostess and could play the harp beautifully.
Anyway, she went insane.'

The flat, unemotional tone of voice in which she added the
last sentence – almost as an afterthought – shocked him.

'What happened to her?'

'She died in an asylum. Her husband tried to care for her
– he painted this picture, by the way – but in the end he
couldn't cope.'

Tia sounded almost disinterested now, but he wasn't fooled.
He couldn't put his finger on it, but there was something going
on here.

'Why are you so interested in this painting?'

For a moment he thought she might not answer. But then
she said, 'It reminds me of someone.'

'Who?'

She shook her head. 'No one you'd know.' Then her face
sharpened. 'I'm leaving now. Don't follow me again.'

'Tia.' He paused, helplessly. 'I don't understand why you're
so angry. I thought that night . . . there was a connection. It felt
true. It meant something.'

'A connection? Well, you certainly scored, I'll give you
that.'

'Scored?'

'Of course. You got to see the gongs, just like you wanted
and then as a little bonus, you got to sleep with the owner as
well. You probably had it planned in advance. Butter me up
and you can visit the gongs whenever you feel like it, right?'

For a moment he thought he had misunderstood. 'Are you
telling me you think that what happened between us was
because I wanted to make sure of future access to the gongs?'

She shrugged.

He was suddenly furious. 'Lady, you've got a problem. But find someone else to discuss your paranoid fantasies with you. I can think of better things to do than hang around here.'

He spun around on his heel but had hardly started to walk away when she said imploringly, 'Wait. Please.'

He stopped but looked over his shoulder, keeping his back turned on her.

'I'm sorry.'

Still he waited.

'Really, I am. You're right. I *am* paranoid. Blame it on some bad history.'

When he still didn't answer, she said, 'Oh, come on. How much more do you want me to grovel?'

He turned and looked at her. Suddenly he felt just slightly apprehensive. He wanted this woman but he wasn't so sure she was good for him. Behind those wide eyes he sensed a complicated inner life. He did not like complicated. Wasn't ready for it.

But then she smiled and he was lost. The rush of feeling that swept through him was so intense, it almost alarmed him.

She nodded. 'There *was* a connection that night. I felt it too.'

'Yes.'

'So you're giving me permission then?' And now her voice was light and teasing.

'Permission to do what?'

'To fall in love with you.'

For just a moment he hesitated but then he drew her towards him.

'Please do,' he said and folded his arms tightly around her.

DAY SIXTY-FOUR

We can cut the Gordian knot of equilibrium and deal with open-ended evolution.

M. Mitchell Waldrop, *Complexity*

She was in love.

She cared for Jon more than she had ever cared for anyone in her life. Instinctively she hesitated placing a label on her emotions, but Tia knew that surely this must be what being in love was all about.

That night at Fluisterwater she had taken him to her bed even though he was little more than a stranger. And now she had taken him into her life, even though she did not really know him. It was frightening how this man had entered her heart and her mind with such devastating ease.

She had been involved in several relationships before. She had even been married once. But these other loves, when she now thought back on them, had been strangely joyless. She had cared for some of these men, had thought that with one or two she had actually managed to dance. But those steps now seemed stiff and predictable with fixed rules governing the movements; utterly lacking in the intensity – the passion – of the dance she was dancing with Jon.

It was frightening: these emotions that were so intense. This was unknown territory. She still marvelled at the way it made her feel just to see him unexpectedly; to run into him as she walked down the campus corridors or to see him from across a crowded room. For a moment all the sounds and voices around her would disappear into liquid silence and she'd wait; wait for him to turn his head and for his eyes to meet hers; wait for that flame of recognition in the dark eyes that said, there you are – you're the one I've been waiting for.

Often she willed herself to stay awake after he had gone to sleep. She'd lie there watching him, wondering what thoughts pulsed behind his eyelids. She would touch his face or run her fingers down his back, while he slept on, unheeding.

Even though he was holding on to the apartment in Drake House, he now spent most of his time at her place. It was a small cottage, which she rented from the university. She had lived alone for so long that it still felt strange to her to open the closet door and see his boots and sneakers tossed in disarray next to her own neatly arranged clumps of shoes; or to see his jacket, worn at the elbows, peeping out from behind her red suit.

She took an adolescent delight in wearing his things; walking around the house dressed in his shirts. She made him swop watches with her, enchanted by the weight of his clunky timepiece on her arm. It was exactly the kind of watch she would never buy. It bristled with knobs and dials and gadgets. It told the time in twelve different countries. It boasted a depth gauge, a compass and could withstand water pressure of up to 150 feet. 'Why,' she asked him one Sunday afternoon as they were trading sections of the papers, 'is this necessary? The closest you get to water is when you take a shower.' And he laughed, and took her wrist and pulled her down onto the sofa beside him and whispered into her ear, 'You shouldn't even try to understand. It's a male thing.'

Sometimes he'd stretch out on the sofa and lie back in her arms, his head heavy on her breast. And she would stroke his hair and look down at him: at the thick brows, the strong nose, the curve of his lips. His was an exciting face. A face that challenged, that seemed to meet life head-on. The face of an adventurer.

At these times he'd insist that she read to him from the book of poetry she had read from that first night at Fluisterwater.

'I have always liked the sound of words as much as their meanings,' he said. 'Besides, when you read to me, I'm reminded of the night when I asked you to translate that poem. The one about evil. You were so serious . . . With the light behind you, there was fire in your hair. And with your pale face, you looked like an angel. It was at that moment that I first knew I must have you.'

He placed his fingers in the hollow of her throat. 'There was a pulse in your throat – right here – racing like mad, and it was all I could do not to touch you . . .'

*   *   *

Jon had little free time, but Tia managed to persuade him to explore the city. 'You can't live here and spend all your time on campus,' she told him. 'The campus is a fortress. It's not real.'

And so she took him into the city's heart. The sky above them was hot and blue but the shadows falling from the tall concrete towers with their broken windows were cool.

There was a time, she told Jon, when downtown Jo'burg was very different: textureless, bland, a city of crystal palaces and lacquered doors. And though it was far, far safer then to walk down its streets, segregated Johannesburg had not been an honest place.

But now the city was pulsing with change. Change in all its glory. Change in all its terror. Change hung in the air like a tangible thing; its presence as strong as the smell of gasoline in your nose. Change was the city's mantra. You could feel it tap-dancing in the minds of those who crowded the sidewalks. You heard it in the voices speaking in twenty-five different languages; in the beat of Mbaqanga and Mpantsula jive. Change was everywhere you looked. You could reach out and pluck it out of the thin air of this mile-high city.

And it was, above all, a city of its time and place. A city of Africa, very much so, despite the skyscrapers, the big hotels, the fancy restaurants and night clubs where South Africa's new black elite party and hustle and try to make up for lost time. It was a city of greed, as it had been a century before when men in the grip of gold fever made the place their own. Now, a hundred years later, the city still lured dreamers and grifters and those desperately searching for a new beginning. By their hundreds of thousands they came, Johannesburg's new citizens. They arrived from dusty rural South African towns or from the rest of the continent's poverty-stricken cities and they created a sea of shanty towns on the Highveld plain.

Africa's power house. A city that disturbs. Enthrals. A place where you can sense the blood under the skin.

Jon was fascinated. 'From over here Europe seems tired and the US self-indulgent. It's as though this city – this country – is keeping creative energy and massive chaos in balance.'

They were sitting on a park bench in the square on Joubert Street. In front of them was a beautiful delicate statue of leaping gazelles – a startling piece of poetry amidst piles of decaying garbage.

She turned to look at him. 'Yes. This is the most exciting place there is. But it's a brutal place.'

'I know,' he said, 'I know. But I believe it's only in places like this; places where you're living on the edge of chaos, where true transformation is possible.'

She was puzzled. 'I don't follow you.'

'Transformation requires an interaction between innovation and disintegration,' he said. 'South Africa is a classic case. You people managed to topple a system, which seemed set in stone, without everything going up in smoke. South Africa is one of those places where the different components don't quite fit, but never degenerate into total disarray either. Scientists call this balance point the edge of chaos.'

'The edge of chaos? That sounds frightening.'

'Yeah, well, it is. Step over the edge and it's darkness. But the edge of chaos is also a very creative place to be. It's where transitions take place. And I'm not just talking political – I'm thinking biological as well. Like when you have wholesale species transformation with years of evolutionary stability suddenly breaking down. That's what can happen on the edge of chaos. Science has a term for it. It's called Complexity. It's a balancing act that's in constant flux.'

Tia looked away from Jon towards the other side of the square. A blood-warm wind was blowing trash across the dirty flagstones. A matt-haired man, barefoot and dressed in a long military-style overcoat, was crouched next to a massive boom box from which came the angry, repetitive beat of a rap song. The man had his ear pressed right up against the speaker.

'A balancing act is a precarious thing,' she said almost to herself.

'Sure. Even the fluttering of a butterfly's wings can trigger an avalanche. And everything is so interconnected that the slightest movement can start a chain reaction. The world is a spider's web – touch one strand and the whole vibrates. That's what Stephen always says.'

She glanced at him. Stephen Yale. Whenever he spoke of Stephen his voice changed, gained an added warmth. It was very subtle – he probably wasn't even aware of it, but she always noticed. It made her feel slightly jealous, which was ridiculous of course – she had never even met the man.

'How long have you known Stephen?'

'Almost fourteen years.'

'How did you meet?'

'We met in grad school,' Jon answered without hesitation. 'Stephen had won a fellowship and had just moved from Britain to the US. We both entered a math contest.'

'Who won?'

'Yours truly. But it was a close-run thing. We became friends afterwards.'

'So what does he do? Is he an academic as well?'

'Stephen doesn't work. He calls himself a full-time listener.'

'Listener?'

Jon smiled wryly. 'It sounds wacky, I know. But Stephen

has this theory that most people don't listen any more. That we're all so overwhelmed by everyday sound pollution, that we've lost our ability to really listen to what's going on around us. We hear, but only superficially. Over the ages we have lost the major part of our hearing skills – anyway, that's what Stephen believes. And he also believes there are only a very small number of people left in the world – initiates – who have retained the listening ability: sort of like a sixth sense. And he's one of them.'

'But I thought you told me he has a hearing problem?'

Jon's voice was suddenly sombre. 'He does. That's what makes it so poignant.'

'Well, if he doesn't work, how does he support himself?'

'Stephen comes from a very wealthy family. They live in this incredible house in Wiltshire and as he grew up he got the whole package: nannies, Eton, Cambridge, a trust fund. His father was a big noise in the City – still is, as far as I can make out – not that Stephen talks about him much.' Jon shrugged. 'Anyway, Stephen won't ever have to work. But he's a highly educated man. After finishing his studies at Cambridge, he did his Ph.D at Carnegie Mellon. That's where we met. He also spent some time at the Santa Fe Institute. And *The Angels' Key* is really his baby. I did the math; he designed the game. It's his whole life. He's obsessed with the idea of perfect tuning.'

Jon turned to her, head to one side. 'Why this sudden interest in Stephen?'

'I was just curious. You talk about him so often.'

'Well, I think of him as a second brother.'

He got to his feet and stretched. The next moment he was pulling her up and into his arms. Underneath her ear she could hear the measured thud of his heart. She felt him press his lips to the top of her head. She felt so close to him. So utterly, utterly content. She needed nothing more than to stand there, to feel his warmth, to quietly match her breathing to his.

She picked up his one hand and turned it over so that it was palm up.

'You have a really long lifeline,' she said and traced with

the tip of her forefinger the crease in his palm, starting thick and strong at the base of the hand and ending in a delicate fan-shaped crescent at the mound of his second finger. 'You're going to be around for a long time.'

'Just so I'm around long enough to create the new scale.'

The way his hand rested in hers: relaxed, the fingers curled slightly inwards, made his hand seem vulnerable. At the wrist the veins stood out clearly: blue-green underneath the softest skin.

'This really turns you on, doesn't it?' she said. 'The idea of creating a brand new musical scale. The challenge of it. That's what captivates you.'

His hand closed. 'I'm captivated by perfection.'

She looked up and into his eyes. His eyes were so dark. The planes of his face were clean and starkly moulded.

He smiled as if in secret. 'No one has ever been able to do this, you see. It will be like a gift to the world. The gift of perfect tuning.'

*   *   *

On some of their excursions, they were accompanied by Ben. Jon had become immensely fond of Ben and the two men spent hours together just talking. Tia became used to seeing them together in the living room of her cottage: the light turned off, the rich cadences of Ben's voice rising and falling in the darkened room. Ben, his head tilted backwards and his eyes fixed on some remote spot, would spin out one tale after another, while Jon leaned forward in his chair, his chin cradled in the palm of his hand, his brows lowered in concentration.

Ben had the ability to bring folklore to life, to make stories that have been transmitted orally from generation to generation, seem not merely quaintly interesting, but imbued with significance. 'They're like the tyre tracks on the moon,' Ben would say. 'Our civilisation left tracks on the surface of the moon: a testament to our intellectual curiosity. Ancient cultures left us stories.'

Ben told Jon about the Shona people and their legendary

hero Makoma and his giant hammer; and of how the Shona believed elephant tusks to be magical, enabling an elephant to foresee the time and place of its death. He told stories of the Venda and the lost city buried underneath their sacred Lake Funduzi. And again and again, at Jon's request, he spoke of the gongs.

'The gongs are just one kind of sacred stone,' Ben told Jon. 'African civilisations have always revered stones that were believed to have the power of healing. The Hottentot god Tsui-Goab created men and women from sacred rock. You will find highly polished rocks everywhere in Africa. Some of these restore virility. Some are used by diviners to boost their mental powers, to aid them in divinatory dreams. And the gongs . . . these are extremely sacred. They can prevent cataclysm if played by an initiate.'

'The gong hammers are a big honour.' Ben rubbed his thumb across the surface of one of the gong hammers that Isaiah had given Jon. 'Isaiah must trust you. If he is the keeper of the stones that means he has to look out for them. He would never have given you the hammers if he thought you might act disrespectfully towards the rocks. In fact,' Ben paused, 'it could mean that Isaiah thinks you have some kind of task or duty to perform.'

'We've asked him several times what it might be,' Tia said. 'He won't tell us.'

Ben shook his head. 'That's not the way it works. You have to follow your own path intuitively and it will lead you to what you have to do.' He replaced the hammer carefully. 'You can be given the tools, but there can be no guide.'

DAY SIXTY-THREE

Great Lakes region
Burundi
Central Africa

The water was brown. It had rained the night before and the river was swollen. Jabulani carefully placed the oar in the water and pushed the boat away from the bank to where the river was flowing more calmly.

That night it had also rained, the night he had lost his family. And the next day the corpses had floated down the Mubarazi River like waterlogged tree trunks.

'Thirsty work,' he remembered one man saying as they had wandered through the streets of the village together where bodies, their hands and feet chopped off, lay amidst rubble and buzzing flies. Some of the victims had been shot, but most had their throats cut or were completely decapitated. As Jabulani searched through the hulks of rotting flesh, he thought the man was probably right. It must have been very tiring to massacre an entire village in the time it takes to eat lunch.

Jabulani pushed his oar deep and the boat slid smoothly away. It was quiet. The women who usually did their washing around here had not yet arrived. In another hour or so, their laughter and chatter would fill the air.

Ahead of him was the underwater canyon where he knew the fish were. He concentrated intensely.

But something was tugging at his subconscious. There was a hum in the air: a strange sound. He looked towards the bank. It wasn't a hum after all – it was his neighbour's radio. The man was sitting on his heels, just where the footpath disappeared into the thicket and next to him, on the ground, was a bright yellow boom box. Jabulani recognised it instantly. Usually it stood in the window of his neighbour's house and it was never, ever switched off. And it was always tuned to the same station: a station that played this strange, strange music. Even in the early morning hours when the station signed off, the radio was left on and Jabulani would lie in his bed listening to the sound of white static drifting out into the still night air. He had come to hate that yellow box and the disturbing music it played.

Jabulani did not know his neighbour at all, even though they had lived next to each other for several years now. The man was from Gitega, a city east of Bujumbura and he had only moved to this place after the massacres. Jabulani looked at the crouched relaxed figure on the bank and lifted his hand in greeting.

For a moment nothing happened. Then the man smiled and from where he was Jabulani could just make out a flash of white teeth. The man slowly lifted his hand but instead of turning his palm outwards in a welcoming gesture, he clenched his fingers into a fist with the forefinger pointed stiffly ahead and the thumb cocked.

DAY SIXTY-TWO

———⋙•❈•⋘———

There is an environment of Minds as well as of Space. The Universe is one . . . a spider's web wherein each mind lives along every line, a vast whispering gallery where . . . though no news travels unchanged yet no secret can be rigorously kept.

C.S. Lewis, *Perelandra*

Everything in the office seemed covered by a film of dust: the plastic specimen trays with soil samples, the long shelves with cardboard boxes holding a jumble of stones and rocks. Even the small man whose office this was seemed to wear a layer of dust. His spectacles were certainly in need of a good polish.

'Are you sure?' Jon glanced down at the two gong hammers on the desk between them.

'What can I tell you?' The small man turned up the palms of his hands. 'They're not that unusual. Old though, I'll grant you that. But that part of the Northern Province is an ancient part of the world. Not far from there you'll find the rock formations of the Barberton Supergroup. Scratch around a little and you can suddenly find yourself holding in your hand something as old as three thousand million years. Some of the oldest fossil evidence of life was discovered over there.'

Jon sighed. He had asked Professor Lange to analyse the composition of the hammers and had fully expected to be told that the stones were rare, outstanding in some way. But the geologist seemed blasé.

'Of course,' Lange said, 'these stones do have a very high quartz content and so do the fragments of the gongs you brought me.' He opened a small brown envelope and shook out the gong fragments onto a sheet of white paper.

'Is that significant?'

Lange shrugged. 'Not for granite. Granite is essentially quartz and feldspar. But it might explain why these rocks are suitable for gongs. Quartz is piezoelectric and when struck, sends out bursts of energy. When you put quartz under tension – for example if you strike it sharply – it produces its own electric current. And when influenced by an electric field, it can vibrate at incredibly rapid frequencies. Tell me, is there a water source close to those gongs?'

'Yeah. Actually there is. That piece of land is called Whispering Water.'

Lange nodded. 'Interesting. There's a theory that fast-flowing underground water will increase the magnetic field of quartz particles in rock. So that would imply that when the gongs get struck, an additional flow of energy is created. Interesting,' he repeated.

'Interesting. But not spectacular.'

Lange smiled. 'You expected something magical, yes?'

'I suppose so.' Jon smiled wryly. 'Something special at least.'

Lange started to wrap the hammers into a piece of soft cloth. 'They're tools. The hands that fashioned these belonged to an age when tools were always special.' He placed the wrapped hammers into Jon's outstretched palm. 'Still,' he added, 'I suppose it's worth remembering that tools are after all only objects. Then – as today – tools are only as special as the mind that guides them.'

*   *   *

As Jon walked from Professor Lange's dusty sanctum to the computer lab, he stretched his stride. He had wasted far too much time at the geology department. He needed to get back to his computer. Stephen had sent him an e-mail earlier that morning that had set his pulse racing. But he still hadn't had a chance to properly check it out. Professor Lange's call had interrupted him and he became distracted. Somehow the gongs always managed to do that: they somehow had the power to deflect his attention away from his real work.

There was no one else in the lab. The rows of computers were silent. He remembered what Lange had said about tools. These computers were also only tools. And the minds that guided them? He grinned as he looked at the mascots and good luck charms which some of the students had placed on top of their workstations. A Barbie doll with a shaven head. Pokémon. A soft toy with fluffy pink whiskers and an unintentional leer in its beady eyes. A stuffed South Park doll. They looked like modern-day gargoyles fending off the evils of a new age.

Placing his satchel on an empty chair, he slid into a chair behind a mercifully unadorned workstation. He logged on and as the screen started to flicker, he waited with that familiar expectant feeling at the pit of his stomach. Which was quite amazing, come to think of it. Thirteen years and his work still managed to excite him.

It hadn't always been that way. When he and Stephen started work all those years ago, the work had been laborious. Mathematical spade work. Mind-numbing number-crunching.

The first breakthrough came when he had realised that the mathematical problem of perfect tuning could be approached as if it were a cipher . . . and that he might be able to devise a computer program to crack it.

It did not, however, take him long to realise that one computer alone was certainly not up to the job. Not for a problem this staggering in complexity. He would have to borrow a page from the DES Internet decryption and make use of distributed computing. What was required was a large number of computers working together on the same project. A very, very large number of computers. Hundreds of thousands of computers. Millions maybe. But where to find all these computers, that was the problem. How were they going to persuade people all over the world to donate computer time to solving a mathematical riddle? Most people would simply not be interested.

And this was when he had a brainwave. Why not devise a game which people would play by connecting their computers to the central computer that was maintaining the master program? Without their even being aware of it, these gamers would be helping to crack the riddle of perfect tuning. While they were playing the game, their computers would be busy calculating solutions as directed by the central computer. So without these people really knowing about it, they and their computers would form part of a giant, global effort to create a new, perfect musical scale. The success of the scheme would depend on attracting as many people as possible to play the game. Every time someone logged in to play *The Angels' Key*, the problem of perfect tuning would be a step closer to being solved.

It had worked beautifully. Of course, if the game had turned out to be unpopular, they would have been stuck. But Stephen had been in charge of designing the game and he had done a fantastic job. They knew they would never be able to compete with the big boys in the console business – the average budget to design a PS2 or Nintendo game was between two and four million dollars. Even some of the other more advanced PC games were far more elaborate than what they'd be able to come up with. But the fact was: most of these other games were boringly predictable. Despite the incredible graphics they were all stuck in the 'quest' or 'shoot-em-up' genre. No surprises. Whereas *The Angels' Key* delivered something new: the music.

From the start he and Stephen had hoped the music generated by the game would be a powerful drawing card but they had never, even in their wildest dreams, expected a response this staggering. The support for the game now was unprecedented. *The Angels' Key* was a killer game. Bigger than *DOOM*. Bigger than *Age of Empires II*. Bigger by far. And it was free: anyone could play. And each time someone logged in to play, a perfect musical scale was one step closer to becoming reality.

Angel music had even made the leap from computer games to the mainstream and the music could now be heard on radio, in live acts, on CD. He wasn't really interested in that side of things, but of course it was all publicity and attracted even more people into playing the game. It made his skin prickle just to think of it: millions of minds and machines all around the globe working in tandem towards creating the perfect *Angel* scale.

And this morning Stephen had e-mailed him with fantastic news. For some inexplicable reason, the speed with which the master computer was making the mathematical calculations had shot forward exponentially, almost out of control. Stephen's e-mail had ended with two jubilant sentences: WHAT'S HAP-PENING?!?! MAN OH MAN OH MAN!!!

Jon tapped out the file name. The screen turned blue. The next moment it was filled with a slowly revolving three-dimensional image. It looked for all the world like a see-through flower with petals and this was the way he and Stephen referred to it: the *Angel* flower. It was a beautiful piece of graphics. Each petal represented a note of the new scale. The flower was constantly growing. He did not know how many notes the new scale would have, but six petals had already formed. Six perfect notes.

At the top of the screen was a colour-coded gauge, which looked somewhat like a thermometer. It was divided into several colours starting with green at the bottom, blue on the second tier, violet on the third tier, yellow on the fourth, orange on the fifth and finally red on the top tier. A tiny black arrow showed how far they still had to go before arriving at the new, perfect musical scale. For almost a year the arrow had hovered in the green and blue zone. Then it had moved on to the violet. And today . . .

He felt his breath catch. This could not be. Since he had checked it the last time six days ago, the arrow had jumped from the bottom of the violet tier to the very top of the yellow tier. It was unbelievable. Simply not possible.

He looked at the graph at the bottom of the screen, which showed the number of players who had logged in since last week. It was slightly up from the week before, but not much. It certainly did not explain this sudden leap forward.

As he sat there watching the brightly coloured gauge, his mind still refusing to believe what he was looking at, he suddenly felt almost a chill. For the first time he was uneasy. Not that this wasn't exciting – it meant they were now much, much closer to their goal – but it was also just a little scary. Any unpredictable development required caution. He liked to know why things happened the way they did, and he had no explanation for this development. Although the number of people playing the game had steadily increased over time, it still did not explain this sudden acceleration in calculation speed. It was as though the number of gamers had crossed some kind of secret threshold to achieve critical mass, kick-starting the process into gaining its own momentum.

The *Angel* flower was revolving slowly, serenely. The gauge glowed with colour.

What's happening. Man oh man oh man.

DAY SIXTY-ONE

It is a tremendous achievement to create a piece of music that incites riot . . . to cause peaceful lovers of music to scream out their agony, to arouse angry emotions and to tempt men . . .

William J. Henderson, Review of Edgar Varèse's
Hyperprism

Tia balanced the tray with its basket of croissants and dainty pitcher of orange juice onto Jon's lap.

'Breakfast in bed,' she said and kissed him. 'And a little something for you.' She handed him the gaily wrapped package.

'Thanks,' he said, surprised. 'What did I do to deserve all of this?'

'You look particularly adorable today, that's all.'

'I don't know that I altogether trust this sudden pampering. What do you want?'

'Dinner tonight at La Dolce Vita. Your treat.'

She sat down on the edge of the bed and looked at him searchingly. She was a little worried about him. Since he came home last night he had seemed to her unusually preoccupied. Almost remote. But he had assured her that nothing was wrong. Quite the opposite in fact. His work had taken a giant leap forward. But she noticed that the frown between his brows did not go away.

'Open it,' she urged and pushed the package towards him.

He smiled at her and touched the bow in her hair. 'You look like a little girl.'

She looked over his shoulder at her reflection in the mirror. She was wearing candy-striped pyjamas.

'Wait till this evening. I'll be wearing the black silk.'

'The one with the spaghetti straps?'

'You bet.'

He started to open the package. She repressed a smile at the over-enthusiastic way in which he tore away at the delicate wrapping paper. If it had been her, she would have removed the pieces of tape very carefully and then have kept the paper to be re-used at a later stage. Astrid caught her out once and had disapproved. 'It shows you're cheap,' she had said loftily.

Jon laughed as he extracted a pair of boxer shorts from the filmy tissue paper. They were silk: fire-truck red with white polka dots and Tia had not been able to resist.

He picked up the tiny cardboard slip that she had placed inside the package and read the message out loud: *'It deserves to be wrapped in silk every day. See you tonight. Love T.'*

Leaning over, he kissed her long on the mouth. 'Thanks, baby,' he said softly. 'We have a date.'

'Are you really OK?' she asked.

'Sure. What could be wrong?'

'I don't know. Since yesterday you've seemed stressed.'

'Just a lot on my mind.'

'You're not supposed to have anything on your mind but me.'

'Amen. So watch me tonight. First we'll have that killer pasta at La Dolce Vita and then . . .'

She smiled and smoothed the hair away from his forehead. 'Who was your first love?'

'Marion Snodgrass,' he answered immediately. 'My dentist's assistant.'

She looked at him suspiciously. 'Is this a true story?'

'Oh, yeah. You never saw a boy as eager to visit the dentist as I was. I had to wear braces. God, I was a sight. But she was a vision in white. Ethereal. Beautiful. Always smiling, always caring. I was truly in love.'

'In love or in lust?'

'I was fifteen – you figure it out.'

'I've always thought a dentist's chair would be the one place where no erotic impulse can survive.'

'Well, it shows how much you know. And you? Who was the first guy to turn you on?'

'Lancelot.'

'Like in Lancelot and Guinevere?'

'Yes, except I saw myself as Elaine.'

'Who's Elaine?'

'Elaine,' Tia said. '"Elaine the fair, Elaine the loveable, Elaine the lily maid of Astolat." She died of unrequited love, you know. Literally died of it. I read Tennyson when I was a teenager and I can still recall that one passage where she meets Lancelot for the first time . . .'

Tia paused and then recited dreamily, '"Seam'd with an ancient swordcut on the cheek, And bruised and bronzed, she lifted up her eyes And loved him, with that love which was her doom."'

'Bruised and bronzed?' Jon sounded dazed.

'Pretty sexy, huh?'

'I'll say. Perhaps I should read Tennyson too.'

'Anyway, there's this one bit where she's watching – furtively – as Lancelot calms his horse. The description of his strong hand on the neck of the restless horse – well, it's pretty powerful stuff.'

Jon put his hands on both sides of her face. 'I'll have to get myself a horse then.'

'At least you already have the scar.'

He was quiet for a moment as he looked down at her. 'What's the worst thing that can happen to someone?' he suddenly asked.

'Oh, I don't know. Being alone. Never finding your love.'

'No,' he said. 'Being alone. Finding, but not recognising your love.'

'Like Lancelot with Elaine.'

'Like Lancelot and Elaine.'

She took her finger and ran it gently down the side of his face, pausing at the small scar that marred the taut line of the jaw. She still couldn't believe this scar was the handiwork of a friend. A best friend.

'We're pretty lucky then,' she said.

'Yeah,' he said. 'Pretty lucky.'

★　　★　　★

But in truth, she thought, watching him get out of bed and shrug into his towelling robe, they were complete opposites. He was, in many respects, an uncomplicated man. There was a clarity to him: she had come to realise that he never doubted himself at the core the way most people do. It wasn't arrogance, it was simply that he was a man completely at ease with himself. Not given to sentimentality or self-analysis, any setbacks that came his way he'd accommodate without going into spasms of guilt or self-remonstration. It was a quality in him she admired greatly. That and his curiosity for the world around him: an appetite for life that was clear-cut, almost aggressively sane.

Not that he was always easy to live with. He was messy. He was easily bored. He could be impatient and dismissive. And he was obsessed with his work. Seriously, seriously obsessed. It was her first encounter with this kind of single-minded extravagant obsession. And at close range it was overwhelming.

Whenever he sat down in front of his laptop, his face would take on an intensely absorbed look. And she, like a neglected wife, jealous of the mistress who had such a hold on him, would sometimes lean over his shoulder, curious and suspicious: the dense tangle of numbers on the screen defeating her comprehension.

It was the one place in his mind she couldn't follow him. And at some level she resented it: resented it because she recognised that it was in his work that Jon found his deepest sense of himself. 'I don't know how to explain it to you,' he once told her, 'but whenever I sit down at my computer and open the file on *The Angels' Key*, I feel as though I've come home. I have the feeling that this is what I was born to do. The problem of perfect tuning is such an exquisite riddle. The mathematical equivalent of a Rembrandt.'

In the mornings after waking up, he did not reach for her, but immediately sat down to check on his e-mail. Usually there would be some long, unintelligible message from his friend Stephen waiting for him, which he'd scan with the anxiety of a gambler checking his lottery numbers.

'I can admire the dedication,' she told him once, 'but I'm wary of the obsession. Obsession carries with it a wing-brush of darkness.'

He had smiled at her impishly. 'Not if it's a magnificent obsession.'

Magnificent obsession. Perfect tuning. When he had first explained the concept to her, she was sceptical.

'You're saying to me that all pianos are off-key?'

'Absolutely.'

'Every single instrument out there?'

'Sure.'

'Even my mother's piano?'

'Afraid so.'

'Well how come I can't hear anything wrong? It sounds perfectly fine to me.'

He made an impatient movement with his hand. 'We're all so used to the flawed version, that it sounds OK to us. Stephen uses the word "ear-washed" and that's really what it is. We've all been ear-washed since birth. But I can assure you: keyboards are all purposely tuned just the tiniest bit off-key, because there's this niggling little mathematical anomaly called the Pythagorean Comma, which is messing up the whole system of tuning. And string instruments like violins and guitars are affected as well. There is no such thing as an instrument achieving tuning perfection. In order to achieve perfection, you have to get rid of the Comma, and if you want to get rid of the Comma, you will have to develop an entirely new musical scale: a scale that is one hundred percent flawless.'

'And that would be difficult?'

'You have no idea how difficult. When Stephen and I took on the challenge of perfect tuning, we were kids at the time; we didn't realise what the hell we were letting ourselves in for. We set out to resolve the imperfection in musical intervals without having to adjust or temper the notes in order to harmonise them. If we had known what we know now, we would never even have tried it, because the truth of it is: there is no possible way to create a perfect musical scale.'

'Except you *are* going to create one.'

'We sure are.'

She shrugged a little petulantly. 'Although that's not quite accurate is it? I mean, you've created this game but the people playing it – they're the ones doing all the work.'

'Oh, yeah?' He lifted an amused eyebrow. 'Give me some credit here, will you. They're not actually solving the problem, *my* program is running *their* computers. They're not even aware of what's going on. But sure, obviously we need people to play the game. But think about it, Tia. One morning we'll wake up and every instrument on this planet will be an instrument that was tuned perfectly. It will be as though we've been looking at a beautiful picture that is just slightly blurred. And all of a sudden, the entire picture will slide into perfect focus. Doesn't it just blow your mind? Isn't it incredibly cool?'

A magnificent obsession. Well, she had to be honest. Sometimes she wished he'd be willing to settle for something less magnificent and less obsessive. Like spending more time with her.

He was now whistling under his breath, the gift and their plans for tonight obviously long gone from his mind. But as he walked towards the bathroom, he suddenly stopped in his stride and looked back at her.

'Oh, shit. I forgot. I won't be able to make it tonight.'

'Why? What's happening?'

'I'm going to that music festival. Remember? The one you said you didn't want to go to.'

'Oh . . . right.' Damn, she thought furiously. He couldn't just give it a miss?

'You OK with that?'

'No. Actually I'm not. I can't see why it's so important.'

'Like I told you. There's this one act I'd really like to hear.' He was adopting that super patient tone of voice that always drove her up the wall. 'Apparently they're really good at mixing *Angel* music with trance. It should be great. I tell you what,' he said with the pleased air of someone who's had a brilliant idea. 'You come with me. We'll celebrate there.'

'I'm a classical girl, remember? Strictly Mozart.'

'Come on, Tia. Take a walk on the wild side.'

She sighed. She really didn't want to go. Although she'd never tell him this to his face, she did not like *Angel* music. She had tried very hard to develop an appreciation for it but without any luck. *Angel* music made her feel agitated. She did not like the aggressive drum and bass rhythms, the eerie, atonal chords, or the bleeps, swooshes and other odd noises generated in the computer's belly. The music was certainly compelling and there was sometimes an otherworldly beauty to it, but she tried to avoid it as much as she could. If it was on radio, she'd turn it off. And whenever Jon played the game on his laptop at home, she'd always find an excuse to leave the room and get out of range of the computer's speakers.

'Please? Pretty please?' He was looking at her appealingly. She wanted to continue holding on to her anger – she had the moral high ground here for goodness' sake – but now he was batting his eyelids in a quite ridiculously affected way and she couldn't help smiling unwillingly.

'I'm going to regret this,' she said. 'I know it.'

*　　*　　*

It felt as though they had been driving forever. Surely they should have been there by now? Tia glanced at Astrid who was hunched over the wheel, muttering to herself. Ben was peering at the road map he had taken from the cubby hole.

So not only was she supposed to have a romantic evening listening to some weird music, she was also expected to do it in the company of both Astrid and Ben. How cosy. She glared at Jon who was sitting next to her. He was happy as a clam; completely oblivious to her resentment.

'You OK, Tia?' Ben was peering at her over his shoulder. He was looking rather stylish in a Madiba shirt à la Nelson Mandela.

'Of course. I just can't believe you want to do this.' She leaned forward and gave him a slight punch against the shoulder. 'Music festivals? They're not you.'

'I'm an anthropologist. This is a field trip. Why are churches empty and rock stadiums full?'

'Enquiring minds want to know.' Jon grinned.

'What?' Tia looked at him.

'Never mind.' He grinned again. 'Outside your frame of reference. But cheer up. It's going to be great. I once went to this gig and some kids put eggs on the front of the stage and by the end of the performance the eggs were cooked. Cool huh?'

'Stunning,' she said sourly. 'And maybe the protein in the brains of those kids were getting fried as well.'

'Hey, what an image.' He grinned, unfazed.

A white minibus with a large *Rock Africa* banner streaming from one of its windows passed them with a screech of tyres. With a sickening swerve of the wheels, Astrid followed and within minutes they were driving into a huge parking lot jam-packed with cars and fleets of white minibus taxis.

The venue for the concert was an enormous disused factory plant on the other side of the road. As they walked towards it, Tia noticed that the dusty windows were painted black. She could hear the roar of the music as they held their hands to be rubber-stamped by a bored-looking attendant sporting a T-shirt emblazoned with the word 'Moby'. Another attendant, his hair died lime green and clad in psychedelic raver wear, led them to the entrance. The music became louder as they walked down the tunnel-like entrance towards the heavy doors. But when they entered the dark cavernous space Tia was unprepared for the sound that rushed at her with a whoosh of energy, like a physical blow to the heart.

The vibration came at her through the soles of her feet. The rhythm crept up her arms and legs; seeped into the grooves of her brain. Tia looked at Jon. He was mouthing something at her, she knew not what. He seemed like a stranger. The white strobe lights blanched his features, only the thick brows standing out sharp and dramatic. Astrid's purple dress shimmered viciously. She smiled and her teeth were phosphorescent white.

The vast space was packed with bodies. There were even some balancing precariously on the rafters high above. The smell of sweat and the sweet, drug smell of dagga hung in the air. Tia could hardly make out the stage. It was a bright shimmering spot in the distance, only to be glimpsed at through a forest of waving arms. The lead singer was bent backwards, her throat forming an arc as if she were abandoning herself to a sublime moment of faith.

Tia recognised the music. It was Mpantsula jive: a hybrid of township jive and Western rock. The hallucinatory, repetitive music throbbed and pulsed. Listening to it you suddenly knew what South Africa was all about: this strange coupling of values and traditions African and Western; this mix uneasy, dangerous and sublimely exciting.

Tia looked at the swaying bodies around her; at the uninhibited faces and hot-looking eyes. The music tugged at her senses but part of her brain was still cool. She would not let herself go completely. She looked down at her wrist-watch but in the shifting light she could not make out the time.

Jon put his hand on her arm. A new act was taking the stage. Jon's mouth formed the word: 'Listen.'

The music had changed. A hum filled the air: swelling and receding; swelling and receding, like the ebb and flow of a spinning top. And underneath the hum grew a thick dense noise: a noise like a sigh, like the breathing of a fatigued long-distance runner. Like fabric tearing, like silk ripping, the sigh gave way to a leap of sound. A sound liberating and ecstatically terrifying. And Tia felt herself responding.

The response left no room for rational thought. Her head was weightless. Her thoughts were strands of light a million years long. She was clutching a wave of sound, riding it out. Someone grabbed her by the waist and held on tight. It was a man, a boy really, his eyes half-closed. 'The music of saints and sinners,' he shouted in her ear, and laughed soundlessly.

There was no break in the wall of music. She did not know how long she stood there in that swirling darkness, inhaling and exhaling along with the driving beat. At times the music spoke of unrelenting alienation. Demon poetry, she thought. But poetry all the same.

When the nausea hit her it was completely unexpected. Her stomach heaved. Her chest felt tight. She motioned to Jon that she needed to go out. Behind her she could feel Ben touching her shoulder as if to make sure she was still there.

An elbow gored into her side. Someone stepped on her foot. The smell of sweating bodies packed close together was overwhelming. There was not enough air to fill her lungs. Not nearly enough air. The faces around her were so incredibly strange. These people were still caught up in the music and she was not and the faces seemed grotesque and distorted.

She stumbled outside and took a large gulp of air. She touched her forehead and found it damp with sweat. Her heart was hammering in her throat. For a second she panicked. Hadn't she read somewhere that people sometimes have epileptic seizures at rock concerts? She couldn't believe how long it took for her breathing to even out.

'You OK?' Jon looked concerned.

She put her hand in his. 'I felt faint in there for a moment. I'll be all right.'

'You sure?'

'Yes. I'll feel better in the car.'

'I can't believe I've actually stood up straight for two hours,' Astrid said as they started walking towards the parking lot. 'I wonder—' Then she stopped and squinted. 'What the hell's that?'

They had turned the corner and in the far end of the parking lot there were flashing lights and a crowd of silent people. As they walked closer they could see two white minibuses parked crazily.

Astrid's face was white. 'Oh, Christ,' she said and turned away, her hand against her mouth. 'Don't look. Don't look.'

Tia pushed past her. Against her back she could feel Jon's urgent hand. She stopped abruptly.

The driver of the one minibus was lying on the wheel. His face was turned away, his one hand pressed against the side window. Even from a distance the gaping hack wounds to the back of his head and neck were clearly visible. Several passengers, some still sitting inside the vans, others lying a few yards away from the buses, had the crumpled, collapsed look of dead people. And near the back tyre of one of the vans was something so wicked, her brain had trouble processing the image.

The stench of charred flesh in her nose. The euphoric smell of gasoline. The corpse was lying stiffly, the burnt-out tyre like a grisly necklace melted into its chest. The eyes white marbles, stiff and wide-open, almost cartoon-like against the black, crackled skin.

It was quiet. No sirens, no noise of weeping. An ambulance, its light flashing and its back doors open, was parked close by the second minibus. Uniformed emergency workers were carrying a stretcher on which lay a young man, his mouth open. He was wearing a light-blue T-shirt with the words PRACTISE SAFER SEX printed on the front. The T-shirt was brown with blood.

Within touching distance of the burnt-out corpse, a young woman was lying on the ground, waiting to be taken away. She was obviously pregnant and had her arms clasped tightly around the hump of her belly. A thin spray of blood fanned out from the side of her stomach, making her arms look wet and slick. It seemed to Tia as though the woman was looking straight at her.

'Ma'am, sir, please move on.' A hand under her elbow propelled Tia away. She looked up into the face of a police officer. He had old, blue eyes. His face was teenager young. 'Move on,' he repeated impatiently. 'Move on.'

'What happened?' she asked, resisting his hand urging her to the side.

The police officer shrugged. 'God knows. Some of the ravers went berserk. For no reason at all. This doesn't seem to be gang or drug-related. But don't worry. We've apprehended everyone involved.'

Tia looked at the faces in the crowd. Many still had that blind, slightly glazed look she had noticed in the eyes of the ravers inside.

She looked back at the pregnant woman. An ambulance worker was kneeling down beside her and Tia could only see the woman's legs, long and shapely and twisted into a relaxed sprawl.

Tia turned to face Jon. His face was white and set. 'Come,' she said and took his hand. 'We can do nothing here.'

Later that night she had difficulty going to sleep. She lay on her back for what seemed like hours, watching the fragile pattern of shadowy leaves on the ceiling. When she finally slid into sleep she started to dream. She saw an ocean of music and a sea of bobbing heads: people swaying and dancing and their skulls chiming like bells. Among them was a young woman with dark eyes and blood on her arms.

Tia jerked awake, her heart hammering in her throat. For a moment she had difficulty breathing. She turned her head sideways and looked at Jon. He was sleeping, his face pressed deeply into the pillow. He sighed, a tired, drawn-out sigh. She brushed her hand gently over his forehead. He frowned and mumbled.

Her heart was slowly settling down. It was only a dream. No need for this sick feeling, which was making her feel afraid.

She turned over on her side. Just a dream, that was all it was. As she closed her eyes resolutely, she vowed not to allow herself to get caught in the grip of a nightmare once again.

DAY SIXTY

The nightmare continued the next morning when she woke up. As she got out of bed she felt woozy and before she knew what was happening, she had walked straight into the bedroom door.

'Hey, watch out.' Jon grabbed her elbow and steadied her. 'You got up too quickly.'

Tia touched her eye where it had slammed into the door. 'I suppose I must have.'

'You OK now?'

'Yes,' she said. But in reality she did not feel OK at all. She had a terrific headache. And the nausea that had gripped her at the music festival the previous day had returned. There was also something wrong with her balance and every sound seemed magnified. She winced at the buzz of Jon's electric razor. Later, in the kitchen, the slices of bread popping up in the toaster sounded like a tiny earthquake.

By the time she arrived at the campus, she was blinking constantly, as though trying to clear dust particles from her eyes. But it didn't help because the prickle was not inside the eye but *behind* her eyes. Somewhere in her skull, somewhere in a moist, dark hollow . . . somewhere she could not get at it.

Fortunately, the students were taking a test today. She would not have been up to teaching class. She felt that unwell.

She poured herself a glass of water from the carafe on the credenza and looked out over the rows of students. They were hunched over their test papers: each student wrapped in a cocoon of quiet concentration.

In the back row sat a girl with a bright red chiffon scarf tied around her throat. She had shoulder-length blonde hair but as she bowed her head to look at the paper in front of her, Tia could see the black roots starting at the scalp. Exposed roots were a clear sign that midterm exams were on hand. The closer the exams, the less attention the students paid to their appearance. The girl held her pen awkwardly and was frowning. She wrote slowly and laboriously, the tip of her tongue peeking through half open teeth. Her pen trailed across the paper: a rustling, dragging sound like a snake moving through dry leaves.

In the seat in front of her sat a man who was in need of a shave. He was thoughtfully rubbing his forefinger across the black stubble on his chin. Back and forth it went; back and forth with rhythmic, rasping regularity.

Tia watched. She was mesmerised by the coarse scratching sound, by the constant to and fro movement of the finger. The student glanced up and saw her staring at him and smiled self-consciously. And thank God, he let his hand fall to the desk where it lay motionless.

But now she became aware of the other sounds in the room. The room was filled with noise but noise that was sly and furtive, like whispered gossip; like women talking to each other with their hands held protectively over their mouths. The stealthy swish of nylon pantyhose as one leg crossed over another. The sluggish rasp of a shirt sleeve on paper. The scrape of a shoe – leather on grit – the sound scratching at her consciousness like splintered glass. Someone sneezed and tiny microbes floated unseen into warm, wet, pink nasal passages, into the glistening tissue of throats from which came the merciless sound of breathing. Breath sucked in, pushed out; sucked in, pushed out; in, out. Relentless.

She was getting angry at the noise. Stupid people. Stupid people making stupid noises. Her rage was suddenly so overwhelming that she felt her hands twitch into two tight fists at her sides. She wanted to shout at them to be quiet. She wanted to put her fist into the half-open mouth of the tow-headed boy at the very end of the first row who was breathing stertorously, dabbing every now and then at his nose with a large yellow handkerchief. She wanted to ram her fist into his slack mouth, to feel the teeth break against her knuckles. To hurt him.

The thought echoed in her head and shocked her into awareness. She felt sick, ashamed of herself. *What was happening to her?* She placed her hand on the top button of her blouse. It was stifling in here. She must remember to report to maintenance that the air conditioning wasn't working. But – it was working, because listen, there was the metallic whine coming from the grate in the ceiling and it was growing into a loud shrill whistle, a long, jagged shard of sound.

And the clock at the back of the room with its bland white face was ticking so precisely, and the long, straight, black legs marched across the face so orderly, so smartly, with such admirable rhythm like two good soldiers, every movement perfectly synchronised. It was good to be punctual, she always prided herself on being punctual. Not like Klio who was always late. Just that five minutes late. And she was always that five minutes early. And then ten minutes wasted, really. But what was ten minutes in a lifetime of minutes. Clocks kept on ticking. Like the clock above the door with its hands moving so quickly across the face in double time now, no triple time, sweeping across the face in a frenzy. Twelve hours disappearing in the time it takes to blink. And now the arms were drooping like melting wax, pearling blackly down the clock face with a soft spluttering hiss . . .

'Ms Theron?'

Her head jerked and her eyes focussed on the student who was standing next to her, holding out his test paper. She took it from him mechanically and looked down at what he had written. She could make no sense of the letters on the page. Black flies clinging to white flypaper.

She managed to nod at him and then the bell went – an explosion in her head – and the students gave her their tests and somehow she had left the classroom and was standing inside the ladies' room throwing cold water on her face and wanting to weep.

She walked into one of the stalls and slapped down the toilet lid. She sat down and placed her head between her knees. The floor underneath her feet was tiled in neat black and white squares. Water was dripping loudly from one of the faucets. Much too loudly. Stop the noise. She couldn't hear herself think. Stop the noise. Wasn't that what Klio had told her? Klio, curled up in the darkest corner of the closet. Klio with her hands over her ears, her face white in the gloom, saying over and over: 'Stop the noise. I can't think. Stop the noise.'

Tia pressed the palm of her hand against her mouth. She closed her eyes tightly. 'Oh, God. Please, God. No.'

*   *   *

Tia looked so pale. Underneath her eyes were dark bruises and her nose seemed strangely pinched. The thick hair lay in matted coils on the white pillow.

'Why didn't you call me?' Jon picked up her hand. It felt sweaty inside his own.

'I didn't want you to know.'

'Why on earth not?' He saw her flinch at the tone of his voice. Get a grip, he told himself. This was not what she needed. But he was feeling scared and feeling scared made him feel powerless. Feeling powerless made him angry. He tried to moderate his voice. 'I could have taken you to a doctor. I'm going to take you anyway.'

'I just wanted to get home and into bed. I've slept for four hours and I'm fine. Really. No sounds jumping out at me any more. Everything sounds normal now. I'm just exhausted, that's all.'

'Why didn't you want me to know?'

'I didn't want you to think I'm crazy.'

'Why would I think that? I would never think that.'

'Jon. I need to tell you something.' He watched as she picked up his hand and placed her own inside his, wrapping his fingers around her fist. It was something she did when she needed reassurance, he had noticed that before. He had always found it endearing but now it made him feel apprehensive.

'I've never really explained to you about Klio.'

'You told me she disappeared.'

'She did. But that wasn't all there was to it.'

He waited.

'You remember that day when you followed me to the museum and you asked me why I'm so interested in that picture of Emmaline Lepworth? And I told you because it reminds me of someone?'

He nodded, puzzled.

'It reminds me of my mother.'

He frowned. 'What do you mean? Isn't that the picture of—'

'Yes, it is. It's the picture of a mad woman.'

It was quiet in the room. Against the window pane was only the despairing sound of a trapped bee frantically seeking escape.

She spoke again. 'Before her disappearance my mother was hypersensitive to sound. She told me it was as though she had giant earphones stuck to her head every single day. Every noise around her got amplified to such an extent that she could hardly function. At times she went a little insane. It was frightening to watch. I've never told this to anyone, but Ben, you understand. I don't want people to remember her as this crazy woman.'

'Go on.'

'I'm so scared. I'm so scared it's happening to me too. What if this is some kind of genetic thing? Or schizophrenia? That's what the psychiatrist said. Schizophrenia.'

He stared at her, momentarily at a loss for words. Those wide lost eyes. They were searching his for an answer. But he had no answer to give.

'Jon?'

'Look, I don't think this is what's happening to you. Probably the explanation is much more prosaic. Maybe you've had a very bad migraine. Yes,' he said warming up to his own explanation, 'that's probably what it is. I sometimes get those, you know, and they're intense. I become really sensitive to sound. I see these auras. I'm nauseous. It's very, very scary. And you were shook up by what we saw after the rock concert yesterday. The stress of that could have brought it on. You had a headache, right?'

She nodded slowly. 'Yes. But what I remember most of all is the anger.'

'Anger?'

'It just came out of nowhere. I noticed this student who was nursing a cold. And I got upset with him. Just like that. Upset isn't the word . . . Jon, I wanted to cause that poor boy physical pain. I could feel the violence inside of me. I really wanted to hurt him.'

He tried to joke but his uneasiness was growing. 'I constantly fantasise about causing my students physical pain.'

She shook her head. 'I don't know . . .'

'Well, look. It's not going to help worrying about it now. Tomorrow we'll go to the doctor and discuss all of this with him. And then we'll decide what to do.'

'I don't want to go to a doctor.'

'I'll be there with you. And I'm sure everything is going to be fine. You'll see.'

'No.'

'Let's talk about it tomorrow.'

She fell back on the pillow and closed her eyes exhaustedly. 'Yes. Tomorrow.'

'Go back to sleep.' He leaned forward and kissed her on the forehead. The skin felt clammy underneath his lips. 'We're going to see this through together, I promise.'

At the door he turned around to look at her. She had turned on her side and all he could see were the matted ringlets of her hair. Her body seemed very small underneath the bedclothes.

He switched off the light and pulled the door softly shut.

★　　★　　★

Inside the living room he looked around him irresolutely, suddenly at a complete loss what to do next. It was as though he was seeing the room for the first time. There was Tia's desk with her Remington typewriter and neat row of medieval poetry books: *The Canterbury Tales*, Walther von der Vogelweide, *Karel ende Elegast*, *Divina Commedia*. Her 'witches' books', as he always joked. There was his own nook, a lot less tidy with books and papers and back-issues of *Rolling Stone* and gaming magazines piled up any which way. On his desk were scattered some Liquorice All Sorts. He was fond of Liquorice All Sorts and often left a trail of candy behind him as he moved from room to room. 'So that you can find me, should you lose me,' he'd always say when Tia complained. Next to the telephone was a coffee cup, carefully placed on top of a coaster. On its rim was a smudge of lipstick.

The telephone. He pulled out the dainty telephone stool, and sat down, his long legs squashed uncomfortably underneath him. Cradling the receiver underneath his chin, he started to dial.

The phone kept ringing in his ear, no one picked up. But then, just as he was about to hang up, the phone clicked and the ringing tone stopped abruptly.

'Hello?'

'Stephen.'

'Hi.' Stephen sounded surprised. But then, the two of them very rarely spoke on the phone. Stephen's hearing problem meant that he tended to avoid the telephone. Not that he wasn't able to conduct a normal conversation on the phone, but it required some effort. E-mail was his preferred mode of communication.

'What's up?'

'Nothing much.'

'What's the matter?'

'Nothing. I just wanted to talk.'

'Something's wrong. I can hear it in your voice. I'm not completely deaf, you know.'

'It's Tia.'

'Oh? What about her?' Stephen didn't sound tremendously interested. Stephen did not believe in relationships: one-night stands were more his style. For this he made no excuses. 'Relationships are messy,' he'd say. 'And messy means time-consuming. Until the *Angel* project's finished, wasting time is not an option.' But now, as he started telling Stephen what had happened to Tia, he could sense Stephen's interest sharpening.

'You say this has happened to the mother as well?'

'Yes. And that's why I'm worried. I'm going to take Tia to the doctor tomorrow. Better to face upfront whatever needs to be faced.'

'Don't do that. A doctor is going to be of no use. They'll just give her tranquillisers, which is the wrong thing to do.'

'What the hell are you talking about?'

'Look, all I'm saying is give her time. Keep an eye on her. If it happens again, OK, then take it from there. But do you really want her doped up? You don't know that there's a correlation between what happened to her and what's happened to the mother . . .'

Jon leaned back, suddenly feeling immensely tired.

'You may be right.'

'I'm always right. Besides, you're talking to a fellow who's constantly living with noises in his head. Drugs don't work. I know, trust me.'

'I do, of course.' Jon spoke quickly, surprised. Stephen never talked about his tinnitus. He rarely mentioned anything about his hearing problems.

'I'll tell Richie you said hi.' Stephen's voice was calm.

'Please do that. I never thought I'd say this, but I quite miss him. How's he doing?'

'He wants to go to Egypt.'

'What?'

'There's this group whose members want to sleep in the sarcophaguses in the pyramids. He wants to join them.'

'Oh, man. Is he serious?'

'Of course. But he's low on funds so I shouldn't worry.'

'Well, call me if he takes off.'

'Will do. So ... Tia ... You're going to follow my advice?'

'Yeah. Like always.'

*   *   *

And it seemed as though Stephen was right. Nothing like what had happened to Tia that day happened again. He was watching her closely, but she seemed fine. 'Sometimes it feels as though my ears are popping,' she told him once, 'you know, like when you go up in a plane. And then the sounds around me will become muted – and I'll hear this sort of hum – but just for a moment or two. So stop worrying.' This didn't sound serious, he had to admit, and as two weeks went by without anything untoward happening, he started to relax. It had probably just been a one-off thing brought on by witnessing the aftermath of those killings. God knows, he felt shaken himself by what had happened. The casual way in which people in this country accepted even the most inhumane violence was staggering. The incident had not even made the news on television.

'Earth calling Jon. Respond please.'

He looked up to find Tia watching him quizzically. She was holding up a long yellow night dress for his inspection. She was shopping for lingerie this morning and he had insisted on coming with her. He knew most men disliked shopping with women, but he was different that way. Women's boutiques intrigued him: the fluttering sales ladies, the soft fabrics and beautiful displays. And the shops had a special fragrance. The scent of women.

'So what do you think?' she asked, impatiently, turning the night dress around so he could see the back as well.

'I think it looks like something my grandmother used to wear.'

She pulled a face. 'So OK. You choose something.'

He thumbed through the garments draped over padded pink and white hangers and pulled out a lace teddy in pale blue silk.

'What about this?'

'I'll have to try it on first.'

'Of course,' he agreed. 'And of course I'll have to come with you. So you can have the benefit of my expert opinion. I've had extensive practice in the field of women's underwear, I'll have you know.'

'I'll bet.' She nudged him in the ribs quite viciously as they started walking in the direction of the dressing rooms. 'It explains a lot. Like why you're not feeling self-conscious in a shop like this.'

'Should I be?'

'Most men would be.'

'I'm not most men.'

She smiled wryly. 'That's for sure.'

And so they walked into the small dressing room, which unexpectedly had a handy bolt on the door, and she tried the teddy on for him and they made love – hurried and fumbling – stifling their laughter as the shop assistant, a pigeon-breasted woman with a worried expression, cooed helpfully from the other side of the door, 'Are you all right in there?'

On their way back to the cottage, he stopped at a street corner flower vendor. 'I feel like buying you flowers,' he said and reached into the mass of riotous colour tumbling from tin containers and plastic buckets.

'Not those.' Tia stopped him as he pulled out a bunch of blood red carnations.

'Why not?' He stood there feeling awkward, the water from the long slimy stems dripping onto his shoes.

'I once read a poem in which carnations are described as

amputated fists. Since then, whenever I see red carnations I think of bloody stumps.'

'Jesus.' He gave a startled laugh. He gestured at a cluster of white African daisies. 'These OK?'

That night as they lay in bed – half-awake, half-asleep – he watched as the breeze softly blew the delicate net curtains into the room. With every gust the air was scented with the smell of the French lavender bush that grew outside. From the direction of the neighbours' house came the sound of Chopin, the faint trill of notes as cool as spring water.

The Delft jug filled with the daisies that he had bought her stood on top of the dresser. The light-blue silk teddy was hooked to the back of the chair and he could see its ghostly reflection in the mirror. Beside him Tia was breathing slowly, deeply. Her hand, sleep-relaxed, was clasped inside his own.

He turned his head on the pillow and looked at her. The sprawling, fragile, bird-like limbs. The pale belly, still gleaming with the sticky snail's trail of passion. The fragrant hair he had wrapped around her throat like a noose. She sighed and turned over and he moved until his body cupped hers and he could feel the angles of her hips against him, the smoothness of the back of her thighs. She reached for his hand and placed it between the warm hollow of her breasts. He closed his eyes to sleep. He couldn't remember ever feeling more content.

The next morning he woke up before her. Quietly, so as not to wake her, he walked into the drawing room to check on his e-mail. There had been another acceleration in computing speed the day before: another anomalous development. But although he was still uneasy about these sudden sprints forward, he had decided to follow Stephen's example and become less freaked out about it all. 'What the hell does it matter that you can't explain it?' Stephen had said the last time he had voiced his concern. 'Think of it as a gift of the gods. What would have taken another year at least, will now only take two months at most. Gift of the gods, I tell you.'

As he logged on, he wondered if Stephen had been able to send through the calculations he had asked for. But when he opened his e-mail, there was no e-mail from Stephen, only a message from Richie.

He was still staring at the screen when he felt Tia's arms around his neck.

'Good morning, sunshine.' She kissed him on the cheek, then nibbled his ear. 'Sleep well?'

'Great.'

'So I was thinking. Maybe, this weekend we could go some place nice. You know where they give massages and facials and leave chocolates on your pillow.'

'The weekend won't be possible.'

'Why not?'

'Richie is coming to visit.' He paused. 'And so is Stephen.'

The Listener

DAY FORTY-SEVEN

Everyone needs a quest as an excuse for living.

**Bruce Chatwin (as quoted by Nicholas Shakespeare
in *Bruce Chatwin*)**

'In the very beginning the world was populated with creatures made up of male-female, male-male and female-female parts. On a whim the gods divided these creatures into their separate halves. Ever since, these divided beings have been searching for the other part of their soul: yearning to be with the one who will make them feel whole again.' His mother stopped talking and her hand, so soft, brushed against his cheek.

'What happens if you don't find the other part of your soul?'

'That would be very sad. But it won't happen to you, Stephen. She's waiting for you – somewhere.'

His mother leaned forward and kissed him on the cheek. 'Now go to sleep.'

And he had turned over on his side and that night a girl – her face pale and indistinct – came to visit him in his dreams. She warmed his heart, took away his fears. And when he woke up he wondered if he would ever find her again.

Maybe he had found her.

He still did not know what she looked like, but he already knew she was special: a listener, like himself.

Not like the others who walked around like sheep, oblivious to the incredible variety of sounds around them. It never ceased to amaze him how people everywhere treated sound with such casual contempt; so completely unaware of its insidious power. Well, that was certainly about to change.

Tia. The name suited her. A tiny shiver of sound: like a bell. Someone else who had also experienced sound like a pain in her heart, her mind, her very bones. Just like he did, that day twenty-one years ago. He was only thirteen then, and he had almost died. But what had happened to him that day had set the course for the rest of his life. He had never told anyone about it. Not even Jon.

Jon. Strange how you can love someone deeply and yet resent him with every fibre of your being. He had always felt this ambivalence towards Jon. Adoration, admiration. Intense envy.

In grad school he had been attracted to the two brothers almost immediately. He was charmed by Richie's intuition – his mystical bent of mind – and fascinated by Jon's genius. At first he tried to compete with Jon, but he soon realised he could never hope to match that burning brilliance. So instead he set out to entice Jon, to seduce him into friendship; because at that stage he already knew he needed help in his quest for perfect tuning. He had known, even while at Cambridge, that he was not up to the job himself. It was such a bitter pill to swallow: the knowledge that he would not be the one to unravel the mystery of perfect tuning; that it would be Jon's privilege to do so. But he had put his envy aside. His immediate concern had been to persuade Jon to take on a project that could well take decades to run to completion. But he needn't have worried. He had presented the problem of perfect tuning as a mathematical challenge and Jon had fallen for it. Jon was intellectually arrogant. It was his one fatal flaw.

Which is what gave him, Stephen, the upper hand. Because Jon's arrogance makes him blind to what the new *Angel* scale really meant, what it's power would be. For such a brilliant man Jon could be quite obtuse.

All that was needed was for him to steer Jon in the direction he wanted him to go and so far that had not been a problem. He knew Jon better than anyone and could usually predict Jon's reactions exactly.

Although it was certainly true that Jon's decision to go to South Africa had shocked the hell out of him. It still made him sick just thinking about it. He would never forgive Jon: it was such a betrayal. When Jon first told him the news, he refused to believe it. They were looking at a year – eighteen months at the most – and their work on the *Angel* scale would be done. The end of the road was in sight. How could Jon casually, on a whim, suddenly decide to go elsewhere? Everything had been going to plan. And then this sudden illogical obsession with prehistoric rocks.

But thank God things were back on track again. Not only that, but the entire process had suddenly speeded up. It didn't bother him that Jon was unable to explain this anomalous development. Gift of the gods, that's what it was. Instead of a year, they were looking at six weeks. In little more than a month they'd be able to start putting the final pieces together.

He had no wish to go to Africa himself. But he had no choice: they were in the home stretch much earlier than he had expected. It was imperative that Jon stay focussed. At this stage of the game, the last thing he needed was for Jon to get sidetracked: certainly not by those stupid gongs. And now there was another reason why he should go to Africa.

He looked down at the sketch pad on the desk in front of him and smiled. He had drawn the outline of a woman's face framed by unruly hair – Jon had mentioned she had thick hair – a generous mouth, the shadow of a delicate nose. No eyes yet. His hand hovered above the sheet of paper, but then he laid down the stick of charcoal with a sigh. It was no use. He'd have to meet her face to face before he'd be able to finish this portrait. He pushed his chair back from his desk and stretched. Then he got up and walked over to the window.

His apartment was on the tenth floor of a portered block

close to Columbia University. From here he had a view of Morningside Park lined on the far side by a ragged row of sad-looking brownstones. It was cold but the clouds were low and the sky outside had the soupy look of water in a fish bowl. The noise of traffic on Amsterdam Avenue reached even this corner flat high up and it felt to him as though the air around him was vibrating with a trembling, shivering rage.

He disliked this city so much. The longer he lived here, the more he longed for dappled light, garden squares, an olive brown Thames, a green and pleasant land. All the clichés of home. Somehow time still flowed linearly on that densely populated little island. In this country, time was a fragmented aberration. He only lived here because of Jon. He had needed to keep Jon close. To make sure Jon's attention never faltered from the work at hand: *The Angels' Key*.

The room was cold, but he did not want to close the sash window. He needed the noise from outside to fill his apartment. Noise was his solace, his opiate. If it was too quiet, he would become painfully aware of the never-ending ringing sound in his ears. Since his accident twenty-one years ago, he had suffered from tinnitus and there was nothing the medical profession could do about it. His head was always filled with noise. The only thing that helped was even more noise. It was like fighting fire with fire. He needed noise to drown out the constant sound that chafed his mind. If he should ever find himself in a sound-proofed room, he'd go mad.

Well, time to start packing. He had asked Richie to pick up the tickets and he should be here any minute. He was paying – Richie didn't have a dime, as usual. But it was better to take him along, otherwise Jon would worry about his little brother. And Richie had been quite useful so far. He was a hacker and knew his way around the insides of a computer.

As he pulled his briefcase towards him, his eyes fell once again on the unfinished sketch on his desk. He picked it up and folded it carefully before pushing it into the inside pocket of his jacket. Now it was close to his heart. As he started packing he realised he was whistling under his breath. A hissing little noise. It sounded expectant. Elated.

DAY FORTY-FIVE

The beautiful one and the savage one: the gods fitted their destinies together like dark and light. They wrestled together, they shared visions and shadows from their souls. They learned to love each other like brothers.

The Epic of Gilgamesh. *The Mythical Quest*, stories retold by Rosalind Kerven

The voice was one of those irritating female voices one hears only in airports. The speaker did not allow her voice to drop at the end of her sentences and the announcement hung in the air, sounding strangely incomplete.

Jon half rose from his seat and looked at Tia. 'That's them. They've landed.'

The arrivals hall was packed. They were squashed against the railings by a crowd of impatient people. It was raining outside and the air in here was thick with the smell of wet coats recently dry-cleaned. A man with his stomach peeping out from behind straining buttons kept poking Tia in the ribs with his umbrella. Every time she looked at him, he would apologise and wink at her. A woman with an incredible load of bags jammed her trolley painfully against Tia's ankles.

'There they are.' Jon's hand urgently pushed her in the small of her back.

Two men were coming towards them through the crush

of people. One was a big man – a very big man. Heavily built, he had stooped, rounded shoulders. As he came closer she could see that his glasses were stained with dirt. Behind the glasses though, the eyes were kind. There was something about him that reminded her of Jon. But with Jon the skin was stretched tightly across the bones. With this man, the strong bone structure was there, but padded by spongy flesh. The colouring too was different. Jon's hair and eyes were black. This man's hair was sandy, his eyes an indeterminate hazel.

But it was the second man who drew and held the attention. Tia noticed the sideways glances from women in the crowd as he pushed his way through. He was tall and walked with a self-assured set to his shoulders. And he was simply the most beautiful man she had ever seen.

The photograph in Jon's office did not do him justice. The black and white of the picture failed to capture the dramatic contrast of the dark blond hair against the sooty eyebrows and lashes and the eyes of a blue so light, they seemed pale in his tanned face. He waved at them, and when he was up close he threw his arms around Jon in a big bear hug.

She stood to one side and watched the three men as they greeted each other. She liked watching men together: the heavy-handed camaraderie, the jocularity, the coded body language, which defined hierarchy and status in a way women could never emulate. The body language of these three men told of long friendship and shared time.

Jon turned around. His face was flushed and happy. 'Tia, get over here, will you. Meet my brother, Richie.'

The sandy-haired man smiled at Tia. He was a very large man indeed, and with none of Jon's grace of movement. He moved awkwardly and did not seem to know what to do with his hands. 'I've heard a lot about you.' When he smiled, his eyes almost closed.

'Good things I hope.'

'That goes without saying. I'm Stephen Yale by the way.' The second man had pushed forward and his hand was now resting in hers. Compared to the relaxed, slightly nasal speech of Jon and Richie, his words sounded startlingly clipped: the cut glass accents of the upper-class Englishman.

Tia looked into his eyes and then looked away. Odd how Jon's eyes, so dark, seemed to draw you in, whereas Stephen's eyes, despite their clarity, were as guarded as reflector lenses bouncing your own image back at you. But he also had an incredibly intense way of looking at one. It was disconcerting, even though Jon had prepared her for this. 'Stephen needs to lip-read a lot. When you talk to him, make sure you look him full in the face.' As Stephen turned away from her she noticed for the first time the tiny ear piece fitting almost invisibly into his right ear.

'Did you bring the gear?' she heard Jon ask.

'Sure,' Richie said, 'but I had no end of trouble at customs here. It took a hell of a lot of explaining to convince them that it's only equipment used for acoustic measuring. I'm sure they think I'm a high tech assassin or something.'

'Well, just as long as you have it. Not that I'm not pleased to see you guys, but it's the equipment I need. Here in South Africa you can't beg, borrow or steal any of that stuff.'

'I still don't understand what you need all of this for,' Stephen said.

'The gongs . . . remember. My readings are too rough. I told you. Up till now the equipment I've used meant I've been working with a butter knife. I need a scalpel.'

'Oh, God. Not those rocks again. I can just see you shuffling around the great savannah in your khaki shorts and pith helmet, clutching a gong hammer: a lonely figure in a prehistoric landscape. Jonathan Falconer, man on a mission . . .'

The remark should have been amusing, but somehow it wasn't. Tia glanced at Jon. He had his arm around Richie's shoulders and seemed completely unconcerned. Well, maybe she was just imagining things. Still, it had certainly sounded to her as though there was an edge to those words.

As they walked through the front entrance in the direction of the car park, Stephen suddenly stopped and abandoned his trolley. 'Just a minute,' he said. He walked over to the flower vendor who was sheltering from the rain in the doorway. The tins and plastic buckets with flowers were covered by a thick sheet of plastic on which the raindrops sparkled like ice. Tia watched as Stephen opened his wallet and fumbled with the unfamiliar notes. The vendor stuck his hand under the plastic and handed him a bunch of flowers wrapped in a yellowed piece of newspaper.

Stephen walked back to where they were waiting. 'Flowers for the lady.' He smiled.

'Thank you.' Tia took the flowers from him gingerly and looked down at the carnations which lay against the white of her blouse like a red stain.

★   ★   ★

The flowers were the first thing she attended to as they got home. Unwrapping the carnations she placed them inside the kitchen sink and opened the tap. She was going to leave the flowers there for the time being until she'd figured out what she was going to do with them. As she flipped the switch on the kettle and took some cups from the cupboard, she could still see the red blooms and floating green stems from the corner of her eye.

She looked across the kitchen counter to where the three men were together in the living room. The cottage suddenly felt impossibly full. While she boiled the water and laid the tray, she stayed on the outskirts of the conversation. Most of it, anyway, was about people and places she knew nothing about.

'I beat your record,' she heard Stephen say.

'Like hell you did.' Jon was laughing.

'I did indeed. I've moved up to level nineteen of the Moon Chamber. You try that.'

Tia's eyes caught Richie's. 'Computer game,' he explained.

'Have they always been this competitive?'

He grinned. 'It's always stopped short of bloodshed.'

'So these are the magic stones.' Stephen's voice was light, almost flippant. She looked over to where he was standing in front of the two large framed photographs that hung on the wall behind Jon's desk. He had his hands in his pockets and was rocking slowly back and forth on his feet.

The photographs were of the rock gongs at Fluisterwater and had been shot by Jon only recently. One picture was a close-up, a study in texture: the weathered stone of the granite rock and a glimpse of silky blue sky in the background. The other picture showed the gongs at nightfall: their dark shapes bulky against a stunning pink and purple sunset.

On the coffee table, cradled in a wooden rest, were the two gong hammers. Jon had had the rest specially made and it now occupied pride of place. Stephen picked up the larger hammer and balanced it on his palm.

'This what you were telling me about?'

'Yes.'

Stephen replaced the gong hammer and shrugged his shoulders. There was, Tia thought, something quite dismissive in that gesture.

Sinking to her heels, she opened a kitchen cupboard and rummaged at the back for some biscuits to serve with the tea. As she got to her feet, the tin of biscuits in her hands, Stephen had entered the tiny kitchen and was right behind her. He did not move away, forcing her to brush past him. He was wearing a cologne but underneath the scent of bergamot, she could smell the tang of his skin.

'Need any help?' He smiled winningly. He even had a dimple, she thought rather sourly. He really was the proverbial answer to a maiden's prayer.

'If you could take the tray for me,' she said as she turned her back on him and reached for a saucer.

'Pardon?'

She looked over her shoulder, surprised. 'The tray. Maybe you can take it for me?'

'Of course,' he said immediately and she suddenly realised that with her back towards him, he had been unable to hear her. For a moment she felt a twinge of sympathy.

She followed him as he left the kitchen and placed the

saucer with biscuits on the coffee table in the living room. Richie immediately started spooning sugar into his mug.

'You and your brother both,' Tia shook her head. 'What's with you and sugar?'

'We were deprived children,' Richie grinned. 'No candy, no cookies when we were bad. Unfortunately, we were bad a lot.' He took a bite out of his biscuit and slouched back in his chair. He had taken off his jacket to expose a shabby-looking tie-dyed T-shirt. Around his neck was a thin gold chain from which dangled what looked like some kind of crystal. Each wrist was encircled with an armband worked out with tiny turquoise beads. With his thick tow-coloured hair falling untidily over his eyes, his long arms and large hands, he looked to her like a friendly grizzly.

Stephen was looking around the room, his glance taking in Jon's knitted tie hanging over the back of a chair, the desk loaded with papers, Jon's satchel propped up against the far wall.

'Looks like you've made quite a home for yourself.' His eyes were speculative under the long lashes. 'This place is neater than any place I've ever seen you live in.' He looked directly at her. 'I don't know how you manage it. The man's such a slob.'

'Never underestimate the power of gentle persuasion.' She sat down on the arm of Jon's chair. 'Scalp massages too. They seem to help.'

'Not so.' Jon placed a lazy arm around her waist. 'Don't let her fool you. This woman's tough. She keeps me in line by cracking the whip.'

Stephen's eyes lingered on her face. 'I can think of worse things.'

His words and tone of voice made her feel uncomfortable. She was relieved when Richie leaned forward, holding out to Jon what looked like a newspaper clipping.

'We brought you something. Front page of yesterday's *New York Times*, no less.'

'All the news that's fit to print.' Jon was staring at the photocopied page, his face grim.

'What is it?' She tried to see over his shoulder.

'Hysteria.'

'Let me read that.' She took the sheet of paper from him. The article in question had been circled with a red marker:

Concern about the harmful effects of Angel music has prompted delegates of COPAK, Concerned Parents Against The Angels' Key, to approve a resolution to 'persuade the music recording industry to reject signing up Angel artists.' This action is based on COPAK's belief that repeated listening to Angel music is inciting children to violence. 'Evidence is mounting of a correlation between violent behavior and Angel music,' so says Dr Oliver Corel, a member of the American Medical Association's Board of Trustees. 'Angel music is no longer confined to the Internet but has gone mainstream and we support COPAK's appeal to the music recording industry to act responsibly. The AMA is getting involved on the premise that violent children already add more than $6 billion each year to the nation's health-care expenditures. The Internet is difficult to police, but we would hope that firm steps can be taken to limit the influence of the game.' COPAK representatives will also be meeting with representatives of the Parents Music Resource Center to discuss strategy.

'Wow, these people mean business.'

'They're fanatics.' Jon's voice was angry. 'They're the same kind of people as those Bible thumpers who preached against Elvis' pelvis. These are people who sue record labels as a hobby. They're kooks.'

'Not quite.' Richie's voice was sombre. 'This is the American Medical Association we're talking about.'

'Yes, and you know as well as I do that a few years ago the AMA asked for song lyrics to be subjected to a rating system. This is just another resolution along the same lines.'

'I'm just saying these are people who can make a lot of noise. They have clout. Remember AC/DC?'

'It doesn't matter.' Stephen's voice was cool.

'You're too complacent, Stephen.'

'It does not matter.' Stephen enunciated every word slowly and carefully.

It was suddenly quiet in the room. Jon had a frown between his eyes.

'Six weeks from now it will all be over. We're just about there.' Stephen looked from Richie to Jon. 'The Comma is about to be eliminated; we're about to create the perfect musical scale. So let them shout. What do we care?'

Jon sighed impatiently. 'Well I care, for Christ's sake. We're not going to abandon everything when the project's done. When it's over I want us to think seriously about pulling the game from the Net and selling it. Make a little money if we can.'

Tia looked at Stephen. His face held an expression that was hard to understand. Boredom, a kind of resigned patience and . . . pity? But his voice when he spoke was smooth: 'You're right, of course.'

Jon placed his mug on the table and got up from beside her. 'I think I should get you guys to the apartment. You must be wiped.'

The plan was for Richie and Stephen to stay in Jon's apartment in Drake House during their visit to South Africa. Just the night before, Jon had removed most of his remaining personal things and had brought them over to the cottage.

She stood on the doorstep as the three men trooped out. As he passed her Stephen took her hand. It was so unexpected she flinched involuntarily.

He smiled faintly and brought her fingers up to his lips with old-fashioned courtesy.

'I'll see you soon,' he said. There was a glimmer in his eyes, but whether of amusement she could not tell.

DAY FORTY-FOUR

Evansville
Pennsylvania
USA

Sebastian slammed the door behind him, but when he looked for the key to lock himself inside his room, it was gone. His mother must have removed it.

He stood motionless for a moment, breathing shallowly. Chill, he told himself. Calm down. But the rage was too great. His hand closed around the alarm clock on his bedside table. With one swing of the arm, he threw it against the wall where it made a sick, twanging sound before shattering into pieces.

Silence. The house was dead silent. But he knew his mother was probably standing at the bottom of the staircase, listening.

He couldn't believe it. She actually wanted him to pee in a bottle so that she could have it checked out. She was convinced he was using drugs and had already searched his room earlier this week, going through all of his private stuff. And now this.

His mom has been on his case ever since he had passed out in the classroom that day. At first she had thought he was suffering from a brain tumour or epilepsy or some such god awful thing and had insisted on taking him to the doctor where he had had to put up with being prodded and poked by the old creep. Just thinking about the man's hearty laugh and sweaty palms made Sebastian's toes curl.

Of course they couldn't find anything wrong with him. He could have told them that. All he needed was to be left alone. But his mom would not let him be. Now she was convinced his 'moods' were because he was taking shit or sniffing glue. Like he needed any of that stuff.

Sebastian slid into his chair and switched on his PC. He turned the volume on the speakers to low. No use ticking his mom off any further. And if anything was guaranteed to get her going it was the sound of an *Angel* power chant. She couldn't stand it; God knows why.

He blinked. His eyes felt as though there were sand in them: an itchy, prickling sensation. And he had that killer headache again.

There was a hesitant knock on the door. Sebastian turned sideways and watched as the door opened slowly.

'Sebastian?'

He glared at her sullenly.

His mother's eyes were watery. 'I'm sorry, Bass. I'm just worried about you. Let's try again, what do you say?'

Her lower lip was trembling. Oh, hell, now she was going to start bawling again.

He nodded and tried to smile. The skin around his lips felt tight. 'Sure.'

'OK then.' She smiled. 'You up for pizza tonight?'

'Great.'

'OK.' Another tremulous smile and she turned around. She did not close the door behind her. Sebastian watched as she descended the staircase.

Stupid cow.

DAY FORTY-ONE

But you can't ignore us. Even if you don't like the ideas behind our music, you have to listen to it because it is everywhere.

Frank Zappa

They were busy washing-up when the doorbell rang.

Jon dropped the tea towel and walked to the front door. Tia, in soapsuds up to her elbows, stayed where she was in front of the sink.

'This looks very domestic.' Richie walked into the kitchen and beamed at her. As always when he smiled, his eyes almost closed. It gave his smile a very sweet quality.

She smiled back at him. She had come to like Richie a lot. He had none of Jon's clear-cut brilliance or his wit. Next to his brother he seemed slightly plodding; a little clumsy. But there was something innately kind and decent about him. He had what was considered that most American of virtues, she thought, 'a willingness of the heart'. And he was interesting company. His head teemed with ideas that were esoteric and fey and far-fetched, but somehow quite wonderful. For one thing, he still hadn't given up on his dream to one day sleep in a sarcophagus. 'Just think of the dreams you'll have in there,' he told her seriously.

'Space cadet,' Jon had once called his brother. There had been affection in his voice, she remembered, but also a hint of indulgent scorn. Jon's ideas were far from mundane, but you always had the feeling that the sharp edge of logic lurked underneath even his most gossamer-like theories. Richie was far less focussed. And unlike Jon and Stephen, *The Angels' Key* was not his life. She also knew he wasn't happy about the cult following that the game was attracting on the Net. 'Not that I'm complaining, really,' he explained to her. 'After all, we need these gamers: without them the problem of perfect tuning will not be solved at the speed it is. Not even distributed computing groups such as the Bovine RC-5 Cooperative or the Infinite Monkeys would have been able to tackle this. It's just that anything which attracts such fanatical devotion is a little scary.' He shrugged. 'Jon and Stephen have no patience with me and they're probably right. It's silly to worry. It's just a game.'

Now, as Tia wiped her hands on a dishcloth, watching Richie as he opened the fridge and took out a carton of milk, she wondered if he ever resented Jon. The affection between the two brothers seemed very real. Nevertheless, it must have been difficult for Richie to grow up alongside Jon: the black and white copy of the dramatic, coloured print. In some respects Jon seemed closer to Stephen than to his own brother. Those two shared a special understanding, even though competitiveness did seem to be the engine fuelling their relationship.

'Come look at my car,' Richie told her and wiped away his milk moustache with the back of one very large hand.

'You bought a car?'

'Sure. We need wheels while we're here. Come see.'

It was a 1973 Mazda that sagged on its wheels. There were patches of rust on the one wing and on the back of the window was an enormous sticker proclaiming 'SURFERS DO IT STANDING UP.' Someone had tried to scrape it off and had only succeeded in scratching the glass.

'I got it really cheap,' Richie said with satisfaction.

'I would hope so.' Jon had joined them outside and was now kicking the tyres dubiously.

Richie held out the keys of the Mazda like a game show host presenting a prize. 'Would you like to take it for a spin?'

'Not really. No.' Jon was not impressed.

But nothing could dampen Richie's enthusiasm. 'It's a great buy,' he stated forcefully as they walked back into the house. 'Everyone's been warning me about car hijackers. With this car I figure we'll be safe. Who'd want to steal a wreck like that? Isn't that right, Stephen?'

Stephen was sitting at Jon's desk in front of the computer. On the screen a big-bosomed female with toxic green hair, dressed in a body-clinging latex suit, was running away from a slavering pack of wolves. Stephen jabbed at the keyboard and the green-haired heroine suddenly grabbed a vine and swung Tarzan-like across a gaping ravine.

Stephen was focussing intensely, hardly acknowledging their presence. His concentration amazed Tia. She couldn't understand this fascination with games. Emulators, X-boxes, *MAME*, *Chu Chu Rocket*. Skinning. PC versus console. *Final Fantasy*. *Earthworm Jim*. *Shenmue*. *Kessen*. A jargon that was alien to her and this was one language she was not keen to learn. Jon called her attitude towards gaming 'snobbish', but it wasn't that. She honestly could not see the attraction. She would watch bemused as Jon sat in front of his computer for hours muttering to himself, shouting at the screen as uninhibited as a small boy.

Maybe it was because she was now living with a computer junky which was making her more observant, but it certainly seemed to her as though everywhere she looked these days, someone was playing a game. And more often than not it was *The Angels' Key*. Jon was a hero to the students. Whenever she walked past the glassed-in lab on her way to Jon's office, she'd see their mesmerised faces, their heads bobbing up and down to the distinctive music. She just didn't understand it. 'Get it,' as Jon would say.

She leaned forward to look more closely at the coloured pixels on the screen.

'This is a crappy game,' Stephen said dispassionately. 'Poor man's *Joanna Dark*. I'm going to switch to *The Key*.' He looked up at Tia. 'Care to play?'

She shook her head and Jon said, 'Tia hasn't even tried it once. I've never been able to change her mind.'

Stephen lifted his brows high against his forehead in exaggerated surprise.

'I just don't like computer games,' she said a little defensively.

'You'll like this one,' he stated with easy certainty and before she could protest, he had vacated his chair and had pushed her down on the seat. She stared at the catchline on the screen: WELCOME TO THE ANGELS' KEY. YOU WILL NEVER LISTEN TO THE WORLD THE SAME WAY AGAIN.

'Now,' Stephen said and leaned forward, his hand on her shoulder, 'this figure here is our hero. His task is to heal and restore mankind's link with the universe. He has to find the Angels' Key. And he has to succeed or the soul of mankind will wander eternally and the world will remain a waste land. Are you with me so far?'

'Yes,' she said. It was hard to concentrate. Stephen's thumb was pressed against her collar bone. She was wearing a tank top and his fingers felt warm where they rested against the bare skin. His breath was against the side of her neck. She hunched her shoulders forward uncomfortably. Not that she actually expected him to look down the front of her shirt but still . . .

'The hero has to solve all these mysteries and puzzles on his journey,' Stephen continued. 'Most of these riddles can be unravelled by making use of magic numbers. And these magic numbers are keyed to magical songs and chants.'

Richie was drawing up a chair and positioning himself so that he could see the screen as well. 'If you get the music right,' he added, 'you can unlock the puzzles. Sometimes the music will place the hero in an ecstatic trance – this is when the music gets really cool. And as you pass from one level to another, the music gets more and more complicated. It's a very interactive game. Towards the end you're composing your own stuff.'

'Now use this key to start,' Stephen placed his fingers on hers. 'There you go.'

She played hesitantly, lost two power chants in the first ten minutes. But it was easy to see what the attraction of the game was.

The hook of the music was startlingly strong. It touched something deep within her. But it was also disturbing. There was no sense of closure: the music never returned to the home key. She felt as though she were constantly willing it to go full circle, holding her breath almost, but just when she thought she had it beat, the harmonic glossy chime would unravel, replaced by a series of jarring, atonal chords.

'Whoops,' Stephen jerked her hand to the side. 'You've got to watch out. You brought our man too close to the shadow. See there?'

'What's the shadow?'

Jon laughed. 'It's one of the things he has to find out. Is it evil? Is it a force from the outside, or is it within him? Should he slay it? Or will he then be slaying himself?'

'Our hero is prone to overweening pride,' Stephen said, 'like those classical Greek heroes who are always overreaching themselves.'

Tia half-turned her head to look at him. 'Usually great sacrifice or even death is required of one who has so offended the gods.'

'Exactly.' Stephen gave her an admiring glance. She was irritated with herself to find a flush of pleasure spreading up her throat and neck. As though she needed his approval.

Tia looked back at the screen. 'It seems sort of cruel. Just as he's about to succeed, he gets whacked by the gods? It doesn't seem fair.'

The music was changing. Underneath the benign overlay of sound was a pulsing rhythm: an aggressive vibrational current. And there was a hum, faint but insistent. It set her teeth on edge.

'Change the tune. Change the tune!' Jon was pumping his elbow into her side.

The music has speeded up. The hum was becoming distinctly dissonant. The music was grating, it felt as though sandpaper was being run across her every nerve end. Her head was aching and it felt as though there were grit in her eyes.

She pushed the mouse violently away from her. 'That's enough. I can't take it any more.'

There was a short silence. Then Jon spoke, 'It's just a game, Tia.'

'I know. Sorry. Guess I'm not used to this.' She looked at Stephen. Something flickered behind the blue eyes.

Jon glanced at the screen and sighed. 'Well,' he said. 'You lost faith. You abandoned our hero. I'm afraid he's had it.' He tapped against the screen. 'See, he's disappearing. First his head . . . now the body; there goes even his spirit horse. He's gone all right.'

Stephen shook his head admonishingly. 'You should take care,' he said. 'You should never lose faith.'

DAY FORTY

He who embarks on the creation of worlds is already tainted with corruption and evil.

Umberto Eco, *Foucault's Pendulum*

He was hiding behind a waxy-leafed magnolia bush and the large white flowers were attracting a lot of bees. One was hovering just in front of his face – a menacing yellow blip – but he could not step aside. The slightest movement on his part and Tia or Jon would spot him.

Stephen could feel the sweat trickling down the side of his face, irritating his skin. But he did not lift his hand. His one foot had pins and needles but he did not shift his weight.

Finally. They were getting back into the car again. Tia was behind the wheel, Jon in the passenger seat. As the car eased carefully onto the road, Stephen slowly let out his pent-up breath.

It had been a close call. They had almost caught him as he was about to let himself into the cottage. He had thought the coast was clear – earlier he had watched as Jon and Tia set out for the university. But something brought them back. Only minutes after leaving, the car had pulled up again and he had had to dive for cover. But it should be safe now.

He walked cautiously up the steps to the front door, the key in his hand. He had made a copy of Jon's key only the day before. It had been no problem whatsoever to lift the key from the side pocket of Jon's satchel. He had waited until Jon was teaching class. He had also made very sure that by the time Jon returned to the office, the key was back in place.

This morning he had woken up as excited as a child going to the amusement park. The idea that he could explore the cottage without Tia or Jon present was exhilarating. He would be able to touch Tia's things, go through Jon's papers. Get a sense of their life together.

It was difficult for him to admit, but he was feeling excluded from Jon's life for the first time ever. Jon usually had someone sharing his bed, but up till now that had made no difference to their relationship. But since Tia came on the scene, there has been a definite change. It was difficult to be precise about it, but he just sensed a kind of emotional withdrawal on Jon's part. He had always been Jon's confidant, the person who knew him best. No more. But he could not be angry with Tia. Or resentful. How can you resent the person who filled your dreams at night, who occupied your mind every day?

The key turned easily in the lock. He walked inside and closed the door behind him. For a moment he stood quietly, listening. The hallway in which he stood was in shadow, but the living room was flooded with light. The curtains were open and in the broad bands of sunshine, he could see slowly twirling motes of dust.

Immediately to his left was the doorway opening into the kitchen. On the drip rack were two turned over mugs. He placed his hand against the coffee maker. A faint trace of heat still clung to the machine. He wondered what it must be like to wake up next to Tia, share breakfast with her, discuss with her your plans for the day. Had Jon become used to it? Had he reached the stage where he was taking the togetherness for granted or was it still new to him, an adventure?

The room he really wanted to see was the bedroom. He had never been inside. Leaving the kitchen, he walked down the short corridor and turned the handle of the closed door at the end of the passage.

There was nothing overtly frilly about the decor, but it was unmistakably a woman's room. Even Jon's heavy boots sticking out from underneath the linen bedspread and the pile of back issues of *Next Generation* on the one bed stand could not detract from the essential femininity of the room. On the wide window sill stood a glass vase filled with apricot-coloured roses. In the far corner was a dark-wooded dressing table. A variety of delicately coloured silk scarves floated down the one side of the oval mirror. A pewter bowl holding an array of earrings, beaded necklaces and other pieces of costume jewellery gleamed in the sunlight filtering through finely meshed net curtains.

He could smell her. Not just her perfume, but the scent of her skin. He inhaled deeply. He placed his hand on the tarnished copper knob of the dressing table drawer and pulled it open.

It was very neat. A powder compact. A tub of hand cream. A pretty floral box with hairclips and next to it a comb and a hairbrush with only a few delicate red hairs clinging to the bristles. Tubes of lipstick arranged in a straight row. He unscrewed the first one in the line and drew it across his wrist. A crimson slash of colour on his skin.

He turned around to look at the bed. It wasn't difficult to guess which was the side she slept on. Her bedside table held several volumes of poetry; a literary magazine; a paperback copy of *Wuthering Heights*. A copy that had obviously been reread many times – the spine was deeply creased. So she was a romantic. He smiled.

Next to the books were photographs in silver-plated frames. There were several of Jon and Tia but he did not allow his eyes to look directly at the smiling images. Instead he picked up a large photograph of Tia – hair cut pixie short – arm in arm with a tall woman with fair hair. This must be the mother. The family resemblance was there if you searched for it.

He suddenly felt a sense of enormous gratitude as he looked at the lovely face of the older woman. She had had the gift. And it looked as though she had passed it on to her daughter. As far as he was concerned, Tia's reaction at the music festival had been a sure sign. The hallucinations, the nausea and, of course, the heightened perception of sound – it was unmistakable. And it was not a one-off, he was convinced of it. It was going to happen to Tia again. Her reaction last night to *The Key* had been interesting to say the least.

He had always known about people like Tia and her mother. The special ones. The ones who were blessed with a premonition of what was to come. People who had a sensitivity to sound, to their environment, that was wonderful and remarkable. The medical profession did not know how to deal with them – labelling them mentally disturbed, doping them out of their minds – never realising that these people were initiates: evolved human beings. Beautiful instruments. Super sensitive antennae.

Listeners.

Not like the brain dead zombies with their empty eyes and empty hearts who walk through life deaf to the stunning array of sounds surrounding them. He'd go to the movies and watch them as they sat there mindlessly chewing their popcorn, not even aware of the background music, even though for the next two or three hours it would cause their heartbeats to fluctuate and turn their adrenaline on and off like a tap. These were people deadened and dulled; the ones who went to sleep with their TVs on; who ran away from silence: constantly turning on the car stereo, the CD player, the radio, wallowing in pounding, aggressive noise. They polluted and wasted and never realised how few completely quiet places were left on this planet. Chattering satellites scarring the heavens. Oceans assaulted by underwater speakers testing for global warming; poisoning the waters as they sent out sound waves that travel right around the globe. Sometimes he wished he could wave a wand and the world would suddenly change into a place in which all sound waves were tangible like long trails of fibre . . . and then: everyone unable to move. Everyone choking, smothering, enmeshed in a dense unforgiving tangle. Maybe then they would stop and listen.

He looked again at the photograph in his hand. The mother

was looking into the camera fearlessly. Thank you, he felt like saying to her. You were remarkable and so is your daughter.

He suddenly had a strong desire to take the photograph with him, but that would be stupidly reckless. He wanted to be able to come back to the cottage again in the future and if he wanted to do that, he should not leave any trace of his visit. After a moment's hesitation he replaced the photograph on the stand, making sure that it stood in exactly the same position he had found it. But he wanted something of Tia's. Something uniquely hers. A little present to himself. Maybe there would be something he could take in the bathroom. Something that would not be missed.

The bathroom led directly off the bedroom. The floor tiles were still slightly wet. A bathcap drooped from one of the shower taps. Two towels were draped over the towel rail. One blue, one pink. Pink for girls. He pressed his face against the fragrant dampness.

On the shelf above the washbasin stood a variety of objects. Tia's birth control pills. A tube of tooth paste. Two toothbrushes, side by side in the same cup. Jon's razor. The washbasin showed a small halfmoon of soap scum close to the rim and he grimaced at the black beard stubble clinging to the sides. Jon could be such an incredible slob. He wondered how a woman as deeply fastidious as Tia could bear to share her space with someone so unconcerned.

There was nothing here that he wanted, but as he was about to leave, his eye fell on the laundry hamper pushed into the corner. Inside, the usual jumble of clothes. A few of Tia's blouses and a pair of slacks. Jon's socks and boxer shorts. His fencing clothes. And some pieces of women's underwear. For a moment his hand hovered over a pistachio-coloured slip, but then he extracted from the pile a pale blue silk teddy. He folded it in two and slipped it into the pocket of his jacket. It might take her a while before she'd notice it had gone, and then it would just be one of those things. And, unlike the photograph, it had no sentimental value. So she'd probably put it out of her mind quite quickly. And because nothing else would be missing, she'd never consider that an intruder might have been inside the house.

As he walked out the front door, locking it behind him, he made himself a promise that he would continue to use this key. And the next time he came, he would attach a bug to the phone so he could monitor their calls. He was already monitoring Jon's web use. At this point he wanted to know what Jon was up to at all times. Not that he expected trouble, but it never hurt to take precautions.

The next few weeks were going to be stressful. Jon was far too relaxed, he needed to sharpen his focus. But it was going to be up to him to make sure that Jon regained his motivation. Living here in South Africa has turned Jon soft. He has lost the hunger. And he had too many distractions: Tia. The gongs. His friendship with Ben. He was going to have to make sure that from now on Jon would concentrate more closely on what it was he was born for: *The Angels' Key.*

DAY THIRTY-NINE

Great Lakes region
Burundi
Central Africa

He was leaving.

Jabulani took the large canvas bag from underneath his bed and packed his good suit and his second pair of shoes. On top he placed the photograph of his daughter and her children.

There was no moon tonight and as he looked out the open door he could scarcely make out the bright phosphorescent yellow blob of the boom box where it stood on a low table inside his neighbour's house, its aerial sticking out the window. For once the radio was quiet.

Jabulani was ashamed to be leaving like this without saying goodbye to anyone, but he could not stay any longer. The dread inside of him was too strong. He had to go to Bujumbura. He needed to talk to Bishop Pierre and tell him of his fears. He had to tell him of the hum that was in the air always, and the devil music. The sickness was spreading. Not only his neighbour was listening to that music; many, many villagers were now doing the same.

He pulled the door of his house shut behind him. He did not have a car and it was going to take him a long time to get to Bujumbura. Maybe he should walk to the petrol station to see if he could get a ride on one of the trucks heading south.

Jabulani did not take the main road. At the edge of the tall grass, where the footpath snaked away into the poisonous green thicket, he paused. With his head cocked to one side, a look of concentration on his face, he seemed to be listening.

DAY THIRTY

The universe is shaped the way it would sound.

Lorin Hollander, *Will You Join the Dance?*

Man, he was tired. Jon yawned and stretched his arms above his head. He couldn't remember the last time he had pushed himself this hard. And all because of Stephen. The man was relentless. He insisted that every spare moment be devoted to the project. By this time it felt to Jon as though he were living in the lab permanently. The only times he was not here were when he had to teach class. But he had made himself a promise that as soon as all of this was over he and Tia would take off and disappear to a beach somewhere. And not talk to Stephen again for a year.

He yawned again and rubbed his eyes. He could understand Stephen's impatience, but he was slowly but surely starting to get fed-up. And it wasn't as if Stephen was burning the midnight oil himself. He was on a date with Astrid tonight, whereas he, Old Faithful, had been stuck behind his computer for the past seven hours. He should be with Tia now. Warm bed, soft sheets. Tia's tiny hands on the small of his back. His mouth against the wetness of her mouth. His hands twisting her hair into a long thick rope . . . Damn, Stephen.

Jon sighed. He supposed he should be fair. At this stage Stephen couldn't really contribute much more to the project.

He'd done all he could. No, it was up to him now to complete the procedure for putting all the parts together. But it sure wasn't fun. Right now his brain was porridge and he felt oxygen-deprived. And he was stiff all over from sitting in one position for so long. At least Stephen had agreed to a fencing match tomorrow. Good. He was going to kick that limey's butt.

He glanced at his watch. Eleven thirty p.m. Time to call it a day. He just wanted to take one last look . . .

He tapped in the code word giving access to the *Angel* flower. And there it was, slowly revolving, its structure becoming more complex by the day with ever more petals forming. It always gave him a buzz just to look at it. Sound given form. A musical scale developing right under his very eyes. When they had started out on the project he had not known what image to expect: the fact that the scale had turned out to be flower-like in appearance was strangely apt. A perfect musical scale giving access to perfect tuning: of course it should be beautiful.

Each of the petals presented a note. He could not project with any certainty how many notes the new scale would have, but based on his calculations and with a little conjecture thrown in, he rather thought it might be ten. That made sense. In Pythagorean numerology, ten would be reduced to One: symbol of all-embracing primordial power and the creative source of the All. The perfect number. So if his calculations were correct, that made it three more petals to go. Only three more notes. Another four, maybe five weeks before the scale would be complete.

He looked at the gauge. The black arrow was stuck midway up the orange tier. Red was next. The final step.

He logged off. As he pulled his satchel towards him, his eyes fell on the thick navy blue folder edged with red, which Richie had left him to read. He grimaced. He had promised Richie he'd take a look, although really, it was a waste of time. But Richie hadn't budged. He was the last person in the world you could ever accuse of nagging, but this time his insistence that Jon read through the file had bordered on pestering.

Jon opened the folder reluctantly. As he had expected, it was filled with photocopied clippings from newspapers and magazines. Some of the articles were in languages other than English and had neat typed-out translations clipped to them. At the top of every page was printed the name and telephone number of an information retrieval agency in New York. The articles all had one thing in common: they were all about *The Angels' Key*.

There were a few articles on the decision of the AMA to support COPAK, but most of the clippings seemed to be first-hand accounts of former *Angels' Key* fans who had now turned against the game. *'I used to be a level 18 warrior, but I am now committed to stopping the destructive influence of this game. Because of The Angels' Key I lost everything. My job. My family.'* Another clipping: *'Every time, after playing a game, I would be hyped up and aggressive. I would go out looking for trouble. I found it. I have just been sentenced to three years for assault and battery.'* One gamer simply stated: *'This game is evil.'*

Not that all the articles were negative. The titles of some of the pieces indicated counter-arguments in favour of the game. *'No to Censorship'; 'Why pick on The Key?' 'Violent behaviour by fans at rock concerts is nothing new. Angel music should not be singled out.'*

Most of the reports seemed to come from reputable, main-stream publications, but there were also some bizarre stories, which seemed to have been lifted from the 'Elvis-spotted-in-Disneyworld' tabloids you could pick up at supermarket check-out counters. People describing visits by aliens who were drawn to the music generated by the game. Time travel expedited by *Angel* power chants. Toddlers becoming full-grown adults in a matter of weeks after listening to *Angel* music in the womb.

Slowly he closed the folder. There was nothing new here. This kind of hysterical reporting had followed the game ever since he and Stephen had placed it on the Net for the first time two years ago. It wasn't so much the clippings that disturbed him, but the fact that Richie was willing to pay for an information retrieval agency from his own pocket. Richie was chronically broke. His willingness to fork out money like this was a sure sign that he was worried. Very worried.

But it was all media hype. That was all. He'd talk to Richie tomorrow and calm him down.

Still, as he stood there in the dark laboratory, the shrouded terminals surrounding him like silent ghosts, he suddenly felt uneasy. Apprehensive.

DAY TWENTY-NINE

Mathematics is music for the mind; music is mathematics for the soul.

Anonymous

The blue silk teddy Jon had given her was missing. She had hunted high and low, but she simply could not find it. It wasn't in her closet. It wasn't in the hamper with the dirty laundry. It hadn't found its way into one of Jon's drawers by mistake. It had simply vanished.

Tia slammed the drawer shut. It was baffling, but more than that – it was her very favourite piece of lingerie. She did not want it to be lost. She sighed, exasperated. Socks she could understand, yes. The one sock in the hamper that goes missing is simply one of the inexplicable mysteries of the universe. But an often-worn piece of clothing doesn't just disappear like this.

She glanced at her watch. She couldn't spend any more time looking for it. She had promised to meet Astrid at the gym and if she didn't get a move on soon, she'd be late.

She grabbed her keys and shrugged into her jacket. Pulling the front door close, she made sure to turn the key carefully in the lock. As she walked to the car she still could not understand how a piece of clothing could simply, inexplicably, vanish without a trace.

★　　★　　★

Astrid was in a petulant mood. 'Fencing is an anachronism,' she said.

Tia hooked her foot behind the leg of one of the plastic bucket chairs that was lined up against the wall of the gym and pulled it towards her. 'You were enthusiastic enough yesterday when you asked to be here.'

Astrid sat down and spread her dress wide, like a ballerina posing. 'I just don't think it has a place in the modern world. You can get on the stair master and burn up more calories in ten minutes than you could in an entire fencing match. Who has time for this?'

'You're missing the point. Jon says it's not so much the physical exercise, it's the mental workout you get from fencing. Anyway, where's your sense of romance? There's just something about a man and a sword, don't you think? Besides, I bet Stephen'll cut a dashing figure in white.'

Astrid hunched a shoulder. 'Oh, Stephen.'

Tia looked at her sideways. This was unexpected. Astrid had been blown away by Stephen. After meeting him for the first time she had told Tia, 'He's gorgeous. There's simply no other word for it. Gorgeous.'

'Yes,' Tia said. 'He knows it too.'

'Don't you like him then?' Astrid was surprised.

'Yes. No. It's not that.'

'Well, I think he's dreamy.' Astrid suddenly giggled. 'Like something from a bad girl's dream.'

But something must have happened to have changed her mind. Astrid had a moody expression on her face.

Tia cleared her throat. 'So how did your date go last night?'

'Not that great, actually.' Astrid paused and bit her finger. 'I don't think Stephen likes women. Not,' she explained hastily, 'that I think he's gay or anything. I just think he's the type who'll lust after a woman, maybe even love her, but never really like her.'

Tia was surprised. She wasn't used to Astrid sounding so stone cold serious.

'What makes you say that?'

'Well, he took me to this restaurant and I ordered salad as a main course. I'm never one to gorge myself on a date, you know. But you know what he said?' Astrid's voice rose. 'He said all women eat green salad and drink human blood.'

'H'mm.' Tia tried not to laugh. 'Those words weren't his by the way.'

'Whose then?'

'Moses Herzog. A fictional character.'

Astrid was not appeased. 'Misogynist creep. Anyway, I did *not* consider this remark a great way to start the evening.'

Jon and Stephen appeared at the far end of the gym. They were both dressed in their white fencing clothes and only the modern running shoes both of them were wearing, Tia thought, struck a wrong note. Otherwise they might have been figures from some cobwebby past where gentlemen still duelled by candlelight and 'honour' was a creed, not a word.

The two men walked onto the piste. They raised their swords in a formal salute, aligning them with their chins. They slid the masks over their faces.

There was something just a little unnerving about the two masked faces, their features just very faintly discernible through the fine black mesh. Tia had once told Jon that whenever he pulled his mask over his face it was as though she did not know him any more.

She smiled to herself. On that occasion he had immediately put on his mask and had chased her around the cottage.

The men engaged and as usual she thrilled to the sense of ritual she has come to associate with fencing. She loved the sense of great discipline and control being exercised; the elegance of movement, the flexible wrists and strong hands, the cadence – everything that made up that restrained but deadly game.

Astrid looked at Tia. 'This stuff turns you on,' she said in the voice of someone who has discovered something in questionable taste.

Tia blushed. 'So?'

'Not that I'm surprised. You've always been a sucker for ritual and ceremony. Tales of chivalry and self-denial. I always said you were born in the wrong century.'

Tia watched as Jon recovered from a lunge: head and body upright, back knee straight and arm flung out behind him to form an almost perfect line from shoulder to wrist.

'They seem evenly matched,' Astrid said.

'Yes.' Tia knew enough now about fencing to know that this was true. Jon's reach seemed to be longer than Stephen's but she saw Stephen shorten the distance by stepping forward into Jon's attack and giving him less room to manoeuvre.

Astrid said, 'It's more aggressive than I thought.'

'It's safe; but it's violent.'

'Stephen talked a lot about you last night.'

'Me?'

'Yes. He wanted to know all about you. What you like, what you don't like. He even wanted to know about your mother.'

'What did you tell him?' Tia couldn't understand why she was feeling apprehensive.

'Just that you were close – and that she had been a pianist. He seemed fascinated by your mother's . . . disappearance . . . wanted to know everything about it, in fact; but I told him I don't really know much about it. Which is true.'

Tia looked back at the piste. Stephen was attacking, straightening his arm from its tucked-in position – not punching from the shoulder but extending the arm with a beautiful fluid movement. She suddenly wondered if Jon had told him about her mother's problem and about her own little nightmare after the music festival. She hoped not. This was private.

'I don't know,' Astrid shook her head. 'Stephen's weird.'

'Weird how?'

'Weird creepy.'

Tia frowned. 'He scared you?'

'Not intentionally.'

There was a shout, whether by Stephen or Jon Tia couldn't

tell. She turned her head back in the direction of the fencers. The tempo of the bout has speeded up. Jon was moving quickly: lunging and recovering, lunging and recovering, kicking forward with the front foot and pushing with his rear leg with such unaccustomed recklessness that she stared. Jon always kept his cool. Always. This was the first time she had seen him lose it. 'Get emotional,' he once told her, 'and it's all over. You'll crash and burn.'

Stephen was angulating his épée to avoid Jon's attack. But then, with great swiftness, he attacked Jon's sword arm. The tip of his blade hit Jon's arm just above the glove.

Stephen had achieved the requisite number of hits. The two men lowered their swords. They moved towards each other and held out their free hands for the final handshake.

Jon was breathing heavily. 'I stank.'

'No you didn't. You did good.' Stephen took his épée and slashed an arc through the air. 'But I did better.'

Jon slapped Stephen across the shoulders with his towel. It was a playful gesture, but there was something in the snap of the towel that made Tia look at him sharply. He turned in the direction of the shower room. 'We'd better get a move on. I have to teach the next class.'

Astrid pulled a face as she watched the two figures disappear behind the swing door. '*Mano a mano*. If you ask me, this whole fencing thing is just a giant testosterone trip.'

'Jon calls it physical chess.'

'Too nerdish a description by half.'

'So, will you be going out on a date with Stephen again?'

'I don't know. Actually, I don't know if he'll want to.'

'Maybe you should give him another chance.'

'Maybe.' Astrid sighed, then dimpled. 'But you're right, he does look kind of cute in those white things. And despite everything, I still think he's sexy as hell.'

The washroom door opened and Stephen came out, his hair wet, but looking as coolly elegant as though he had stepped out of a *GQ* fashion plate.

Astrid picked up her handbag and settled the strap on her

shoulder. She smoothed her hair and touched her bottom lip with the tip of her tongue.

'It's a pity duels are passé,' she said as Stephen came up to them. She smiled slowly and tried to link her arm through his. 'Otherwise I'd call on you to defend my honour.'

Stephen looked at Astrid with a complete lack of expression. After a moment or two she flushed slightly and removed her arm.

'And you, would you like a duel fought in your honour?' Stephen had turned to Tia. His tone was intimate.

'Are you volunteering?' she asked and was immediately furious with herself for perpetuating the situation.

'Of course. Gives me a chance to swing from chandeliers and leap across tables.'

'I suppose I'll call on Jon if I need to.'

'Well . . .' he paused theatrically, 'you saw his form today.'

Astrid, determinedly nonchalant, tried to reenter the conversation. 'True. Perhaps you should reconsider, Tia.' She smiled tentatively at Stephen.

Stephen leaned over casually towards Astrid and flicked his fingers sharply, leaving a tiny, angry red mark on her cheekbone.

Astrid gasped.

'Sorry,' Stephen said unconcernedly. 'I thought I saw something on your face.'

★　　★　　★

The woman's face was a perfect oval. She was looking over her shoulder. There was the hint of a swell of breast underneath one uplifted arm, and from below the veil that was draped around her hips the faint bulge of her abdomen showed. In the corner of the sketch were the unfinished outlines of a man looking on: there was something stealthy in the way his head was bent forward, in the way his hand pushed aside the heavy fall of fabric in front of him.

'Bathsheba,' Stephen said. 'And David.'

Tia looked up. Stephen was standing slightly behind her, a cup of tea in his hand. He was looking down at the sketch pad, which lay open on her lap.

They were having tea at the cottage and she had been idly turning over the pages of Stephen's sketch pad, impressed by what she saw. The majority of the sketches were in charcoal but there were also a few in pen: one of two fencers, the figures drawn with clean strokes, and a clever sketch of Richie. But what had drawn her interest was this unfinished but meticulously crafted sketch of a woman bathing.

'Of course, she knows David's watching her.' Stephen took a bite from his biscuit.

Tia looked back at the face of the woman. Sure enough, there was something knowing in those elongated cat's eyes, something self-conscious in the way in which her hand was letting loose the curls on top of her head.

'Women like being watched,' Stephen said. 'All women.'

Tia stared at him.

Stephen pursed his lips. 'Even when they're all alone – brushing their hair, putting on their lipstick, even in sleep – women act as though they're being watched. It's what women are all about. It defines everything about them.'

He sat down on the sofa, stretching his long legs in front of him and placing his arms behind his head. His every gesture was as elegantly self-conscious as though he were posing for a luxury goods commercial. Even when dressed casually he looked like he had just stepped out of a gentlemen's shop on Savile Row.

Tia shut the sketch pad quietly. She deliberately looked Stephen up and down, letting her eyes travel slowly from the dark blond hair falling over his forehead, to the crisply starched open-necked shirt, to the immaculately tailored Sulka jacket with just the right amount of cuff showing, to the tan trousers, all the way down to the carefully crossed ankles and the full brogues. She took her time. Then she looked him straight in the eye. 'Not just women like being watched, it seems,' she said, her tone deliberately rude.

He laughed, showing a pink tongue. 'Touché.'

'Excuse me,' she said, 'I have some calls to make.'

'Of course,' he nodded, but with a look that said he knew she was running away from the situation.

Later that evening as Richie and Jon went outside to get the car, Stephen lingered beside her in the doorway. The night air coming through the open doorway was chilly. Tia shivered.

Someone in the street was throwing a party. There were a number of cars parked right onto the sidewalk and she could hear the loud beat of a Brenda Fassie song played through powerful speakers.

'I notice you're wearing Jon's watch,' Stephen said.

She put her right hand protectively over her left wrist. 'I gave him mine.'

'Very romantic.'

There was no irony in his voice. His face showed nothing but friendly interest.

'Well, so long.' Then, as he started to turn away, he said: 'You do know, don't you, that I gave Jon that watch as a gift for his birthday?'

★　　★　　★

'Why?' Jon asked her when she gave him back his watch the same evening.

'It's too heavy for my arm,' she said.

DAY TWENTY-EIGHT

The classification of the constituents of a chaos, nothing less here is essayed.

Herman Melville, *Moby Dick*

She was skittish. Much as he'd like to say otherwise, Tia was definitely avoiding him.

Stephen couldn't understand it. He usually had absolutely no problem where women were concerned. But he seemed to be unable to get a hold on the one woman who really mattered.

Maybe it was just because she hadn't really had the chance to get to know him properly. It was impossible to find any opportunity to be alone with her. Jon was always there and if not Jon, Richie. But maybe he'd be able to get close to her when they got to Fluisterwater tomorrow. It would be the first time they'd been in each other's company for two days on end. Even with the brothers around, he should be able to create an opportunity to be alone with her.

Not that he wanted to go to Fluisterwater. The last place he wished for Jon to be right now was near those fucking gongs. But Jon had insisted. So vehemently, in fact, that he had decided to back down. And it was true that Jon was looking exhausted. Maybe he was pushing Jon too hard. A break might not be such a bad thing after all: give Jon a chance to recharge his batteries. And they wouldn't be gone for long: only two days.

He was just thankful that Ben had pulled out of the trip. Ben did not like him, of that he was convinced. He sensed a deep distrust there which the exquisite manners, the perfect courtesy, could not hide. That was OK. He wasn't crazy about the old man either. And he was not about to forget that Ben was to blame for Jon's ridiculous detour. If Ben hadn't appeared on the scene, Jon would never have known about the gongs. And Ben had continued to fan the flames of Jon's interest. He would not forget that. Or forgive. Yes, Ben would do well to stay out of his way.

But if a visit to Fluisterwater was inevitable, at least he should try to turn it to his advantage. Two days in Tia's company. He would make them count.

Last night, after they all had dinner together, he had watched her furtively as she sat reading, her head a glowing flower on the slender breakable stem of her white neck. Her hair was up and above the low collar of her blouse he could see the knobbly jutting hardness of her spine: pieces of petrified stone in a forest of soft skin. Wistful mouth. Peach-downed cheek. The long filmy skirt she was wearing flowing over the slight curve of her hip, the sweet line of her thigh. Around her ankle she wore a thin gold chain. Her feet were bare, slightly soiled with dust. The desire to touch her, to slip his hands underneath the silky blouse, feel the shape of her back, the warm weight of her breasts, had stabbed at him, sharp as a freshly made wound. And then she had looked up and she was smiling. For one breathless, heart-stopping moment he had thought her smile was meant for him. Until he sensed Jon behind him and noticed that her eyes were looking past his shoulder.

But that would all change. It was just a matter of time.

Stephen sighed and patted his forehead with his handkerchief. He was sweating, it was very hot in here. He turned around on the bar stool and winked at one of the female bartenders. The funky-looking blinking name tag pinned to her breast said her name was Joela. Young, very pretty and, if she continued working in this club, she'd be deaf within the year. The music was so loud she had to put her head right up close to his to hear his order above the pulsating bass lines, the insistent, sweatdown hard-edged techno. As she walked to the other side of the bar to get him his Scotch, communicating with her fellow bartender through what looked like a complicated set of hand signals, he kept his eyes on her and wondered casually whether he should ask her to leave with him when the club closed. Which would not be for another four hours but it might be worth the wait. Her perfect skin was a lovely, coffee-cream colour. Her black hair was a mass of beaded plaits. She had that kind of elfin beauty that appealed to him. He was a sucker for slender-wristed, doe-eyed women. And she would certainly be game. There was something decidedly flirtatious in the way she placed her hand on his before placing his drink on the counter in front of him. Yes, he might just let Joela take him home.

He took a sip of his drink and looked around him. The place was rammed. The doorman had told him there were already more than five hundred clubbers inside. He could well believe it. The sweating, gyrating, shuddering bodies were shoulder to shoulder. Many had been inside the club for nine hours straight, their heads thrown back, their eyes unblinking. And outside they were still queuing up.

The club itself had a throwback seventies look: slick walls, a reflecting black lacquered floor, mirrorballs dripping a cold rainbow of blue and pink light. The music was a blend of discotechhouse, ranging from deep and hard trance all the way to hi-NRG. And certainly quite a few of the boys were dressed in rock-chick clothes.

He watched the sweat-slicked bodies, the gleaming eyes and teeth. He watched the bodies jerking to the assault of 220 skull-jarring dance beats per minute. And he thought how it was the same everywhere. New York. London. He couldn't even remember how many clubs he had visited over the years. All of them so different, so alike. All of the faces so different, so alike. But always the same emptiness. The same addiction. The same wanton waste of what is sacred. And in this country it was even more unforgivable. Because South Africa was actually one of the few places in the world where it was still possible to find absolute quiet. Some of the deepest worked out mines in the world were here: empty, gutted cathedrals of silence. Not that he would find escape even there. For him there was no hiding place: the ringing sound in his ears made sure of that. Only in a place like this could it be masked. But he carried it with him always. An aural stigma. A divine mark of what had happened to him on that day in spring twenty-one years ago.

Pain. He would never forget the pain. It would be coming his way again and this time he was ready for it. Pain was good. In pain was transformation. Pain gives access to truth and stunning beauty.

Tia would understand this. She would have the courage to grasp the truth with both hands.

He had paid two more visits to the cottage in her absence. He had needed to plant the bug that would enable him to listen in on Jon's phone conversations, but the visits to the cottage were also a form of self-indulgence. Just touching Tia's things, placing his head on her pillow, reading from the book she was reading, calmed his mind. But his appetite was growing and he has been toying with the idea of paying a visit to the cottage at night. Sleep is the most private of experiences. He wanted to be there, watching her. It would be taking a risk, but Jon was such a sound sleeper, he wouldn't wake up if you dropped a bomb next to the bed. And he'd be very quiet.

But the role of voyeur was not really what he had in mind. He wanted the right to put his arm around Tia and draw her close. She would be the keeper at the gate: warding off loneliness and solitude. And they would make the leap together when that hour arrived. Because she was a listener and so was he.

'Will you have another?'

He looked up to find Joela's face only inches from his. She really was quite amazingly pretty. And as he looked into her eyes, he saw her pupils swelling. He smiled. This was a sure thing.

As she poured him his shot, he placed his hand inside the inside pocket of his jacket and pulled out his pen and the book. Since coming to South Africa he has kept a journal. Tia would approve of that. The last time he had actually used pen and paper to express himself must have been in college. Since then word processing programs, printers and floppy disks had been his tools. But he knew Tia did not like computers and the time was approaching when he would want her to read his thoughts. And she was right: there truly was something immensely satisfying in the feel of paper beneath his palm; the scratch of a pen keeping up with his thoughts. It was an intimate feeling.

'If you like . . . you can do that in the chill-out space.' Joela was motioning with her hands.

'What?' He wasn't sure he had heard her correctly. The DJ had switched to a reworked version of an old Donna Summer tune featuring some throbbing falsetto male vocals which made any verbal communication almost impossible.

'Chill-out space. Upstairs. Quieter. So you can write.' She gestured at the pen and the book, which he had opened in front of him.

He leaned over and placed his mouth right next to her cheek. Her tiny earlobe felt soft. She was wearing a heavy, spicy perfume.

'No. I'll stay here. It's perfect here.'

She obviously thought he was staying because of her, because she suddenly gave a pleased, lop-sided smile; unpretentious, with not a hint of studied coquetry. It was delightful. He leaned forward again and cupped his hand across her ear. 'We'll talk later.' She smiled again, nodded her assent.

As she turned in the direction of another customer, he picked up his pen. The page in front of him was bathed in pulsating pink and blue light. He wrote slowly and the words seemed to float across the paper:

In ancient times man was a fly walking across the piano keys of the universe. He made no sound.

But that has changed.

Stephen smiled. He was getting better at this. The words sounded almost poetic. Or was it prophetic? He smiled again.

Our fragile blue planet is spinning through space like a tumescent, pulsating drop of sound. Earth: pumped up and wired. Feverishly vibrating.

He paused, delighted with the image and with his own eloquence.

Welcome to my mind.

DAY TWENTY-SEVEN

*Never before has there been a moment so simultaneously perilous
and promising. We are the first species to have taken our evolution
into our own hands.*

Carl Sagan, Broca's Brain

Tia looked over at Jon. While waiting for her to finish dressing,
he was lying on his stomach on top of the bed, looking down
to where a book was lying open on the floor. She couldn't
understand how anyone could read that way, but it was one
of his favourite things to do.

'Have you been looking for something?'

'H'mm?' he said absent-mindedly, not even glancing up.

'Are you missing something? Have you been going through
my things?'

This got his attention. 'Going through your things? What
do you mean?'

Tia looked down into the drawer of her dressing table.
Maybe she was becoming completely paranoid, but it certainly
seemed to her as though her stuff had been . . . rearranged,
somehow. She always kept her powder compact in the far
right corner. It was now pushed behind the tray of lipsticks.
Her box with hairclips was usually on top of the box with
safety pins, not underneath. And this was bizarre, but she
had the feeling that someone had cleaned her hairbrush for

her? The bristles showed not even one stray hair spun around the base.

There were also other tiny things. Like the cardigan she had searched for earlier this morning. It was made of cotton and in summer it usually lived on the very top of her pile of sweaters. But when she had looked for it in her closet, she hadn't been able to lay her hand on it straight away, because it was placed not on top, but in the middle of the stack of woollies.

'I think someone's been rifling through my things.'

'Are you sure?'

But she wasn't sure, of course. She was a creature of habit, and was meticulous about her environment, but could she really swear that a sweater she hadn't worn for a while was not in the place it was supposed to be?

'Is anything missing?'

'My blue teddy. Remember, I told you. The one you got me.'

Jon pushed himself up on his elbows. 'Pretty strange burglar this. Breaking and entering without leaving any trace to . . . wait for it, steal a panty.'

'Funny.'

'I still think you misplaced it. Or left it at Fluisterwater.'

She thought for a moment. 'That could be.'

'Well, you'll be able to check later today. What time are we leaving, by the way?'

'I thought we'd set out just after lunch.'

'Good. That will give Stephen time for a kip. Richie told me he was out all night and didn't come home until late this morning, looking really busted.' Jon grinned. 'I think one can draw the obvious conclusion.'

She didn't respond. Stephen's tomcatting was not something she felt like discussing.

'Anyway, I'm looking forward to going to Fluisterwater. I want Richie to see the gongs. And, man, will it be good to get out of the lab for two days.'

Tia sighed. She herself was less excited about the trip. And she knew why. It was Stephen. The idea of him walking through the rooms at Fluisterwater, touching her mother's things, while smiling that asymmetrical smile of his; going into the garden, making himself at home in one of the big paisley-covered armchairs in front of the fire – there was just something about the idea she resisted, that seemed wrong somehow.

'Tia? Are you OK with this?'

'Of course. Why wouldn't I be?'

'You look strange.'

'That's flattering.'

'No, really. Like you have the toothache.'

'No, I'm fine.' She paused, tried to inject some enthusiasm into her voice. 'It should be fun.'

*　　*　　*

Jon and Stephen were singing. Loudly. Loudly and off-key. They had been singing on and off along with the car radio ever since they left Johannesburg. This time the Rolling Stones were serving as inspiration. Jon's off-key baritone and Stephen's tenor blended startlingly well with Mick Jagger's raucous vocals.

Tia glanced at the rearview mirror. The two men were hanging onto each other's shoulders. She turned her head sideways and caught Richie smiling at her.

'Children,' he said. 'They've always been like this, ever since grad school.'

'They liked music?'

'They like noise.'

Tia reached over to the radio and turned the volume down, ignoring the shouts of protest coming from the back seat.

'Noise?'

'Yeah. I sometimes thought the walls of their room would buckle underneath the blast of all that sound. Even in the lab they'd sit there hacking code with earphones blasting away. I was surprised their brains didn't start dripping through their ears. Acid Rock mostly.'

'Richie was into Donovan.' Stephen affected a falsetto voice. 'They call me Mellow Yellow. Jeez.'

'Those were the days,' Jon's voice was nostalgic. 'We never slept. Didn't seem to need it. Music banging off the walls. It was a really wild time, I tell you. Eating pizza and drinking Coke. A lot of Coke. But I mean really a lot.'

'For a while Jon and I grew beards,' Stephen sounded amused. 'And I must admit, our standards of personal hygiene slipped a bit.'

'Oh, Lord, yes. Unwashed socks, unwashed crockery, body odour, fungus in the fridge.'

'So what happened?' Tia asked.

'We grew old.'

'Real old.'

'Yeah. It's sad.'

Tia looked in the rearview mirror again. Stephen and Jon were smiling at each other. She recognised the expression on their faces. She had seen it a few times before when the three men were together. It wasn't exactly a secretive expression, but it bordered on being so. It made her feel excluded. It told of camaraderie and things beyond her ken. Sometimes the three men were like members of a tiny tribe with their own alien customs. Certainly their own language. *Oscillator. Fast Fourier transform. Fractional noises. Random phenomena. Polanskian adaptive tuning.* There were times when they would talk about their work and she would look on, struggling to follow the conversation that dazzled and shimmered between them.

She looked in front of her again. The road stretched straight ahead for as far as she could see. On both sides was yellow grassland interspersed with patches of maize browned by the sun. Every few miles they would pass by a homestead: large and squat with a corrugated iron roof, or see in the distance the gaunt outline of a steel windmill. She never saw any signs of life. No children running around in the front yard. No farmer standing on his stoep scanning the sky for clouds. It was as though they were passing through a land abandoned and forgotten. As though some awful calamity had taken place, which had made those who lived there leave their homes forever.

She brought her thoughts back to the car. Richie was

talking. 'Spinoza called mathematics the music of the soul. You can't get more cool than that.'

Stephen disagreed. 'Pythagoras said a stone is frozen music. Now that's super cool.'

'It may be super cool, but it doesn't make much sense.' After Tia had spoken she was ashamed of herself. She must have sounded ill-humoured. And all because she was feeling jealous.

Her eyes caught Stephen's in the mirror. He was smiling. A knowing, pointed smile. As though he knew exactly what she was thinking. She did not like the feeling. Stephen was not a person she wanted inside her head.

Jon protested. 'Hey, why diss Pythagoras. You're the one who's into poetry – what's wrong with you?'

'Actually,' Stephen said coolly, 'it's not just poetry and it does make sense. All matter is made up of wave functions. A fundamental property of a wave is vibration. Sound is vibration. So Pythagoras could very well argue that a stone is made up of sound.'

Richie said, 'In a sense the entire universe is frozen music.'

'Well, OK then,' Tia said sullenly, 'but you guys seem to have an awful lot of faith in a man who was so weird he wouldn't eat beans because he believed them to have a soul.'

'Wow, cool.'

'Supercool.'

'Mega cool.'

Tia laughed unwillingly. 'You're impossible. Are all mathematicians this spaced out?'

Jon said, 'It goes with the territory.'

'And I'll have you know,' Richie added, 'it's not being spaced out, it's being cool.'

Stephen smiled. 'And mathematicians are really cool guys.'

★   ★   ★

They arrived at Fluisterwater just after dark. Tonight there had been no lingering sunset. It was as though a hand, clumsy and careless, had snuffed out the light with one casual gesture.

After unpacking the alarming number of bags and suitcases that Stephen and Richie had brought with them, as well as the portable generator and technical equipment – an intricate and troublesome mess of tripods and chrome dials and yards and yards of black cord – they opened a bottle of wine and Jon made a fire.

As the flames burnt redly in the hearth and threw long shadows on the walls, they told each other ghost stories: tales of creaking mansions, a headless rider on a dark horse, shadows on the moon, a raven carrying a thread of gold in its blood-stained beak. The firelight gleamed off Richie's glasses, burnt gold in Stephen's hair, lit Jon's face from below so that his eyes seemed heavy-lidded and brooding.

'I propose a toast,' Stephen said and raised his glass. He looked at Jon. 'To my friend, my comrade in arms—'

Richie put down his glass and started to stroke the air with his hand as though playing an imaginary violin.

'—who can also be a real pain in the arse when he cares to be—'

'Hear, hear.'

'—I wish you well. May you slay all your demons, may you fulfil all your promises, may you live life ecstatically. And may the force be with you.' Stephen lifted his glass.

Tia looked over at Jon. His face was flushed.

Richie laughed. 'You're supposed to respond in kind,' he said to Jon. He started humming ironically, 'You're the wind beneath my wings.'

Jon lifted his glass slowly. The light glinted off the crystal in his hand. For a moment it was quiet as he and Stephen looked at each other.

Tia felt an odd sensation as she watched the two men: Jon so dark and Stephen so fair and yet something in the two profiles that were so alike.

'Thank you.' Jon paused. 'To *The Angels' Key*.'

'To the Quest.' Richie clinked his glass loudly against Jon's.

'A perfect musical scale.' He turned his head and smiled at Tia. 'It's your turn now.'

She raised her glass. 'To my knights in shining armour. May you find your grail.'

'Well,' Stephen lifted an eyebrow. 'This calls for another toast: to friendship.'

And to her surprise, he hooked his arm through Jon's so that they drank from their glasses while locked in embrace. The gesture should have looked corny, but it didn't. There was a kind of ritualistic aspect to it, as though they had done this before.

It was then that she became aware of the insistent vibration that seemed to creep into the room through the barrier of closed windows and heavy drapes.

She drew the velvet curtain to one side and opened the window. With her palms pressing down on the window sill, she looked out into the darkness. The muscular sound of drums was much louder now.

The three men joined her at the open window and for a while they stood there listening in silence. The darkness outside was intense but alive. She had the feeling that if she pushed her hand into the blackness outside the window she would feel the sound – a tangible thing – running through her fingers like an electric current.

Even after they had gone to bed, the drums continued playing: the beat shifting and changing but never stopping. She was puzzled. Sometimes shows of traditional drumming were put on for tourists who were visiting the private nature reserve run by her neighbours, but never had she heard the drums played with such intensity for so long. And it sounded close. There was a small informal squatters' settlement not that far to the south. But the drums sounded even closer than that.

Beside her in the bed Jon moved restlessly. 'Don't these guys know when to give it a rest? What time is it?'

She peered at the clock on her bedside table. 'Three o' clock exactly.'

'Jesus.' Jon sighed. 'What's the occasion, do you think?'

'I don't know. It must be something special.'

He grunted. She looked over at him. Usually Jon tumbled into sleep the minute his head touched the pillow. Except here at Fluisterwater. He was always restless here. And tonight he had that insistent rhythm to contend with as well.

She pushed herself upright. 'Roll over. I'll give you a neck massage.'

Her fingers moved across his neck and back and after a while she heard him sigh sleepily and his breathing slowed.

She leaned back against the pillows and stared at the wall. No sleep for her. The incessant drumbeat made her feel anxious, short of breath. The heavy darkness was claustrophobic. Maybe she should get up and make herself a cup of cocoa. There were some marshmallows left in the cupboard. Yes, cocoa and marshmallows. That was sure to put her to sleep.

She slid out of bed and in the darkness searched for her nightgown. She finally found it in a heap on the floor. The fabric was so silky, it had slid off the foot of the bed where she had placed it.

There was only a tiny sliver of a moon tonight and the house was dark. She walked slowly down the passage, keeping her hand on the wall to guide her. As she turned the corner towards the living room, she noticed a glow.

Inside the living room the fire was burning brightly. Stephen was sprawled out on the sofa, his feet resting on the one sofa arm, his head on the other.

'Hi,' he said calmly, unsurprised, as if he had known she would come and was waiting for her. He did not get up, merely looked at her.

'Hi.' She felt awkward standing there, shifting her balance from one foot to another.

'You can't sleep either?'

'No.'

He swung his legs down and moved to one corner of the sofa. 'Come sit by me.'

She paused. A tête-à-tête in front of a flickering fire was not what she wished for. And she wasn't dressed properly.

But it would look foolish if she were to scamper off like a frightened virgin. She walked over, but sat down in the armchair opposite him.

He looked amused, but merely said, 'Do you often have difficulty sleeping?'

'Yes. I suppose I do. And then, I seem to dream a lot. And the dreams sometimes wake me up.' She felt slightly embarrassed – as if she were admitting to some peculiar failing. And the intent way in which he looked at her when she spoke was uncomfortable. She knew he was only lip-reading, but she found the unblinking stare discomfiting.

'Me, I seldom dream. But I might in this house. I think in this house dreams will come easily to me.' He glanced at her sideways from underneath long lashes. 'I think I shall be dreaming to please you.'

'What an odd thing to say.' Her voice was sharp.

He smiled. Reaching his hand into the pocket of his robe, he took out a packet of cigarettes.

'Smoke?'

She shook her head. She watched as he lit a cigarette and took the first drag. He had a way of covering the lower half of his face with his palm whenever he brought the cigarette to his mouth. It gave him a guarded, watchful look.

'I was lying here looking at the carvings of the angels on that mantelpiece,' Stephen nodded towards the stone fireplace. 'Why are the faces so damaged?'

She smiled. 'You've stumbled onto a family secret. My mother told me that when my father got upset, he would take his walking stick and beat it ferociously against the angels' faces.'

Stephen had been drawing on his cigarette as she spoke. He coughed and looked at her disbelievingly. 'You're joking?'

'Afraid not. Some men keep punching bags in the cellar. My father assaulted angels. I can hardly remember him, you know. He died when I was so little. But my mother assured me he was quite normal in other respects.'

'I envy people who never knew their father. It leaves

them free to invent in their heads the parent they'd like to have had.'

She looked at him curiously. For the first time since meeting him, she had the impression that he was speaking without monitoring himself. He was looking past her, the cigarette burning between his fingers unheeded.

'You don't get along with your father?' she said gently.

'He's a cruel bastard. I detest him.'

'And your mother?'

'She ran out on me and my father when I was twelve. She was a weak woman.'

'At least you won't make the same mistakes with your kids one day.'

'Oh, I won't have children.' The armour was back in place; the face smoothly self-assured once more.

'Don't you like kids?'

'I do, very much. But according to my doctor there isn't a snowball's chance I'll ever have any.'

'I'm sorry,' she said awkwardly.

'Don't be. In this day and age you'd have to be mad to bring children into the world, don't you think? Besides most people make lousy parents.'

She didn't answer. He put his head to one side and looked at her consideringly. 'But your mother sounds as if she were a really special person.'

'She was, yes. Of course, sometimes I got angry with her. She could be impetuous, unthinking. She would do things without pausing to reflect on where they might lead to.'

He gave her a flickering smile. 'You know what they say: visionaries rush in where angels fear to tread.'

He leaned forward and tipped the ash of his cigarette into the fire. 'They found no trace of her? She simply vanished?'

'Yes.'

'And she had been living here permanently?'

'Yes, towards the end. She was passionate about this house. This place.'

'What drew her to it?'

'She tried to explain it to me, but I couldn't really be bothered with listening to her closely. Today I'm sorry I didn't pay more attention . . . But Jon tells me you grew up in a wonderful house yourself.'

He grimaced. 'The house is much admired. Certain sections are open to the public, so I grew up with gawking day trippers traipsing through the hall. The house dates from the early seventeenth century, but was burnt down almost completely in 1850. That's when they added the west wing and a truly hideous octagon temple.'

'You sound as if you don't care for it at all.'

'It's dead, lifeless. Not like this house. In this place I sense a gathering of forces.'

'You sound just like my mother.' She smiled. 'She told me once that at Fluisterwater duality will be resolved: that good and evil will be united here – at this place – into a harmonising force.' She added rather helplessly, 'Whatever that might mean.'

He turned his face to one side, and blew out a delicate cloud of smoke. 'Interesting. But then, what is good and what is evil?'

Tia spoke haltingly. 'The wilful intent to harm. Taking pleasure in pain . . . that's evil, I suppose.'

Stephen's eyes narrowed against the smoke curling up from the tip of his cigarette. 'Every now and then,' he said, 'evil suddenly bursts out to overwhelm good. As it did in Germany in World War Two. As it did in Bosnia. The Indonesians have an expression for that: *mata kelap*, the darkening of the eye. It's painful, but it usually leads to a necessary transformation.'

'You're talking about people suffering. How can that ever be necessary?'

Stephen sighed. 'It never ceases to amaze me, this fear people have of violent change: this dread at the idea of life ending in one enormous, sudden moment of terror. And yet people fritter their lives away every day – killing off their existence little by little – interested only in vapid, trivial things and events. That's not life. That's a slow and squalid suicide. And besides, violence can be a creative force.'

'Violence can never be creative.'

'Of course it can. Evolution is violent. The evolutionary journey is littered with death. Along the way evolution brings with it massive extinction of species. But that's good. That's as it should be. Consider this – if single-celled beings had found a way to stop evolution so that they could establish and maintain themselves as the dominant life-forms on earth, the whole of mankind would never have evolved. There will always be some things that need to be killed off to make way for the new.'

The fire crackled and hissed. Tia put her fingers to her temples. Her face was hot from the fire.

Stephen spoke carefully. 'Evil lies beyond grotesque behaviour; it encompasses more than simply unspeakable events. I think there's only one thing that is truly wicked. And that's trying to hold back what has to happen. Fighting change.'

'Jon says uncontrolled change can lead to disintegration just as well as to transformation.'

Stephen smiled and lifted his one eyebrow in an elegant and obviously well-practised gesture. 'Oh? But then, Jon is a little timid.'

'Timid? Timid is certainly not a word I'd ever associate with Jon.' She was surprised to find that she was angry.

'OK. Maybe not timid. But you know the joke about the guy reaching two signposts and the one saying "This way to paradise" and the other saying "This way to a lecture on paradise"? Well, Jon is the fellow who'd choose the lecture. Jon has a mathematician's soul. He'll tell you different, but he likes sharp edges and clarity. Chaos, fuzziness, that's not for my friend Jon.'

'Your friend.' Tia's voice was icy.

'Yes,' he said emphatically. 'My friend. I love him. I don't think there's anyone I love more. Don't you ever forget it.'

There was something so raw and dangerous in his voice that she shrank back. But then his face relaxed into a smile and all of a sudden he looked charming and normal and very nice.

'Besides,' he added, 'Jon's a genius. Me, I'm just a chappie who writes computer games.'

She didn't answer, she was still shaken. And his next words were so unexpected, it threw her off-balance again.

'Would you be able to take someone's life? In self-defence, of course.'

She was jarred by the question. Car hijackings and random violence had become such a part of everyday life in Jo'burg that many of her friends now carried handguns in their bags. Astrid has been urging her for months to learn how to use a gun. So far, she had resisted. 'What's the use,' she told Astrid, 'if you know you'll never be able to take the life of another person – no matter what.' Astrid was impatient. 'That's just a cop-out. You have to take responsibility for yourself.'

Stephen was watching her with smooth eyes. His question hung in the air between them. The silence went on and on.

He smiled.

He got up from the sofa and before she had time to move, he bent over her, his hands resting on both sides of her on the arms of the chair. His face was so close she could see the stubble on his jaw and the fine lines around his eyes. The hair on his chest was a pale gold.

'I've enjoyed our conversation,' he said.

She felt herself blinking. Her throat was tight and dry. And then the drums stopped. The sudden silence was a shock.

Stephen looked at her for a long moment. He slowly straightened. 'Sleep well.'

She didn't answer but got up from the chair quickly, moving swiftly away from him. Halfway to the door she turned around and looked back to where he was standing in front of the fire. He had his hands in his pockets and was rocking slowly back and forth on his feet.

Stephen smiled charmingly. 'Don't dream too much.' His voice was slightly mocking.

She managed to find her voice. 'And you.'

'Oh, I know I'll be dreaming.' His eyes lingered on her face. 'I won't be able to stop myself.'

Without a word she turned around and walked out the door, conscious of his eyes following her.

DAY TWENTY-SIX: MORNING

'Laugh not so lightly, O King, for in these stones is a mystery and healing virtue.'

Merlin speaking to Arnelios in the *History of Britain* by Geoffrey of Monmouth, 1136 (as quoted by D. Cowan and A. Silk in *Ancient Energies of the Earth*)

The next morning Tia overslept. By the time she got up to take a shower, the men had already finished breakfast and were packing their equipment into backpacks.

As she came out the bathroom after her shower, she noticed that the door to the bedroom was slightly ajar. Through the tiny opening she could see Jon leaning over a fat folder that was lying open on the bed in front of him. The expression on his face was troubled.

She pushed open the door and he slammed the folder shut with a swiftness that surprised her.

'Hi,' she said, feeling awkward for no reason.

'Hi.' He turned around and placed the folder carefully inside the drawer of the bed table.

'What's that?' She gestured to the drawer.

'Nothing. Just work.' He paused. 'You'd better hurry,' he added abruptly. 'The guys are waiting.'

'Let me get my sunglasses.'

She waited until he had left the room and slid open the

drawer. The folder was navy blue, rimmed in red and in the right-hand corner the words ANGELS' KEY were written in bold, capital letters. The contents of the folder peeped coyly around the edges. She put out her hand to open it.

'Tia?' Stephen's voice came from the passage outside the door. 'Are you ready? We're leaving now.'

'Yes,' she said and closed the drawer quickly. 'I'm coming.'

★   ★   ★

Outside, it was chilly. The grass crackled under their feet as they walked in single file towards the edge of the garden. They let themselves out by the wooden gate and crossed the stream of water, which on this morning was flowing cold and sluggish and with hardly a whisper.

Tia blew into her hands in an attempt to warm them. She looked up into the sky. There wasn't a cloud to be seen, just miles of endless blue. The knee-high grass was tinder-dry.

It was so quiet. Not even a bird-call disturbed the gleaming silence. The only sounds were their feet moving clumsily and their breaths, already slightly laboured from the weight of the heavy backpacks. Jon and Stephen walked in front. She and Richie lagged behind.

Richie stopped for a moment to rearrange his backpack. Tia saw thick red marks at the side of his neck where the straps had bitten into the flesh. As she waited for him to readjust his load, she turned her head and looked back in the direction of the house.

Last night she had thought she could sense negative forces strung out like a force field in the darkness. In the bright light of day those fears now seemed silly. In the distance Fluisterwater was serene and peaceful in the early sunlight. It was just a simple farm house: sturdy walls, thick thatched roof, solid doors and windows.

Richie said, 'I can't wait to see those gongs.'

'Not long now.'

He made a small unintelligible sound somewhere between

a grunt and a sigh, which nevertheless managed to convey a sense of immense delight and satisfaction. His spectacles were askew and the tip of his nose was shiny. His eyes behind the thick glass lenses were screwed up against the sun.

She really did like him so much. He was comfortable to be with. Dependable. Like a kind of shaggy St Bernard. And he looked – she glanced at him again – so very 'huggable'.

He caught her glance and smiled, his eyes almost closing. 'Sometimes you have this look,' he said, 'as though you're not made for this world. As though you should be protected or something.'

'I'm not the fragile flower you think I am.'

'That's what Stephen says,' Richie answered unexpectedly. 'Eyes of a fawn and a ferocious heart. That's what he says about you.'

She was silent for a moment as she pondered this. She wasn't quite sure what to make of it. She did know that she disliked the feeling that she had been discussed behind her back.

She looked ahead to where Stephen and Jon were walking ahead, side by side.

'You guys talk to each other about everything, don't you. You're really close.'

'H'mm. Although we're really not alike at all.'

She looked at him, surprised. 'You are too. As far as I can see you've got the same interests: gaming, computer junkies all three of you—'

'That's true enough, as far as it goes. But Jon is the brain, Stephen is the mystic and I'm the flake.' His tone of voice was strangely resigned and he spoke without any hint of bitterness, but there was a sadness in his eyes.

'What are you talking about? I know Jon values your work.'

He smiled. 'I'm blessed in having Jon as my big brother. He's rescued me out of so many scrapes and he's given structure to my life – as far as he can. Our parents died early as you know, and ever since then he's watched out for me. He's had his work cut out for him, I can tell you. My generation did one of two things: we either lived the whole American-Psycho-Bright-Lights-Big-City bullshit, or we dropped out. I dropped out. But big time. I bummed around, sold T-shirts, got tattooed a lot. One year I attended *Burning Man* in the Black Rock Desert. That's where I became interested in computers. I started to hang out on-line with some "script kiddies" who introduced me to some very weird chat rooms. Here I hooked up with a bunch of scary crackers. Not good news at all.'

'Crackers?'

'Criminal hackers. Cyber criminals illegally entering sites. Shutting them down, or vandalising them. Even stealing credit card numbers. Anyway, I landed in a world of trouble. Unfortunately, I pulled Jon in there with me. For a while the FBI thought he was the master mind – you know, evil computer science professor planning cyber domination.' Richie shrugged. 'To top it off, along the way I managed to develop a very nasty little drug habit. Couldn't avoid that little rite of passage, now could I? Jon's the one who got me clean. It was a hellish time for me and a very tough time for him. One day I hope to repay him somehow. I'm chronically out of pocket, so it won't be in money, that's for sure – but maybe some day I can make a contribution. Help him get what he really wants.'

'And Stephen?'

'What about him?'

'What does Stephen really want? Besides achieving perfect tuning, I mean.'

Richie frowned. 'That's a good question. I've known Stephen for years, and I love him, but I still don't know who he really is. He's a complicated guy. He had a near-death experience as a child, which turned into an epiphany for him. Ever since that day he's been obsessed with sound. I don't quite understand it myself and he doesn't like talking about it. But of the three of us, he's probably the one who has the truest understanding of music. The fact that he's partly deaf doesn't matter. He's a searcher.'

It was quiet between them. Then he said, 'By the way, I've been meaning to tell you. I'm really pleased about you and Jon.

It's not his style to fall hard, but let me tell you, he's crazy about you. And Stephen approves as well.'

'How nice of him.' She did not try to keep the sarcasm out of her voice.

Richie shook his head. 'Sorry, that came out wrong. It's just that very few of Jon's relationships with women were ever serious. And that was just fine with Stephen. Anything that took Jon away from *The Key* was not to his liking. When it came to women, he'd make sure Jon's attention did not wander too far from the work at hand. I think his biggest fear was the pitter-patter of tiny feet, lawnchairs and Jon happily drowning in baby food and mortgages. He wasn't about to let that happen.'

'You mean he sabotaged Jon's relationships?'

'That's a little harsh. And I can't blame Stephen for the bust-up of Jon's affairs – Jon was quite capable of messing them up himself. Anyway, Stephen really seems to like you. As for Jon – he's a goner. And I'm thrilled for him.'

She relaxed. The mood between them was easy again. 'Thanks.' She put her hand on his. 'I'm glad you're my friend, Richie.'

'Always. And if you ever need me, let me know.'

'I will.' She laughed, slightly uncomfortable.

'I mean it, Tia. I'm serious. OK?'

She looked into the kindly eyes. 'OK.'

*   *   *

After another hour of walking, the bulky shape of the giant rock pile and the black slash of the ravine appeared on the horizon. And then the four gongs finally came into view.

While the men unpacked their rucksacks, carefully lay-ing out equipment on spread-open oil sheets, Tia wandered off towards the ravine. It was deceptive this landscape: one moment the earth was completely flat and arid and then all of a sudden you happen on this enormous steep plunge down to a riverbed below. She knew that down there was water, even though she could not see it for the dense vegetation.

Gingerly, holding onto the sturdy branch of a mopane tree, she peered over the edge and then drew back quickly.

'We should have a wonderful view from up there.'

Stephen was standing behind her, so close. She wondered that she hadn't heard him coming towards her. This was yet another way in which he and Jon were alike. They both moved quietly.

Stephen pointed at the towering outcrop of rock that drooped impossibly over the lip of the ravine.

'Yes,' she agreed. 'I've always thought the view from up there would be spectacular.'

'So, let's climb up.'

She shook her head; gave a step backwards.

'What's the matter?' Stephen looked at her quizzically. 'Are you scared of heights?'

'No,' she said sharply. 'Nothing like that.'

'So come on then.' He held out his hand.

Tia hung back. She looked at the pile of rocks. It was very high.

He folded his arms across his chest and looked her up and down. 'You really are scared of heights, aren't you? Terrified.' There was something in his voice she couldn't fathom: a note of disappointment; even a slight contempt.

She looked again at the rocky outcrop. The jagged edges of rock were etched against the blue of the sky with the clarity of a pencil stroke. She swallowed and turned her head to find Stephen watching her with an alert expression in his eyes.

She took a deep breath. 'OK. Let's go.'

She felt shivery and the muscles in her throat jumped with fear. She climbed slowly and carefully, but her palms felt slippery as they searched for holds in the cracks of weathered rock and once or twice she stopped, her eyes squeezed shut, holding her breath as though that would still the panic that was bubbling just below the surface. She didn't want to think about what she was doing, because she knew that if she did she might succumb to debilitating, sobbing terror.

Ahead of her, Stephen climbed easily and gracefully: stopping at every ledge to look back at her, smiling his cat-like smile, his eyes daring her to follow him. Damn him, she thought, her anger a welcome relief to the fear. This was a test, she knew it. Some stupid test he wanted her to pass. She should have refused to play along. God, she was pathetic. Trying to impress a man she didn't like and didn't trust. Why the hell should she care what he thought of her?

She winced as the muscles in her upper arms stretched painfully as she reached for the next rock shelf. Then, for one awful heart-stopping moment her foot couldn't find a resting place and she scrabbled frantically to secure safe footing, her breath leaving her mouth in a kind of sob.

She was trembling when she reached the top. She placed her fingers, wet with sweat, in Stephen's cool palm as he pulled her up.

'See,' he said, gesturing to the panorama that stretched out around them. 'Didn't I tell you it would be worth it?'

She refused to walk closer to the edge. Enough was enough. She pushed her back against the rock wall. The flat crest on which they stood was about ten feet in width, strewn with small boulders. Tiny pockets of vegetation grew from the crevices and cracks in the rock face. The wind up here was stronger than below and strands of hair whipped across her mouth.

She sank to her heels – collapsed was more like it – keeping her back against the rock. On her one arm was a bloody scratch where the skin had been broken by the sharp thorns of a bush as she had pulled herself upward. Her blouse clung soggily to her body.

Stephen was sitting unconcernedly on the very edge, his legs swinging over the lip of the ledge. Just looking at him sitting there without any anchorage for his legs or arms, made her feel sick and anxious. He slipped his hand under his sweater and she could see the outline of his fingers as they searched for the packet of cigarettes that made a bulge under the wool.

The tiny flame of the cigarette lighter sparked once, twice. He took a drag from his cigarette, keeping his hand cupped to shield it from the sudden gusts of wind.

For a while they sat quietly, not saying anything. The smell of the tobacco from his cigarette was not unpleasant, strangely calming. After a while her heart stopped rattling away in her chest like a mad thing and she was actually able to look around her.

You could see for miles. Part of the ravine was right below them and she could not see it, but it also stretched away to the left. From this height, it made an extraordinary impression: the landscape so flat and then this steep-sided gash into the ground; as though the ravine had not been worn away by running water – was not the result of a gradual process – but rather the product of one dramatic moment when the earth had been put under tremendous strain and had torn open painfully.

She turned her head, a little stiffly, to see if she could see the gongs and Jon and Richie. But they were on the other side of the rock pile, screened from her view. It was the strangest feeling. She and Stephen might have been the only man and woman in the world, marooned up here in their eyrie high above a land that had existed since the dawn of time. The landscape was a jumble of colours – yellow, brown, brick red – and only gradually did the eye separate the tawny hues into grass and soil, bushy slopes and outcrops of sunburnt rock: the product of ancient geologic forces.

When Stephen spoke, she jumped a little. It had been so quiet between them, the sound of his voice was unexpected.

'Africa. Cradle of Humankind.'

His face was serene, but she thought there was just the faintest trace of mockery clinging to his words.

'You're not really interested in the gongs, are you?'

He shrugged. 'They're Jon's little hobby. Indiana Jones meets the Age of Aquarius. Frankly, I don't see what the fuss is about. But hey, if it keeps Jon happy . . .'

He paused. 'It's just that these gongs seem to me to be an anachronism. Their time is past.' He glanced at her. 'Don't get me wrong, but I suppose that's what freaks me out about the whole of this continent. The twenty-first century is all about individuals from right across the globe becoming linked through communication – to such an extent that they'll cease to be members of individual communities. The world has become a huge spider's web with every strand connected. Touch one strand and the whole vibrates. Those who do not link up – like much of Africa – will be forgotten. They will be forgotten because they will not form part of this new planetary superstructure. They'll find themselves adrift in an alien world.'

His calm certainty irritated her. 'You do realise what this thesis of yours amounts to . . . eventually.'

There was a smile in his eyes. 'No,' he said. 'I don't know what it amounts to . . . eventually. Tell me.'

She knew he was laughing at her and felt foolish. 'If you take the argument to its fullest extent,' she said repressively, 'it means that the individual will no longer be important. You're saying that it'll all come down to collective intelligence.'

His eyes glinted. 'That's a rather melodramatic way of putting it. But yes, the name of the game will be collaboration: a massive interaction of minds . . . and machines. I hate to break this to you, but the age of the lone hero slaying the dragons is over.'

'You're wrong. I know you're wrong. And as for Africa – don't be so sure. She might surprise you one day.'

He raised a disbelieving eyebrow. She watched as he stubbed out his cigarette. He sighed. 'The one thing about this place, though. If you sit here long enough, time appears out of joint. You know what I mean?'

She was unwilling to indulge him. 'No,' she said. But in actual fact she did know what he meant. The landscape had that effect on one. As though what was, what is, and what is to be, had congealed into one never-changing, silent moment.

He gave her a sidelong glance. 'What's the matter?'

'Nothing. Let's go down.'

'I could stay here forever,' he said, as though he hadn't heard her. 'Never go back to the real world again.'

'What's so bad about the real world?'

He was silent for a moment. Then he said, 'When I was a boy I almost died. But during that experience, I also lived through the one truly ecstatic moment of my life. But it was only for a moment. And ever since then life has seemed flattened, dulled to me.'

She frowned. 'I would have thought a brush with death would heighten, not take away from your appreciation of life.'

'You'd think so, wouldn't you. No. Just the opposite. I'm constantly seeking to reinvent my life with mystery and beauty: but I'm beginning to think – no, I know – I won't find that kind of passion in this reality. Passion is only present in sex and death and music. The rest is exhaustion and chaos.'

There was such a weary contempt in his words, she felt oddly shaken.

'I can't accept that.'

He looked all at once immensely bored and irritated. With one swift movement he had pushed himself backward and to his feet.

'Come take a look,' he said, holding out his hand. 'Come on,' he said impatiently when she did not respond.

She edged forward until she was just behind him. He turned around and gripped her arm, pulling her right up against him, at the same time pushing her slightly forward. He had a pebble in his hand and he threw it over the edge. She watched with dreadful fascination as it fell down, down, down, bumping on its way against the rock face and then spinning away until it disappeared into the vegetation.

'It would be easy to loose your footing here,' Stephen said. 'To slip.'

'I want to get down now.' Her voice sounded small.

'Right at this moment,' he said, 'don't you feel more alive, more aware?'

She didn't answer; couldn't really.

'Tia.' He paused. 'I would never let you fall. I would catch you.'

His eyes were slitted against the light and the dark eyebrows swooped away beautifully and dramatically above his eye sockets like the wings of a gull. His face was mask-like – blank – but, she realised with a rather sick sense of surprise, he was turned on by the situation. There was a sheen of sweat on his cheekbones. His excitement clung like an invisible miasma to his skin. His grip on her arm was tight, but his thumb was very slowly and softly rubbing against her wrist.

She did not struggle, did not speak. She was paralysed and it made her feel ashamed and humiliated. Why couldn't she just twist away angrily, or even better, laugh at him and turn his evil little game into a joke . . . but she was quite, quite unable to even utter a word.

He drew back.

'OK,' he said softly, '*now* we can go down.'

The thought that she would soon have solid ground under her feet, was all that sustained her on the descent. When she finally lowered herself down the last ledge, her legs were rubber.

'Well done,' Stephen said casually. 'I knew you could do it.'

She turned away without answering. She saw Jon and Richie coming towards them. Jon had a concerned expression on his face. He knew of her fear of heights.

'What did you do that for?' He placed his arms around her shoulders and half-turned towards Stephen. 'Didn't she tell you she was scared?' He looked down at her. 'That was a stupid thing to do. If you're nervous, you can fall.' He stared at her, gave her a little shake. 'What did you do that for?'

From the corner of her eye, she saw Stephen watching them. 'Because I wanted to. It's something I had to do.'

She extricated herself from Jon's embrace and walked over to where she saw her backpack. She bent over and picked it up.

'Where are you going?' Jon asked.

'I'm going to leave you guys now. I have to go back. I have . . . some stuff to do.'

'We're probably going to be busy here for quite a while.'

'That's OK.' She hoisted the rucksack onto her back. 'I'll expect you when I see you.'

She couldn't wait to get away, but when the initial, over-whelming impulse to escape started to fade, she turned around. In the distance she could see the boulders. There was something about their outlines that seemed unusual. She put her hand to her eyes to shield them from the glare.

The rocks had sprouted antennae-like structures. Thin and spidery and black, they looked like alien growths. She could see the figures of the men moving in front of the rocks. Jon had a large object in his hand and Stephen and Richie were busy rigging up something at the foot of one of the gongs.

The wind was much stronger now. It tugged at her scarf. She put her hand to her hair. Her eyes were tearing.

DAY TWENTY-SIX: EVENING

There's music in all things, if men had ears; Their earth is but an echo of the spheres.

George Gordon, Lord Byron, *Don Juan*, Canto 15.5

The house was dead quiet. Everyone was asleep. And, thank God, there was no sound of drums tonight. But as was always the case when he was at Fluisterwater, Jon was feeling anxious and restless. And after staring into the darkness for an hour, with the sound of Tia's even breathing making him feel only more wide awake, he had decided he could just as well use the time to work. It was a good opportunity to look at the data he and Richie had collected from the rock gongs earlier that day. Especially with Stephen asleep. It would be easier to study the data without Stephen around to make churlish remarks and dismissive comments.

He tapped on the computer keys and stared frowningly at the screen. After manipulating all of the data he had gleaned from the gongs, what he had basically ended up with were nine notes: *C,D,E-flat,E,G,A,B-flat,B,D*. Not that exciting a result, really. If you should play these notes on a keyboard they would sound odd: not musical at all. But still . . .

He tapped on the keys again. The only aspect that was remarkable about all of this, was that each of the gongs had the same identical notes carved out of them. Only these nine notes, nothing else. But there was something strangely familiar about these notes . . . something that was tugging at his unconscious. They reminded him of something, but what? He concentrated hard, staring at the computer screen, his eyes aching, but it was of no use. The feeling that he should know what this was all about was slipping away from him.

It was probably nothing. He yawned and shut the lid on his laptop. He should get back to bed and really try to get some sleep. He needed his rest: he was planning to make one last trip to the gongs tomorrow before they headed back to Jo'burg.

In the bedroom door he hesitated for a moment and then walked softly over to Tia's side of the bed. The curtains were open and there was enough light that he could see her quite clearly. She had her arms around the pillow in a kind of embrace. The heavy hair was pulled back from her face by a bow and she looked disturbingly young and vulnerable. She was smiling slightly and he wondered if she was dreaming.

The strength of his feelings for her still had the power to surprise him. He truly loved this woman, even though he did not always understand her. She was an intensely private person: he rather doubted he'd ever get to know her through and through. And she was a bundle of contradictions: powerfully feminine, with a spiky mind. Water and steel her make-up. An old soul who could be unsettlingly childlike. An unknown melody that reminded him of every other melody. A key who could unlock a puzzle, if only he knew which puzzle to look for. The more he got to know her, the more she fascinated him. And it seemed Stephen thought so too. He had noticed the way Stephen has been looking at her. And something had happened between Stephen and Tia today. When the two of them got back from their climb he had sensed that something was amiss. Tia's face so white and shuttered. And her early return to the house. It made him wonder.

He shook his head. This was nonsense. Stephen was his best friend. Tia was his love. The last thing he should be was jealous.

He leaned forward to tuck the sheet close around her. She

turned slightly in her sleep and once again she smiled. She must be dreaming.

About what?

Whom?

DAY TWENTY-FIVE

━━━━◆━━━━

> . . . *I began to look at the DNA molecule in a very specific light. The four nitrogenous bases, the triplet RNA codons, the sixty-four possible combinations of bases and the twenty-two signals at the amino-acid stage of development – all this was beginning to look remarkably like a biochemical manifestation of the heptatonic musical scale.*

Michael Hayes, *The Infinite Harmony*

Driefontein was a small town fifteen miles to the north of Fluisterwater and served as a supply centre for neighbouring farms. During the week the town's streets were dead and there was little sign of life in the tiny houses with their deep verandahs.

But on weekends, when farmers from miles around drove in to stock up on supplies, the town came alive. As Tia turned the car into the main street she realised that she had hit Saturday morning rush-hour traffic. It was going to be difficult getting a parking space among the dozens of pick-up trucks lining the sides of the road. After circling the block a few times, she saw an old 1950s diesel Mercedes swing out from behind a tree. She accelerated and narrowly beat a large truck with a crate of chickens on the back to the parking spot. The woman behind the wheel of the truck merely looked resigned.

Tia had decided against joining the men as they set out for the gongs this morning. After her climbing adventure with

209

Stephen the day before, she was in no hurry to spend more time in his company. And besides, she was looking forward to having the day to herself. The three men together could sometimes be just a little overwhelming.

After stocking up on some groceries, she was thirsty and decided to have a milkshake in the town's only tea room. As it was Saturday, the place was packed. A group of farmers sat at the table next to hers, gesticulating forcefully. The men were dressed in khaki shorts, velskoene, long socks up to their knees, and sweat-stained hats pulled low over their foreheads. Their voices were deep and they uttered their words slowly and with care. She suddenly had the strongest sense of déjà vu. Surely when she was a child she had walked into this very same shop. Her hand had been in her mother's hand and Klio had been walking slowly so as to accommodate Tia's tiny steps. They had walked past a group of men who had looked very much like these farmers here and surely these men were having the exact same conversation . . .

She finished her milkshake and a slice of guilt-inducing tipsy tart. Stepping out into the street, her eye fell on the storefront of a tiny shop in an alley leading off the main road. It was just visible from where she stood. Isaiah's muti shop.

Through the dusty fly-spotted windows, she glimpsed rows of glass jars and brown paper bags. She pushed the door open and a bell rattled above her head. Inside the shop the air was close, as though it had been a long time since any window had been opened to fresh air. The ceiling was very low. She had to duck her head to avoid the animal skins and dried ostrich feet hanging from the ceiling.

Isaiah was sitting cross-legged on a wide stool behind the wooden counter, wearing the two crossed strips of skin of the fully-initiated sangoma. They ran from shoulder to waist. His eyes were half-closed and his hands were on his knees, the fingers pointed upwards like closed flowerbuds. As she entered the shop, he simply nodded at her.

It was not a big place and it hadn't changed much since the last time she visited, probably more than two years before.

Behind Isaiah hung a beaded curtain, which probably led to another room. In this front room, the shelves ran unevenly along the wall and held a bizarre collection of objects. There were tins and jars filled with seeds and herbs. Barks and roots, untidily wrapped in newspaper, shared shelf space with pebbles and animal skulls and small plastic toys. At the back of the shop was a glass display case, which was home to a sleepy-looking brown snake. On the shelf above it a stuffed monkey head screamed silently: its mouth open, the incisor teeth bared.

Several drums, their edges touched by a strip of sunlight, were stacked next to each other in a long row. Tia knew there were izangoma who wielded the drum like a magic tool, bringing themselves face to face with the spirits of their ancestors. As she looked at the drums, quietly leaning against each other, it was difficult to imagine their power.

She picked up a two-headed drum, its heads joined together by thin strips of leather. She gently slapped the palm of her hand onto the dried oxskin surface. It made a soft thud, and dust rose from the drum's heads in a slow puff of air.

She looked at Isaiah. 'Why were the drums playing the other night?'

He regarded her calmly. 'Darkness is coming. The drums know it. And the witch is here. He has come.'

She frowned. He had used the word umthakhati. Unlike the izangoma – the diviners – or the inyanga – medicine men – abathakathi practised black withcraft and were greatly feared. According to traditional custom, witches have to be killed. In the Northern Province especially, witch burnings were not uncommon. In fact, it had become such a problem that many police stations in the north now had a witchcraft unit permanently attached to them.

'This witch,' Tia asked, 'he lives in your tribe?'

Isaiah shook his head.

She opened her mouth to ask more, but he closed his eyes, ending the conversation as effectively as shutting a door between them.

On top of the table in front of her was an antelope skin

and spread out on the skin were several small ivory-coloured objects. She picked one up and rolled it in her palm. It was a dingaka bone, a divining bone. Some divining bones were made of ivory, but the one in her hand was the knuckle-bone of a sheep or ox that had been cooked clean. As a child she had played with dingaka bones just like these and Isaiah had explained to her that in the hands of a medicine man they were powerful tools for finding out what ailed a patient, for locating a missing item or for identifying witches.

It was just the kind of thing that Richie would find interesting and his birthday was coming up. She opened her handbag.

'Imalini?' she asked Isaiah in Zulu. 'How much?'

'Ten rands.'

As she searched for her wallet, she took out the stack of photographs that she had just had developed and placed them on the counter. One of the slick, glossy prints slid out from underneath the others.

She felt a tug on her sleeve. 'Who is that?'

'Stephen. Jon's friend.' She was surprised by the look on Isaiah's face. His upper lip was slightly drawn back.

'Friend?' Isaiah's voice was very quiet.

'Yes,' she said, puzzled. 'You must stop by the house. I will introduce you.'

'No.' He stared at her for one moment and she had the impression that he wanted to say something to her. He put out his hand as if to hold her back.

'What?' she asked, suddenly alarmed. 'What is it?'

But then he blinked and his eyes became blank. With a lovely, graceful motion he got up from the stool and opened a cupboard behind him. When he turned around he had a bag in his hands made of some kind of antelope skin. It had seen a lot of wear: there were bald patches where the hair had worn away. He opened the bag and took out two darkly polished beer pots. The pots were marked with white crosses.

'For you,' he said. 'And for Jon.'

She crossed her hands and picked up one of the pots. She

rubbed her palm over its smoothness. These were not like the beer pots that were turned out for the tourist trade: cheap, factory-made replicas. The beer pot in her hands was old and dark with age. Beer was used in all major rituals and these two pots had obviously been kept in use. A yeasty whiff still clung to them.

'Thank you.'

Isaiah nodded. 'Put them at your door. For protection.'

'Protection?'

He nodded again.

She stared at him, slightly at a loss. 'Isaiah—'

'Ten rands,' he said briskly and pointed at the divining bone still clutched in her fingers. She had the strong impression that he wanted her to leave, even though his face was as smooth and still as any of the masks lining the wall.

She handed him the ten rands and picked up the pots – their value incalculable – and cradled them in her arms. Isaiah had his eyes closed again, and after a slight moment of hesitation, she stepped out the door. After the dim light inside, the glare in the street was blinding.

Just before she crossed the road, she gave a last glance backward. Isaiah was gone. The stool was empty. But the beaded curtain behind the counter, its beaded strings shimmering dully in the gloom, was swaying slightly.

*   *   *

She spent most of the rest of the day in Driefontein's only cinema, watching *Brigadoon* in the company of a gaggle of white-haired ladies. After the movie she had another milkshake and it was dark by the time she returned to Fluisterwater.

She turned the car into the dirt road leading up to the house, past the open iron gate and saw in the distance, outlined against the lesser blackness of the horizon, the bulky form of the house and the strong sweep of the roof. The windows were dark. There was no sign of life. The men had not yet returned from the gongs.

The wheels of the car crunched over the loose pebbles in the road and the dust hung in a transparent red cloud in front of the headlights. She suddenly realised that she was pushing down on the brake pedal and that the car was slowing down to little more than a crawl. She looked at the squat blackness of the walls. There was a strange reluctance in her to approach the house. She did not want to have to stop the car, walk up those shallow steps, push open the heavy door . . .

She pulled the car into the carport and killed the engine. For a few moments she sat quietly, watching the peculiar jerking motion of the white hands of the clock on the dashboard. Then, taking a deep breath, she got out of the car, slammed the door behind her, and walked quickly towards the front door.

The house felt very dark and empty without the men. She switched on one of the table lamps and hung her jacket behind the door. Richie's guitar was propped up between two pillows on the sofa. Stephen's sketch book was face down on the seat of one of the armchairs. Jon's laptop computer was set up on the telephone table.

She walked through to the bedroom and stood looking around her, not sure what to do next. Jon's sweater was lying on the floor and she knelt down to pick it up. As she got to her feet, her eye fell on the half-open drawer of the night table. Inside she could just see a hint of blue.

The drawer of the bedside table opened smoothly. As she took out the folder she found herself glancing backwards guiltily, like someone afraid of being caught snooping. The bulging folder felt awkward in her hands. She opened it.

It was filled with photocopied clippings from newspapers and magazines. And they all dealt with *The Angels' Key*. Many were in languages other than English and had translations clipped to the back. At the top of every page was printed the name of an information retrieval agency. The clippings came from a wide range of publications: the *Bangkok Post*, *Der Spiegel*, *Le Monde*, *Neue Zürcher Zeitung*.

Tia frowned. Of course she was aware of the controversy surrounding the game, but seeing all these clippings together was somehow altogether more disturbing than she would have thought.

At the bottom of the pile were a large number of fullscap sheets. They appeared to be print-outs that had been lifted straight from some Internet bulletin boards created by *Angels' Key* fans. One of the bulletin boards seemed to be devoted to poetry, of all things. But as she started to read, she could feel herself grimacing at the sly, but deliberately childlike words staring up at her. The poem was titled *The Gift*:

> daddy, hold my hand
> daddy, you never liked me
> your screwed up, seesaw kiddie
> such a disappointment
> such a waste
> let me make amends daddy
> give you a pretty present
> a red flower blooming in your forehead
> head. dead. dead. dead. dead.

The other poems were along the same lines, if decidedly less subtle: misogynist fantasies; imaginative images of torture and bloodlust. Chainsaws seemed to feature prominently. The 'poets' were identified by such names as 'bumcrack baby' and 'maggot mother'.

Somewhere in the house behind her a door slammed shut. She jerked her head upright and looked almost fearfully over her shoulder. But then the white lace curtains framing the windows came to life like two startled birds. It was only the wind.

She looked back at the print-out in her hand. She felt slightly nauseous. Placing it with the rest of the clippings, she closed the folder and pushed it away from her. She felt like Pandora, or like a character from *Poltergeist* who had found a host of demons lurking behind an ordinary-looking closet door. Maybe she should talk to Jon about this, although he was so touchy when it came to criticism of *The Key* . . .

She replaced the folder carefully into the drawer and walked back into the living room. Her mind still on the folder, she poured herself a glass of wine and stopped in front of Jon's laptop. It was open and the screen saver showed a haunted house and a tiny bat leaving the attic with a flap of an outsized wing. Two owls, perched on the branch of a withered tree, made a screeching noise.

For a moment she stared at the image. Then, after slight hesitation, she sat down on the telephone chair and tapped on one of the keys. The screen saver disappeared.

She placed her finger on the mouse and clicked on the icon that would give her access to the Internet. The modem screeched cacophonically. Carefully she typed in the URL: www.angelskey.com.

The screen blinked, turned a deep aqua. WELCOME TO THE ANGELS' KEY. YOU WILL NEVER LISTEN TO THE WORLD THE SAME WAY AGAIN.

Music was coming from the miniature inbuilt speakers: a slow steady rhythm, like a heart beat.

Taking a deep breath she clicked on the moss-encrusted door with its huge padlocks. It swung open and a long, twisting passage glimmering with wet stretched into the darkness. Waiting in the gloom, a woman – her face veiled, the outlines of her body clearly visible underneath a long, gauzy robe – crooked a finger and beckoned: Come with me . . .

Against her will Tia was starting to enjoy herself. It was strangely satisfying to plot the tiny red-hatted hero's course as he wandered through desolate stretches of barren waste-land, through cities adrift in spiritual confusion, through dusty libraries and echoing rooms. She was surprised at how involved she became in the little figure's shape-shifting flights as he rode the spirit of his sacrificed horse between earth, sky and the underworld: fighting demons, resisting sirens. She was faring much better this time than when she had played the game that first time with Stephen. And the music was egging her on. Each time she wanted to log off, the music seduced her into playing just one more cycle, and then another one . . .

But suddenly she winced as a groaning, protesting sound – an atonal screech – sliced into her skull and placed pressure on her eardrums. She tried to move the cursor to the exit icon, but it seemed stuck. She stood up, pushed the chair backwards and stretched out her hand towards the power switch – anything to stop the assault on her ears – but before her fingers could reach the switch, another sound exploded in her brain and sent her reeling backwards. Her hand swept violently across the table and the glass of red wine fell to the floor: the crystal shattering into a million pieces, the wine splashing blood against the white of the wall.

The edges of the windows were starting to glow – yellow and orange – but the panes themselves were black. The air was thick with the smell of decay: piles and piles of putrefying garbage and gutters overflowing with excrement. It sickened her, made her gag. She started to run, to try to get away, but she could hardly move her legs and when she looked down, black mud was clinging to her feet. The mud made sucking noises that became louder and louder until all she could hear was a gluttonous slobbering noise that pressed wetly against her skin. Madness, such was madness.

And then she was outside and for just a moment the kiss of the wind against her cheek steadied her. Sweat formed wet patches under her arms. She opened her mouth to call for help, but the sound that passed her lips was so terrible, she clamped her teeth together.

But there, in the distance, she could see something. She found herself walking towards it and the night sky was suddenly bright as day. The speck on the horizon became bigger – it was a bird – an African vulture. Clumsily it hopped around on dirty pink legs and pecked at the shape in the grass, the shape that became a body. There was something in the form of the head that was familiar. But she found to her surprise that she could not recognise the face, even though the vulture had left most of it untouched. But the eyes were pulpy hollows and therefore she could not remember who it was she was looking at. She tried and tried but the features refused to take on the form of memory. The vulture screeched and the sound lingered. Echo upon echo.

She realised she was lost. Where was she? She looked up into the sky and the sun had disappeared and the stars were all wrong. She searched for the four bright Pointers of the Southern Cross, but they weren't there. The blackness was studded with a slew of twinkling stars but they were stars unfamiliar to her. Instead of the huge pinwheel of the Milky Way, these stars were pushed together into a long thin funnel that drained into a vast sea of black matter. She turned around to try to find the house again but it had disappeared and around her was only emptiness.

The air was starting to sparkle, to hum. The sound was terrifyingly beautiful. She wanted to drown herself in it, to wrap the sound around her like a cloak. To hold on to it forever.

But out of the hum was growing a steady rhythm, a rhythm that grew more and more pronounced. It pushed against her, jostled her, knocked her down. She fell and, even though she put out her hands to stop herself from falling, she was tumbling into nothingness.

Voices and in the distance three figures black against the yellow oblong of light behind them.

'Jon,' she shouted, but her voice broke. 'Jon, help me.' And then his arms were around her and she was clinging to him and the words tumbled from her mouth and she was trying to make him understand the horror of it all.

★   ★   ★

When she finally stopped talking, Jon said to Richie, 'Help me get her into the house.'

Richie nodded and slipped his arm around her. With Richie on the one side of her, Jon on the other and Stephen bringing up the rear, she slowly walked up the steps of the verandah.

At the bedroom door Jon turned around, 'Guys—' She saw him look at Stephen. 'Excuse us.'

Richie closed the door behind them and Jon sat down on

the bed with her in his arms. For the longest time he simply held her. His sweater was comfortingly rough against her cheek.

'I thought I was dying,' she said. 'I thought I was lost. I couldn't find my way back to the house. Where did you find me?'

He was silent for a moment. 'Not far. As a matter of fact, you were still in the garden.'

'It can't be. I was lost.'

'Hush,' he kissed her on the forehead. 'Don't think about it now.'

She concentrated on regulating her breathing. After a while she got up and walked to the bathroom. She splashed some water onto her face. When she returned to the bedroom, she ignored Jon's outstretched arms and sat down in a chair so that she could face him directly.

'There's something wrong with that computer game,' she said.

'What are you talking about?' His voice was still gentle, but there was an expression in his eyes that she could not fathom.

'I think you know.'

'Well I don't.'

'*The Angels' Key* is making people aggressive. Violently aggressive.'

'Oh, for God's sake,' he said and the note in his voice was one of pure exasperation.

Tia stood up and walked to the night table. She yanked the drawer out as far as the stop. Then she took the folder out of the drawer and threw it at him. The clippings cascaded onto the bed.

'So you explain this to me. Why are you collecting these? And why are you hiding them from me?'

His face was expressionless. He didn't answer.

'Jon,' she realised how exhausted she was. 'Talk to me.'

He blinked. He leaned forward and put his elbows on his knees. 'All right,' he said. 'All right. I'll be straight with you. This isn't my folder. It's Richie's. He's had a bee in his bonnet about this for a long time now. But Tia, this is nonsense.' He gestured with his hand at the clippings. 'Most of these people are fanatics. Kooks.'

'But some of these are first-hand accounts.' She picked up a newspaper cutting from amongst the pile. 'People talking about what happened to them while they were playing the game, or listening to *Angel* music. They come from all over. They can't all be kooks.'

'Look. I'm not saying that people don't experience strong emotions when they listen to *Angel* music. But that's the case with all music. If you start arguing like you do, you're going to have to ban everything: starting with Country and Western. All those tears in beers songs have been linked to an increase in suicides. I mean come on. Garth Brooks as the Evil One? Where are you going to draw the line?'

'But these poems . . .', she picked up a print-out. 'Have you read them? They're sick.'

He sighed. 'Tia . . . you never surf the Net. These poems are not that unusual. There's a lot of scary stuff out there. I'm a fan but even I have to admit the Net is a playground for the disaffected and disgruntled. You'll find some very creepy people crawling around cyberspace. They range from teenage delinquents to the truly disturbed. You can't blame this kind of sick fantasy,' he gestured at the print-out in her hand, 'on *Angel* music. It's not fair.'

She dropped her hand in her lap. She felt frustrated. 'I know *The Key* is what's driving me crazy. I know it's what's making me hear those terrible sounds; what's causing those hallucinations . . . It happened at that music festival as well . . . and that was the first time I was exposed to *Angel* music for any real length of time. Jon, I know it. Please believe me.'

He stretched out his hand and touched her cheek. 'You're still very upset by what happened tonight.' He paused. 'Frankly, I think it's time you saw a doctor. I wasn't that worried after the first attack you had after the festival, but now with this . . . breakdown . . . and with your mother's history . . .'

She looked at him bitterly. 'You think I'm out of my mind.'

'I'm worried about you.'

'Well don't be.' The exhaustion was suddenly too much for her. 'And now, if you don't mind, I'm going to go to bed.' She caught a glimpse of herself in the mirror behind him. White face, staring eyes, dirt on one cheekbone.

She swallowed and tried to sound dignified. 'I'm really very tired.'

★. ★ ★

When she woke up the next morning she was still tired, so tired she couldn't lift her hand. Inside of her was a tremendous sadness. She sensed tears running from the corner of her eyes and down onto the pillow.

She got up slowly. It took her several minutes just to put her arms through the sleeves of her nightgown. She felt like an old, old woman.

As she walked down the passage, she heard music. She entered the drawing room and saw Stephen sitting at the piano.

His face was half-averted. In repose his face seemed withdrawn, the expression slightly austere. The flat morning light gave his profile a pristine clarity, like a sharp-nibbed drawing in Indian ink. The music alternated between joyful ecstasy and haunting melancholy; his left hand trilling almost trance-like on the home key.

He looked up and saw her standing there, watching him. He let his hands fall into his lap.

She cleared her throat. 'That was lovely. Was that your own composition?'

He smiled and nodded and in his eyes was an expression, warm and uncomplicated. 'The closest one can get to God. Music.'

Getting up from the chair, he closed the lid on the piano and ran his hand along the surface. 'What a beautiful instrument. Computer music, which is what I normally work with, offers more freedom of choice with respect to tuning, but an instrument like this has such a mellow voice.'

'My mother would have agreed with you.' And suddenly she was overcome with such longing for her mother. In her mind she imagined again the sound of notes following each other with formal and dizzying perfection. How many, many times had she stood here, just like this, listening to Klio practising her scales – a long, spiralling thread of sound carrying on and on and on . . .

'Don't be sad.' Stephen was looking at her, compassion in his eyes.

'No.'

His hands were gentle as he led her to the sofa.

'Where's Jon?' she asked. 'And Richie?'

'They'll be back any minute. They left some of their equipment at the gongs yesterday and went back this morning to retrieve it.'

He took a pillow from one of the chairs, fluffed it and inserted it behind her back. 'There. How are you feeling?'

She tried to speak, but suddenly her lower lip trembled.

'Hey, what's wrong?' He took her hand in his.

'Stephen,' the words came out in a rush. 'Do you think I'm going crazy? I think Jon thinks I'm going crazy like my mother.' She pressed her hand against her mouth.

'I'm certain he thinks nothing of the sort.'

'He does too. He wants me to see a doctor when we get to Jo'burg.'

'Tell me what happened to you. Tell me everything.'

'Yes,' she said. 'It all started with the music festival.' It was such a relief to talk about it, even though it was difficult finding the right words to explain the angst, the fear. Her narrative was interrupted by long pauses, but Stephen didn't seem to mind. He didn't say anything; he just listened patiently while keeping his eyes on her face. Every now and then he nodded.

'That first time – the day after the festival – it was like I was the only hearing person in a world filled with deaf people,' she said, feeling spent. 'I looked at those students, at their unknowing eyes and I never felt so alone in my entire life. And now it's happened again.'

She took a tissue out of her pocket and blew her nose sharply. 'And there was this hum last night. I don't know how to describe it: it was this dreadful combination of terror and beauty. But I know I will never, ever forget what it sounded like.' She paused and looked him full in the face. 'So what's happening to me? Do you think I'm mad?'

'No, sweetheart, I don't.'

'So how do you explain it?'

'You're not mad. You have a gift. And your mother had it too.'

'What do you mean?'

'We live in an age of sound.' Stephen spoke slowly. She had the feeling that he was counting his words very carefully – as though unsure of how much he should tell her. 'Think about it,' he said, his eyes oddly watchful. 'Man has never, in his entire history, been exposed to as many sounds as he is today. We've also made great advances in acoustic technology. But our technology has made us deaf to what sound – and music especially – is really all about. We think of sound as air vibrations. We think of music as entertainment. And we take it for granted, because music is so accessible to us. It's on tap. But you can imagine what it was like thousands of years ago. How quiet it was and how rare and precious music was then. Modern man has lost sight of the sacred side of music. We're also creating enormous sound pollution. It's impossible to find any place quiet anywhere. And no one really listens any more. You said you felt like the only hearing person in a roomful of deaf people. That's about what it is. You're one of the few people around who are still able to really listen. You show a sensitivity to sound that most people simply don't possess any more. People underestimate sound. The trembling of a butterfly's wings can trigger an avalanche on the far side of the world. You should think of yourself as one of the select few who can sense the wings move.'

She was silent, trying to come to terms with what he was saying.

'And what about *The Angels' Key*?'

'What about it?'

'I think *The Angels' Key* is what's behind all of my problems.'

His voice was reproachful. 'You sound like Richie now. There's nothing wrong with *The Key* as such, believe me. And if you think the game is to blame, how do you explain your mother's problems? She never listened to *Angel* music, did she?'

Tia was silent. This was true, of course. Klio only ever listened to classical music. And she certainly never played any computer games.

He leaned over and gently brushed a stray tendril away from her forehead. 'Medical science knows about people like you: people who are hypersensitive to sound. It's rare, what's happening to you, but there are other documented cases. Unfortunately it's often misdiagnosed as a mental illness. But you shouldn't feel alone: there are others out there who share your gift: fellow listeners. Obviously your mother was a listener as well. And sometimes it gets too much for people like you and you suffer from sound overload. But really, you should look at it as a rare and precious talent.'

'But what about the hallucinations?'

'They're not hallucinations, they're aural images.' He lifted an eyebrow. 'In another culture, in another time, you would have been a person of great importance. Nine hundred years ago Hildegard von Bingen experienced what you did. And shamans have had this gift since the beginning of time: the incredible ability to use sound as a vehicle to go into a trance and take a magical flight into another reality.'

He sounded wistful. 'I wish you could take me with you.'

'Believe me, you don't.'

'No, I do.' He hesitated. 'Actually, I've experienced something similar once. Only once.'

She looked at him sharply. 'Something similar?'

'Remember . . . I told you I had a near-death experience as a child.'

'Yes.'

'That's when it happened.'

'I don't understand. What *did* happen?'

'It's difficult for me to talk about it. Suffice it to say that it was this experience which turned me into a listener. I understand what you're going through.'

There was a silence between them. Then she said, 'At least one thing is clear to me now.'

'What's that?'

'I think I know what happened to my mother. Last night I was completely disoriented. I didn't have a clue where I was. I think something like that must have happened to my mother. But she wasn't as lucky as me. She may have wandered off for miles and miles . . .' Tia swallowed. 'It must have been awful for her. There are still predators out there, you know. Leopards. And at night it's dangerous terrain. I can't stand thinking about it: all alone, lost, her head filled with these sounds—'

'Shh. Don't think about it.'

His voice suddenly changed and became deliberately brisk. 'Would you like to know what I've been doing all morning?' He gestured to the sketch pad on the table.

She nodded, glad for a change in topic.

He got up unhurriedly and walked across to the table. When he placed the pad in front of her she was surprised and a little disturbed to find herself looking at her own face.

It was an idealised depiction of her features. Certainly the jaw was more defined and the eyes bigger with the lashes immensely thick and dark. And there was something in the corner of the mouth and something in the eyes Tia did not recognise in herself. She did not believe she possessed those qualities. The eyes looked out of the picture fearlessly, and the set of the lips indicated someone who brooked no self-doubt. A faint smile lurked in the eyes and they reminded her of someone else, but she couldn't think who.

He had signed the sketch. His signature was dark and sprawling. The Y of Yale reached back to interlock with the S of Stephen: like the limbs of two lovers reaching out for each other.

She pushed the pad away from her.

'Do you like it?' Stephen asked.

She looked at the sketch again. From where she had pushed it to the corner of the sofa, it now seemed as though the eyes were fixed on a spot behind her. She suddenly knew of whom she was reminded. It was Klio looking out of those eyes.

'It's flattering.'

'It's the way I see you.'

He stood up. 'I promised those guys I'd have lunch ready when they get back. Do you feel well enough to help me?'

'Sure.'

'That's my girl,' he smiled approvingly. 'You're strong, you know.'

'Tough as nails, that's me.' But she wondered how she was able to smile, when she really felt like weeping.

As she walked in the direction of the kitchen, she suddenly spotted the two beer pots Isaiah had given her the day before. They were balanced next to each other on the wide window sill. 'Oh, I had forgotten about those.'

'Jon took them out of your car this morning. What are they?'

'A gift. From a friend.'

Stephen touched the cross on the surface of one of the pots. 'Do they have a religious significance?'

'Religious, but not Christian. The cross is a very, very old African symbol – it was used long before the missionaries came. It stands as a mark of protection. If the ancestral spirits see this mark, they may watch over you. Isaiah said I should leave them at the door.'

Stephen frowned slightly. 'At the door? They must be valuable. Aren't you worried they might get knocked over?'

She hesitated. 'You're right. Better keep them safe.'

She picked up the pots and, standing on tip-toe, placed them on top of the tall stinkwood display case. 'They'll be safe there.'

As she turned around, she found Stephen right beside her. 'Remember, I'm here for you whenever you want to talk.' He placed his hand on hers.

'Thanks.' She returned the pressure of his hand briefly.

His eyes suddenly looked past her. 'Jon,' his voice was light. 'You're back.'

She turned around to see Jon standing quietly in the doorway.

'Look,' Stephen said, 'our girl's much better.'

'I see,' Jon said.

DAY TWENTY-THREE

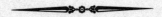

In the following weeks, as I looked deeper and deeper into the workings of the genetic code, I became convinced that God himself was a musician.

Michael Hayes, *The Infinite Harmony*

A near-death experience. No, not near death. Near life. An experience so ecstatic, he would forever be haunted by it.

In the beginning was the Word, and the Word was with God, and the Word was God.

The Word. Sound.

The tool with which cosmos was created out of chaos. The ancient Chinese believed the origin of the universe to lie in an inaudible sacred sound. In the Upanishads it says the syllable OM is the universe itself.

Tia had spoken of a hum: he knew it was the sound he had been searching for his entire life. And now he knew for certain she had heard it as well. It was now irrevocably part of her soul. Everything had changed for her, just as it had changed for him that day, long ago, when sound and music became the deepest part of him: the essential part of him. The day he had looked onto the face of God.

Twenty-one years ago. A lovely spring night in Wiltshire.

★   ★   ★

'Stephen. Ste-e-phen.' The girl's voice was sweet, but teasing. She flipped her black hair from her forehead and smiled at him, her gleaming lips parting slightly. She was only thirteen, but already she had the full breasts and rounded hips of a woman.

He watched her warily. He did not understand her sudden friendliness. Earlier this evening she and that coven of witches she called her friends had sniggered at him as he had asked her to dance. And then her boyfriend Clive, the Neanderthal rugger bugger, had threatened him. He hadn't known about the boyfriend, would not have dared approach her if he had. At fourteen, he was still small, slightly-built – certainly no match for Clive who played front row forward for the first rugby team. He made it a practice to stay as far away as he could from the school's jocks and their casual cruelty. He despised them: their crudeness, the sweaty locker room camaraderie, which seemed to be as essential to their wellbeing as oxygen. He knew they could never measure up to his intelligence. What's more, they knew it too.

This party tonight was to celebrate the birthday of the school's star football striker. Ordinarily he would not have dreamt of coming here and, truth to be told, he would not have been invited. But his father and Mr Norris were partners at the same bank and he and the birthday boy were both given no choice in the matter.

The girl smiled again and pulled her shoulders slightly backward. Her long hair brushed silkily against her bare shoulders. She had a tiny mole just below her collarbone. Her breasts strained against the thin cotton of her dress. She wasn't wearing a bra.

She turned slowly away from him, but looked back over her shoulder, that faint smile still on her lips. 'Come on.' The smile widened. 'I want to show you something.'

He followed her hesitantly back into the house. Earlier tonight he had sought refuge in the garden. He urgently needed to get away from the necking, the ecstasy, and the music. An enormous sound system, rigged up in one corner of the vast living room, has been pumping out amplified music at an incredible volume all night. Of course, as might have been expected from this crowd, the music itself was excruciatingly bad. Olivia Newton John. Boney M. Rod Stewart. He couldn't believe anyone would willingly listen to such pap.

But as he entered the house, he realised the mood of the party had changed. Saccharine pop had given way to heavy metal. Not that he considered this an improvement. He could feel the floorboards vibrate underneath his feet. The girl in front of him was swaying her hips to the beat. Even the chandelier in the ceiling was trembling. The spiky wooden chandelier was in keeping with the rest of the ersatz gothic decor of the house. Mrs Norris seemed to have a fondness for heavy tapestries, stained glass windows, steep arches and stone floors. There was even a gargoyle smirking from the top of every door. As he followed the girl down a corridor, he caught a glimpse of himself in a large silvered mirror. Navy blazer and tie. Flannel pants. Black lace-up leather shoes. The other boys were wearing jeans, windbreakers and trainers.

At the entrance to the living room, she stopped. He slowed his pace. He didn't really feel like going in there. To begin with, Clive might still be inside.

The girl was watching him, her eyebrows lifted in disdain. 'Come on. Are you afraid?' A flirtatious smile and then she disappeared through the doorway. After a moment's hesitation he followed.

The bone-jarring music had stopped. It was suddenly strangely quiet. The girl was standing next to Clive. She brought her hand up to her mouth and blew him a kiss. He realised that everyone in the room was looking at him. He could feel his face growing warm under the gaze of all those eyes. And then he realised something else. He was being surrounded. The doorway behind him was now blocked by three boys and on either side of him a circle was forming. Some of the faces around him were grinning. Others seemed just slightly apprehensive. A blonde girl, clinging to the arm of a red-haired boy with a pugnacious expression, giggled nervously.

A large boy with a crewcut moved towards him and pushed his face close to his.

'You're a pretty little sissy, aren't you?' He placed his hand against Stephen's chest and pushed.

'Think you're better than us, don't you?' Another blow against his chest. Harder this time.

'Trying to steal my mate's girl, then?' The boy stretched out his hand and flicked Stephen on the nose.

'What's the matter. Cat got your tongue? Why don't you answer me?' A fist landed against his head and this time the ferocity of the blow took his breath. His cheek was on fire, his ear stung.

He tried to speak but no words would leave his mouth. Behind him someone laughed delightedly – a vicious, sadistic little snigger. The expression in the eyes of the face in front of him made him go cold. Deep inside of him he could feel the terror growing.

He wouldn't give them the satisfaction.

'Why should I talk to someone who clearly has the IQ of a slug?' He uttered the words meticulously.

The expression of disbelief on the boy's face was almost comical. 'What?' The boy leaned forward. 'You fucking pansy.' A fist sailed through the air and connected just above his kidneys. The pain was so stunning, he bit down on his tongue and tasted blood. The next moment he was seized from behind in a neck lock. He couldn't see who it was, but he smelled the sweat on the skin of his attacker and felt nauseous. He tried to wrest free from the merciless grip around his neck, but the person behind him was heavier and taller. And then pain flared through the lower part of his body with such stupendous intensity, it left him slack-jawed. Someone had kicked him in the balls.

The pain in his groin was unbelievable. Tears came to his eyes. The arm around his neck was squeezing ever tighter. He felt lightheaded and at the periphery of his vision he saw flashes of light. He was vaguely aware that he was being marched towards the far end of the room. Rough hands were tying his arms behind his back – using his own tie as rope. Something heavy was placed on his legs, pinning him down. And now his face was dragged up against the amplifier. The next moment earphones were placed over his head and ears.

He looked up, his limbs weak with pain. From his position on the floor, the bodies around him seemed elongated, the faces peering down at him large and flat.

Everything was muted now. The boy with the crewcut was talking to him, but he could not make out the words – the sound deadened by the rubber insulation of the headphones. He moved his eyes from face to face. The expressions in the eyes looking down at him seemed only mildly interested.

He was afraid. He was so very, very afraid. If only he could hear. If only—

The earphones crackled. The music was faint.

He twisted his head and looked backwards. Clive was standing with his hand on the volume knob. He was grinning.

The music was much louder now.

Louder, much louder. It seemed to fill every hollow in his body. His ears were aching.

He tensed his body, strained his hands against the knots of the tie. His heart was beating like a trip-hammer. His ears. Pain.

Louder. Louder. His ears. Oh God, his ears.

Louder.

His head was shaking. Dribble trickled from the corner of his mouth.

Louder. Louder. Louder. The pain in his ears was unbearable.

An explosion of sound ripped through his head. His eyeballs bulged. He could feel blood running from his nose. His mouth stretched wide. He screamed. He could not hear himself scream but his body jerked and vaguely he knew that he had soiled himself. And then silence.

Oxygen was leaving his brain. Bright lights flashed inside his head. Neurons in his eye and brain were firing at random.

Red as blood the carpet underneath his cheek. The walls so white they made his head hurt. Above him the tall stained glass window shimmered, the jewel colours dazzling. He looked back at the wall and his retina carried with it the image of red and blue and yellow and transferred it onto the white of the wall: a delicate lacework pattern; real, but not real, like a divine imprint. And from the silence came a sound: a sound unlike anything he had ever heard or would ever hear again. A hum. It seeped into his mind, was sucked into his bones. Stardust floating through his veins. The beauty of it brought tears to his eyes. Someone had freed his hands. He looked down at them and he could see the bones like glittering dendrites glowing through gossamer skin.

He was floating now. The light around him bright as day. But the hum was growing fainter. No. Don't leave me. He was weeping. He stretched out his hand to grasp it, to bring it close to his heart, but the sound had dissipated. He was left only with the memory of it: a glimmering, aural shadow.

The throat-catching hospital smell. The prick of a needle against his skin. Gleaming, tiled walls. A voice said, 'He's losing consciousness again.' Blackness.

★ ★ ★

Afterwards, when he was recovering, he had told them about the light and the humming sound and the doctor had explained to his father that these were all neurological symptoms of a near-death experience. That what his son was describing – bright lights, the hum – were only hallucinations as powerful opiates were released by the brain to relieve the extreme stress of dying. Stephen did not understand what that meant and he did not care. He had lost the hearing in his one ear and would suffer from tinnitus for the rest of his life. But that was as nothing to him. He was possessed by the memory of the sound he had heard. He wanted it back: that ecstatic, humming sound. He wanted to hear it again. Would do anything to hear it again. He would search for it, even if it took him all his life.

The sacred sound. The Music of the Spheres.

As in the beginning. With the Word.

merely uncomprehendingly sympathetic. He was not even horrified.

'You don't need a doctor,' he told her. 'This is exciting. An aural adventure.'

'Stephen.' She looked at him helplessly. 'Don't you know how scared I am?'

'Most things in life that are truly worthwhile are terrible in some way or another. Beauty can be terrible. Truth always is.' The long lashes shuttered his eyes for a second. 'But you must embrace these experiences – not shy away from them. And I know you, you take your fences cleanly. You'll go for it.'

'I'm not the person you think I am,' she said exasperated. 'I'm scared of just about everything.'

'Nonsense. You're a risk-taker at heart. And this gift of yours: it requires sacrifice.'

She was still not quite at ease with him. Sometimes she would recognise in him something that was sincere and spontaneous, and drop her guard. And then his emotional antennae would pick up on this response coming from her and immediately he'd try to manoeuvre his way into her confidence; attempt to create a feeling of intimacy between them. A feeling of intimacy with which she was not comfortable. Still, despite her misgivings, she realised she was slowly coming to depend on him.

As for Richie, he had disappointed her. The folder with the clippings was his. She knew he shared her own suspicions and misgivings about the game. But Richie was reticent; evasive.

'It's probably just coincidence,' he said. 'Like Jon says: where do you draw the line? So if *Angel* music is not good for you, what about Heavy Metal? Techno? Rap?' He glanced at her, his face troubled. 'Can't throw out the baby with the bathwater, you know.'

'Richie . . .' she paused frustrated; unsure of how to continue. 'You once said if I needed you I could call on you.'

'I did.' His eyes wouldn't meet hers.

'Will you make me a promise?'

He looked at her warily. 'What is it?'

'I can't ask this of Jon and Stephen: they're too—' How to describe the two men's single-mindedness when it came to *The Key*: fanatical? '. . . too enthusiastic,' she finally said. 'So I have to ask this of you, because I don't care what you say, I know you're worried.'

She took a deep breath. 'Will you promise me that if you feel that something about that game is seriously wrong, that you will terminate it? That you will put an end to it?'

There was a long silence. He was staring in front of him, his eyes unseeing.

'Richie?'

He turned his head slowly and looked at her. 'I hear you.'

'Promise you will?' She held her breath.

He stared at her for one long moment. Then he nodded slowly, wearily. 'Yes, I promise.'

★ ★ ★

But if anything, it seemed to her as if the men were increasing their efforts to bring the project to a close. Since returning from Fluisterwater, they had worked hard, spending long hours together in the lab. When they returned to the cottage for dinner, their conversation bristled with unfamiliar terms and technical jargon that kept her at arm's length. She'd lie in bed and drowsily listen to their voices coming from the living room; the words strung together like some secret code she did not know how to break.

And something else was happening. At first she did not notice it, but slowly it became clear that below the surface of daily banter and friendship flowing like a sparkling river, there was black water stirring at the bottom.

The tension came from Jon. He was short with Stephen, sometimes to the point of rudeness. Stephen never responded in kind. When Jon was belligerent, he was patient. When Jon made a crack at his expense, he only smiled. In fact, Tia thought, it seemed as though he would go to any lengths to keep Jon happy.

And then the tension came to a head.

The men were working in the living room. She was in her bedroom, watching the news on television.

The camera panned over a steamy green landscape, showing a long line of refugees. They were mostly slender-necked women walking with unconscious grace while carrying children on their hips and balancing bundles wrapped in cloth on top of their heads. They were refugees from the renewed violence in Burundi. Almost the entire population of a small village close to the Mubarazi River had been massacred. For one stomach churning moment the camera focussed on dismembered bodies lying in pools of blood and vomit; surrounded by a poignant mish-mash of household articles: a kettle, a blanket, a phosphorescent yellow boom box, its aerial snapped in half like a broken twig.

The horror of it was overwhelming. When the camera zoomed in on a tiny orphan crying listlessly, a horrible gash on one chubby cheek, she couldn't bear it any longer and flipped the switch on the remote. The screen went blank. It was then that she heard the voices.

The curtains on the tall window next to the dressing table were drawn, but the window itself was open. The voices were indistinct, but there was something about the intensity with which the words were spoken that drew her attention. The voices were low, but the words were razor blades slashing through the soft air.

Next to her room, outside, was the tiny patio. The curtain at the window formed a screen, but from where she sat she could just see a long shadow creeping over the terracotta tiles. The shadow stopped moving. Someone was leaning his shoulders against the wall. She saw an arm rise and the red glow of a cigarette. Stephen.

He spoke and his voice sounded irritable, the words even more clipped than usual. 'Richie's always worried. He's losing his grip. Don't tell me he's getting to you too.'

The other voice was too low for her to make out every word; it came from the far side of the patio. But she knew it was Jon.

There was a pause and she thought she heard Jon say the words 'pushing too hard'.

Stephen sighed impatiently but she sensed a note of real agitation, almost panic in his voice.

'We're at a crucial stage of the project. We don't have time for this nonsense.'

Jon said something about 'running a few tests', but Tia could not make out the rest. The only other words she could hear for certain were the words, 'Richie insists . . . not too much to ask for.'

Stephen flicked his cigarette away from him. She saw the red tip flying through the darkness before fizzing out in the grass.

'Shit,' he said tightly, 'I am tired of weakness.'

Jon's answer was almost inaudible, but she could sense the tension running through his words. She heard the sound of shoes scratching on tiles and then Jon's voice coming from right outside her window. She had never heard his voice this cold.

'It's not weakness. Let's give him the chance to set his mind at rest.'

The silence between the two men was as tense as a shout. Stephen's shadow slid to the side. He was moving away from the wall.

Jon spoke again. 'If you don't agree, Stephen, it ends now. Right this minute. I promise you I will stop all work immediately. He's my brother. He deserves my consideration.'

Silence once more. Silence as dangerous as a poised mamba.

But when Stephen finally spoke his voice was soothing.

'Come on. This is too intense. Richie wants to run tests. Fine. No problem. When does he want to start?'

Jon's voice was still cold. 'After we get back from Fluisterwater this weekend.'

'We're still going? We got back only ten days ago. And it's a hell of a drive for a birthday party.'

'Well, that's where Richie wants the party to be. And it's his birthday after all. He gets to call the shots.'

'He seems to call the shots a lot these days. But OK, OK. As long as we get back to the lab straight away.'

'One more thing,' Jon said. 'Stay away from Tia.'

It was so unexpected, she almost gave an audible gasp. She held her breath. It seemed impossible that they would not hear the beat of her heart through the curtain.

'What are you saying?' Stephen's voice was wary. 'You know I'd never do anything to hurt you. Don't you trust me?'

'I trust Tia.'

'Jon – What's wrong with you? We're friends, remember?'

There was a long silence.

'I'm sorry.' Jon suddenly sounded incredibly weary. 'You're right. I'm sorry.'

Stephen sighed, an explosive sound like a valve blowing off steam. 'Forget it. Let's go inside.'

Their footsteps echoed flatly on the clay tiles. They stomped their feet outside the door on the entrance mat. And then it was quiet.

DAY FOURTEEN

'. . . the Pythagoreans . . . look for numerical relationships in audible concords, and never get as far as formulating the problem and asking which numerical relations are concordant and why.'

'But that would be a fearsome job,' he protested.

'A useful one, none the less,' I said, 'when the object is to discover what is right and good; though not otherwise.'

Plato, *The Republic.*

He was jealous. It was that simple. Jon couldn't remember ever feeling this way before, but there it was. He was jealous of his best friend and his lover.

It was illogical. Nothing was going on between them, he knew that; of course, he did. But they seemed to spend a lot of time together. And unfortunately, Stephen has sided with Tia on the issue of whether she should seek medical advice. He himself felt strongly that she should, but Stephen had managed to persuade her not to. And it was almost as if Stephen was suggesting that some kind of bond now existed between him and Tia.

The idea of it made him crazy. It was presumptuous and dishonest. What did Stephen really know about Tia? Did he know that in her most private moments she could be as ribald and as bawdy as a sailor? That she actually liked spiders and insects and would forever herd them gently outside whenever they strayed into the house? That her solemness could vanish in a moment of startlingly raucous laughter? Did he know what she looked like when she towelled her hair dry, her slender arms held high, the slight S-curve of her spine a visual image of such immense power it could make your mouth go dry? No, Stephen knew nothing of this. Only he knew what it felt like to go to sleep with Tia pressing up against him, writing her name on his back with her finger; to wake up to her mouth on him, her head a heavy weight on his abdomen. Stephen had not memorised her secret places: the tiny dent behind her earlobe, the soft, soft skin right next to the hollow of her armpit. Stephen had no knowledge of the bitter taste of her fingertips; the way her hair could spark with electricity. No, Stephen knew nothing of this.

So why was he jealous? Why did suspicion gnaw at him so? There was nothing there. Nothing to be concerned about. He had to get a grip. His relationship with Tia and a thirteen-year-old friendship were at stake.

What's more, his jealousy was turning him spiteful. He knew Stephen did not want to go to Fluisterwater again: he resented any minute spent away from the lab. And he had a point, of course. This close to the finishing line, they should not allow themselves to become distracted. To be honest, he wasn't that keen on going himself, but Richie had set his heart on celebrating his birthday at Fluisterwater and his jealousy of Stephen had made him throw his support behind his brother.

And then there were the tests. Stephen did not want to waste time on those integrity tests Richie was insisting they run. The tests were going to set them back a week at least, but again he had supported Richie. And again his motives weren't pure. Ostensibly he was backing Richie because he believed those tests to be necessary. In reality, he was simply trying to irritate Stephen. He felt slightly ashamed of himself: it was as though he and Richie were ganging up on their best friend.

He would make an effort tomorrow to be nice to Stephen and put his suspicions and jealousy aside. It was a special day after all. His brother's birthday. Some of Richie's previous birthdays had been less than happy occasions. Richie stoned. Or in rehab. Whereas this birthday would be a happy day. He'd make sure of it. Yes, he would make a real effort.

DAY TWELVE

OM. This eternal Word is all: what was, what is and what shall be, and what beyond is in eternity. All is OM.

Mandukya Upanishad

Richie's birthday was a big success. Tia was surprised, she had nursed misgivings about the whole thing. They were all irritable these days and the idea of the four of them together for two days in close proximity at Fluisterwater had seemed daunting. But she needn't have worried. For the first time in almost two weeks there was no static between the four of them: everything was as it used to be.

They had clowned around like children. She smiled as she thought of Richie's efforts to teach her the Lotus position. She had collapsed into a heap of giggles, much to his exasperation. The men had held an armpit-noise contest, which Jon won convincingly. And now after a birthday dinner of soup and pasta, they were having chocolate cake, roasted marshmallows and champagne while Richie opened his presents.

Jon's gift was a Far Side mug imprinted with the School for the Gifted joke. Stephen had bought Richie an exquisite scarf; cashmere on the inside, paisley silk on the outside. But she was able to say without reservation that her gift was undoubtedly the one that gave Richie the most pleasure.

She had taken the divining bone, which she had bought

from Isaiah two weeks ago, to a jeweller and had asked for it to be made into a key ring. Richie was enthralled. He listened spellbound as she explained to him that there were four different kinds of dingaka bones and that they were magic bones, which, in the hands of a medicine man, were tools for solving all kinds of puzzles.

He touched the ivory-coloured bone reverentially. 'So this bone tells the truth?'

'If you know how to read it.'

From his pocket Richie took the keys for the Mazda and attached them carefully to the key ring, the tiny bone swinging gently from the thin silver chain. Behind him on the wall his shadow, huge and misshapen, mimicked his gestures. 'Thanks,' he said and gave her a big hug. 'Thanks.' And on the wall behind him his shadow dipped.

After they had emptied the bottle of champagne, they went out into the garden to look at the stars. They lay on their backs, staring up into the blackness, their hands linked with each other. They tried to spot satellites and followed their path as they trailed through the sky: an army of whispering spies. In Jo'burg the stars were fuzzy, muted by the light glow coming from the city, but here at Fluisterwater they took your breath. As Tia looked up at them from within that chilly dark garden, their silver sparkle seemed chaste and remote and ancient. This night, she thought, this night I shall remember always.

Inside the house she took out the camera. 'Stand next to Richie there,' she told Jon. 'I want a picture of all of us together.'

Stephen immediately turned towards the camera with easy self-assurance. Richie laughed open-mouthed. 'Come on,' he said and tucked his arm around Jon's shoulders.

Tia looked through the view finder. The three faces seemed tiny and far away. Placing the camera on the mantelpiece, she set it on automatic and darted back to stand next to Jon.

'Say cheese,' she said as the shutter clicked.

*   *   *

She woke up to one zinger of a hangover.

'Oh, God,' she said weakly. 'Pills. Drugs.'

Jon looked amused. 'Could it be that you had a wee bit too much to drink last night, my sweetheart?'

She glared at him through slit eyes. He was looking more relaxed and clear-eyed than he had any right to.

'Listen,' he sat down on the edge of the bed next to her and the mattress dipped underneath his weight, 'the guys and I are on our way into town to fill up the cars. Stephen and Richie are taking the Mazda and I'm taking your car. Will you be OK by yourself?'

She nodded, winced at the pain in her head. 'Sure.'

'We shouldn't be too long. Get dressed, OK? When we get back we're taking off for Jo'burg straight away. Richie needs to start running those tests as soon as possible so we can get on with the job.'

Her mouth was blotting paper and she groaned as she got out of bed. The house was very silent without the men. In the living room she grimaced at the empty wine glasses with their purple stains; the ashtray with its dirty collection of cigarette butts.

She opened the side cabinet where Klio used to keep her music collection and let her fingers run past the the long row of CDs. Horowitz' Complete Master work recordings of Franz Liszt. Jon Cage's Chance Music standing cheek by jowl with a recording of Lowell Lieberman's *Second Symphony*. Stravinsky's *Firebird*. David Fanshawe's *African Sanctus*. Even a collection of Paul McCartney hits with the man himself staring out from the cover with that angelic but sensual face.

Some of her own CDs, bought when she was in high school and at college, were mixed in with her mother's collection. She hadn't listened to these recordings in years. Sinéad O'Connor. P.J. Harvey. The Beach Boys? Surfing, California girls and T-birds. In those days she hadn't known what a T-bird was. But the song's message – fun, sun, irrepressible optimism – had seemed very American to her, and very appealing. But she rather doubted she could cope with such determined cheerfulness just now. After hesitating for a moment, she selected the next disc on.

She slid the disc into the CD player and walked out the door to the sound of Schubert's ballet music from *Rosamunde*.

★   ★   ★

The music followed her as she stepped back into the bedroom. She didn't feel like a shower this morning. A warm, fragrant bath was what she needed. But that meant using the en-suite bathroom, leading off Klio's bedroom.

The drapes in Klio's room were drawn. The room was in shadow and the air in the room was dead air. She pulled the drapes aside and pushed back the window. From this room one could hear the stream at the bottom of the garden and the sound of water whispering. It was the reason her mother had chosen this room for her own.

The tiny pink and peach bathroom, which opened off the bedroom, was a late addition to the house. It was an enclosed bathroom with no window and no natural light. From the centre of the low ceiling hung a fringed lamp from which dangled tiny purple prisms.

If swimsuit manufacturers insisted on dressing rooms like this, Tia thought, as she watched herself in the mirror, they'd make a fortune. The dim light made her eyes look luminous, her skin smooth. It was like watching a picture of herself painted by a slightly myopic artist. She unbuttoned her nightdress and it fell to her feet with a soft rustle.

She turned away from the mirror. There were two prints in gold-leaf frames hanging behind the door. They were prints from Hieronymus Bosch's *Garden of Delights*. The pictures looked wrong for the room. In that feminine glowing room the finely drawn details of sadism and torture seemed incongruous.

Tia stretched out her hand. Her finger traced the outlines of the frail pink figures in torment, the fantastic growths, the dead fish, the rat, the two ears with the blade stuck between them.

She stopped and drew back. She had looked at those prints a hundred times before, but today she noticed for the first time that the tortured figures were being tormented by musical instruments: one tiny figure crucified on a harp, another tied to a lute, yet another closed up in a drum. She had never focussed on this aspect of the painting before.

She shivered slightly and turned her back resolutely on the pictures. She opened the taps and hot water rushed out. Soon the tiny bathroom was filled with steam. Small beads of moisture fogged up the mirror and dripped down its surface like tears.

Behind the frilly skirt of the small vanity table she found a glass bottle filled with coral-coloured bath salts. The salts were caked solid. She had to shake the bottle and knock it vigorously on the bottom to get any of it out. The last person to have used that bottle would have been her mother.

She turned off the taps and lowered herself into the water. Through the closed bathroom door she could hear, faintly, violin and piano in sweet harmony.

She closed her eyes. The water folded around her body as comforting as an embrace.

Her thoughts roamed and wandered with delicious senseless abandon. She was walking through a night as dark and as rich as boiling chocolate. Jon was at her side. Underneath their feet was sand, the colour of chalk. She could hear the ocean and see the curl of the surf. The air was heavy with the scent of cloves. Maybe, somewhere out there in the darkness, tiny flower buds were waiting to be handpicked by beautiful women with demure eyes.

Jon was kissing her and his lips against hers were so soft. His breath was sweet. Underneath her palms his skin felt smooth. His lashes were dark and his eyes were blue.

Blue?

Tia jerked her eyes open. Her heart was racing in her throat. It was quiet: the music had stopped. The record must have reached its end. She wondered how long she had been lying there; the water in the bath was only lukewarm.

She reached over and pulled the plug from the tub. Just as the water started its escape with a greedy slurping gurgle, she thought she heard another sound. Like someone opening and closing a drawer.

She shoved the plug back into its hole and the water stopped its downward spiral. She strained her ears in the silence. But the only sound to be heard was the sound of her own breathing.

She pushed herself upright and stepped carefully out of the bath. She took the large towel and wrapped it around her, folding and tucking the end into itself to keep it from slipping. Then she opened the door and stepped into the room.

Stephen straightened up from where he had been bending over the open drawer in front of him. In his hands he held a flimsy piece of underwear: a silky scrap of a thing.

Tia blinked in the sudden strong glare of natural light. After the soft light of the bathroom everything seemed sharp-edged. For a moment she thought she was imagining things. But then Stephen pushed the drawer to and the snap of the drawer as it slid shut was as abrupt as a pistol shot.

'What are you doing?' Her voice was high. She felt a tiny flame of anger running through her.

He didn't answer. He calmly propped his shoulders against the wall and looked at her, his arms folded across his chest.

'This,' she said, stumbling over her words, 'this is my mother's room – these are her things. You have no right.'

The light was from behind him and she couldn't see his expression clearly. His silence seemed brooding.

'Get out.' Her voice trembled.

He moved away from the closet, but did not walk towards the door but walked straight at her. Before she knew what was happening he had crossed the space between them and his hands were on her shoulders and he was pushing her up against the wall. His hands were cool on her skin, still damp and warm from the bath. The plasterwork of the wall behind her felt cold against her shoulder blades.

'Jon,' she said, 'Jon will—'

'Jon isn't here,' he interrupted her. 'I came back before them. It's just you and me.' His eyes were very blue. Ice blue.

He brought his mouth to her ear. 'Don't you know,' he said, 'how close Jon and I are? Don't you know we share everything . . . everything.'

She froze. 'Get away from me.' She heard her voice rise. She swallowed and tried to stay calm. 'Let me go.'

'I'm the only one who really understands you, Tia. You and me . . .' His voice was no more than a whisper, '. . . there's this strong attraction between us. You feel it too. I know it.'

And, God help her, she did. She felt her breasts tighten. But along with the attraction was also revulsion. A revulsion so strong it made the hairs on her neck rise, made her feel cold.

She twisted sharply in his grasp and brought her elbow up into his face with a sudden, vicious gesture. He made a muffled sound and moved back. There was blood running from his nose.

She grabbed at the slipping towel and ran for the door. He did not follow her. Slamming her bedroom door shut, she turned the key. Then she put her ear to the door and listened.

'Tia.'

She made no answer; breathed shallowly.

'Tia. I do not want you to tell Jon.' He was speaking slowly, enunciating every word with precision. She could hear him clearly; he was standing right by the door.

'Don't you hurt Jon. No purpose will be served by telling him. If you try to come between us . . .' His voice trailed off.

'Are you threatening me?'

'Don't do it.' His voice had a warning note to it. 'It will be a wicked thing to do. Destroying this friendship will be an evil act.'

She waited. The sound of blood rushing in her ears. And then the sound of his footsteps moving away from the door, moving further and further away. And then silence.

It was now so quiet the rhythmic ticking of the old-fashioned clock on the shelf next to the bed sounded loud.

She closed her eyes tightly to force back the tears. But still she tasted salt in her mouth and her eyes were burning.

$$\star \quad \star \quad \star$$

Jon reversed the car into a tight parking space at the back of B block, and switched off the engine.

He turned sideways to face her. 'So, are you going to tell me what's wrong?'

'What do you mean?'

'You've hardly said two words on the way in from Fluisterwater.'

'I'm just tired, that's all.'

'Hey,' his voice was puzzled. 'It's me, remember? I know something's wrong. Why won't you talk to me?'

She looked out the window and bit her lip. She remembered the coldness in Stephen's voice: 'Destroying this friendship will be an evil act.' And could she really claim to be the innocent victim here? Maybe, without her even being consciously aware of it, she had been giving off signals.

As if reading her thoughts Jon said very quietly, 'It's Stephen, isn't it? Is there something you need to tell me, Tia?'

Her heart jumped. She looked him in the eye and hesitated for just a second too long.

His eyes narrowed. 'My God, I've been wondering about the two of you.' Jon's voice was savage. 'Such buddies these days. Don't think I haven't noticed.'

His anger was completely unexpected. One moment he was still talking to her normally, the next she could hear him fighting to keep control of his voice. She watched in shock as a thick blue vein pulsed above his left eye.

She found her voice at last. 'Jon, please. It's not what you think—'

He yanked open the car door. 'Spare me.'

She grabbed desperately for his arm. 'Let me explain, please. Nothing happened.'

He looked at her without any expression. 'I'm late.' He got out of the car and slammed the door behind him.

It was all happening too quickly. She should have run after him, but her mind seemed slow on the uptake. She merely stared dumbfounded after him as he crossed the parking lot and disappeared through the revolving door.

He did not look back once.

★   ★   ★

The day dragged by. The students seemed even more listless than usual on a Monday. She couldn't remember ever feeling more wretched.

But apart from feeling miserable, she was also slowly becoming angry. He hadn't allowed her to explain; hadn't even given her the benefit of the doubt. She was angry at him, but she was also afraid. She was afraid she was losing him.

It was getting late. Dusk had long since fallen. She glanced out the window of her office. From here she could see all the way to the car park. The lot had emptied but her car was still there where he had parked it that morning, the maroon colour a sickly orange under the yellow overhead lights.

She took a deep breath and picked up her handbag. Well, she supposed it was a case of Mohammed and the mountain . . .

She crossed the skywalk and walked down the long empty corridors, her heels clicking on the shiny linoleum. The door to his office was locked and no light shone through the window above the door. Her heart sank.

She turned the corner. There was light coming from the computer lab. Through the glass partition she could see Jon standing with his back towards her. Next to him, on the chair in front of the computer sat Richie. He was leaning over the keyboard, peering short-sightedly at the screen. When she entered the lab he looked up at her. He had taken off his glasses and his eyes seemed small and pink-rimmed.

'Hi,' she said addressing Richie directly, 'How's it going?'

He shrugged. 'I started running the tests only this afternoon. Too soon to know.'

She looked at Jon. 'Are you ready to go home?' She was standing so close to him, his elbow was touching hers, but there was no warmth in his eyes when he looked at her.

'No. I'm helping Richie.'

Richie, sublimely oblivious to the undercurrents of the situation, shook his head. 'No need,' he said. 'I'm packing up myself. I'll work from the apartment tonight.'

For a moment Jon hesitated, but then he shrugged and picked up his satchel. Without waiting to see if she was following, he started to walk out the door.

Tia gave Richie a brief salute. 'See you tomorrow.'

'Sure,' he smiled, his eyes almost closing. As she stepped out she looked back over her shoulder. Her last impression was of him clumsily pushing papers into his bag, while simultaneously trying to shrug into his jacket. Typically Richie. Some of the papers had slipped from his hands and were cascading to the floor. She couldn't help but smile.

Jon didn't look at her or say a word as they walked out to the car. He unlocked the passenger door and waited for her to get in, his gaze fixed somewhere in the distance.

He drove smoothly: no sudden braking, no sharp acceleration. But still there was a kind of quiet aggression in the careful way in which he drove. The silent suburban streets were illuminated by street lights placed at even intervals from each other. From the corner of her eye she could see Jon's profile and the play of light on his face each time they passed by one of the lamp posts: light, shadow, light, shadow, light.

She felt her throat close. She wanted him back. She so wanted things to be the way they used to be. She reached out a tentative hand and placed it on his knee. Jon did not respond. Didn't even glance at her.

She heard the drone of a police helicopter patrolling the area and for one brief moment the inside of the car was lit as brightly as daylight. Then the helicopter moved on, its searchlight probing the shadows of other streets. She slid her hand down Jon's thigh, rubbing her palm against his leg.

When he stopped the car outside the front door of the cottage, she leaned over and put her hands on both sides of his face. 'Jon. Nothing happened.'

His eyes stared into hers unblinkingly. Then the lids closed palely, the lashes forming dark half-moons on his cheeks.

She placed her lips on his and for one moment he did not respond, his lips lying cold and chaste against her own. But then he suddenly returned her kiss with an urgency that startled her, his hands gripping her so tightly it hurt.

It was too desperate, she thought. As though they might never be in each other's arms again and needed to imprint on their senses the contours of each other's bodies, the texture of each other's skin, the taste of each other's kisses. It was too desperate – but she clung to him because she sensed that he was allowing himself to become vulnerable to her once more.

They stumbled into the bedroom holding on to each other and undressed each other with quiet urgency. The curtains were open and moonlight fell in silver splashes onto the bed.

He pushed her down almost roughly and placed his hands underneath her hips, pulling them up towards him. Brushing the heavy hair away from her shoulders he kissed her at the side of her neck and she felt like stretching and moaning and arching her back. He kissed her lips and she tasted the inside of his mouth and the slow burn crept across her body.

Gently, very gently, she moved her fingers in a tapping motion across his arms, his shoulder blades, all the way down his spine to where she knew a small patch of dark, baby-fine hair grew in the curve of his back. He was licking the hollow in her throat, moving his tongue sideways towards her armpit and then down; his tongue barely touching her skin.

His eyes were black as pitch. He placed his one arm across her shoulders. He cupped the palm of his other hand and placed it on her throat.

The phone rang.

Jon's body stiffened. For a few seconds they lay motionless, listening to the phone as it kept on ringing. Finally, Jon stretched out his arm and hooked his fingers around the receiver.

'Hello?' A pause. 'Richie?'

Tia heard herself make a small sound of protest. Placing her hand over Jon's, she brought the receiver to her mouth. 'Richie. This is not a good time. Call tomorrow.'

For a moment she felt Jon resist as he tried to wrench the receiver from her hand. She tightened her grip on the receiver but stretched out her other hand and caressed his neck, sliding her fingers between his hair.

The resistance was starting to leave his body, she could feel it. She continued moving her hips underneath him, drawing him on. She lifted herself a few inches off the bed and pressed her breasts against his chest. His hand dropped away from the phone and he lowered his head to kiss her.

She tried to replace the receiver on the stand, fumbled and felt the phone slip from her hand. She could hear Richie's voice. The words were faint but she could make out Jon's name. She reached over and yanked the cord from the jack.

Jon's breath was touching her skin. She turned towards him in the soft darkness and buried her face in his neck.

DAY ELEVEN

Oh, where will you go
and with what ship?
the earth is fire
the earth is stone,
and if you try to flee from the city that burns,
then I flee with you
like a woman hand in hand

N.P. Van Wyk Louw, From: *Ballade van die Bose*
(Ballad of Evil)

The police found Richie's body a few yards away from his car. The Mazda was parked a block away from Drake House in a makeshift parking lot littered with broken bottles and trash. He had been dead, they said, for at least six hours.

The police were not the first on the scene. A newspaper seller, a small boy of ten, had noticed Richie's arm peeping from behind a garbage can and had investigated. What he saw, made him run screaming to the grocery store on the corner of the street.

Richie's name and address were in the notebook that he always carried in the inner pocket of his jacket. When the police knocked on the door of the apartment, Stephen opened, still in his pyjama shorts and with shaving cream on his face.

Stephen's voice, as he recounted what had happened, was

hesitant. But his words meant nothing to Jon. His brother was dead. Richie was dead. But these were just words. They were empty, meaningless. They hardly made any sound. He stared at Stephen's face in front of him. There was a line running from the cheekbone to the chin. Strange, he had never noticed that before. And suddenly he knew what Stephen was going to look like as an old man.

Tia's eyes were sick. She was sitting on the very edge of the bench to which a police officer had escorted them when they arrived at the police station almost an hour ago. She had placed her hand on his, but she was shivering continuously, as if in the grip of a fever.

The police officer who had interviewed them had been sympathetic but in a hurry. With a minimum of fuss he explained that Richie's throat had been cut. The cut was very deep, extending all the way from the lobe of the right to the lobe of the left ear. 'Probably robbery,' the officer said, 'or a botched carjacking. The keys to the car are missing. Although I have to say,' he shrugged, 'the car doesn't look as if it's worth stealing.' He had offered them coffee, made them take a seat and had promised to be right back.

Tia looked at Stephen. 'You didn't notice he was gone?'

'I told you: he came back from the lab and worked at his computer for about an hour or so. Then he called Jon on the phone. But I think he had difficulty getting through or something.'

Jon saw Tia flinch. And suddenly he felt such anger towards her, he wanted to slap her face. The thought shocked him. He was being unfair, he knew that. But he couldn't help it. If she had allowed him to take that call . . .

Stephen's voice was patient. 'Shortly after he had made the call he said he was going to drive over to the cottage to talk to Jon. I didn't think anything of it. It was already late and I went to bed. When I woke up this morning I just assumed he had stayed over with you guys rather than drive back at that time of night.'

Tia didn't answer. She turned her head away. After a while

she picked up the ashtray on the low coffee table and started spinning it round and around the smooth surface of the table. It was getting on Jon's nerves. He wanted her to stop. Now. Immediately.

'Excuse me, are you the relatives of Richard Falconer?' Jon looked up from the spinning ashtray to find yet another police officer standing in front of them. This one was dressed in plain clothes. He had shrewd eyes but a diffident way of speaking.

'I am,' he started to rise to his feet.

'I'm very sorry for your loss. Very sorry.' The man held out his hand. 'My name is Detective Vermeulen. I've been assigned to your brother's case.'

He had difficulty concentrating on the man's words. He spoke so quickly and so softly. He was now telling them that Richie's glasses had been found not far from the body. They were broken and it looked as though someone had stepped on them on purpose.

'How poor was his eyesight?' Vermeulen asked.

'Very. He must have been helpless without his glasses.'

This was no exaggeration. As far back as Jon could remember, Richie had had problems with his vision. He often thought his brother must have been born with a tiny pair of spectacles already fixed to his nose. The pebble glasses had made him a ready target among other kids and he often returned home after school, his glasses broken, the buttons on his shirt torn off. Only in high school, when Richie had reached his full height – a head taller than even the teachers – did the teasing and bullying stop. But his eyesight had deteriorated steadily over the years. Only the other day Stephen had hidden Richie's glasses as a prank and Richie had moved through the room like a man walking under water.

Richie's wallet was missing, as well as his car keys. 'If we find these items,' Vermeulen said, 'the wallet and the keys – we'll find the killer.'

'But you will find him?'

Vermeulen sighed. 'Mr Falconer, we have one of the highest – if not *the* highest – violent crime rates in the world. We are understaffed and overstretched.' He paused and sighed again. 'We'll do our best.'

It was past noon by the time they were able to leave the station.

'So,' Stephen said, 'I'll see you guys later.' He had a pinched look to his nostrils. His hands were balled into fists inside the pockets of his jeans.

Jon nodded. A part of him wanted to tell Stephen to come with them, but he couldn't bring himself to utter the words. He stared after the tall figure, walking with such easy grace, until it became a mere spot in the distance. He stood there until Stephen finally turned a corner and disappeared from view.

They were silent all the way back to the cottage. Tia drove and he got out before she had finished parking the car.

Inside the cottage he stopped in front of the pinboard attached to the wall above his desk. A snapshot of Richie and Tia was stuck to the one corner. Someone had tacked it up against the board rather carelessly: a pin with a small, red head was stuck through one of Tia's eyes. It gave her a startlingly malevolent look. He took the photograph down and looked at if for a few seconds.

Tia was facing the camera. The wind had blown wisps of hair across her mouth. Richie was looking down at her. He had his arm around her shoulders in a protective hug.

'Jon.'

He turned around. Tia was standing in the door, the keys of the car in her hand. Her eyes were stricken.

'What?'

'I'm sorry.'

He suddenly felt fatigued beyond belief. 'I'm going to lie down.' Without looking at her he walked into the bedroom and stretched himself out on the bed. He turned on his side and closed his eyes.

And that night he lay awake looking into darkness. His head was pounding. He was afraid to go to sleep. Afraid of seeing Richie lying on his back, looking up at the sky with dry wide-open eyes.

DAY NINE

[Music] whispers to us dim secrets that startle our wonder as to who we are, and for what, whence and whereto.

Ralph Waldo Emerson, *Journals*, 1836–38

The day of Richie's funeral dawned fresh and lovely. Feathery white cirrus clouds streaked the horizon. A light breeze was blowing and the air smelt clean.

The small funeral procession wound its way towards West Park cemetery and passed by neat houses and gardens in which flowers bloomed extravagantly: roses redder than red, and white marguerites and flowers Tia did not recognise that were butterscotch yellow.

The funeral procession moved very slowly through the stone gate posts and the wooden gates at the entrance to West Park. It stopped briefly and then continued until the row of cars reached the highest ridge of the cemetery.

The back of the hearse opened and Jon, Stephen, Ben and one of Jon's colleagues at work fell in line on both sides of the coffin.

There weren't many people at the grave site. Astrid was there, a few of Jon's colleagues and a book store owner who had befriended Richie. And Jon had agreed to a minister.

The soil around the grave was almost orange. Dust, fine

as flour, clung to the shoes of the mourners as they crowded around the opening in the ground.

The minister started to speak and Tia looked past him into the distance.

Richie's grave was in a lovely spot. It was so high here that one had a long, long view over the suburbs of Emmarentia and Linden with their unpretentious houses and emerald gardens and many trees.

Astrid was standing opposite her. Tia could see she was weeping. She was biting on her handkerchief and her shoulders were shaking.

Stephen looked like an angel. He was wearing a dark suit and a cream shirt and charcoal tie. The breeze ruffled his hair and the hair fell in golden wisps over his forehead.

Jon's eyes were black hollows. Tia gave him one of the white flowers she held in her arms and he placed it on the coffin as it was being lowered.

There was to be no reception afterwards. One by one the mourners left the grave site. Tia heard car doors opening and slamming, and engines turned on quietly.

Ben came up to her. For the first time he looked like the elderly man he was. The polished ebony of his skin seemed dulled. 'You must look after him,' he said to her and nodded his head to where Jon was standing.

'I will.' He nodded again and gave her a kiss, dry as paper. She took his arm and walked him to his car and waited till he had driven off. Then she turned around and walked back to the grave, her high heels sinking into the soft turf.

Stephen and Jon were standing at the side of the grave, facing each other. The sun was in her eyes and she couldn't see their expressions but there was something in their body language – something so menacing – it made her stop in her tracks.

'It's over,' she heard Jon say. His voice was dead. 'I'm ending it. I should have done it long ago.'

Stephen was leaning slightly forward, as if assuming a fencing position. 'You don't mean that.'

'Yes, I do.' The words exploded with venom. 'We should never have messed with this thing in the first place.'

'Jon.' Stephen's voice was a plea. He stepped forward and held out his hand as if to place it on Jon's arm.

Jon moved his shoulders violently. He lifted his arm and slapped Stephen hard across the face with his open palm.

Stephen's head snapped backwards. Without touching his face, he said quietly, 'You have no idea what *The Angels' Key* is all about. You think too small. You always have.'

Without another word Jon turned around and walked past her. His face was so white it shocked her.

She looked back at Stephen. Jon's hand had left a red mark on his cheek and there was blood on his lip. He saw her looking at him and all emotion left his face. Reaching his hand inside his jacket, he took out his dark glasses. In almost exactly the same words Ben had used he said: 'Look after him.' For a moment he paused, his head turned towards the grave. Then he walked away with long strides.

The wind sighed through the row of dark cypresses. A large bee circled the white flowers that lay on the grave like fallen stars.

*   *   *

'So what was that all about?'

'What do you mean?'

'I mean what was that with you and Stephen?'

It was as though he were looking at a stranger. He didn't recognise her. He felt remote from her, even as he noticed how pale she was. How burning her eyes. Black was not her colour, actually. The delicate freckles on her collarbone stood out sharply against her skin. Her skin seemed sallow.

'It has nothing to do with you.'

'What then?'

He turned away from her and started putting his papers together. 'I have to go back to the lab.'

'What?' Her voice rose sharply.

He hoisted his satchel over his shoulder. 'Don't wait up for me. I don't know when I'll be back. I might end up having to spend the night there.'

'You just buried your brother. How can you even think about *The Key* at a time like this? You already spent all day yesterday in the lab. This is grotesque. What's wrong with you?'

'I'll call you later.'

'Fine. Go. Just go.' She threw her handbag violently onto the table. It slid across the smooth surface and fell off the edge. The contents of the handbag – keys, lipstick, powder compact – scattered across the floor. The next moment she had slammed the bedroom door behind her.

Grotesque. On the way to the lab Jon thought back on Tia's words. He couldn't disagree with her. His behaviour must seem bizarre. But he was doing this as a kind of homage to Richie. He wanted to finish those tests on Richie's behalf. When Richie had first mentioned the tests, he had not believed them to be at all necessary. It was just one of Richie's harebrained ideas again. And of course he hadn't really bothered keeping his scepticism hidden from his brother. He now felt terrible when he thought of it. Poor Richie – always the one whose ideas were treated with kindly contempt. And still Richie had stuck to his guns with that kind of dogged determination he always displayed when he felt strongly about something.

What was more, it now seemed Richie was right.

Yesterday in the lab he had stumbled onto something he could not explain. But of one thing he was certain: instead of merely humouring Richie, he should have paid attention.

What made him feel sick with apprehension was that Stephen obviously knew what was going on. He had confronted Stephen at the cemetery with what he had discovered and Stephen's reaction had confirmed his suspicions. Something was very seriously wrong. And Stephen didn't want him to know.

The lab was empty except for two students in the corner with Walkmans clamped to their heads. He nodded at them and sat down behind his terminal.

As he logged on, he felt his stomach clench in uneasy anticipation. He took a deep breath and tried to stem the rising tide of panic within him. Calm, the thing here was to stay calm.

All those years ago, when he had first decided to make use of distributed computing in order to crack the problem of perfect tuning, he had used the DES Internet decryption as his model. Basically, what he had ended up doing was to break down the stupendously complicated mathematical problem of perfect tuning into many small parts. He had placed code for solving these small problems on a central computer, so that when people logged in to the Internet to play the game, their computers would download the code. Each of these computers would then send its solution of a tiny part of the puzzle via the Internet back to the central computer, where all these small solutions were collated. Of course, he had also made sure to create a backdoor with which to access the programettes if he should ever have need of it. It was a standard safety procedure.

Except . . . the backdoor was no longer working.

A virus might be responsible, and that had been his first thought yesterday when he first discovered the problem.

It wasn't a virus.

What he saw on the screen made him sit quietly.

He tasted salt in his mouth. No, it wasn't salt.

It was fear.

*　　*　　*

The ringing of the phone on the bedside table woke her. Tia winced as she opened her eyes. She must have slept in the full glare of the midday sun that fell onto the bed. Her body was sticky and underneath her armpits she could feel the prick of sweat. For a moment she was disoriented.

The phone was still ringing. She picked up the receiver, and all she heard was the thump, thump of loud music in her ear. An impatient voice came on the line.

'I'm looking for Tia Theron.'

'This is she.'

'There's a guy here—' He must have turned his face away from the mouthpiece, because she couldn't hear his next words. It was already difficult hearing him above the sound of the drums in the background.

'Excuse me?' She sat up straight in the bed.

'Oh, yeah. Says his name's Jon. He's had too much to drink and he doesn't want to drive back by himself. Can you come by and pick him up?'

He gave her an address in Hillbrow and then said irritably, 'Get here quick, will you? I don't want this guy puking all over everything.'

When she stood up she realised she felt more fatigued than before she had had her nap. Her mind was sluggish. She seemed unable to concentrate on the message she had just received. Or maybe she simply did not want to think about it. She looked at her watch. It was already almost six o' clock.

As she pulled the front door closed behind her, the sky was changing colour. The sun was losing its sting and the day was rapidly cooling. The city was easing into the Blue Hour. The tranquil hour, she always thought. The time when children were called in from the gardens; when young girls primped in front of their mirrors, their party clothes laid out on their beds; when weary commuters streamed out of the city towards the smoky townships of Soweto and Alexandra where shebeen-owners were polishing glasses and checking on supplies of alcohol and home-made beer. It was the good hour when hope and anticipation still hung in the air and the evening's disappointments and failed plans were yet unrealised.

Despite the phone call, despite the memory of Richie's funeral lurking at the edge of her mind, the tranquillity of the hour stayed with her as she got into the car and drove in the direction of the remote glittering tower and the ridge of lights at its base. It was only when she turned the car into the streets of Hillbrow itself, puzzling over the map spread out on the passenger seat beside her, that she felt anxiety crinkle her forehead and narrow her eyes.

Through the closed car windows she could hear the unrelenting beat of boom boxes, and gusts of shrill laughter. Hillbrow was a city within a city: a place for people to lose themselves in. Here the sky was bluish-green and on the horizon, red, as though there was a city burning.

Every now and then she saw the reflection of the car, ghost-like, as she passed by the empty facades of abandoned buildings, graffiti-splashed and wrapped in razor wire. Prostitutes peered from the shadowy doorways like shy butterflies. The sidewalks were packed with people who did not seem to care where they were going; their feet moving unhurriedly. The streets were glazed with the shiny stains of neon lights.

She was waiting at a set of traffic lights, when a man shuffled up to the car. He did not hold out his hand for money or try to clean her windshield. He simply leaned against the car, his face only inches away from hers. Through the curved glass of the windshield she could see small drops of greenish pus in the corners of his eyes and there was dribble on his chin. He held her eyes unblinkingly.

The lights changed and he stepped back. Looking in her rearview mirror, she saw him stare after her until she turned left and the silent watching figure disappeared from view. What was it about him that had so disturbed her? He was just another of the city's lost nomads she saw every day. But his appearance at her car window had seemed as significant as a prophecy. There had been something in his eyes of which she was nerve-end conscious. Something that gave her the same feeling she would have had, had she woken up to the sound of a stranger in her room clearing his throat.

By the time she found the address she was looking for, she was tense and jumpy and angry with Jon. She locked the car and activated the alarm. Then she walked in the direction of the scabby doorway and the broken neon sign, which told that this was the No Exit Club.

As she approached the doorway she looked down a small

alley leading off to the left. It held garbage cans that were beginning to disgorge their contents: a sad collection of bottles, wet tea bags, and what looked like a used condom. She drew a deep breath before putting her shoulder against the door. She did not want to touch the doorknob with its smeared smudges of fingerprints and palm marks. How on earth did Jon land up in a place like this?

The sweating walls inside were painted orange. The music was turned up very loud: a pounding of drums and a voice, slick as gel, uttering one word over and over again like a mantra.

There weren't many people in the club, it was still far too early for real business, and she spotted Jon at once. He was sitting by himself at a table, clutching at the edge with both hands as though afraid of falling over. When he saw her coming towards him, he gave her the sweetest smile.

She refused to notice. She sat down opposite him and shouted across the heavy beat of the drums: 'What the hell are you doing here?' She knew she was being too aggressive – he had buried his brother only that morning, for God's sake – but she was feeling scared and she did not like feeling scared.

He pushed out his head towards her and squinted and then opened his eyes wide as though he had difficulty focussing. 'I am having,' he said clearly without the faintest slur to his words, 'a little drink.' And he started to laugh, weakly at first, and then louder until he threw back his head and was howling with mirth. Each time when it seemed as though he might get a grip on himself, he would look at her and start laughing anew and she could only sit there silently watching him, with this cold, cold ache in her heart.

The music stopped as abruptly as though someone had pulled a plug. The sound of his voice, hitting the sudden quiet like an alarm must have shocked him, because he stopped laughing.

'Jon,' she said, 'what's wrong? Tell me.'

He put his finger to his lips. He leaned forward and said in an exaggerated whisper: 'Such a clever girl. You were right all along. Are you happy now? Why don't you say it? Why don't you say I told you so?'

★ ★ ★

Jon picked up the whisky glass from the table in front of him and drank deeply. Some of the liquid ran down the corner of his mouth.

'You're drunk.'

'That I am, that I am.' He nodded his head sagely at the glass in his hands. But then he looked at her and there was so much despair in his eyes, she felt the breath catch in her throat.

She got up and walked around the table. Sliding her hands under his arms, she helped him to his feet. 'Let's get out of here. Have you paid the bill?'

He nodded. As they moved towards the door, he swayed against her.

They staggered through the club door and Jon took a greedy gulp of the petrol fumed night air. He suddenly lurched to the side away from her and slapped one of the garbage lids onto the ground. The next moment he was throwing up with loud, rasping regularity.

For a moment she stood appalled. Then she hurried over to him and held his head as he cried and retched at the same time until finally his stomach heaved uselessly.

He sank to his knees and she sat down on her heels beside him and put her arms around his shoulders. She held him tight as he put his face against hers. His breath tasted sour and his cheeks were wet with tears.

'I'm so sorry,' he said. 'So sorry.'

She put her hands on both sides of his face and kissed him on the mouth. 'I want to take you home,' she said. 'Please, Jon, let me take you home.'

'No.' He pointed vaguely to the fast-food restaurant on the opposite side of the road. 'Coffee.'

'It's too dangerous here,' she started saying, but he was already crossing the road and she had no choice but to follow.

268

They entered the grimy restaurant and she left him sitting at a corner table on a vinyl-covered stool shaped like a hamburger. She walked over to the serving counter.

'A coffee, please.'

The girl behind the counter was young but the stoop to her shoulders told of boredom and fatigue. When she handed Tia the Styrofoam cup, she said in a monotone voice as if repeating a recitation learnt by heart: 'Management says to accept their apologies. From next month the Styrofoam cups will be replaced by environmentally-friendly recycled paper cups.' She pushed the change over the counter. 'Have a nice day.'

Tia walked back to Jon and he took the coffee from her with a hand that trembled. He did not add milk or his usual six spoonfuls of sugar.

'Now tell me,' she said, after he had taken a few sips, 'what you meant by saying that in there, about my being right. Right about what?'

He placed his cup carefully on the table. Behind his shoulder, through the window, she saw a video arcade sign flashing on and off. She saw the yellow lights of cars and the white scream of an ambulance driving past, and many people floating down the sidewalks like figures in a dream.

'Tell me,' she said.

And there, in that unlovely place, with the smell of French fries and old cooking oil hovering in the air, he did.

★　　★　　★

'You were right,' Jon said. '*The Angels' Key* is a trap. It leads to violence. I know that now.'

There was a long silence.

'But you told me it can't be.' Her voice sounded slow, stupid to her ears.

'I was trying to convince myself as much as you. But in my heart of hearts I knew. I wish I could look you in the eyes now and tell you I never suspected a thing. But that would be a lie. I have sensed that something was very wrong for a while now, but I refused to own up to it. I did not want to destroy everything I'd believed in for thirteen years. It's such a deeply elegant program. It's like I have this beautiful perfect flower in my hands. How can I hack it to pieces? How can I dismember something so flawless? I couldn't bring myself to give up the idea of perfect tuning.'

He paused. 'I was too greedy.'

Picking up the Styrofoam cup, he started to carve tiny marks in the rim with the nail of his thumb. There were small yellow marks on his collar, which she now realised were spots of vomit.

'Richie—' he stopped and took a deep breath. 'Richie had been concerned about reports linking violent behaviour with *Angel* music right from the start. That's why he kept that file. He was actually paying out of his own pocket for an information retrieval agency to keep track of all the reports. At first these negative reports represented only a trickle, but lately they've become a flood. People becoming mentally unhinged and violent. People suffering memory loss. Crowds at *Angel* concerts acting increasingly destructive. Because these incidents are far-flung – and because anti-social behaviour at rock concerts is so common – it's not that easy to see the pattern: unless you start looking for it. And the evidence keeps getting more and more compelling as the new *Angel* scale continues to form.'

'Well then, stop it. Stop it from forming.'

'I can't.'

'What do you mean you can't?'

He looked at her silently. The lids of his eyes were inflamed. The vigour, the energy she always associated with him was there no more and he looked old and tired and the flesh around his jaw seemed veined and soft as putty.

'You forget,' he said, 'about the game.'

She waited with sick certainty for him to continue.

'As we speak, people everywhere in the world are sitting in front of their terminals downloading the game. They'll sit there for hours. And while they're playing, the new scale moves ever closer to completion.'

'So pull the plug.'

He didn't answer, just shook his head.

'Why not?'

'Stephen and I are co-authors of the game. Neither one of us can unilaterally pull the game from the Net. Even if I did just that, he'd simply have it back on the next day and legally there's nothing I can do to stop him. He's been paying for the webspace not me. And he refuses to end it. Besides which, there's no time for legal wrangling. There's no time. We've run out of time.'

She spoke carefully, trying to control her voice. 'So you can't remove the game itself. Surely you can sabotage the program behind the game? So that the scale won't continue to grow?'

'I don't have the means any more to do that.'

The silence stretched out between them.

'I had a backdoor, but it's not working any more. At first I thought it was a bug.' His voice tautened. 'It wasn't.'

'What then?'

'Someone got in ahead of me. Someone is shutting me out.'

'Stephen.' Why was she whispering?

'I never thought he'd do this to me.' Jon's voice was blurred. 'He must have planned this a long, long time ago: months before I even considered something might be wrong.'

'Have you talked to him?'

'Yes. At the funeral. And also on the phone. The last time he hung up on me: he refuses to listen. He won't even consider terminating the game. We're so close you see.'

Another long silence.

She reached out and took his hand. 'That's what's really scaring you, isn't it? The fact that you're so close.'

'If it's already affecting so many people adversely, what's going to happen when the new scale is finished? How will people react to the music then? Do you know how many people all over the world are exposed to *Angel* music? How many ordinary people could potentially become violently aggressive? I'm not even talking about your usual delinquents or cybercreeps who are already pretty disturbed to begin with, or about people who find themselves in countries or societies where the situation is volatile. I'm talking about ordinary people. Just ordinary people. And we're not talking about hundreds of thousands of people. We're talking millions. Many millions. Even if only a fraction of these people are affected, it will still be devastating.'

She looked past his shoulder out the window into the gleaming street. A woman with a baby on her hip was reading the menu that was posted at the entrance; her lips moving soundlessly. The baby was fretful. Tia saw it frown and yawn and wriggle under its mother's arm. The woman put her finger in the baby's mouth and it quieted down. Its lashes drooped and its eyes closed. The woman finished reading the menu and shrugged. Then she turned away and started walking down the street, the baby's head bobbing up and down on her shoulder. Tia followed them with her eyes until they disappeared into the blaze of light and movement.

She looked back across the table at Jon.

'The *Angel* scale is not yet completed.'

'No. But we're very, very close.'

'How close?'

'It's impossible to say. Days. If we're lucky . . . a week.'

'Can you stop it? Even without the backdoor?'

'I don't know.'

'But there's a chance?'

He smiled and a ghost of the old Jon looked through his eyes. 'There's always a chance . . .'

She got up from her chair and held out her hand. 'I want you to show me. Take me to the lab. I want to see for myself.'

'Yes,' he said.

As they walked back to the car, she was only dimly aware of the surge of the traffic – uneven – like blood pushing through a faulty valve. She looked up at the steep outline of the Hillbrow tower and at the grey walls of the leaning apartment blocks and it seemed to her as though this was some decayed, destroyed city of the future she was looking at. And in her mind she heard a sound: a humming sound – the sound a wet finger makes when you rub it slowly round and around the thin rim of a fragile crystal glass.

★   ★   ★

The eighth floor was deserted and the lab was dark and empty of people. Jon pushed open the door and without switching on the fluorescent overhead lights, sat down in front of one of the terminals.

'Every time someone logs in to play *The Angels' Key* that person downloads a programmette.' He spoke in a startlingly uninflected, unemotional tone of voice. 'When Stephen and I first put *The Angels' Key* on the Net, I left a secret access code in every programmette so that I'd be able to update the code whenever I needed.'

He bent his face towards hers. Behind the sheen of his eyes seemed to lie a terrible blackness.

'This afternoon I accessed the central host computer and tried to distribute new patches to the programmettes, using the secret access code. The idea was that every computer logging in would then have its programmette altered. The problem was, none of the programmettes responded. Stephen has distributed a modified version that is shutting me out.'

Jon's hands moved over the keyboard. The screen flickered and then filled with the image of the *Angel* flower, slowly revolving.

As she watched, the flower suddenly started to change shape, unfurling from a tight, three-dimensional bud into two, long, drawn-out strips connected to each other by eight smaller lines in between. It looked like a ladder, she thought, a ladder, which was missing some of its supports.

'What is it I'm looking at?'

'You're looking at the new, perfect musical scale. Each of these eight lines represents a musical note. They are the notes that will form part of the future scale. Now you can see the scale isn't finished yet—', Jon touched his finger to the screen, 'there are gaps – missing notes, but as soon as these notes are formed, the new scale will be fully completed. Perfect tuning will be a reality.'

'How many notes to go?'

'I think – no, I'm almost sure – there will be ten notes. That makes it two to go.'

Tia looked at the gauge at the top of the screen. The arrow was hovering right where the yellow tier connected with the red.

'This is going to sound stupid,' she said. 'But if you're unable to simply terminate the game, can't you change it? Make it boring, somehow? You know, so people won't be interested in playing *The Key* any more?'

He shook his head. 'That's not stupid at all. But it would be impossible. People aren't playing because of the game plot or the graphics; they're playing because they're hooked on the music. And the music is based on the partial solution to the mathematical problem.'

'I don't follow.'

'See, the key to the problem of perfect tuning is that it contains within itself its own solution. As the small parts of the problem are solved, you get better approximations to the final solution. You get new scales. And each small solution uses the previous one for solving itself. Almost as if by playing approximations to itself, the true scale gets to know itself better. The point is: we were able to wire the solutions into the game as a continually increasing reward. And there's no way of changing that.'

He rubbed his eyes tiredly. 'No. There's only one way out.'

'What?'

'I have to find another scale: another scale that will perfectly break the symmetry of the new, *Angel* scale. A scale that is powerful enough to suppress the *Angel* scale. And I have to find it before it's too late.'

He tapped a key and the ladder folded back into itself to form the revolving *Angel* flower.

'Turn it off.' She looked away from the screen and out the window. There was a thin film of black dust where the moon touched the windowsill. From where she sat she could see it clearly.

'So we have a week. Approximately.'

'If we're lucky. And if we don't have another sudden unexplained acceleration in computing speed.' He brushed his hand across his forehead. 'New gamers are logging in on *The Angels' Key* every day. It's impossible for me to predict how soon the new scale will be completed.'

He paused. 'But it will be soon. Very soon.'

DAY EIGHT

Evansville
Pennsylvania
United States

The gun was heavy. It dragged at the fabric of his jacket. Maybe he should have left it in his locker, but he liked the feel of it against him. Sebastian touched the bulge above his heart.

He couldn't believe how easy it was to get a hold of the .22-cal. handgun. Chuckie Durco had set him up with a straw buyer who had offered him his choice of a Bryco 9mm semi-automatic and the .22. He would have liked the Bryco, but the price was way above what he had available to spend. Still, the .22 was better than nothing.

Sebastian picked listlessly at the hamburger on his plate. He never seemed to be hungry any more. The only thing he was able to keep in were Honey Nut Cheerios. Anything else made him wanna puke.

He sighed. His head was aching as usual and the din in the cafeteria seemed to echo inside his head. These days it often felt to him as though his head was this hollow cave, in which sounds zinged around like those shuriken stars he'd read about in *Neuromancer*. And there was the hum. It was with him always. And he was tired. He hadn't gone to bed at all last night but had stayed up for hours trying to guide his hero through the Valley of Despond. It had been the hardest part of the hero's journey yet and he had lost three magic numbers and two shaman songs during the long trek. And even after nine hours of playing he still hadn't been able to leave the valley's deadly terrain behind.

Across from him, at the other side of the cafeteria, Cecily McFee and Holly Sykes were sitting down at the end of a long table. Cecily's hair had that incredible golden sheen which never ceased to amaze him. She looked up and saw him watching her. She turned her head and whispered something into Holly's ear. The two of them looked back at him and sniggered.

He felt his face grow warm. He knew the tips of his ears were probably red: a dead give-away. His heart was suddenly hammering away in his throat and his fists were opening and closing as though he had no control over his hands.

Frigid bitches. A lesson, that's what they needed. A lesson. He blinked rapidly; his head felt as though it were splitting in half. What if he were to pull the .22 right now, right this minute and pump it into her pretty white neck. He could see how the bullet would slam into her chest. Would the force be strong enough to spin her around? And how much blood would there be? Like a geyser, violently spraying everything in sight with sticky red stuff? Or maybe it would be more like a slowly spreading stain, growing bigger and bigger.

His mouth filled with saliva. He swallowed convulsively. His fingers rested on his chest, underneath his jacket. He could feel the short hard grip of the gun beneath his palm.

The bell went off – a nerve-jangling burst of sound – and his entire body jerked. For a moment longer he sat there with his hand on his heart, his eyes like stones in his head.

OK. OK. He let out a deep breath. OK. He stood up and pushed his chair aside. As he walked towards the door he balled his hands into fists to try and stop them from trembling.

The Scale

DAY SEVEN

Our Sages tell us that . . . in the world to come the musical key will contain more notes. Furthermore, in the time of Mashiach, the musical scale will contain an additional note . . . and at the time of the Revival of the Dead . . . the scale will contain ten notes.

M. Glazerson, *Music and Kabbalah*

The beep, beep of her alarm clock plucked Tia from her sleep. She scrambled upright.

The room was dark. She had set her alarm for four a.m. Next to her the bed was empty: Jon was still at the lab. For a moment she sat still, waiting for her heart to slow down. She'd had that same nightmare again. Someone in the shadows. Someone watching her. Walking up to the bed. Touching her face.

She switched on the bedside light and threw the bed clothes to one side. Then, as she had done the day before, she got up and got dressed. So as not to wake the neighbours, she let the car run silently down the driveway into the street before switching on the engine.

And then she was driving through quiet, silent streets: past houses where no light shone from the windows and past dark gardens and deserted parks. And all she knew, all she had ever known, was the sound of tyres on the tarred surface of the road and the yellow pools of light from the streetlights flitting past her window.

As though her body were still sleeping between the soft sheets of the bed and this were but her shadow walking through a dream, she saw the dark bulky outline of the university in front of her, felt the movement of the elevator, listened to its slow whine in the empty building and walked into the lab where Jon looked up from his terminal with eyes so fatigued they seemed drugged. The symbols on the screen in front of him glowed: an intricate, mathematical tapestry that was constantly changing as he unravelled the strands that held it together; as he started over and over again like some mad weaver who would not be satisfied.

They hunched over the terminal together, pressing their bodies close together: the two of them alone in that big sleeping cathedral, and the air filled with the sounds of silence: strange creaking, clanging noises that echoed in the vast empty spaces.

Jon's cheekbones stood out sharply and the thick lashes and brows were startlingly black against the translucent whiteness of his skin. His eyes had a queer glow in them. It reminded her of the dark medieval passion burning in the fanatic eyes of a martyred saint.

She watched as Jon's sinewy fingers tapped out a complicated rhythmic composition on the computer keys.

'He's blocking me,' Jon said with stiff lips. 'Stephen's blocking me.'

On the screen in front of him was the *Angel* flower, a star-like cluster of white petals. Tia stared at the feverish white image. The flower seemed to vibrate with a demented energy.

Jon's hands moved; the tap of the keys was sharp and hurried. One of the petals turned red, detached itself from the cluster and floated silently upwards. When it reached the left-side corner of the screen it turned into a bright green circle.

Jon's fingers moved again, this time much more quickly. Another petal drifted upwards, and another circle joined the first.

She was holding her breath. The expression on Jon's face was one of anxious hope.

But then, just as the third petal detached itself, one of the round circles at the top of the screen started to dissolve: turning from green to red and then from circle to petal before drifting back into the heart of the revolving white cluster.

Jon was muttering under his breath. His fingers tapped out an urgent, desperate tattoo. But the tiny green circles were fading away one after the other. As soon as Jon managed to detach one petal, a circle at the top of the screen would float back into the orbit of the flower. With terrible regularity, with terrible implacability, the petals drifted back into each other's embrace like poisoned steel splinters drawn to a magnet.

'He's blocking me. I can't get past him.'

And Jon's fingers raced with manic urgency across the keys while she watched with growing hopelessness this keyboard to keyboard duel: two phantom swords crossing in the darkness.

DAY SIX: MORNING

Great Lakes region
Burundi
Central Africa

From afar the village seemed completely peaceful, Jabulani thought. Only the broken bridge, its wooden slats sticking up crazily, gave any hint of what had happened here. That and the long dusty red fingers of hard-packed earth, which marked the location of the mass graves. They were easy to spot: no grass grew on these filled-in trenches.

The last time such a great killing had taken place, he had been present when it happened and he would never forget the sights and smells of that time. The sweet odour of blood. The sticky noise made by the black flies. Corpses in the street.

This time it was different. He had been in Bujumbura when violence swept through the village. And it had taken him weeks to gather up the courage to return. By now everything would have been cleaned up.

But the presence of evil still hung in the air and the village had emptied itself of people. As he walked through the silent streets, past the battered door frames, the broken windows and shell-pocked walls, Jabulani knew that this time the village would not come to life again.

His house was destroyed. He looked at the roofless shell and the black stains left by fire around the window frames, and could hardly believe he had once lived here. On the opposite side of the road, his neighbour's house seemed strangely unscathed. But as he pushed open the door, he saw that the interior was in shambles. Only the large table below the window, where the man used to sit in the morning, drinking his coffee and listening to his yellow radio, had been left intact.

Jabulani walked out the house and into what remained of the village square. The sun was warm, but he hugged himself. And then he became aware of the sound.

He looked around him, but he could not find the source. He started to walk towards the river, wondering what it was that he had heard. And then, all of a sudden, it seemed to him as though everything around him was humming; as though a deep throated hum was emanating from every rock and leaf, seeping from the very ground on which he stood. The trees were vibrating; the air was alive; the water hummed as it rushed over the cliffs.

He started to run. Even though his bad knee hurt him and his breath became fire in his chest, he did not stop until he had reached the ridge on the outside of town.

He turned around. In the distance the village seemed quiet. Sunlight reflected off the white bell tower of the church. The air was completely still.

The killing was over. Why then did he feel as though the worst was yet to come?

DAY SIX: EVENING

One of the greatest of the mysteries of the science of sound is the strange phenomenon known as Pythagoras' comma, which since time immemorial has been to man a symbol of his fallen state of imperfection.

David Tame, *The Secret Power of Music*

It was late. The library was almost empty.

Tia walked slowly down the narrow aisle, her finger moving across the leather spines of the row of books in front of her. She had almost reached the end of the shelf when that nagging feeling of being watched came over her. She stopped and looked to the side. The aisle stretched long and empty ahead of her.

She turned and walked around the corner towards the next aisle. Just as she stepped out from behind the book shelf, she thought she saw something move from the corner of her eye. But when she jerked her head back, there was no one there. And it was quiet. The only sound was the humming of the fluorescent tube lights.

You have no idea what The Angels' Key is really about. You think too small. You always have.

Stephen's words at Richie's grave site. They had been scratching at her mind ever since.

She reached for a big encyclopaedic volume and took

another, smaller leather bound book from the shelf as well. With the books heavy in her arms, she walked past the low coffee tables with their untidy piles of magazines, past the tables with chairs haphazardly drawn to the side, past the empty carrels until she reached the reading room. She slid the heavy volumes onto one of the desks.

The pages were rice paper thin and edged with gold. She flipped the pages over until she found the section marked with an ornate, thickly printed P. She was looking for the term 'Pythagorean Comma.' She knew that this odd-sounding phenomenon was at the heart of the mystery of perfect tuning. The root of all evil as far as she was concerned.

Jon had called it a mathematical blip, a flaw. Mathematics was not her strong suit, that's for sure, but she was willing to give it a try. Moving her forefinger slowly down the page she silently mouthed the entry words: pastoral, pyiba, pyipar, pyknon . . .

Her finger came to rest on the next entry: Pythagoras.

Greek philosopher and mathematician. Sixth century BC. Born on the island of Samos. Best known for major contributions to astronomy, geometry and the theory of music. Subject of numerous legends such as that he had a gold shin bone and that he was named after the Pythia, the oracle at Delphi, who prophesied that mankind would be immeasurably enriched by his wisdom.

Pythagoras discovered that all music can be reduced to numbers and mathematical ratios and concluded that these exact same ratios can be applied to the universe and all phenomena within it. Pythagoras distinguished between three kinds of music: musica instrumentalis, commonplace music; musica humana, the unheard music made by each human organism (especially the harmonious or inharmonious music between soul and body); and the Music of the Spheres: the harmonic relationships between heavenly bodies, which produce divine music as the bodies rush through space. The divine music cannot be heard by human beings as long as mankind is in its fallen state.

Tia shook her head. Interesting but hardly illuminating. Her eyes wandered to the following section: a discussion of pythagorean numerology and neopythagoreanism. She allowed her eyes to skip swiftly over the sentences until she reached the second to last entry in the column.

Modern keyboard instruments are all purposely tuned slightly off key. Only the octaves are perfect: the fifths, thirds, fourths and so forth are tempered in order to accommodate the Pythagorean Comma. This interval is mathematically expressed by the ratio 531, 441: 524, 288. See Interval

This sounded a lot more promising. She quickly paged towards the front part of the book until she found the page listing the entry for 'Interval, calculation of'.

After working her way through long demanding paragraphs dense with references to 'just intonation', 'microtones', 'expressive intonation', 'mean-tone system' and even something called 'The Wolf', she stopped, appalled and irritated.

Without much hope she opened the second and smaller book. This volume was written in a style that was more accessible. 'Pythagorean Comma' did not appear as an entry word, but 'Sacred Sound' did. She smoothed her hand across the paper and started to read.

The sacred writings of the ancient mystery schools of Egypt, Rome, Tibet and India indicate that the knowledge of sound was a highly developed science. It was based on the understanding that vibration lies at the heart of all the matter and all the energy in the universe.

It is worth noting that this belief has found modern expression in the work of certain scientists working in the field of particle physics who are of the opinion that the structure of the atom can be reduced to ratios and numbers, which mirror the harmonic principles of music. These scientists propose that atoms react as though they have resonance and that the very nature of matter is a harmonic one; thus echoing the thoughts of the sages of ancient times. Furthermore, Pythagoras's theory of harmonics bears a strong resemblance to twenty-first century wave theory.

According to Eastern traditions, man's fallen state is the result of his musical misalignment with the shabda – the sacred sound that emanates from the spiritual source that created the physical universe. The phenomenon known as the Pythagorean Comma has become a sign of this tonal misalignment and a symbol of man's fall from grace. The Pythagorean Comma is a constant reminder that the harmony of mortal music is flawed . . . and so is man.

If the Pythagorean Comma is ever eliminated, the world will be in possession of a perfect musical scale and, according to mythology, the Music of the Spheres will become audible. It is predicted that this momentous development may be signalled by a period of great turmoil.

There was an odd ripping sound behind her back. Tia gave a small shriek and spun around.

The student standing behind her was staring at her, his mouth open. He was pudgy and in his one hand he held a sweating can of Coke. The forefinger of the other hand was still locked inside the ring at the top of the can.

'Sorry,' she took a deep breath. 'Just a bit jumpy.'

'Sure,' he looked at her doubtfully. As he moved away, he took another puzzled look over his shoulder before walking towards the elevator.

Everything was quiet now, but somehow she still had that feeling that she was not alone. There was someone else here, watching her . . . someone biding his time.

Through the large window ahead of her was the dark shape of the main building in the far distance and a pinpoint of light against the smooth blackness of the wall. She wondered if the light she was looking at was light coming from the lab where Jon was.

She needed to get out of here. Shrugging into her jacket,

she picked up her bag, but then realised that she had not yet finished reading the very last paragraph in the book that lay open on the desk. Still standing, she read the closing sentences:

It is said that should man ever succeed in finding a perfect system of tuning, he will find perfect truth. It is also said that perfect truth is not for man to seek.

★　　★　　★

As she hurried from the library towards the main building, cutting across the empty quadrangle lit by yellow security lights, she could feel her shoulder blades hunching forward apprehensively. She looked back over her shoulder. There was no one there.

At the main entrance she fumbled for her security card and passed it through the electronic scanner. The tiny red eye looked at her unblinkingly. But just as she was getting ready to run the card through again, it turned to green and the glass door opened underneath her weight with a faint moan.

The building was quiet. Towards her right the long wide corridor stretched silent and deserted and disappeared into a shadowy stairwell. Tia tilted her head back and looked up into the space above her; up to where the big skylight on the very top floor floated in the murk. She could see no light coming from any of the offices looking out onto the well.

She turned to her left and started walking past dark deserted lecture halls and administrative offices. The tall glass windows that lined the wall opposite her seemed almost white in the silvery gloom. In front of her was the waiting elevator: its doors open.

The elevator was so slow. It felt like forever before the doors slid open on the eighth floor. She blinked in the gloom. Without any of the electrical lights switched on and with only small slit-like windows in the walls, it was almost dark here. Behind her the elevator doors closed smoothly and she could hear the whine as it descended.

She turned the corner and headed in the direction of the skywalk. The click of her heels on the linoleum tiles was loud as she walked down a long narrow hallway past smooth silent doors. Just before she entered the skywalk she looked over her shoulder. In the distance was a yellow oblong of light. The elevator had returned to the eighth floor. Its doors were open.

She increased her pace, almost skipping now in her haste. She couldn't shake the feeling that there was someone or something just behind her. Something malevolent. She almost ran into the glass and Perspex tunnel. After the empty echoing space of dark corridors and gleaming floors, the well-lit skywalk seemed blindingly bright. And there, thank God, was the lab. She could see through the large glass windows into the room where the shrouded terminals stood lined up like a ghostly army.

There was no sign of Jon.

Just as her breath caught in her throat, she felt a hand on her arm. She screamed.

'Hey, it's me.' Jon was staring at her. 'What's wrong?'

'Someone . . . someone's following me.'

He peered into the long passage behind her.

'I don't see anyone.'

'I tell you, someone's out there.'

'OK, look.' He pulled her into the lab. 'I'll lock the door. See?'

Sinking down on one of the chairs, she tried to get a grip on herself. She looked fearfully over her shoulder. God, she felt so exposed with those enormous glass windows. Anyone could be watching them from the shelter of one of the many doors lining the long, dimly lit corridor.

'What's this?'

'What?' She looked back to where Jon was staring frowningly at his computer screen.

'Someone's trying to reach me. Let's see who it is.' He clicked on the tiny spinning icon on the screen.

The message was short: *On-line. Pyth Central. Now.*

Jon's face was grim. 'It's Stephen. He wants us to set up a real-time conference on the central computer.'

She felt her scalp contract. 'Where is he?'

'What do you mean? He's at his computer.'

'Yes, but where? Could he be around here? Anywhere close by?'

'Why would he be? You don't think he's the one who's been following you?'

'Maybe.'

Jon shrugged his shoulders impatiently and turned back towards the screen. As he waited for the hook-up to go through he said, 'Stephen's wacky but not violent. And as for stalking you . . . why the hell would he bother? He knows he can just walk in here. I've been leaving him messages begging him to meet with me. There's no need for him to hide.'

'How do you know he's not violent?'

'Because I know. I know Stephen.'

Hello, Jon. The words appeared on the screen slowly; as if typed with effort.

Jon's fingers tapped out in reply: 'Why won't you help me?'

Tia is with you, right? Hi Tia.

She reached over the keyboard and brushed Jon's hands aside. 'Answer Jon's question. Why are you doing this?'

Ask me nicely.

She hesitated. 'Please.'

A long pause.

From the very beginning I knew what would happen if we created a new musical scale. I could not do it by myself. Needed Jon. I dared him to solve the riddle of perfect tuning. Knew he wouldn't be able to resist.

She typed again, her fingers feeling clumsy. 'People are being hurt by the game. More people will get hurt. Why won't you stop it? Stop it.' She hesitated, glanced at Jon. 'For me, please.'

Moments passed.

For you I would do anything. But not this. And too late now. Not up to me any more.

She was aware of her heart beating in her throat.

'You're insane.'

I thought better of you, Tia. I'm not mad. I believe in destiny. And I want to help it along. This is not a tragedy. Mata kelap. The darkening of the eye.

'What the hell's he talking about?' Jon moved violently in his seat. 'I don't understand.'

Tia stared at the tiny flickering cursor. It looked like a luminous blob of white spittle. And in her mind came the memory of Stephen sitting opposite her in front of a flickering fire, his voice dreamy: 'The Indonesians have an expression for that: *mata kelap*, "the darkening of the eye". It's painful, but it usually leads to a necessary transformation.'

New words were forming: *The violence is of no account: a necessary waste product.*

Jon, has it ever occurred to you that the Pythagorean Comma doesn't only bear a startling resemblance to a cipher: but that it IS an encrypted message? A message about resonance phenomena? You and I are true believers: we know the universe and everything in it is made up of complicated systems that have multiple resonances that interact. The Comma describes a way to excite the fundamental, universal resonances for all natural systems. Isn't it stupendous? Isn't it glorious?

Jon was staring at the screen, his hands hanging nervelessly by his side. 'No,' he said as if to himself.

She placed her hand on his arm. 'What's going on? What's he saying?'

Jon did not even glance at her. The words were now appearing on the screen rapidly.

The Angels' Key is pumping additional energy into the human collective. The earth is starting to hum, Jon. The Pythagorean Comma will be the perfect energy conduit. We're standing at the brink of chaos. A new level of complexity. The next step in evolution.

Jon's hands moved: 'You're out of your mind.'

No, Jon. Think about what I'm saying. You know I'm right. You know it.

'I will stop you.'

Unstoppable. I am not evil. You are for trying to stop what has to be.

Long moments passed. Then the words: *I'll be in touch. Keep the faith.*

Tia stared at Jon. 'What was that?'

Jon's face was bloodless. 'He's insane. He's lost it.'

'Why? What did he say?'

'It's a totally crazy idea. He seems to think the Pythagorean Comma is the encrypted master program of the universe.'

'What of it?'

'Tia, Stephen believes the Pythagorean Comma holds the key to the building blocks of the universe. If the Comma starts to disappear and a new scale begins to form, that means the building blocks are starting to give way. What he's saying is that we're not just dealing with the scale in the computer game – we're also dealing with a vast scale on a cosmic level.'

She tried to make sense of this. 'But that's rubbish, right?'

'What the fuck do you think? Of course it is.'

'So why are you so angry?'

'I'm not.'

'Yes, you are. And you're scared.'

'Look,' he took a deep breath and she could hear him trying to calm his voice. 'I'm not disputing that modern man's activities – his resonance patterns – are impacting on the whole of this planet. We're creating excessive sound and excessive communication and this in turn is creating excessive feedback: global feedback. Stephen's right. The earth is humming: but this is hardly a new idea. It was already proven a few years ago by Japanese geophysicists. They identified a number of notes over two octaves that make up the earth's background hum: a kind of low frequency noise. There's no question that the sound pollution we create around us will inevitably have long-term consequences for our environment. But it will take time, a lot of time: the degradation of a planet does not happen overnight. Stephen, however, believes *The Angels' Key* is adding to the sound pollution tremendously – that it is feeding massive additional energy into the human collective – which is causing the earth to vibrate and hum even more strongly. He thinks we're approaching meltdown – and that it's just around the corner.'

'What do you mean by meltdown? What will happen?'

'Environmental catastrophe. Earthquakes, tidal waves. Avalanches. Disaster and death on an evolutionary scale. Stephen's insane,' he repeated. 'This is not possible.'

'What's insane is not so much that he believes in this stuff, but that he wants it to happen anyway. Why would he want that?'

'He thinks we're standing at the edge of chaos. That we could be entering the next level of complexity.'

'The next step in evolution?'

'Yes – whatever the hell that might be. And he thinks the violent psychotic behaviour of people who are affected by the game forms part and parcel of the whole process. Remember what he said about violence being a waste product? If you stick with his argument, he's right, of course. There's no getting away from the fact that violence is a necessary step in the evolutionary process. History is filled with examples where evolution has brought about annihilation of entire species.'

'The darkening of the eye.' She was whispering. 'First violence, then transformation.'

Jon said furiously, 'This is crap. I refuse to be distracted by the fantasies of a sick man. Just because Stephen's off his rocker, doesn't mean we have to go there. We have enough to contend with as it is.' He paused. 'But this is a complication. I was still hoping I could talk some sense into him and get him to help me stop the game. But if Stephen has these ga-ga Armageddon fantasies, he's never going to listen to reason now.'

'I've never trusted these things, you know,' she said, suddenly vehement. 'This mess just proves me right.'

'What things?'

'Computers.'

'Oh, hell.' His voice was rough. 'That's a goddamn simplistic way of thinking. This is not a computer gone crazy. There's no ghost in the machine. *I* am the ghost in the machine.'

The contempt in his voice made her chest feel tight. And then, to her dismay, she sensed tears – wet and warm – on her eyelids.

The next moment he was pulling her into his arms, kissing her face. 'I'm so sorry.' He kissed her eyelids gently. 'I never want to hurt you. I love you so much. You'll never know how much. You're my life, don't you know that?'

She closed her eyes and leaned against him. She did not want to move. She just wanted them to stay as they were, with the feel of his body against hers, so comforting, and with her face pressed against the musky warmth of his skin.

Opening her eyes at last, she looked past his shoulder. Stephen's words were still staring up from the computer screen: *the darkening of the eye.*

DAY FIVE

So when the last and dreadful Hour
This crumbling Pageant shall devour,
The TRUMPET shall be heard on high,
The Dead shall live, the Living die,
And MUSICK shall untune the Sky.

John Dryden, *A Song for St Cecilia's Day,* **1687**

Mata kelap.

He saw people, whole armies of people. Some had eyes that
were sad and lost. Some had eyes that were empty and vulgar.
But they all walked through the dirty streets of their diseased
cities unsuspecting and uncomprehending. Beneath their feet
the pavement cracked open in bloody veins but they did not
see. In their ears was a beautiful maddening sound, but they
did not hear. Only he, Stephen, was able to hear it; was able
to comprehend its glory.

Stop, he shouted at them. Stop. Listen. Don't you feel it,
don't you know what's happening? Listen, for once just stop
and really listen. Beneath his feet the earth sighed and he felt
it bunch like a giant muscle. Don't you feel it, he shouted
soundlessly. It's happening.

He turned around and saw across continents and across
time and distance and there were people running through
black grass. They had long thin necks, their hearts and organs

seemed exquisitely fragile inside the delicate sculpture of their ribs. They were in the grip of a dark passion that was bearing them relentlessly forwards. And the movement started small, but it was spreading from continent to continent. Because the world is a spider's web with every strand connected.

And now he was alone. Underneath his feet was ice. He looked down and underneath the ice, like flies in amber, were faces. The eyes were open, the hands pressed against the ice, palms upwards. They were casualties of war. The women, he could see, had had their breasts sliced off and the wounds were raw pink flowers. He heard weeping and when he looked up he saw angels sitting on every rooftop, cradling their bruised wings in their laps. But it didn't matter, none of this mattered, because the air was filling with a wondrous sound. The sound he'd been waiting to hear for the past twenty-one years. A sound on the other side of silence.

The world was moving into a new dimension. It would require sacrifice. Evolution is a brutal business. Things die. Precious things disappear forever.

He knew Jon thought he was out of his mind; barking – a candidate for a straitjacket. But Jon was a small thinker. He was worried about people hurting themselves and others. He was fixated on the violence, unable to see the big picture. A perfect musical scale would inevitably lead to the brink of chaos, but only at the edge of chaos would change – necessary change – take place. *Mata kelap.*

He had no fear of what was about to happen. He and Tia were both initiates. Listeners. They'd survive. As it says in the book of Revelation: *And I heard a voice from heaven, as the voice of many waters, and as the voice of a great thunder. And I heard the voice of harpers harping with their harps: And they sang a new song . . . and no man could learn that song but the hundred and forty and four thousand, which were redeemed from the earth . . .*

He and Tia both, they would be redeemed: able to learn the new song.

But Tia shouldn't be with Jon. She should be with him. He was the one who really understood her. He had been keeping an eye on both Jon and Tia: staying close. He listened in on their phone calls, monitored Jon's activities on the Net. And at night he visited Tia while she slept. He'd watch her. Listen to her breathing. And before leaving, he'd go right up to the bed: touch her face, just lightly. Even in sleep, her face was troubled. And at day she looked tired. In the library he had noticed how the skin around her eyes was dark and bruised-looking. He knew what was happening. As the new scale was approaching completion, she was experiencing more moments of heightened perception. He wished he could tell her not to fight it. She was part of a miracle: the Music of the Spheres was becoming audible to her. But she might find the experience unbearable. Soon she might think she was going insane.

Maybe she would.

But then – as he well knew – madness was a divine state of grace.

DAY FOUR

The key to the universe is no longer of use to anyone, because the exquisite edifice it once unlocked has crumbled into nothingness.

Jamie James, *The Music of the Spheres*

The shutters at Lepworth House were up and the near-empty rooms were in shadow. The museum was closed to the public, readying itself for major renovations that were planned to commence at the end of the month. But Tia had managed to persuade the caretakers to let her in one last time. She hadn't walked through these rooms in almost three months, but she used to be a frequent visitor and they still remembered her.

There were packing cases in every room, some half-filled, others still flat-packed. Some of the paintings had been taken down from the walls, leaving squares of dust against the off-white walls. As she walked up the stairs to the second floor, Tia wondered if she had made the trip in vain.

But no. Emmaline Lepworth was waiting for her. There she was, still in her spot at the far end of the long wide passage, her mouth still silently screaming, her eyes pouring tears, her large slender hands covering her ears in desperation. A Listener who could not bear to listen any longer.

Tia closed her eyes. It was so quiet here. From outside came the faint swishing sound of the gardener's rake as he gathered together the first fugitive leaves of autumn. But in here the air was completely still.

She hadn't told Jon, but that faint dizzying hum that had been her constant companion ever since her breakdown at Fluisterwater, had suddenly worsened. Over the past forty-eight hours she had experienced several periods of heightened perception.

She would find herself standing on the corner of a busy street, unable to move: an insect caught in a sticky web of noise. Around her were the sounds of sorrow and laughter; the sounds of the dying and the living: ambulances wailing, police cars screaming, the shrill voices of schoolchildren at a bus stop, the frenzied chatter of a group of young women in bright suits, the footfall of commuters hurrying, hurrying, the sound of a car backfiring or a gunshot, the crunching, metallic sound of destruction as a yellow caterpillar bit into the concrete foundations of a condemned building. And everywhere the sound of music and its throbbing incessant beat; pounding, pounding. Sounds that streamed into her head, entering every cavity of her body until it felt as though her body was overflowing with sound, as though her skull, like a vessel springing leaks, would give way and sound would pour from her ears and her open mouth and leave her head in a long, bloody, gummed-up stream of undigested noise.

Tia opened her eyes. Emmaline stared back at her in silent agony, offering no help.

She turned her back on the picture and slowly closed the shutters, which she had opened on her arrival. As she walked away from the mistress of Lepworth House, her footsteps sounding dull and tired against the uncarpeted plank floors, she remembered her last visit here. It was the day Jon had followed her. She could still recall the puzzlement on his face as he gestured at the picture. 'Why are you so interested in this painting?' And she had answered, 'It reminds me of someone.'

Tia turned around and looked back down the passage, back to where the gold leaf of Emmaline's picture frame managed to reflect the afternoon sunshine pouring through a tiny crack in one of the shutters. And as she stood there in that quiet, darkened hall she thought:

'It reminds me of myself.'

DAY THREE

Evansville
Pennsylvania
United States

His parents and Ray had left early that morning with the Masons for the annual company picnic. They hadn't even tried to persuade him to go along. Thank God they were finally getting the message to just leave him be.

Sebastian sat hunched over his keyboard. He was shivering continuously. His room was dark except for the glare of his computer screen. He never opened his curtains any more if he could help it. And by now his mom knew better than to mess around in his room. She had even returned his key and accepted the fact that he kept his door continually locked now.

His teeth were chattering and his hand was trembling so badly he could hardly steer the mouse. He tried to focus, but his head was aching so much today and the hum in his ears was deafening.

Something was out there watching him, he knew it. Since yesterday he had been aware of the fact that someone, something was following him. Something that would rip his heart out with one blow, that would feast on his brain. He could see it now: some creature with red eyes and a hooked claw for a hand.

But he had his gun. He was never without it any more. And he would use it. He would blast the shit out of anything that so much as touched his door. Let that door handle so much as move an inch. Just an inch . . .

*   *   *

st of the computers in the lab were draped in dust covers.
ly Jon's screen was a bright square in the darkness.

He leaned forward to look at Tia. Her eyes were wide
 scared.

'OK. So you know Pythagoras formulated a theory based on
 idea that music – divine music – is produced as the planets
h through space: the Music of the Spheres.'

'But we can't hear this music.'

'No. According to Pythagoras, only evolved human beings
 hear the harmony of the spheres. Anyway, Pythagoras
v the relationships between the spheres in terms of musical
ervals. From the earth to the moon was a whole step, from
 moon to Mercury a half step; from Mercury to Venus
other half step; from Venus to the sun was a minor third –
t equals three half steps – from the Sun to Mars a whole
p; Mars to Jupiter, a half step: Jupiter to Saturn another half
p until you reach the region of the fixed stars beyond Saturn:
t's another minor third. It's like a row of musical notes:
D,E-flat,E,G,A,B-flat,B,D.' He paused. 'Like a scale.'

'So?'

'Richie and I found these exact same notes in the rock gongs
Fluisterwater.'

'That's . . . interesting,' she said uncertainly.

'It's way more than just interesting. When I discovered those
es, I kept having the feeling that I was missing something.
re was something about them that rang a bell but I never
e the connection with the Music of the Spheres. But then,
ver even considered that they could form a scale because if
should play them on a keyboard, they would sound rather
ge: not at all musical. But Tia . . . I think I've found it.'

Found what?'

I think I've found the scale that will break the symmetry
e *Angel* scale.'

What?' He could see the blood draining from her face.

DAY THREE: EVENING

*There is geometry in the humming of the strings. There is music
in the spacings of the spheres.*

Pythagoras

The walls of the bedroom were bathed in a wash of light. It
was keeping Jon awake. He'd close his eyes, but still sense the
light on the other side of his burning eyelids: a glow, blood red,
instead of darkness.

Beside him on the bed, Tia stirred. 'You should try to sleep.'
Her voice was listless. He was worried about her. For the past
two days she had looked sick. But then, he supposed he didn't
look his best either.

'I can't sleep with that light on.'

'I'll complain to the Scotts tomorrow.'

'Leave them be. They're scared.' He knew it would be
impossible to talk to the Scotts. They were Tia's neighbours
and two days earlier they had been burgled. The house was
trashed; their dog's throat cut. Along with a roll of barbed wire
on the wall and a massive electronic gate, they had installed
several high voltage spotlights around the house. One of these
was painting the wall of their bedroom yellow.

He felt Tia stretch out her arm and place her hand against
his palm. His fingers were a good two digits longer than hers.
He splayed their fingers apart and held their hands high and saw

against the faintly lit wall the shadow of the two hands locked together: a broken-winged origami bird.

'Do you remember that poem you read to me that first night at Fluisterwater? *The Ballad of Evil*? The one that starts with Evil saying, "Do you know me? Have you looked into the mirror and do you know yourself?" '

'Yes.'

He placed his arm over his forehead, his hand masking his eyes. 'I think about that poem a great deal these days.'

She was quiet. And he did not really expect an answer. What could she say to him? Earlier today the arrow on the gauge had moved a hair's breadth into the red zone. And the line image of the *Angel* scale had changed. Instead of eight notes, the scale now had nine. Only one note left to go.

'It feels so long ago.'

'What does?' He turned his head on the pillow to look at her.

'That first visit to Fluisterwater. I remember how reluctant I was to take you there. And then . . . you were so excited to see the gongs. Do you realise it's only been three months? But doesn't it feel to you like another lifetime?'

The gongs. When was the last time he had thought of them? All of that – Fluisterwater itself – seemed unreal now. She was right. It did feel like another lifetime. Like a mirage belonging to a different reality. A place untouched by *The Angels' Key*.

It was quiet between them again. He was exhausted. His limbs felt heavy and his eyelids were starting to droop.

'Jon . . .'

'What?'

'I was in the library recently . . .'

She paused. He waited for her to continue. He knew her by this time. She wanted to say something to him, but she was afraid of his reaction, he could sense it.

'What is it, Tia?'

She sat up and crossed her legs. In the uncertain light he could not see the expression in her eyes but her voice when

she spoke was hesitant. 'Look, I know you don'[...] apocalyptic theory of Stephen's—'

'Damn straight.'

'But in the library I read this bit about th[...] Comma—'

'The *Pythagorean Comma*? What on earth ma[...] on that?'

'I was curious. I know it's what lies at the [...] *Angels' Key* and I thought it's high time I learn [...] Anyway, in this book I read, it says that centuri[...] ancient civilisations believed—'

'You're quoting folklore at me now?'

'Let me finish.' Her voice was suddenly sharp. 'I[...] ever in possession of a perfect musical scale, it says, [...] the Spheres will become audible and this event will [...] by great turmoil.'

He was so tired. He just didn't have the energ[...] 'People are becoming violent, Tia. My game is tu[...] dangerously violent. That's what we should focus [...] don't think we should worry ourselves overly mu[...] damn Music of the Spheres – Jesus.' He suddenly je[...] so abruptly, Tia pulled back in alarm.

'What?' she asked, her voice fearful.

He didn't answer; swung his feet over the [...] bed.

'Where are you going?'

But he only shook his head. The next mom[...] the room.

In the living room he sank on his heels ne[...] table. Picking up the two gong hammers fron[...] rest, he balanced them in his palms. For a long[...] he simply stared at them. 'You can be given the[...] can be no guide.' He spoke slowly, wondering[...] to where Tia was watching him from the do[...] clutched around her nervously, her eyes unc[...]

'Jon?'

'Get dressed. We're going back to the la[...]

'Yes. The *Angel* scale represents one side of the cipher. The rock gong scale might be the counter key with which to lock up the puzzle.'

'How?'

He hesitated. 'This is complicated. See if you can follow me, OK?'

She nodded. He placed his hand on hers, forced himself to speak slowly.

'OK. The traditional view in physics is that sound waves are linear waves that do not interact with each other, but can stimulate resonances in other objects. However, if you throw this model out the window, and subscribe to the idea of chaos theory, like I do, then all waves, even sound, are non-linear. OK so far?'

'Yes.'

'Good. So this would mean that the frequencies in the *Angel* scale interact, as well as resonate, with each other. So all the tones have to be present to complete the full scale. When all the necessary tones are present, you get feedback between these modes, which drowns out all other frequencies, allowing for a single dominant configuration. Now, I discovered that the components of the rock gong scale also interact with the frequencies within itself. Therefore, what I'm hoping for, is that when you combine the rock gong scale with the *Angel* scale that the gong scale will break the symmetry of the *Angel* scale by absorbing and releasing the energy to stabilise and diffuse the feedback from the *Angel* scale.'

He looked into her eyes. He could see she was struggling to make sense of his words. 'To put it very simply,' he said, 'the rock gong scale will neutralise the *Angel* scale.'

'Neutralise. As in counterbalance?'

'Yes – at least for as long as the *Angel* scale remains incomplete. Right at this moment, both scales have nine notes. If the *Angel* scale should be completed first, it will destroy the rock gong scale. But I won't allow that to happen.'

He moved his hands swiftly over the keys. 'I'm going to release a new programmette containing the tones I've measured from the gong, which will interact with the old programette. If I'm right, this new programmette will provide missing tones to the incomplete *Angel* scale to provide stability. The two scales will become locked in perpetual duel, perfectly balanced. At least I hope so.'

He took a deep breath. 'Only one way of knowing for sure.'

The screen bloomed white with the revolving *Angel* flower. Nothing happened at first. Then, without warning, one of the petals turned red, detached itself from the cluster and glided effortlessly to the top. When it reached the left-side corner of the screen it turned into a bright green circle.

Another petal drifted upwards, another circle formed.

And another. The three green circles sat neatly next to each other. Not one had drifted downward again.

He turned his head: his eyes met hers. In her eyes he could see the hope that was also touching his own mind.

Another petal detached itself. Another.

Another. And another.

And another and another. Nine perfect circles sat in a straight line at the top of the screen.

Tia put her hands to her ears, her gestures strangely hesitant, as though if she were to touch her head too abruptly, it might break apart like an egg. The expression on her face made him feel sharply apprehensive again. 'What's wrong?'

Slowly she turned her head first one way then the other. 'Nothing's wrong.' Her voice filled with joyful disbelief. 'The humming. It's stopped. Stopped!'

He looked at her face, her eyes; he touched her lips. He placed his palms on both sides of her face and started to laugh. She was laughing with him. The laughter started from deep within her and he laughed at the happy face he held between his hands: at the joyous eyes and the delicate web of laughter lines around them.

*　　*　　*

He was screaming. He couldn't stop screaming. Someone was pounding on the door, and outside he heard a voice urgently asking him if he was all right. But he couldn't speak, and he couldn't stop the awful keening sound coming from his mouth.

He took his arm and brushed it across the desk, sending the computer crashing to the floor. Pain. Terrible, terrible pain. His heart was breaking. He felt such loneliness as he had not felt since that day his mother had walked out the house without even so much as a backward glance. She had betrayed him. Everyone in his life was always betraying him. Tia. Now Jon. Such incredible emptiness.

He closed his eyes. He saw Tia falling backwards: her face white, her mouth a red gash in her face. Her hair streaming past her shoulders, a dark red cloud. But now her face was morphing into someone different: her green eyes turning black.

Jon. Jon was the one who was falling.

DAY TWO

6 A.M. US EASTERN STANDARD TIME

Evansville
Pennsylvania
United States

Sebastian lifted his head. He had fallen asleep in front of his keyboard. For the first time ever he had actually gone to sleep while playing *The Angels' Key*. For some reason the game had not been able to hold his attention and it seemed he must have passed out.

He peered around him. Through a chink in the curtains he could just see a sliver of sunshine. The house was quiet, though. Everybody must still be sleeping.

He peeked his head out his bedroom door. Yeah. No one else was up yet. His father's snoring came through the walls like friendly thunder. Ray's door on the other side of the hallway was half-open and he could see from here that his little brother was still asleep. The kid was lying on his back, his mouth half-open. Sebastian stared at him as though seeing his brother for the first time. There was just the hint of stubble on Ray's baby chin: his kid brother was growing up. He couldn't remember when was the last time they had actually spoken to each other. It might be nice to hang again; this afternoon maybe.

Sebastian lifted an arm and sniffed at himself. His pits needed a soap. When was the last time he had taken a shower?

He walked back into his room. Opening his closet, he took out a fresh T-shirt, a pair of pants. He hesitated. As he did every morning, he took out the gun from inside the elaborate chemistry set his grandparents had given him for his last birthday. He had never used the set, but he knew it was the one place his mother would never think of looking. For a moment he stared at the gun. Then he slowly replaced it in its hiding place. He didn't think he would need it today.

He walked over to the window and yanked at the drapes. Sunlight streamed into the room and he blinked his eyes against the bright yellow glare.

DAY TWO: AFTERNOON

There is what I would call the hero's journey . . . to bring forth in his life something that was never beheld before.

Joseph Campbell, *The Hero's Journey*

Jon picked up her overnight bag and carried it to the car. He clicked the trunk shut and turned to look at her.

'Have you got your plane ticket?'

Tia nodded. 'I wish I didn't have to go to this stupid conference. I want to stay with you.'

'You'll be back tomorrow. And you have to pay your dues. Earn your bread. I'll be here waiting for you.' His face was pale, there were deep shadows under his eyes. He had spent all of yesterday in the lab. He had needed to secure the main computer and stabilise and monitor the spread of the new programmettes.

But now he yawned. 'I'm wiped. I think I'll go crash.'

'So you'll be at the cottage all the time?'

He hesitated. 'I have to talk to Stephen.'

'No,' she said vehemently. 'Don't do that.'

'I've destroyed thirteen years of his life. Stephen is not an evil man. But obviously he needs help. A lot of help. I can't just walk away from him. Before I met you I had never been that close to anyone else in my life. I loved Richie, but with Stephen . . . it was something totally different. Can you understand that?'

'At least promise me you'll wait until I get back tomorrow. We'll go together. Promise me, Jon. Otherwise I'm not going.'

'OK. Promise.' He pulled her close. 'I love you, Tia.'

With his face only inches from hers, she looked at him intently, seeing as for the first time the hooded almond-shaped eyes, the strong nose and sensual mouth, the black hair curling away from his forehead. *El Caballero de la mano en el Pecho.*

Emotion overwhelmed her. 'I should go.'

'Tia.'

She waited. The sun was hot on her bare arms and as she narrowed her eyes against the glare, Jon's face seemed white and smooth. For a moment he seemed a stranger.

'I almost managed it, you know.'

'Managed what?'

'To give the world something unique. Something wonderful.'

'Yes.'

'It would have been really cool, wouldn't it. Perfect tuning.'

'Yes.'

'Too bad it wasn't meant to be.' He smiled, a smile full of sorrow.

She stretched out her hand to him, wishing to tell him that she understood, that she was so very sorry . . .

'Shh. It's OK.' He took her hand and placed it on his lips. She felt his mouth move against her fingers.

'Hurry back,' he said.

★   ★   ★

As the car moved slowly down the dirt road towards the gate, he raised his hand in farewell. Tia honked and shouted something from the window but he could not make out the words. And then she had turned the car onto the tarred surface of the road and he was only able to hear the engine of the car as it accelerated out of view.

315

Turning around he walked back into the cottage. His legs felt like lead and he was slightly lightheaded from exhaustion.

Inside the living room, he collapsed onto the couch. The room had an airless feel to it. On the window ledge was a small, cut-glass vase with stagnant green water and the shrivelled-up remains of a rose. And there was dust on the surface of the coffee table, on the edges of the bookshelves. Very unlike Tia. She was not content unless her environment gleamed. But then, the last few days had not exactly allowed her much time for domesticity. And suddenly he missed her, missed her dreadfully, even though she had been with him only moments before and the scent of her perfume was still hanging in the air.

God, he was tired. He couldn't remember ever feeling this fatigued. But he knew he would not be able to go to sleep. His thoughts would not let him.

The game had lost its power. The rock gong scale had, without any doubt, managed to break the symmetry of the *Angel* scale. The two scales were now keeping each other in perfect balance. Why then was he unable to relax?

He was sure the music no longer had the ability to incite violence in those who played the game, but there was something else nagging at him. 'The darkening of the eye.' Despite his professed scorn, he had been unable to dislodge Stephen's words from his mind. He had tried to ignore the thoughts that were plaguing him, but they were insidious. He hadn't told Tia of his fears. Since yesterday she'd been so happy, he didn't have the heart to spoil her mood. And he did not want to upset her needlessly. It might be that he was simply tired; that the nervousness he was feeling was because his mind was still overactive and would not yet allow him to declare victory: a natural enough reaction after such a hard-fought battle.

Last night, in an attempt to calm his misgivings, he had surfed the Net in search of information. But if he was looking for reassurance, he did not find it. The results of even such a casual search had been far from comforting. Still, none of it was conclusive.

Placing his hand inside his shirt pocket, he extracted a folded print-out of an article from a back copy of *New Scientist*. It was one of several articles he had retrieved last night.

He unfolded the piece of paper, and his eyes skimmed over the first paragraph: *'A moderate earthquake in California last year was preceded by a mysterious electromagnetic hum, says a geoscientist from Stanford University. This is the second time . . .'*

He lowered the piece of paper and stared in front of him, his eyes unseeing; his mind churning.

Sound had incredible power – it was a truth he accepted as absolutely as he accepted the axiom that oxygen was necessary for breathing. And it had always been his contention that sound pollution would one day lead to serious environmental damage. He had even written academic papers on the issue. But he could never subscribe to Stephen's apocalyptic vision of sound as the catalyst for a complete global meltdown. That was a bridge too far. That was lunacy . . . wasn't it?

The phone on the other side of the room suddenly rang loudly, causing him to jump. He sat still, waiting for the answering machine to kick in. He didn't feel like talking to anyone right now.

'Jon. Pick up.'

He stiffened. It was Stephen. The machine made Stephen's voice sound flat and tinny, but even so the note of pure rage running through the words was impossible to miss.

'I know you're there. Pick up.'

Jon got to his feet and walked over to the phone, staring at the instrument.

'Fuck you. Pick up. You owe me that at least.'

He lifted the receiver. 'Stephen.'

'Himself. Time to talk.'

'Don't you think the time for talking is over? You had the chance to help me put an end to something evil and you turned your back.'

'Evil? You're one to talk. Tell me, how does it feel to have maimed something so beautiful?'

Jon could hear Stephen's breathing on the other end of the line. When Stephen spoke again his voice was slightly trembling.

'Take a good look at yourself, Jon. In this little drama you get to wear both the white and the black hat. First building up something of exquisite power and then deliberately smashing it. Ironic isn't it? First hero, then villain. Although from your pathetically blinkered point of view you probably see it as the other way around.'

'What is it you want, Stephen?'

'Oh, no, my friend. I think it's a question of what *you* want.'

Jon was silent. The anger had disappeared but there was now something in Stephen's voice far more unpleasant than any outburst of temper.

Stephen's voice became sly. 'You've been surfing the Net rather frantically since yesterday. Why this sudden interest in natural disasters?'

The idea that Stephen has been monitoring him was highly unpleasant, but before he could respond, Stephen continued. 'Your mind is fighting the idea, but in your heart you know.'

'What is it you think I know?' The words were supposed to sound jeering, but they came out wrong. They sounded scared. *He* sounded scared.

'The scale, Jon. The scale in the computer game was only a reflection of the greater cosmic scale. A surrogate for the real thing.'

Jon didn't answer. Stephen was mentally unstable. He was listening to a disturbed person. He should remember that. Keep a grip on himself. What Stephen was suggesting was not possible . . .

'You've managed to stop the scale in *The Angels' Key* from growing, Jon. But the cosmic scale is out of your reach. The clock can never be turned back on the cosmic scale. The past two years have been bad ones: that flood in Bangladesh – remember? The earthquake in Silicon valley? And as I'm sure you now realise after your research last night on the Net, the number of earthquakes, tsunamis and other natural disasters has been increasing over the past few years . . . not dramatically, but pretty steadily. Why do you think that is?'

He sat there, the receiver to his ear, listening to Stephen's voice and he thought how odd it was that he should suddenly feel so completely detached from what was happening. But when he touched his forehead, the tips of his fingers were ice.

'The fabric of the environment is tearing, Jon. The stress created by sound pollution is too much. The building blocks are starting to disintegrate. With or without the help of the game.'

'You don't know what you're talking about.'

'I'm talking about a chaos cascade. *The Angels' Key* accelerated the process enormously, but even without the game the process of apocalyptic environmental decay will continue.'

'You can't believe any of this.'

'Can't I? Let's pretend we had never created *The Angels' Key*. The world would still be at tremendous risk from sound pollution, right? Granted, to reach meltdown would have taken a long, long time. Another millennium maybe? But then you came along. You created *The Angels' Key* and all of a sudden the game quantum-leaped the entire process of decay. And even though the game has stopped, the genie is out of the bottle: too much *Angel* music was played.'

Jon did not respond. He was cold and his hand was clenched around the receiver so tightly, his fingers were cramping. But he was completely unable to relax his grip.

'Too much excess energy has already been released into the environment, Jon. The end is near. Without the game it will take longer, yes. Another fifty, sixty years? But it will happen. And it will happen because people will continue to abuse sound. It will happen because it is impossible to switch off the overload of sound generated every day by the good people of this earth. The planet is drenched in sound and will continue to soak up energy in the future. Man's sound pollution is unlocking the puzzle of perfect tuning as surely as *The Angels' Key* used to do.'

'No!'

'Accept the unacceptable, Jon. The Pythagorean Comma is the master key to the universe. With *The Angels' Key* you had the opportunity to turn that key, but you didn't have the guts. But the key will turn without your assistance. And there is no way of stopping it.'

'There's always a way.'

'Not this time. There's no cure. There's no way you can flip a switch and suddenly turn the planet quiet. The process has its own momentum now. Without *The Angels' Key* it's going to take a few decades longer. But you haven't stopped the transformation, you've only slowed it down. It will happen. Even though you and I may no longer be around.'

'Stephen—'

'And keep this in mind. You were the architect *of The Angels' Key* and it was the game which kicked the entire process into fast-forward. Just imagine, years from now you'll be cold and dead, but your children will have to live through the chaos cascade pushed into high gear by their own father. The world will move into a new dimension . . .'

Stephen paused, his breathing shallow and sharp. 'How's that for a legacy?'

DAY ONE

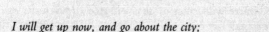

I will get up now, and go about the city;
In the streets and in the squares I will seek him whom my
*   soul loves.*
I sought him, but I didn't find him.

The Song of Songs, 3:2 *The World English Bible* (WEB)

Against the one wall of the lounge at Johannesburg Airport was a long row of payphones. Tia picked up a receiver and dialled, putting her one hand over her free ear to try and block out the noise of footsteps and bustle and airport announcements.

The answering machine at the cottage was still on. Earlier today, after she had finished her speech at the conference in Cape Town, she had called repeatedly from her hotel room but there had been no answer at either the cottage or at Jon's office.

She retrieved the car from the overnight parking lot and turned it onto the M2 highway. She put her foot down on the pedal, ignoring the speed limit that was posted every other mile. It was hot inside the car, so hot that she opened the windows and the wind rushed in, whipping her hair across her face, rustling the papers on the back seat. On the horizon a bank of thick white cumulo-nimbus clouds was massing together. There would be a storm before the day was over.

The pinprick of anxiety was growing into a nagging doubt. She couldn't wait to get home.

The tall black towers of Jo'burg came into view, poking into a sky that was slowly turning from blue to violet in anticipation of the coming storm. She could see the big letters of the wraparound Vodacom sign on the top of the Ponte building. And there was the glass facade of the old Stock Exchange, which always looked to her like the bulky back panel of a television set. In the plane she had wished for the moment when the city's skyline would materialise on the horizon in front of her and she'd know that she was close to home. But now, as she drove into its heart, the city suddenly seemed alien to her: a bizarre wilderness of glass and steel; a place she could not possibly call her own.

As she parked the car outside the cottage, she looked expectantly at the door. But the door did not open in welcome. It was only at this moment that she realised how much she had depended on seeing his tall figure come down the steps towards her, seeing him brush away the hair falling over his forehead and give her that small secretive smile; how much she had looked forward to feeling his hands in her hair, to hearing his voice. When she entered the lobby there was no answer when she called out. The disappointment was so strong, it stabbed at her.

The curtains were open. The kitchen did not look as though it had been used in all the time she had been away. The bed was made and the bathroom was pristine.

Without knowing what she was looking for, she opened the closet door in the bedroom. Jon's shirts were stacked neatly on top of each other. His good jacket was there, but next to it hung an empty hanger. Jon had taken his tweed jacket with him. She picked up his green sweater and for a moment she put her face against the soft wool. The scent of him clung to the fibres – as elusive as a fleeting thought.

Even Jon's desk was neat, showing none of the usual anarchic mess of papers and magazines and folders. His satchel stood propped up against the wall, the stencilled skull on its canvas exterior grinning at her foolishly. But his laptop was gone and something else was missing. She couldn't place her finger on it. What was it?

She walked over to the phone and dialled Jon's office. A disembodied female voice invited her to leave a voice mail message. Tia replaced the receiver, picked it up immediately and dialled the number for the department secretary, Anne de Vries.

'Anne, is Jon there?'

'He didn't come in today, Tia. Where are you, are you still in Cape Town?'

'No. I'm back. You're sure he's not in the lab?'

'Positive. I passed by there only a few minutes ago myself. But if I see him, I'll be sure to tell him you called.'

'Please. Tell him to call me urgently.' Tia replaced the receiver slowly.

It was then that she spotted the blinking red light of the answering machine. She pressed the playback button. The tape started to rewind. It was taking a long time. The message must be a very lengthy one, or else she had neglected to erase some of her earlier messages. Finally the tape stopped.

Stephen's voice said: 'Jon, pick up.'

★　　★　　★

Tia was sitting on the very edge of the couch, listening to the taped conversation for the third time. It was nearing the end.

'Just imagine, years from now you'll be cold and dead, but your children will have to live through the chaos cascade pushed into high gear by their own father. The world will move into a new dimension. How's that for a legacy?'

'I'm not listening to this any longer. This is insanity.'

'No, it's genius. True genius.' And suddenly Stephen was shouting, his voice sickeningly shrill. 'You coward. You arrogant bastard. I'm right. Admit it, you conceited prick. I'm right. I'm right.'

The tape clicked loudly and immediately started rewinding again.

Tia realised she was shivering. The hatred in Stephen's voice had been a tangible thing. The feeling of dread that now stabbed at her mind was so strong, it blotted out every other emotion.

She picked up the phone and dialled Stephen's number at Drake House. Jon had promised her he wouldn't go to Stephen, but after this conversation he may have decided to settle the matter face to face after all. But no one answered. The phone kept on ringing. She realised she wasn't even sure if Stephen was still living at Drake House.

There was only one way of finding out.

As she was about to step out the front door she looked back at the room. Again she had the feeling that something was missing.

And then she knew. The gong hammers were gone. The wooden rest was empty. Isaiah's gift to Jon was nowhere to be seen.

★   ★   ★

Twenty minutes later she inched the nose of the car into the sparse shade of a stunted acacia tree. The heat was now so oppressive that she scanned the sky, anxious for the first drops of rain that would bring relief. She felt her blouse stick clammily to her body and when she got out of the car there was a large sweat stain on the vinyl back of the driver's seat.

The margarine-coloured lobby was cool after the heat in the car. She glanced at the black board with the Bakelite letters that hung on the wall next to the entrance. She noticed that the names 'S. Yale and R. Falconer' were still among the names of the occupants of the building.

The door to the mailbox for Yale and Falconer was open, hanging half-mast on its hinges. She peeked inside. It held only a flier for pizza delivery and an open invitation to attend a street festival.

The elevator seemed to be out of order and she had to walk up four flights in a dank stairwell. There was no response to her knock on the door. When she knocked a second time, a woman opened the door at the end of the hall and peered out. Behind her Tia caught a glimpse of a shadowy hall with yellow wallpaper and a light with a cheap green plastic lampshade. The radio in her apartment was switched on and Tia could hear Boy George asking petulantly, 'Do you really want to hurt me?'

The woman squinted at her. 'You looking for Stephen? You his friend?'

Tia hesitated. 'Yes,' she said uncertainly.

'Spare key's under the doormat.' The woman started to close the door.

'Wait,' Tia said. 'Is he in?'

The woman stared at her. 'How would I know?' She lifted her hands, palms upwards and the bracelets on her slender wrists jangled.

Tia sat down on her heels and reached under the mat for the key. As she fitted it to the lock, it stuck and she thought for a second that it was the wrong key, but then it turned and the door swung open.

The apartment had the forlorn look of a place that was about to be vacated. The closet doors stood wide open and the shelves were empty. There was an overflowing waste bin in the bathroom, but no towels on the rails.

On top of one of the single beds was a suitcase, the lid open. On the bed, next to the open suitcase, stood Stephen's briefcase.

She put her thumbs on both locks and they opened with a click. Inside the briefcase were a few loose pencils and pens. A book of Leonard Cohen's poetry. Four CDs: The Clash's *Sandinista*; Yo-Yo Ma's rendition of Bach's Sonatas 1,2, and 3, Scott Walker's *Tilt* and a recording of Jean-Claude Risset's *Mutations I*. There was also a plane ticket. She opened it and noticed that Stephen had booked himself a first class ticket on British Airways, leaving for London the following evening.

She rummaged through the rest of the papers. One of the sheets of paper was slightly larger than the rest and dog-eared. She pulled it out from between the others.

It was the portrait Stephen had made of her that day at

Fluisterwater. The charcoal was smudged. The outline of her face was out-of-focus. It was as if someone had dragged a dismissive palm across the surface of the sketch. She stared at the face on the paper for a moment. The smudged eyes looked blandly back at her.

She was still staring at the picture when she heard something in the corridor outside the front door. The shuffle of shoes. She tensed – her eyes fixed on the doorknob, hardly breathing. But then a key scraped in a lock on the other side of the hall. A door slammed shut.

Taking a deep relieved breath she turned her back on the front door again. Once more she gave her attention to the briefcase.

At the bottom of the case was a book with a soft pebbled leather cover. She opened it. It seemed to be some kind of journal and she recognised Stephen's handwriting. Most of the pages were filled with technical jargon, but there were also entries of a personal nature. Even though she did not allow her eyes to more than skim over the content, her attention was repeatedly caught by her own name. But she ignored it and turned resolutely to the last entry. All she was interested in was finding out whether Stephen had met with Jon the previous day.

But the very last entry was dated three days before. The words seemed barely coherent. It spoke of pain. Terrible pain. Feeling guilty, she closed the cover on those anguished sentences. She had intruded on something intensely private, not meant for other eyes.

Her eye fell on the open suitcase. The clothes inside were neatly folded. She recognised the white shirt with the pale cream stripes that Stephen had worn for Richie's funeral and next to it Stephen's favourite black sweater. A piece of blue silk peeped out from underneath the black wool. She frowned and pushed the sweater out of the way. It was her blue teddy. The one that went missing. As she picked it up, a small green plastic bag slid from its silky folds. She opened the bag and shook out the contents into her hand.

'His glasses were broken,' Detective Vermeulen had said, 'as though someone had stepped on them on purpose.' She remembered the expression on the detective's face; as though he was telling them something obscene. And he had continued, his voice soft and embarrassed, and had told them of Richie's wallet that was missing and the keys to the car. 'If we find these items,' Vermeulen had said, '—the wallet and the car keys – we'll find the killer.'

Tia looked at the contents of the green bag that lay in her hand. Car keys. Just ordinary car keys. Keys that were strung together on a key ring: a key ring attached to an ivory-coloured piece of bone.

She closed her eyes and saw firelight and crystal glasses brimming with champagne and Richie's party hat throwing strange shadows on the wall. Richie opening a tiny package. The delight in his eyes as he rubbed the divining bone between his fingers; his voice filled with almost childish awe: 'So this bone tells the truth.' And she had answered, 'If you know how to read it.'

Tia opened her eyes. She was clenching the keys in her hand so tightly that when she opened her fist, there were red welts on her palm. She looked at the tiny ivory-coloured bone. The bone that tells the truth.

The truth. She now knew the truth.

She had to find Jon. She picked up the phone and dialled Jon's number at the university once again. After a few rings there was a click and then his voice mail message came on the line.

'Jon,' she said and was shocked at the note of desperation in her voice. 'Are you there, pick up.' But the line stayed quiet. There was just the faint swish of recording tape in her ear.

The gong hammers. They were not in the cottage. Jon must have taken them with him. So maybe he was at Fluisterwater. But when she dialled the number for Fluisterwater, no one answered. She could not bring herself to hang up. Maybe, if she held on long enough, there would be a click and his voice, drowsy from an afternoon nap, would speak into her ear. 'Tia,'

he'd say, 'Come to me. I've missed you so.' But still the phone
rang and rang: the loneliest sound in the world.

She opened her handbag and slid the keys into the side
pocket where, like a poisonous thing of the night, it slithered
from sight between her handkerchief and wallet. She hesitated
for a moment and then picked up Stephen's journal and added
it to the keys in her bag.

As she placed her hand on the doorknob, she was surprised
to see it trembling only a very little.

★　　★　　★

Outside the sky had turned purple. A long flicker of light
ran across the horizon and she could hear the low rumble of
thunder. The storm was about to break.

As she slid behind the steering wheel, a few fat drops
spattered against the windscreen. And then suddenly, the rain
came down – thunder rain and thick as glue – hissing and boiling
as it struck the steaming blacktop. The rain was coming down
so heavily that she could hardly see through the glistening sheet
of water cascading down the windscreen. The crash of thunder
was loud and long flashes of lightning shimmered outside the
windows.

She looked into her rearview mirror. Johannesburg was disappearing from view: the city's glass towers and squatter shacks
vanishing like a mirage behind a glistening veil of water.

DAY ZERO

The eternal silence of these infinite spaces terrifies me.

Blaise Pascal, *Pensées* **206 (392)**

She knew he wasn't in the house even before she entered. The house was dark and the curtains drawn shut against the blackness of the veld and a sky burning up with stars. It was already after midnight and there was no reason to suppose that he wasn't in bed sleeping. But the feeling that she was too late was overwhelming. As she sat in the car, looking at the pale windows and listening to the tic-tic of the cooling engine, she suddenly knew that the house was empty.

But Jon had been here. Through the side window she could see his car parked inside the garage. The key underneath the pot plant was gone and when she placed her hand on the doorknob, it swung open to the touch.

She walked from room to room and there were signs of Jon's presence everywhere. The bed was unmade. In the kitchen sink was the coffee mug that he had given Richie for his birthday with a small pool of black water and yellow cream in its depths. The hot water tap in the bathroom was dripping, the tiny sound glinting roundly in the darkness. It was a temperamental tap and in the past she had scolded Jon who never could be bothered with closing it properly.

But there was no sign of the gong hammers. Jon must have

them on him still. Maybe he was visiting the rock gongs? But it was so late. What was he doing out there alone in the darkness?

She lingered at Jon's desk. It was a mess. Books and folders were scattered across the surface. A half-empty bag of liquorice all-sorts sagged against the base of the desk lamp and a few pieces of sticky candy had fallen out. She picked up one of the sweating pieces. Her fingers were stained black.

Jon's chair was pushed back from the table. The laptop was open and the screen saver on. She pressed one of the keys and the screen saver dissolved. As she watched, Jon's e-mail record appeared on the screen.

She stared at the 'Mail Sent' column. Jon had sent Stephen an e-mail only five hours before. Her mouth suddenly dry, she clicked on the 'Read' button. The screen blinked and the message opened.

Dear Stephen,

You wanted me to acknowledge you're right. Well, here it is: you're right. Accept the unacceptable, you said. I have. I accept that the world is under tremendous threat: like some fragile crystal glass that will shatter within the next few decades because of the never-ending onslaught of sound. And yes, I accept that The Angels' Key had added to the pollution enormously. Do you feel better now? Do you feel healed by the fact that I accept the guilt?

But know this: I am not going to sit back and fold my hands in resignation. I've decided to write a new computer game – only this time it will be based on the rock gong scale not the Angel scale. As I write this, I'm at Fluisterwater. I drove here earlier today to speak to Isaiah. I gave him back the gong hammers and asked him to start playing the gongs regularly. An instance of technology reaching out to primitive power, you might say. My computer and his rocks: a two-pronged attack. If the gongs are played continuously the balance might hold. Oh, I can just imagine you shaking your head: I mean, come on, how can the sound of four gongs combat global sound pollution, right? But you've never understood the potency of the gongs. And even a single sound has enormous power and can influence other sounds. Just like a spider's web. Touch one strand and the whole vibrates. You taught me that, remember? The sound of a few gongs may be enough to start with. At least until I have my game up and running – whenever that might be.

Earlier today you called me hero as well as villain. I'm neither. I'm someone who got blinded by the search. I thought it was all about relentless perfection. It wasn't. It was about perfect imperfection. You understood that and so, I think, did Richie. But there's no such thing as evil music. I still believe that. There's just wanting too much.

Stephen, I loved you like a brother. I still do. Despite everything I know there's an unbreakable bond between us. And I need your help in this new quest. You and me and Richie. When we joined hands we were unstoppable.

Join hands with me now?

Jon.

Holding her breath, Tia clicked on the 'Mail Received' button. But the box was empty. There was no return message from Stephen.

Suddenly she was tired: tired enough to sleep for a thousand years. Walking into the bedroom, she wanted nothing more than to lie down on her bed. And there, amongst the tangled sheets with Jon's smell on them still, she went to sleep.

★   ★   ★

The first thing she saw as she woke up was the alarm clock. It was just after three o'clock in the morning. The house was quiet, but the quiet was tense, as if the house was holding its breath.

She got out of bed and pulled the curtain away from the window. It was still pitch black outside. And Jon had not yet returned.

The anxiety came flooding back. If he had indeed set out for the gongs, maybe he got lost in the dark, maybe he was hurt.

Possibilities – one more frightening than the other – crowded her imagination. And lurking in the deepest recesses of her mind was the image of Stephen . . .

But she refused to acknowledge that fear. Yes, Stephen was dangerous. Yes, he had – God only knows why – killed Richie. But there existed between Stephen and Jon a bond so strong. She remembered the look on Stephen's face when he had told her, 'I love Jon. Don't you ever forget it.' And she hadn't. Stephen would not hurt Jon. Would not harm him. She just had to repeat that thought to herself often enough and it would be true.

Daylight was still another two hours away. But she couldn't just sit around here waiting while Jon might be needing her. She took a jacket from the closet, wrapping it around her. She picked up a pair of sneakers and reached down to remove her high-heeled shoes. She stared for a moment at the fragile-looking pumps, at the ridiculous heels. Jon had been with her when she had bought these. He had helped her as she had tried them on and she remembered how his hand had lingered on her calf. She felt her eyes burn and shook her head. This surely was not the time.

She scribbled a quick note to Jon to let him know that she was out looking for him and attached the yellow sticky to his computer screen. From the top shelf in the kitchen she took the flashlight that she kept in case of power cuts. She was just about to let herself out of the house when a sudden thought brought her up short.

She crossed over to where her handbag was and rummaged around until she found Richie's keys. She slipped them into the pocket of her skirt. As she walked to the door, she could feel the weight of the keys where they brushed against her leg. Without a backward glance, she pulled the heavy door shut behind her.

The row of tall poplar trees rose up from the blackness like ghosts, their leaves rustling in the slight breeze. It was very dark, the moon hidden by thick cloud. She switched on the flashlight and the tiny pool of yellow light darted back and forth, as though it had a life of its own, as though her hand could not steady its erratic course. The restless yellow beam played across a clump of knotted vygies and the tiny, purple flowers seemed dull in the artificial light. A rock flashed white before again receding into darkness. For a split second she saw the curled jagged leaves of an aloe; a fantastic shape amongst the shadows.

She negotiated the stream carefully and the light in her hand skated across the surface of the water, unable to penetrate the deeper blackness below. As she opened the tiny white gate at the bottom of the garden, she looked back at the house.

The bedroom window from which she had pulled the curtains gaped. She suddenly had the feeling that she was being watched, that behind those velvet drapes stood a silent figure. For a moment she stood still, her body tense. But then, with a quick shake of her head she dismissed this fanciful thought. As if on cue, the moon broke out from behind a cloud and bathed the stone walls in a soothing milky light.

★   ★   ★

She had been this way so many times before with Jon, but the darkness slowed her down. And even though she still recognised familiar landmarks, they seemed different from the way in which she remembered them. The darkness played havoc with her perceptions of time and distance. It was as though someone had rearranged the landscape, but only slightly so, just enough to be unsettling.

From time to time she stopped and shouted Jon's name. Each time the sound of her own voice startled her and once a bird flew up from the grass right from underneath her feet, producing a moment of pure terror.

She must have walked for nearly an hour when she noticed the faintest glimmer of pinkish light on the eastern horizon, but the sky above her was still black as ink.

When she finally saw the towering rock pile in the distance, she slowed her pace. She was so close to the gongs now, but instead of running towards them, she wanted to stop walking, to delay the moment of actually reaching them. What if she should get there and find no sign of Jon? What if she called out and no voice answered? What then?

The sky had the shimmer of a pearl and long fingers of light streaked the horizon. But the shadows in the crevices at the base of the gongs were deep and dark. The gongs . . .

For a moment she stood as though someone had punched her hard in the stomach. She found that she was actually bent over in disbelief. Her eyes were seeing, but her brain was refusing to process the image.

Someone had defaced the rocks. They had been spray-painted with glistening white and red paint. The spray-painted symbols sprawled over the grey surface of the gongs and looked like a living growth, like an out of control cancer. The paint had a kind of phosphorescent quality to it and appeared luminous in the uncertain light.

As if in a trance, she walked towards the gongs, holding out her one hand. The paint had dried, it left no residue when she rubbed her fingers against the rock's surface. At the foot of the gongs lay several aluminium spray cans. The grass was trampled and blotched with white and red streaks. There was something indescribably vile about the scene. A holy place defiled.

The symbols and figures glared up unrepentantly from the surface of the rocks. The figures snaked across and around the boulders, but what at first sight had seemed like indiscriminate vandalism now appeared to be something different. There was method to this madness.

She walked from one boulder to the other and back again, her lips soundlessly forming the numbers: 531, 441: 524, 288.

The numbers had been spray-painted over and over. The symbols tugged at her memory, she knew what this was, she did, if only she could remember . . . and then it came to her: it was the mathematical expression of the Pythagorean Comma.

She looked in the direction of the one boulder that lay on its side a little way off. It seemed to be the only rock that was unscarred. As she started to walk towards it, she tripped and fell clumsily to her knees.

Behind her a twig snapped. A shoe scraped against a pebble. She froze.

She turned her head, stiff as a mechanical doll's, and looked over her shoulder.

Stephen was standing a few paces behind her. His stance was relaxed: one hand in the pocket of his trousers, his head turned slightly to the side.

For a moment she couldn't think, couldn't breathe. Then Stephen walked slowly towards her. She looked up at him, crouched at his feet, awkwardly balanced on her heels.

'Tia. Somehow I knew you'd come. So what do you think?' He gestured to the rocks with their spray-painted scars.

'You did that?'

'Childish of me, wasn't it? Only way I could think of to get back at those fucking things.' Stephen's smile didn't reach his eyes. 'I was always worried about these gongs. I didn't know why but I knew there was just something about them.'

Tia got to her feet and realised she had her hand clamped to her mouth in the classic gesture of horror. Like the heroine in a melodrama. Maybe, like those damsels in distress, it would be easier just to let her legs give way beneath her, to faint and then she'd wake up and Jon would be there holding her, smoothing the hair from her forehead and she'd be safe.

Something, some twinge of shame brushed her mind and made her straighten her back. When she spoke again, her voice was almost steady.

'Where's Jon?'

He didn't answer. Just watched her quizzically, rocking back and forth on his heels.

'You killed Richie.'

There was a long silence. He watched her with bright, glittering eyes. Then he said softly, 'Did I now?'

She slipped her hand into her skirt pocket and took out Richie's keys. 'I found this.'

He looked at the keys dangling from her fingers. He made no attempt to reach for them, but even so she pushed the keys quickly back into the pocket, as though afraid he might snatch them from her.

'Tia.' He shook his head in mock disapproval. 'You've been snooping around.'

'Why? Why kill Richie?'

'I had to.' He sounded as defensive as a child caught out in a naughty prank. 'He wouldn't listen. He insisted on running those tests. As a matter of fact, I think you had something to do with it. He told me he had made you a promise.'

Will you promise me that if you feel that something about that game is seriously wrong, that you will terminate it? That you will put an end to it?

I hear you.

Stephen was nodding. 'Yes, if you want to blame anyone for Richie's death, blame yourself. Because of you he insisted on running those tests. I knew it was only a matter of time before he'd find out that I had distributed a modified version to keep him and Jon out. I just didn't think he'd get on to it so quickly. That night when he called you – he was going to tell Jon. I couldn't have that. Jon would think I had betrayed him.'

'Jon found out about your betrayal, anyway. He found out about the backdoor.'

'Yes. I thought Richie's death would buy me some time. But who could have imagined that Jon would get back to those tests on the very day he buried his brother?'

Stephen smiled at her. It was not a pleasant smile. She started backing away from him slowly.

'Sweet Tia. You've been my Achilles heel all along. Jon sensed the way I felt about you. If it weren't for you, my relationship with Jon would still be intact. Richie would not have run those tests and he and Jon would probably still be working on the project, none the wiser.'

She continued moving backwards and Stephen followed slowly, his eyes never leaving her face. Her shoulder blade bumped into something hard and she found herself pressed up against the rock gong, the skin on her back contracting at the feel of the cold rock.

until she could feel the rock wall, solid and safe, behind her back.

He was breathing hard and his face glistened with sweat. His dark blond hair fell over his forehead. Across his cheek the blood from the deep gash was a dull brown. She looked at the blue eyes under the dark brows, at the long beautiful mouth, and she thought, he has the face of an angel.

'Do you remember when we were up here the last time? I told you then that I would never let you fall.' His words came out in gasps.

'Yes.'

'I meant every word.'

She did not want to look at him. She looked past his shoulder to where a hawk was hovering in the air, almost motionless. It must have spotted its prey down below.

'The first time Jon told me about your gift, I knew you were meant for me. Later, when I saw you there at the airport was sure of it. I recognised you as the one. The other half of my soul. But you did not recognise me. Why not?'

'Jon—' Her voice was a croak.

He made a gesture, so violent that she shrank back. 'No. love Jon like a brother. He and I, we're one and the same. t I know now that he was weak. The transformation ahead red him. But you—' There was an expression on his face raw that she averted her eyes. 'I thought I saw something you that no one else was able to see. I thought you were less: that you would take my hand and we would make the together.'

She tried to concentrate but her brain felt stupid. She looked his shoulder again to see if she could find the hawk, but she not see it anywhere in that blue expanse.

Dry your tears.' His thumb brushed gently across her

he hadn't realised she was crying. But now the tears were ng down her cheeks and everything around her was ing in a vivid blur of shape and colour. Great sobs were g her chest: harsh and ugly.

'But I'm the only one who understands you, Tia. I'm the only one who understands your gift. You're a listener, like me. I see something in you that no-one else can see. Take my hand.'

'No.' Her voice was a hoarse whisper.

'I've watched over you. You knew I was watching you, didn't you. You wanted it – like all women. It made you feel desired. It made you feel safe.'

He gripped her face with his hand and moved her head gently to and fro. His forefinger pressed into the corner of her mouth, causing her to swallow convulsively.

'You loved me once,' he said.

'I've never loved you.'

'Listen.' He put his fingers to his lips. 'Don't you hear it?'

She stared wildly, moving her head from left to right. 'What?' she asked. 'What?'

'The sound of my heart breaking.' And he started to laugh.

She tried to stem the rising hysteria within her. 'Where's Jon?' she said again.

'Jon.' Stephen looked away from her. He gave a step backward. His face had changed subtly. Something passed behind his eyes, like a stranger moving within. His mouth seemed almost slack. The arrogance, the self-assurance that was such an integral part of his physical beauty disappeared in front of her eyes.

'Jon thought he could find a way out. He was wrong. He did not count on me.'

'He wanted you to join hands with him, Stephen.'

'He did, didn't he. His mistake.' The expression in his eyes made her go cold.

She was shivering and she balled her fists and pushed them into the pockets of her skirt. Her fingers brushed and then closed around the cold edges of Richie's keys. The tiny divining bone pressed into the palm of her hand. Taking a deep breath, she placed her one foot slightly in front of the other and tensed her muscles.

Stephen suddenly smiled. It made him look charming and sane and made the situation seemed utterly surreal.

'You're not thinking of trying to run past me, are you?' He lifted his eyebrow teasingly. He slid his hand into the inner pocket of his jacket and brought out a knife. The casualness of the gesture shocked her.

The knife seemed small. Somehow a knife used for killing should be big and jagged; should be able to rip through shower curtains and hack through flesh. Not small and trim and elegant-looking.

She wondered, with an odd kind of curiosity, whether this was the knife with which he had killed Richie. Had he pulled that thin blade across the softest part of Richie's throat?

'I'm sorry we won't be around to see it, Tia. The burning wind, the blood. The world: one vast, open mouth, screaming itself into silence. But it's coming.'

She saw, disbelievingly, that there were tears trickling from the corners of his eyes. 'But I wanted to be there, Tia. I wanted to hear the new sound, look on the face of God.' He brought his hand up to his face and closed his eyes as he wiped the tears from his lashes.

She pushed herself violently away from the rock and brought up her knee. Stephen slumped forward, his one hand clutching at his groin. He looked up at her, his eyebrows pushed up high against his forehead.

She brought her hand forward in a swooping, stabbing motion. She held in her fist Richie's keys and she was aiming for Stephen's eye. The fear moved inside her skull like a skittering rat. But the sickening thought of the thin point of the key slicing into the soft gelatinous mass of his eyeball made her hesitate for just a second.

Stephen jerked his head and her hand left a bloody gash across his cheek. He shouted. As she sprinted past him she sensed the knife in his hand and felt it burn across her skin. She looked down at her breast and saw against the white of her blouse the blood; dark and red, like a carnation in full bloom. And then she was past him, and running, running . . . She could hear him

stumbling after her, and the terror suddenly overwhelmed and she screamed long and uncontrollably, and the scream s the silence into a million pieces and the sound of her own te horrified her.

She found herself, winded and gasping, at the bottom the giant rock pile that overhung the lip of the ravine. hesitated, then stretched out her hand and hooked her fi over the edge of a ledge and pulled herself up. And up again fingers scrabbled desperately, found places to grip on the sla broken rock and she felt her calf muscles stretch painfully a foot slipped on some loose pebbles. Her blouse was wet blood where Stephen's knife had cut through the skin. trickled into her eyes and her elbows and knees were s raw as she pulled up the lower half of her body onto yet ledge. She climbed with a wild urgency that left no r any thought.

But when she looked down over her shoulder th hit her like a lungful of poisoned air. It was too high too high. She looked up and the clouds above her h so steeply and so drunkenly that she thought they w crashing down upon her. It was too high up here. and edged her one foot back. But then she heard shale falling down. He was following her.

His voice was hoarse. He was reciting someth Bible – something she remembered vaguely from h Sunday school classes – Revelation? He spoke in fashion of a child delivering a nursery rhyme: ' voice from heaven, as the voice of many wat voice of a great thunder. And I heard the v harping with their harps and they sang a nev voice came out in breathless gasps.

She knew she couldn't escape him. SI brush her ankle and she screamed and ki even as she pulled herself up the highest l sensation that she was falling backwards in was helping her up from behind, steadyin she could lean on it to support herself

'Don't.' There was such tenderness in his voice that her heart ached and she closed her eyes briefly. He leaned forward and held out his arms as if to comfort her.

When she lunged at him, pushing violently against his shoulder, putting her full weight behind it, there was surprise on his face.

But he did not resist, did not even grab for the edge. And as he fell she thought she heard him say her name.

EPILOGUE

And they will hear a far-off music, a beautiful, cosmic music, that will lift them . . . beyond this little world with its fearful dreams. That music will draw closer and yet closer with its message of hope and becoming. That music is the Song of the Stars. Indaba.

Sanusi (high sangoma) Credo Mutwa, *Song of the Stars*

ROCK GONGS: THE HEALING SOUND
by Dirk Lubbe
The Johannesburg Post

December 22

JOHANNESBURG – *They spend their days playing rock gongs: ancient stones struck like bells and believed to have the magical power to heal. For centuries the rocks were played when the people needed rain; when peace was sought, when the land had to be healed. An unexpected revival of this ancient rite is sweeping the African continent. From as far afield as the Ivory Coast, down to the southernmost tip of Africa, traditional healers are practising a ritual that had seemed on the verge of extinction.*

Reports from the continent's capitals confirm the rumours that gongs are being played constantly. 'The reason for the unexpected upsurge in gong-playing is unknown,' says Olivia Temba, anthropologist at the University of Nigeria. 'We think it may have been triggered by the regular playing of a cluster of gongs in the Northern Province of South Africa. But the sudden subsequent playing of rock gongs across the breadth and width of the African continent seems to be a spontaneous phenomenon, not coordinated in any way.'

Tia smiled and placed the newspaper clipping back in the envelope. She made a mental note to herself to thank Ben for sending it to her. Here at Fluisterwater it was not easy to get hold of the Johannesburg papers. Not that she was really trying.

She placed her hands on the table in front of her and heaved herself to her feet. These days she felt like a beached whale. The closing weeks of her pregnancy were supremely uncomfortable. She had difficulty sleeping and was constantly bumping into things.

She stood quietly at the window, looking out at the garden and the sunburnt veld stretching into the distance. It was late morning, and the day was heating up. And it was quiet. In the cities people would even now be congregating in public places to welcome in the New Year that evening with as much noise as they could possibly manage. But out here, New Year's Eve would pass very much like any other day.

Fluisterwater was tranquil again and it has been for many months. The search and rescue teams, volunteers and hordes of reporters had long since left.

For a moment her thoughts went back to the days following Jon's disappearance. Terrible days. Days of despair. Days of waiting by the phone; of calling hospitals and morgues; of watching with growing hopelessness as a search party combed the stretch of land between the house and the gongs. The search had rarely let up. Even at night the police, neighbours and townspeople had explored undergrowth, ravines and hollow caves: their searchlights turning the blackness yellow. A helicopter and trained dogs had been brought in from the towns of Nelspruit and Pietersburg. The police had placed ads in the newspapers.

But no sign of Jon.

The most obvious suspect was Stephen – if indeed there

had been foul play. 'It may be that your boyfriend simply got lost in the darkness,' the one detective told her. 'At night it's very dangerous out there. And he's American, right? This isn't Disneyworld. Maybe he doesn't realise the animals out here don't wear cute little outfits.' He laughed, pleased with this witty observation.

Tia felt like shouting at him. With difficulty she managed to keep her voice even. 'He's made the trip to the gongs several times before. I doubt he'd get lost, even in the dark. I'm sure Stephen had something to do with it.'

'So what is it you're saying? You think Mr Yale attacked your boyfriend without leaving any – and I mean any – trace whatsoever?'

She shrugged hopelessly. 'Jon would not have expected any danger from Stephen. He didn't know that Stephen had killed Richie.' She paused as she remembered Jon's plea to Stephen, *'Join hands with me'*. 'And he may have thought Stephen was looking for reconciliation.'

The policeman sniffed, unconvinced. 'Well, for now we'll stick to what we know for sure.'

Which was very little. And after three weeks interest had started to wane. The press left, then the volunteers and finally the police. No sign remained of the full-scale but fruitless search which had taken place within Fluisterwater's borders.

Although fruitless was probably not the correct word, Tia thought, turning away from the window and walking towards the kitchen. At the end of the first week they had found some remains. She was actually present when the bones were discovered, but it was immediately clear to her that their search for Jon was not over. These bones must have been lying out there for a long time. They did not appear sinister or repellent. They were bleached white with the sun – picked completely clean of any tissue. The dental records had since confirmed that they belonged to Klio. Her first emotion had been one of relief. Sadness as well. But first and foremost relief – tremendous relief – at finally knowing.

She had decided to stay on at Fluisterwater for her pregnancy and she might even stay longer. She felt safe at Fluisterwater. Sometimes she imagined the hum was touching her mind again. Although that's probably all it was: imagination. But at night she would lie in bed and hear the rocks sing. Isaiah was following Jon's instructions to the letter. The gongs were played regularly. She found it calming, this throbbing pulse in the darkness. And now, according to the clipping Ben had sent her, the playing of these gongs had set off a beneficial chain reaction of healing sound across the continent. It was like an incantation, she thought. Like a charm against the powers of destruction.

And there was another reason she did not want to leave Fluisterwater. This was the last place where Jon was seen alive and therefore she did not want to leave.

Tia sighed. Ben was certainly not happy with her decision to stay here on her own, although he'd given up trying to change her mind.

She entered the kitchen and took a pitcher of ice water from the fridge. She was feeling very thirsty today and restless. Carrying the glass of water with her, she entered the living room and sat down in one of the armchairs.

She supposed Ben was right. It was lonely here, but then, she was never really alone. Fluisterwater had become a place of ghosts, but they were the ghosts of people she loved. She would hear music and look up and see the top of Klio's head as she bent over the piano. And then she'd turn around and there was Jon standing in the doorway, looking at her with those dark eyes and that small secretive smile of his she loved so much.

But oh, she missed him. And suddenly she felt a sense of loss so strong, her throat ached with unshed tears. She closed her eyes tiredly and the four walls of the living room disappeared and she was sitting next to Jon again. She felt his body close to hers, his hand in her hand. He was talking animatedly, explaining, gesturing. But she wasn't listening to his words. She was watching his face – his wonderful face. His eyes were so dark. But no avarice in those eyes. No apathy. Just intense curiosity and an appetite for life. She looked down at his hand, turned it around so it lay palm upwards.

You have a really long lifeline. You're going to be around for a long time.

Just so I'm around long enough to create the new scale.

Tia opened her eyes and for a moment the living room with its worn furnishings, the books against the wall, the piano seemed foreign to her. She felt lightheaded, dislocated in time.

But then she felt a strong kick in her womb and it brought her back to reality with a rush. Smiling, she placed her hand on the bulge of her abdomen and felt suddenly anchored and utterly at peace.

*   *   *

Ben opened the hatchback of his car and placed the bag of groceries in the boot.

The sun was about to set: the light harsh and yellow. In the air was the smell of dust and sweat. On the outside wall of the grocery shop, someone had spray-painted with a flamboyant hand: AFRICA IS NO PLACE FOR SISSIES. From within came the sound of a sound system pumping out songs by Splash and Patricia Majalisa: *into engiyenzayo ngiyijwayelema!* 'I have the courage to perservere because I have been doing it all my life!'

Ben got behind the wheel of his car and turned the key in the ignition. To the north, the black curl of an elevated highway carried a relentless stream of trucks and boxy cars and sweating motorists. Even through the closed car window he could hear the surge and ebb of snarled traffic; as monotonously regular as surf splashing on sand. In the lavender sky above, a silver wing glinted and the drone of a jet engine came to him from thousands of feet above the earth.

Ben turned the wheel and slowly manoeuvred the car into the road, carefully avoiding a straggling swaying group of revellers. This group had obviously decided to get a headstart on the evening's celebrations. One of the girls, a pretty redhead dressed in a hot pink dress, looked at Ben and blew him a kiss. Precariously balanced on her high heels, she looked like a beautiful but clumsy flamingo.

The red of her hair made him think of Tia. They spoke on the phone regularly but he hadn't seen her in months.

Ben's thoughts went back to the last time he had visited Tia at Fluisterwater. It was not a good memory. It still distressed him to think of that visit. During his stay, she had spoken calmly, her voice eerily serene.

'Jon will be back. I know he will.'

Her face was pale and to contradict her would have been cruel. But in his own mind he had little doubt. Jon was no longer alive.

'He'll be back,' Tia repeated. 'You know it too, don't you?'

He couldn't stop himself from involuntarily shaking his head.

'Don't shake your head like that.' Her voice trembled. 'I can't give up on him, Ben. One should never give up. It's an act of faith: like lighting a candle in the window.'

And for the rest of his three-day visit they had kept to safer topics. She talked about her pregnancy and seemed happy, excited at the prospect of having a baby. She talked about the baby constantly, wondering if it would be a boy 'with Jon's eyes' or a little girl she'd name after Klio. She was also racing to finish her book before the birth of the baby. It was nearing completion. 'I only have to decide if it's going to end happily,' she told him.

She did not discuss Jon's disappearance with him again and not once did she mention Stephen's name; at least not until the very last night of his visit.

Ben turned his car up his driveway and parked it in the garage. As he unlocked the front door of his house, he heard laughter and the bass of a sound system coming from further down the road. A New Year's Eve party was in full swing.

The house was dark and he did not switch on any lights until he reached his study. He had a lovely bottle of Krug champagne on ice, but he rather doubted he would stay awake to see in the new year. And it did seem rather a waste to open the bottle when there was no one there to share it with him.

He walked over to his liquor cabinet and took down a bottle of Dunhill whisky instead and listened appreciatively to the oily trickle of sound as the liquid filled the glass. He closed the door to the cabinet and took his glass with him as he stepped out onto the verandah.

It was beautiful outside. The moon, a big yellow disk, floated in a sky the colour of wine. The fragrance of his tea roses hovered sweetly in the air. Maybe he should pick some to put on Richie's grave tomorrow. Tia had asked him to place flowers on the grave for the new year: 'Anything but red carnations,' she had said.

Ben walked down the shallow steps and towards the fishpond. Here it was quiet, but a few hours from now – he glanced at his watch – the neighbourhood would explode with noise: crackers and the honking of cars, as the clock struck midnight.

He wondered how Tia would be celebrating this New Year's Eve all alone at Fluisterwater. He was worried about her out there on her own. The last night he had spent at Fluisterwater – the night before his departure – he had asked her to return with him to Johannesburg.

'It's too isolated here. I'm concerned about your safety.'

Despite her pregnancy her face seemed thin; her eyes enormous in her face. But at his words she smiled faintly and gestured at the door. 'You see that? I have another beer pot just like that at my back door. Isaiah says as long as they're at my door posts no harm can come to me or the baby.'

For a while it was quiet between them. Then she looked him full in the face. 'Isaiah was pleased to hear that Stephen had been cremated, you know. "Witches should be burnt," he said. He promised I shall feel no trace of Stephen's presence here.'

It was the first time she had mentioned Stephen's name. Her voice was steady but something in her eyes made him ask sharply, 'Tia, what's wrong?'

She placed her hand over her mouth as though she might forcibly keep herself from speaking.

'Tia . . .' He was alarmed.

349

She opened her eyes. 'I have never told this to anyone, you understand.'

He waited.

'I wish . . . I wish, I could be sure in my own heart that I was still in danger from Stephen at that final moment when I pushed him and he fell.' She swallowed. 'I can't tell you how often I relive that moment, over and over. I need only close my eyes to see Stephen leaning forward, opening his arms as though reaching for me, but with something in that gesture, which seems so protective. Ben, I don't think he would have hurt me.'

'You don't know that. He killed Richie. He may have killed Jon. He was out to harm you.'

'Was he? I don't know any more. But what I do know is that if he were alive now he could tell us what had happened to Jon: I'm sure of it. Because of me, we may never know. How can I forgive myself for that?'

He hugged her. 'Don't you blame yourself for anything.'

'But I do. I do blame myself.' She leaned over and opened the drawer of the table. 'I want to give you something.'

'What is it?'

In her hands she held a book with a pebbled leather cover. 'I don't want this near me.' She held it out at him. 'But I can't just throw it away. It's Stephen's journal. You keep it. Keep it until Jon gets back. He'll know what to do with it.'

The next morning as she said goodbye to him, she seemed more cheerful. 'I'm fine, really. Don't worry about me. Soon I'll have my baby in my arms and I know it's going to be wonderful.' And she smiled, the lost look in her eyes dispelled by genuine delight.

That was four months ago. He hadn't seen her since.

The fishpond needed cleaning. Ben picked up a stick and poked at the water. A dank smell came from its depths. The pond was filled with green scum and the tiny marble figure of Cupid was stained with a thin patina of grime. He would have to tend to it soon.

A warm wind suddenly shook the trees around him and

the branches above his head swayed restlessly. There was a slightly acrid smell in the air, which Ben knew came from open fires burning in the neighbouring township of Alexandra. In the northern suburbs that smell was a familiar one. It was a reproachful reminder that out there existed another world: a world of poverty that could be casually brutal, and dark and chaotic. As a young man and an activist he had once been a part of that world that lies outside the boundaries of well tended lawns and pretty houses. It still took his breath away to think how completely his life had been transformed since then. Change, when it came, could be heart-stoppingly swift.

He turned around to look at his house. He could see across the dark lawn through the french doors into the study: the warm yellow glow of the lamps, the dark gleam of his desk. It seemed far away; almost out of reach.

He shivered and drew his jacket against his body. As he walked back to his study, he lengthened his stride. To his left, he could see the black outline of his shadow hugging his footsteps.

Inside the house he closed the french doors tight and pulled the curtains close. As he reached out to turn off the lamp on his desk, his elbow knocked over a book balanced on the very edge of the table. It fell soundlessly to the carpet.

The leather felt cool against his palm. Stephen's journal. He had read through the entire thing several times already and what he had read haunted him. He often thought of this man, whose most private thoughts he now held here in his hands. He often thought about what Stephen believed in so passionately: about the process being only postponed, not stopped. About people abusing sound and unlocking the puzzle of perfect tuning slowly, but just as surely, as the computer game used to do. About the tenth note of a perfect cosmic scale growing stealthily and invisibly every day.

The journal fell open in his hands. On the page underneath his fist Stephen had written: *I think about the driving beat that never ceases; how it's hammering away at our fragile planet — and I*

*wonder how it is that everyone around me seems oblivious. Am I the
only one who hears?'*

The prose on some of these pages approached the ecstatic
fervour of a mystical vision. And there were passages dedicated
to Tia: lyrical and achingly sweet. One of the last entries in the
journal consisted merely of a few lines of poetry:

> *'Cupid shall guard the Door
> the more to please us,
> And keep out Time and Death
> when they would seize us:
> Time and Death shall depart,
> And say in flying,
> Love has found out a way
> to Live by Dying.'*

Below these lines Stephen had written in a cramped fist: *In my
heart I know this to be true.*

At the back of the book, pushed between binding and
stitching was a photograph. Ben took it out and looked at the
four faces captured in glossy silence.

Richie was laughing open-mouthed. On his head he had
what looked like a party hat. Stephen was giving the camera
that devastating, asymmetrical smile of his; head tilted to the
side with studied grace. Jon had his arm around Tia's waist,
drawing her close. Tia's face had the expectant look and wide
eyes of someone anticipating the flash from the camera.

So much had happened since this picture was taken. Ben
stared at the photograph and felt suddenly old. Sometimes it
was hard not to lose faith.

Lowering the photograph to the desk, he reached out
to switch off the light, but the phone started to ring. The
voice on the other end was female: brisk and official sounding.

'May I speak to Professor Ben Mbuyazi?'

'This is he.' Ben sat down in the chair behind his desk.

'Oh good. This is Nurse Venter of the Driefontein hospital.

I'm calling with regard to one of our patients who was admitted earlier today: a Ms Tia Theron.'

Ben felt himself suddenly short of breath. Tia. She wasn't due to deliver for another five weeks. Something must be wrong.

'Is she all right?'

'Oh, yes. But she asked me to let you know that she's given birth to a baby boy at six minutes past seven o'clock this evening.'

'The baby . . . Is the baby all right?' He was stumbling over his words.

'The baby is under observation in the neonatal unit but we don't believe there's anything to worry about. He had quite a good birth weight.' She paused and he could hear some papers rustling. 'Yes, here it is. 2,65 kg. The baby will be fine, Professor. And the mother is doing very well.'

Ben leaned back against his chair, feeling suddenly weak. 'Please tell Tia I'll drive over tomorrow to see her. And thank you for letting me know.'

'Not at all,' Nurse Venter said cheerfully. 'Oh, and Ms Theron specifically wanted me to give you the following message.'

'What is it?' he asked when she did not continue.

Nurse Venter had a smile in her voice. 'She said to tell you the baby has Jon's eyes.'

A boy. Jon had a son. As Ben replaced the receiver, he realised he was smiling, even though his eyes were suddenly moist. He swivelled around in his chair and looked out the window. The garden outside was black but in his mind's eye he saw a picture of a sky that was crystalline blue, grass that was green and sweet-smelling and a tiny toddler moving across the vast expanse of lawn on uncertain pudgy legs. He could hear it shriek with delight as it moved forward awkwardly, arms outstretched, the tiny hands searching, exploring: everything new and curious and wonderful.

He would install a swing, Ben thought, from one of the branches of the big blue gum tree at the end of the garden. A rope swing with a tyre. And later there would be a tree house in that tree – a special, private place – where a little boy with dark eyes could play and dream when he came to visit. And the garden and the house would be filled with life and laughter.

One should never give up, Tia had said. It's like lighting a candle in the window.

Ben got up from his chair and walked across the room, his tread light. He switched off the large standing lamp next to his armchair; then the light sconces against the walls. The room went dark.

At the door he paused and gave a last look back. A fierce beam of moonlight fell onto his desk, giving the cover of Stephen's journal a glassy sheen, touching the edges of the photograph with its four faces smiling into the darkness.